Black Hand of Sangarie

Black Hand of Sangarie

T. Olsen

sequel to *Shadows of Old Town*

iv

Dedication

To my mom, for always being proud of me no matter what, to my sister for being my biggest fan, and to my grandparents… because I miss you and I wish you could have seen this.

Table of Contents

Acknowledgements... Kind Of

I don't have an agent to thank.

Or a publisher.

I've seen a lot of "How I Got Published" posts on social media, and many of them resulted in moans of soul-crushing defeat from myself and my fellow writers. So I wanted to write about how I queried off and on for almost 20 years, with seven different manuscripts, and how I planned on getting that agent and getting a big five (four?) publishing deal, then... didn't.

Spells.

No, not spellcheck. Spells.

I created this foolproof spell for publishing a book, and soon I will have all the orders coming in, reviews stacking up, and movie deals in the wings. You too can publish a book with this Very Easy manipulation of causality and fate. Here's what you'll need:

A dusty, vanilla scented candle to represent the smell of books.

A miniature book stitched together with thread soaked in your tears, the pages of which are made from your first rejection letter, and the cover cut from an old library card.

A dried rose petal from the grave of someone you looked up to, who had persistence.

Then you recite a prayer over the ingredients and burn the book and the rose petal in the flame of the candle. Done.

Seriously, though. My author journey has been a story of hope, rejection, wavering determination, and questionable luck. It's a tale about how hard *I* worked, and how much effort it took, and how I constantly wanted to give up—and *did* give up a couple of times—but always went back to writing and improving myself. Because that's what authors do.

When I started, I thought I was brilliant. My friends all loved my books. My fledgling writing group thought my work was A+. And my very first query (sent to Baen publishing, because I didn't realize I needed an agent) came back after thirteen months with a lovely rejection letter about how they weren't looking for this kind of book right now, but my characters were relatable, the interpersonal relationships were very natural, and the conflict made sense. They had a few tips for fight scenes, but otherwise they said it was "a really good story."

Well, I'd make short work of this whole publishing thing.

Hahahahahahahaha...

In the 20 years I've been trying to "get published" I've learned a lot about my writing, about myself, and about this process. I have a lot more disappointment to go through, but I can share my struggle and I can acknowledge what I've accomplished. Because I do consider it a great accomplishment.

The first thing I learned was that I'm not special. I'm a very good writer in a veritable sea of very good writers. That was humbling. That was intimidating. That was a little bit disappointing, but ultimately necessary to build my thicker skin. Lots of people are very good. That won't get you published. And there are brilliant books that will *never* get published, just like there are books that make thousands that should have been printed on toilet paper because that's about all they're good for. Skill helps on the road to success, but it's not a key that will open that door. Sometimes it takes a little luck.

The next thing I learned is that I'm not able to edit my own novels. This took longer to realize. I still fight it to this day, even knowing better. I write *great* first drafts. My words are polished. But authors have blind spots. When I look back over 20 years of querying and over 30 years of writing, I can see the huge jump in quality that happened once I found critique partners that wrote at my own skill level. And once I started *listening* to them. (Thank you, dear friends.)

And then there were the craft books. I thought I knew my shit, mainly because my English and creative writing teachers had always said I had a sense for these things. (I did it, Mrs. Olbertson, aren't you proud?) I picked up my first craft book, which was Stephen King's *On Writing*, about halfway through my query journey. It cracked open a little piece of my brain where my muse had been imprisoned. It was like I'd been keeping her in a cave, toiling away, chained to a desk, and now there was this whole world of process and knowledge available for me to explore.

I consumed a whole list of craft books. Every book, no matter how little it resonated with my writing style, taught me something. Learning and trying out these techniques helped me internalize good habits with my writing. It helped me be a better critique partner. And most of all it helped me realize that writing really is a craft and not a talent. A talent just happens, but a craft can be improved upon.

But you know all this, right? You came here for the secret to how I got published, not for a list of rehashed advice on becoming an author.

The secret is a combination of opportunity and serendipity. You create the opportunity and wait for the serendipity. Some people have really high levels of opportunity—like industry connections, or money, or fame—and they only require a tiny bit of serendipity. Like so little that as long as a bus splashes puddle water in their face, that's close enough to magically get them where they need to go.

Other people must fight for every glimmer of opportunity. Hundreds of queries, dozens of pitch events or conventions, and endless years of honing their craft. Then they just have to hope the bus of serendipity waits long enough for them to make it to the right bus stop, but it starts pulling away and they have to run after it and make a leap onto 12th street and grab the hand of someone reaching from the window, then be pulled inside where they fall into a panting heap and realize they lost their bus fare so they're thrown right back out at the next stop. Because serendipity doesn't give a shit.

The reality is most people miss the bus. But if you stop going to the bus stop, you'll never get on it. Sometimes I go days, weeks, or months without going to the bus stop. Then I put my running shoes back on, duct tape my bus fare to my arm, and get ready to jump.

I'm right there with you. I'm begging for reviews, fumbling through marketing, lurking on social media, and taking every rejection like a punch to the chest.

But I'm there. And being there is how you make this dream come true. Keep writing. Keep building your craft. Storytelling is so very personal. That's your broken soul on the page, and it's hard to sell that to someone and be rejected. It feels like it should be easier than this, but it's not.

How did I get published? I made my own opportunities… and I'm still ready to grab that serendipity bus when it rushes by. So this is my way of acknowledging *myself*. My work. My doubts and insecurities. And this is me saying: I fucking *did* it.

1 – Chasing Rue

I stood on a roof in the light of the full moon, my back against a chimney, eating a sweet roll as I waited for my young protege to complete her hit. Ruena was fourteen now, and while she'd improved by leaps and bounds over the last five years she still had a clumsy streak and a habit of getting distracted.

Two sounds came to me from the dark street below—one shortly after the other. The first was the distinctive clink of an armored boot on cobbled stone that told me a Copperguard was nearby. The second was the sharp bang of a window frame being dropped into place.

The Six be damned. I jammed the last of the honeyed bread into my mouth and pressed into the deep shadow of the chimney, maintaining my view of the street below.

Rue peeked around the corner of the alley just as the Copper stepped out and looked in the direction the noise had come from. They both stared at each other for a long moment, Rue's arms full of wrapped packages clearly stamped with the warehouse's brand, her long dark braid falling over her shoulder. Then she ducked back into the alley and the Copper shouted for her to stop as he took off after her.

Damned and damned again.

I brushed the crumbs off my fingers and quickly plotted a path across the rooftops to keep pace with them without being seen.

The rooftops of Sangarie were referred to as the Thieves Way. Little bridges and handholds were carefully placed to make travel easier for those who wished to remain unseen and move quickly, and any halfway decent thief had the roofs in their district memorized, as well as a good deal of those in the adjacent districts. I was able to jump the narrow alleys and wind my way along after them, although it took a lot more

1

energy than merely chasing them on the street would have. The frantic trill of a whistle from Rue's pursuer hastened me on.

After a few minutes the lone Copperguard was joined by two others and they were pressing Rue hard, closing in. She couldn't use one of the secret entrances to the underground if there was a chance of her being seen. It was against guild law, and I'd been very clear about not ignoring that particular rule. It was flustering her, because she was indecisive at the corners and checking her tail too much instead of putting distance behind her. At this rate, they'd catch her in the next few blocks.

If they caught her, they'd have her up against the Warden's bench by morning. Thieves in Old Town district were dealt with mercilessly. That was mostly my fault, since the Warden was still sore about having lost the chance to hang me five years ago. She was also well aware of my favoritism for Old Town, even though I was no longer its enforcer. Rue wouldn't get any leniency.

I, however, was nearly untouchable. The Warden wouldn't dare risk a war with the guild by hanging one of the Hands of the Master for petty theft. Or at least that's what I hoped.

I cursed and took a shortcut over a roof to get ahead of the Coppers, then swung down a metal drain pipe and darted out into the street in front of them, puffing to catch my breath and raising my arms to block the way.

"I surrender!"

The Coppers clattered to a stop, glancing past me in confusion as Rue popped around a corner. The first one growled and made to go around, but I stepped in front of him, a little breathless from the run. "You caught me. Good on you."

"Get out of the way, asshole."

One of the other Coppers, younger and skinnier than the others, gasped and his eyes widened. "That's Gray! He's worth more than a hundred thieves to the Warden."

I raised my eyebrow and hoped that was an exaggeration.

The one who'd been trying to shove his way around me paused and squinted in my direction. His nose was red from a love of drink and most of his teeth were black. I didn't recognize him, so he must be new to Old Town. I watched the struggle on his face as he weighed taking the bait handed to him and chasing after his original quarry. Hopefully he

2

wouldn't realize how useless it was to bring me in for absolutely nothing.

The young one came up with a length of thin chain and cuffs, then grabbed my upraised arm and wrenched it down to click the cuff around my wrist behind my back. He was nearly quivering in excitement. The black-toothed guard took one last look down the empty street beyond, then grumbled under his breath as he fell into line.

I sighed and let them drag my other arm back as well, fighting my instinct to resist. They weren't gentle, and as the young guard finished securing the chains behind me the third, who'd been silent thus far, stepped forward and grabbed a fistful of my hair, dragging my head back.

The first knot of anxiety began to gnaw at my gut. This one I recognized. Shit. What was his name? Margus. He had a black beard, neatly trimmed and waxed, and a scar along one cheek that was also my fault a long time ago. I'd gotten much better at throwing knives since then.

His voice was low and filled with menace. "I know what you're doing, and it was a foolish move."

"I don't know what you're talking about."

His grip tightened and my eyes watered. He leaned in very close. "One wrong step and I'll claim you were trying to escape."

Oh yes. Margus definitely knew I wasn't to be touched, and it grated on him. I grinned back. "Wouldn't dream of it."

He let go and cuffed the back of my head, staggering me. I glanced forward as I caught my balance and noticed Rue watching from around a corner. Stupid kid. I'd given her the chance to run and she was still hanging around.

The young guard pushed me ahead of him, holding the end of the thin chain behind me. I started walking, keeping my head down and my eyes sharp. Before we'd gone a full block I caught sight of Ruena on the rooftops ahead of us. She'd ditched her take somewhere and was keeping pace with our steady plod.

She better not be thinking of trying to help me. I glanced at Margus and he glared back. I needed to make sure she understood this was on purpose. That I had everything under control.

3

I pitched my voice loud enough to carry through the moonlit streets. "I can't believe I was so *clumsy* back there. I made so much noise stealing from that poor warehouse manager."

Rue's head popped over the edge of a parapet wall above and she scowled back. I didn't stare and risk alerting the guards to her presence, but I kept watching for her, making sure my voice was loud enough she could hear me clearly. Since I had her undivided attention for once, I was going to make the most of it. "I should have checked for Coppers before making off. And I definitely took too long picking the lock. I didn't practice like my boss told me to."

I caught the sound of her indignant snort as Margus prodded me in the side with his spear. "Shut the fuck up."

He probably thought I was mocking him. I noticed Rue's shadowy form on the rooftops ahead of us, jumping from one building to another. With the bright moonlight, the guards would see her too if they happened to look up, but at least she was being quiet. It was worrying that she hadn't yet broken off and gotten out of the area, and I tried to think of a better way to shoo her. "I hope this chat with the Warden doesn't take long. Hopefully someone sends word to the *guildmaster*."

The shaft of Margus's spear thwacked across my gut. The breath whooshed out of me and I hunched over and staggered to keep my feet, the chain pulling tight as I instinctively tried to bring my arms around and couldn't. Pain spread across my abdomen and I sucked in air while trying not to throw up. That sweet roll wouldn't taste nearly as good coming back up.

He shoved me against the wall of the closest building, setting the length of his spear under my chin to push my head back until we were face to face. His dark eyes bore into mine and his teeth were clenched so hard I could hear them grinding, pulling the skin tight over his cheeks and making his scar almost glow in the moonlight.

My paranoia flared up. Years of running and hiding from the Coppers was so ingrained that I had to force myself not to fight back. I'd pushed him too far.

"Keep your mouth shut, scum. You utter another word and I'll knock your brains out and drag you to the Warden by your feet."

He knew better than to actually kill me, but he had a lot of buried resentment I was leaning on. I nodded, trying to appear humbled and probably failing. It wasn't an expression I was good at, especially when my adrenaline was running high.

He stared into my face a few more moments, his breath smelling of whatever meat he'd eaten last, and probably hoping I'd resist. When he finally released the pressure on my throat and stepped back, I risked a glance at the rooftops.

No sign of Ruena. I sighed in relief and fell into step behind the black-toothed guard.

I expected to be taken to the holding cells in Old Town, but we passed the turn and I wondered if they were marching me straight through to Varinston and the Warden's jail instead. It was a long walk to the central districts, and one I wasn't looking forward to. However, as we crossed into the Lower Yard to the south with its numerous warehouses and ship storage, it became apparent I was wrong again.

Maybe Old Town was just full. Wouldn't be the first time a dock riot or tavern brawl had the cells at capacity, although I couldn't recall either going on at the moment.

Movement caught my eye above and I saw a thin, awkwardly graceful figure leap from one rooftop to another in the gleaming moonlight. Damn her. Why couldn't she just go home? I bit my lip to keep from trying to distract the guards, as they were already having none of that.

A few blocks later there was the sound of falling tiles and a string of curses in Rue's hissing tone. I sighed and looked at the guard ahead of me.

He was the older one that had originally caught her in the act, and he was still on high alert. He hefted his spear and turned toward the alley where another muffled thud sounded. This would turn out very badly if they took *both* of us in. The Warden couldn't do much to me, but if she thought I was protecting Rue, she'd gleefully order a morning hanging in the Old Town market and give me a front row seat. My mind raced trying to think of how to keep that guard busy long enough to let Rue get away, or at least get herself hidden again.

The black-toothed guard was moving now.

It was a bad decision, but I didn't have a lot of options. I darted to the end of my thin chain, then kicked the Copper in the ass hard enough to stagger him.

A few things happened at once. The chain was yanked back by the younger guard and I stumbled to keep my feet, the forward guard shouted a curse as he glared back at me, and the shaft of Margus's spear came flying toward my head.

I was still catching my balance as I saw it coming, so all I could do was close my eyes and flinch away, taking it across the side of my face hard enough to make my ears ring. Even with my eyes closed I saw stars, and crashed to the cobbles as they slipped out from under me. If I could have cradled my head in my hands, I would have, but they were chained behind me and I had to settle for resting my forehead on the street and fighting back the fresh bout of nausea.

I think the guards were arguing with each other. That's what it sounded like at any rate as the noise faded in and out. I shifted my jaw and tried to lift my head off the street, but it made the dizziness even worse. That damn kid was going to be picking pockets on the docks for the rest of her life once I got out of this.

The point of the spear was thrust into a crack in the cobbles next to my head, and I flinched at the spray of gravel chips it sent out.

"Just try to run."

"Nope." I blinked and swallowed thickly. "I think I'm good."

He gripped my arm and dragged me to my feet. I swayed as I found my balance, and my head started pounding.

"Please. Run." He leaned closer. Close enough his breath was hot on my face. "The Warden will understand when I tell her you slipped and fell into the river. The weight of your chains dragged you under, made it impossible to retrieve your body."

I resisted the urge to look at the rooftops, instead fixing my gaze on a stain on the orange-colored Copperguard emblem over Margus's armor. It was probably gravy judging by his breath. All I had to do was shut up and play along.

Margus growled, breathing heavily as he waited for me to make a move, then finally gestured at the others to keep going. They half shoved, half dragged me into motion down the dark street.

A few blocks later I realized why we were in this district as we arrived at the old, unused holding cells for the Lower Yard. Years ago new ones had been built that were larger and not prone to leakage from the river while the old ones had been retired and relegated as storage, though everyone knew it was still people that were stored there.

It was a place to put someone to lose them while the baroness looked the other way.

2 – Lower Yard

The iron door squealed as the black-toothed guard opened it, and I could smell the dampness and the rust as I was shoved inside. It was dark, and the further in we went the more smells presented themselves. Refuse, urine, blood maybe, and then the rotting stench of something decaying in water. Maybe I shouldn't have eaten that sweet bread at all.

My headache was getting worse and my gut felt bruised, but my greatest concern right now was why *this* was where they were taking me. If it was an intimidation tactic, it was working. The black-toothed guard held an oily torch in the lead, casting wavering light through the bars to either side, and small things scurried out of sight.

I gagged as we neared a cell, and a quick glance into it showed me nothing except a person-sized pile of rags in the far corner. It didn't move and I doubted it had in quite a while.

Margus unlocked the cell across from it with a rusty ring of keys, then stood aside. The black-toothed one was holding his sleeve over his mouth, looking around the central corridor in disgust. It was the young one behind me that seemed hesitant. He stammered softly until the words finally formed, uncertain and shaking.

"Is this right? Are you sure we should be bringing him here?"

I resisted the urge to agree with him out loud. It wouldn't help my cause.

Margus's eyes narrowed and he stabbed his finger at the open cell door.

The young one sighed and steered me in, then removed the manacles around my wrists and backed out. The door slammed shut with a screech and a deafening clang, and Margus locked it.

I wiped a hand across my jaw and looked at my fingers, expecting to see blood, and was relieved when I didn't. The cell wasn't deep enough to prevent that spear from reaching me, so I chewed on the smartass comments I wanted to make. Instead I went for all business.

"The guild already knows about this." Maybe… if a beggar had happened to see us. Because my insufferable little thief was probably watching from outside instead of reporting it.

Margus sneered. "You're just in holding until the Warden can process you. Standard procedure."

I sucked in an angry breath and immediately regretted it as the rotting stench burned my nostrils. The gag reflex nearly won out, but I wrestled it down, clipping off my words as I tried to breathe as little of the rancid air as possible. "The guildmaster won't be happy."

He moved closer, his hand flexing on the shaft of his spear. "I don't care. Enjoy the company."

The youngest guard was already at the end of the hall and Margus spit on the stones at my feet before following him. The black-toothed guard chuckled and hooked a thumb across the corridor at the pile of rags. "Nobody came for that one either." Then he followed after the others, taking the smoking torch with him.

I stood quietly as they left. A litany of curses ran through my head, but it would only entertain them more if I spluttered and protested. The outside door squealed shut and I was left in the dark with the smell.

I looked around, catching a faint glimpse of stars from a narrow, barred skylight in the middle of the corridor ceiling that let in enough moonlight to let me see blurry shapes in the dark. There were no windows in the cells, but there was one over the main door on the other side of the building. The brief look I'd taken before they left with the torch had revealed the floor to be covered in grime and sodden piles of the-Six-knew-what. Definitely not someplace I wanted to sit down.

Although I desperately wanted to sit down. My gut was killing me and my head was pounding.

A tiny squeak came from off to my left and I strained to place it again amidst the other noises of dripping water, then something moved across the top of my foot. I cursed and kicked it off, backing into the door and kicking randomly out in front of me. "Fucking rats."

I slowed my breathing again and cleared my head. They hadn't taken anything from me. I had all my knives, my picks, my pouches. I didn't

9

imagine an experienced guard would have overlooked that, so I could only assume they didn't care.

Or they were hoping I'd use them.

Well, at least I could get out of the cell and away from my decaying friend. I slipped a couple of picks from the lining of my belt and wrapped my arms through the bars of the door, feeling for the keyhole in the dark. It was old and rusty, and I had to press myself against the greasy bars to get a good angle. It took five minutes and a snapped pick, but I was finally able to push it open, wincing as it screeched long and loud.

I waited, but nobody came running.

Then I slipped out of the cell and crept toward the door leading outside, cursing as I stepped on something in the dark that was too soft for my imagination. Maybe it was just mud and gravel. When I finally reached the front of the room and leaned against the grimy door to listen, the tiny barred window set above it let me make out the sighing and shifting noise of what I assumed was the youngest guard, left to watch their prisoner. I ran my fingers over the inside of the door, but could find no keyhole, so I wouldn't be able to pick it from here. I doubted I could take the hinges in the state they were in, so the only way I was getting out through that door was if someone opened it.

Fuck. I looked back the way I'd come, trying to peer into the dark and see any other source of moonlight where there might be a window low enough to reach.

Ruena's exaggerated whisper floated down from the hole in the middle of the ceiling. "Gray? Are you alive?"

With a glance at the door behind me, I made my way to stand below the grate, disgusted with the squelch under my boots. "I ought to beat you senseless."

Her voice rose in indignation. "I followed to *help* you."

"To help me do what? Fly? Why didn't you go for Senyr?"

"Senyr would've lectured me all the way here."

I glared up at the barred hole, just able to make out the dark blob of her head against the darker sky. "As well he should."

"And he'll lecture you too."

It was true. I'd miscalculated and gotten myself in a little deeper than I expected. While technically Senyr and I were of equal rank now, we'd never shaken that mentor-student relationship. He absolutely would chew my ass for this.

"How's your face?" she whispered.

I took a deep breath and immediately regretted it as the smell of decay filled my nose. My face ached like someone had hit it with a fucking pole, but I didn't want to distract her. "It's fine."

"Can I get you out?"

"Just go and get someone who can negotiate for me. This place is a rusted box of rot, and I don't want to end up sleeping here." Temporarily *or* permanently.

"Fine. But you should look in that cell in front of you. There's something magic in there."

I frowned and looked instinctively, but the inside of the jail was still dark. "Are you fucking kidding me?"

There was no response from above.

"Rue?"

Still nothing. Now she finally listens.

I wrinkled my nose at the cell containing what was most likely a rancid corpse, bloated by stale river water. Rue's ability to see magic had gotten us both out of some tight spots in the past, and into more trouble than I cared to recall. Whatever she saw in there was probably more on the trouble side.

If she wasn't fucking with me. She'd hit that age where the hero worship was wearing off and she was finding joy in the stories of my less successful exploits. She was also picking up my bad habits. Sending my mentor digging through rotting garbage for made up treasure was something I absolutely would have done at her age, then laughed about with my friends.

But what if she was right?

I sighed and moved to the cell where the worst of the stench was coming from. I could barely see the bars in front of me in the dark, and felt for the lock plate on the door. It was even more rusted than the one I'd already opened. I pulled a couple of picks from my dwindling supply and started poking around in it.

I took my time, not wanting to break any more. Good picks weren't cheap. Eventually the lock grated loose and I pulled the door open. If she was fucking with me, I'd give her to the beggars.

11

My gift was touch based, and anything low-powered enough to go unnoticed by guards wouldn't show up for me unless I got my bare hands on it. I took a handkerchief out and held it over my nose as I kicked at shadows of refuse in the little cell, peering at the floor in the dark with a faint hope that whatever she'd seen was out in the open. A few things turned under my boot, and I set a finger on each of them, but they just felt slimy.

After a good fifteen minutes I looked at the corpse pile and sighed. It was tempting just to wait until she came back and ask her where exactly it was, but she'd have Senyr with her and he wouldn't let her climb onto the roof and talk with me, and the guards certainly wouldn't give us some quality time alone in here. If I was going to find anything it'd be now. On my own.

I held the cloth firmly over my mouth and nose, then tugged at the rags covering the lumpy corpse. They stuck. I pulled a little harder and it started to peel away, then came loose all at once along with what looked like part of a rib cage.

I staggered back and vomited that sweet roll all over the other side of the cell, resisting the urge to wipe my fingers off on my pants so I didn't get corpse juice on myself. When my stomach was settled again, I glared at the pile of rotting flesh and caught the twinkle of moonlight off a hard reflective surface.

"Well damn…"

I crept closer, tilting my head to catch a glimpse of it again in the dark. Sure enough, something was nestled in the remains. About the size of a nut. If I had to hazard a guess, they'd kept it from the guards by swallowing it and I'd managed to pull apart enough of the chest cavity to expose it.

The thought started the gag reflex again and I paused to regain control before squatting in front of the corpse. I just had to do it. Don't think about it, just do it. Pretend it was only mud.

I hooked my fingers in the sludge around the thing and felt the tingle of magic. She'd been right. As I pulled it out, a delicate corroded chain dragged along behind it, then swung free and flicked gore on my pants. I backed away from the corpse, retreating into the central corridor and doing my best not to throw up again.

"Disgusting."

12

The necklace sat heavy in my fingers, sending tingly waves of magic into them as I grimaced at the black sludge. I should have used a stick or something to poke it out first.

Off to my left, just at the corner of my vision, something moved.

I froze and tipped my head just a fraction of an inch in that direction, trying to widen my field of vision without drawing attention to it. The aisle between cells ended somewhere down there, but it was lost in shadow. As I peered closer, an irrational panic crawled through my chest. A feeling I hadn't felt so strongly in years. The shadows around me rippled like drifting fog and the faint moonlight coming from the barred skylight above vanished, sinking the jail into true darkness.

A long, low sigh reached my ears and a slight breeze tickled the back of my neck. My heart stuttered against the inside of my ribs and I spun and took a hesitant step away. My clean hand reached for a knife at the small of my back. Then the moonlight once again showed the faint outlines of cell bars and the debris strewn floor, where nothing moved but the rats.

The heavy sound of the main door being unlocked startled me, and I quickly wrapped the necklace in my handkerchief and shoved it into the top of my boot before the guards pushed open the heavy squeaking door.

I was letting my nerves dredge up old fears when I needed to pay attention. Diplomatic immunity or not, I was walking a thin line by throwing myself at the mercy of these men. I glanced once more at the back of the building, hidden by deep shadow, but there was no movement that I could see. Nothing but silent, empty cells.

The jail brightened somewhat as a guard brought a torch into the doorway while other figures waited in the dark street behind him. As he raised it up, I saw Margus's neatly trimmed black beard and the scar on his cheek. He looked surprised for a moment, then grinned. "He's escaped his cell, ma'am."

Ma'am? My gut dropped. He'd brought the Warden.

3 – The Warden

The Warden's raspy voice pierced through the dark with an easy tone of authority. "Well, bring him out."

Margus stepped to one side of the doorway, beckoning me with his finger.

I could stay in here, make them waste time coming in to catch me again. It might buy Rue time to fetch someone to help me. Of course it would really piss off the Warden, and if I didn't waste *enough* time, she might decide to do something about it. My best chance was to be polite.

I grimaced and walked toward him.

As I went to pass him he clapped a hand under my upper arm, and a guard just outside reached for the other as I crossed the threshold. They stopped me a couple of paces outside the door, under the light of the moon and stars and at least a dozen torches held by Silvers and Coppers. Directly across from the door stood the Warden.

She was a head taller than me, and much bulkier. She didn't have the half plate with the tabard like the other guards, instead wearing a custom fitted shirt of scale mail with the symbol of the baroness, leather pants that showed off muscular thighs beneath the hem of the shirt, and scaled boots that went nearly to her knees. It all moved so easily on her that she may as well have been wearing cotton. Her nose was crooked, and her black hair, streaked with gray these days, was bound into a bun behind her head with a leather cord, pulling her face into an even more severe expression. A longsword hung at her side and a fancy dagger was sheathed at her belt.

Her delighted gaze was locked on me, and her voice grated in my ears. "I've been waiting a very long time for you to fuck up again."

I wasn't sure what to say. I thought about denying that I was trying to escape, but she'd twist that however she wanted anyway. I thought about

14

trying to charm her, but rumor had it she wasn't interested in men, charming or otherwise. I even thought about trying to make a break for it, but there were a lot of guards here.

In the end I just chuckled weakly and tried not to sound like I was worried. "I'm sure someone from the guild will be along shortly to sort all this out."

Her lip curled. "I hope not." She started forward, a hunger burning in her eyes that brought to mind some of the more crazy Red Hands.

I tugged back, but the guards held me tight. If I went for a knife, she'd kill me for sure, but I didn't want to just stand here and let her do whatever those eyes were imagining.

Senyr's calm voice came out of the dark. "It looks like we're just in time."

I blew out in relief, the tension draining from my muscles.

The Warden narrowed her eyes as he walked into the circle of torchlight with Ruena in tow. Another figure strode along behind them, and when that one lifted his head I recognized Neffrey, one of the highest ranking beggars. Maybe one of the beggars *had* seen me being brought in.

Senyr came to a stop and slowly took in the guards surrounding the front of the old holding cells. "This is a lot of muscle for one diplomatic prisoner."

"He was trying to escape."

I spoke up. "Ah. No. I was actually just avoiding the rats that lived in my cell. Didn't even try to leave the building." Although I might have, if there'd been a clear way to do that.

Senyr strolled into the ring of guards, leaving Rue and Neffrey at the edge. He ignored me and spoke directly to the Warden. "You and I both know he didn't do enough to risk the peace of this city. You'll have to throw him back this time."

She returned a glare, then jutted her chin beyond him. "Then give me that one. My guards say he was protecting one of the lesser thieves who was caught holding pilfered goods. A girl. He interfered with them doing their job."

Rue shrank back against Neffrey, who pushed her away with a growl.

I looked to Senyr, my mouth open to protest, but he raised a hand at me and I bit it back. It wouldn't be helpful. I knew he wouldn't give her over to them if he could help it, but my jaw still tightened. I'd face the Warden myself if I had to make that choice.

"I don't think that's going to happen either. We have plans for the girl."

The Warden's lip curled in disgust. "I don't give a fuck about your plans."

"There must be some compromise to be had. We aren't unreasonable." He gestured vaguely in my direction again. "We understand how insufferable he can be."

"Hey," I protested.

The Warden shifted her eyes in my direction, the eager light flaring briefly. "Let me have a pound of flesh."

I scowled. "Excuse me?"

Senyr turned his gaze on me as well, his expression blank. "Very well, you can have a few minutes to beat on one another. But no weapons, and I don't want him killed or crippled."

She grinned. "Deal."

I glared at Senyr. "No. No deal."

Senyr turned and casually rejoined Rue and Neffrey. "Don't you dare pull your knives, Gray."

The guards shoved me into a widening circle of armored men. The Warden was unstrapping her longsword and handing it to one of the Silvers along with her dagger.

I went cold. "You expect me to fist-fight the Warden?"

She stepped into the ring of guards, cracking her knuckles and rolling her neck and shoulders. She even bounced a little on the balls of her feet. She was well-trained in hand-to-hand combat, a consistent winner in the festival arenas, and the commander of every guard in the city. I just knew how to brawl in the taverns, and I'd already been smacked around by the Coppers as they brought me in.

"How am I supposed to beat her?"

Senyr spoke up, his hand on Rue's shoulder to hold her in place. "I don't expect you to beat her. I expect you not to die."

I swallowed the lump in my throat and crouched in a defensive position. My instincts screamed at me to draw my knives, and my fingers twitched with the urge, but I didn't. If I cheated right now, Senyr might very well give me over. Or the guards around us would rip me to pieces.

The Warden began circling, forcing me to match her. She dipped closer, then away, always moving, her thick hands balled into fists and held up in front of her chest. The muscles on her bare forearms were corded, and her shoulders rounded.

There was no world where this didn't end with me in a whole lot of pain. I just needed to try to stay away from—

She darted in, faster than I thought possible for someone so large.

I dodged a punch, ducked under a swing, then threw myself to the ground to avoid the backswing. Gravel flew as I rolled to my feet and skittered away from the fist already moving toward my head. Two more came in quick succession and I stumbled back, barely avoiding them.

I'd lost my good footing, and when she leaped forward and hooked a fist toward my middle, I couldn't bend away quite enough and it slammed into my side. I dropped to one knee, hissing at the instant pain in my ribs, and pressed an arm to my side as I pushed myself back to my feet to lurch away.

Rue's voice came from somewhere behind me. "Hit her back, Gray!"

I growled, "Shut it, kid."

The Warden leaped forward again and I dodged the first punch, and brushed away the second, but the third caught me on the jaw and snapped my head to the side. Blood pooled in my mouth and I spit it out as I staggered to keep my feet and blinked away the sparkles in my vision. The headache I'd been nursing from earlier tripled.

I had to at least hit her once. This was just sad. I pulled up my fists and crouched lower, planting my boots in the gravel so I could move however I needed to.

She darted in and I shifted sideways, twisting to put my weight into a full right hook. She had scale mail on, so the only way I was doing this without breaking my hand was to punch her in the face or a limb, and I chose the face. My knuckles cracked with the force of it, and spit flew from her mouth after the impact, but she took it and grinned back at me.

Oh… shit. I shook out my bruised knuckles and danced away.

She lunged forward, swinging for my head. I slid to the side, not seeing her other meaty fist until it hooked into my gut, driving the breath

17

out of my chest entirely. Then her fist came down on my shoulder and drove me face first into the cobbles.

I curled up on the street and tried unsuccessfully to suck in air. Maybe if I just huddled here and waited Senyr would stop her from killing me.

Fingers hooked under the back collar of my vest and yanked me upright. I took in a few shaky breaths, the torchlit street spinning, then shrugged off her hand and raised my arms to protect myself. Everything seemed to be tipping to one side and I stumbled to follow it.

She came at me again and I crossed my arms in front of my face, grunting as she landed two gut punches in quick succession. One arm came down instinctively to protect myself, and the third punch cracked across my jaw.

Then I was on the ground again, lying on my back with my arms flung out to keep myself from sliding off the street, staring up at the blurry stars as they spun in circles. I choked and coughed at the blood filling my mouth from the cuts on the inside of my cheek. People were yelling and laughing.

Her face came into my spinning gaze.

I swallowed the blood and croaked, "I'm done."

She crouched low, her face close to mine. "Someday you'll fuck up again, and I'll be here... waiting to stretch your neck. You can't hide behind your guild forever."

Senyr's voice boomed from the sidelines. "I think that's enough."

Her eyes blazed and she pushed herself up, leaving my narrowed field of vision.

Then Senyr was there, his brow furrowed as he stared down at me. He reached out a hand.

I ignored it and closed my eyes. "I'll stay here."

He sighed and gripped my forearm, pulling me into a seated position.

It hurt. I hunched up and spit more blood out of my mouth as I waited for the street to stop spinning. "I hate you."

"Then stop being such a pain in the ass." His voice lowered as he shifted closer to my ear. "I can't believe you thought you'd just walk out of here. You're lucky she didn't get here faster or she'd have flayed you alive before I could stop her."

"Blame the runt. I was protecting her."

"I know." He ducked under my arm and someone ducked under the other–Neffrey by the smell–and together they heaved me to my feet. He continued speaking in a low grumble. "Next time think of some other way to protect her, or I doubt I can help you."

I didn't bother answering. The street tilted again, then eased back to level, leaving me with a pounding headache and wobbling knees. The guards and the Warden had all left and Rue was biting her lip so hard I was surprised she didn't have blood running down her chin too. She wiped the back of her hand across her cheek and turned away.

4 – The Elf Returns

It was a long walk to the underground and then to my apartment. Senyr and Neffrey came along, one to either side of me, and occasionally one of them would reach out to steady me when I started tilting a little. Ruena walked ahead of us, her arms crossed tightly over her chest and her head down. She was obviously feeling pretty bad about the whole chain of events, but I let it go for now in favor of concentrating on walking. It had been a long time since I'd had the sense beaten out of me like that.

As we approached my room, Ruena slowed until we were almost on top of her. Rather than step aside to allow us to pass, she extended her arms to better fill the corridor and blocked our way. She glanced up at me with watery eyes and a nervous expression. "Big magic ahead."

I tried to push past her, but she stubbornly kept her arm in front of me. Movement caught my eye and a cloaked and hooded figure stepped out of the shadows of the rough-hewn stone opposite my door. It stopped in the middle of the corridor and stood waiting.

The hair rose on the back of my neck and I took Ruena's arm just below the shoulder and dragged her back, ignoring her hissing protests, until she was behind Senyr and myself. Neffrey had already slipped a few feet away and stood against the wall. The panic from earlier was still close to the surface and I stubbornly shook it away so I could protect myself and Ruena however I'd need to.

The figure glided toward us, making no sound, and a tingle of magic washed over me as it neared. Strong magic. Very strong for me to feel it from paces away. I raised a hand. "Stop right there."

It did, and its gloved hands slowly went to the hood and pushed it back to reveal Nissa's greenish tinted skin, her emerald eyes shining in the dim lamplight.

I let out my breath in relief.

Ruena shouldered her way past me and I clutched my ribs, grimacing at the sudden spike of pain.

She flung herself into the elf's arms. Nissa's cold expression softened and she wrapped her arms around the teen, squeezing briefly. "You have grown so much, child."

They were roughly the same size now. Elves were a foot or so smaller than humans on average, and Rue was small for a fourteen year old girl. Maybe another effect of her elfish blood. Her pearly eyes closed and she sighed as she squeezed Nissa in return.

The elf's hair was still a vibrant white, although the long braid looked to have been chopped off and what remained was now a few inches long and windswept. Her delicately pointed ears swept back and were adorned with a few silver rings at the tip of each. There was a new scar that ran up her jaw to the front of her right ear.

Her new look made me uncomfortable, and I was confused why, until I remembered the vision given to me by the stone five years ago. This was what she'd looked like on top of the baroness's manor, standing with Rue and I before—

Her gaze lifted to mine and her lips drew together in a frown. "What happened to your face?"

I scowled back, the pain of my beating reasserting itself and helping to banish the memories. "Had a polite talk with the Warden."

She slipped away from Ruena's embrace and pulled a dented tin from a satchel at her side. "How have you survived for the last five years without elfish magic to fix you?"

As she moved forward the tingle of magic crawled over my skin and I stepped back instinctively. I didn't remember her very presence being this strong, but our time together had been distractingly stressful, and once in the labyrinth there had been no shortage of magic playing havoc with my senses. Still... just having her stand a couple of paces away shouldn't be affecting me this much.

She hesitated, rolling the tin in her fingers, then responded quietly. "I told you I would return when it was time."

Time for Sangarie to be destroyed.

I'd never mentioned the vision to anyone, not even her. When I'd first touched the stone we were sent to retrieve in the shadow labyrinth it showed me what happened in Sangarie to turn it into an ash-covered ruin littered with portals to other times. I saw myself, carrying the stone through the baroness's manor, all the way to the top. Then holding it aloft as it exploded in a blinding burst to end everything.

I was an idiot. Of course it was the stone I was sensing, not her. She'd brought it with her.

I swallowed the lump that rose in my throat, pushing back the images from the vision. Nissa knew the stone was involved in the destruction we'd seen in the labyrinth. She didn't yet know I'd caused it... would cause it. Somehow.

My voice came out huskier than I intended. "Why come back here?"

"Destiny."

I chuckled, reaching to rub my hand over my face and remembering at the last moment that my face was bruised and bloody. I let it drop to my side. "You have it with you."

She raised her eyebrow and tilted her head, her troubled expression clearing a little. "That is why you hesitate."

I grunted and flicked my gaze away. She'd expected a warmer reunion? Our time together had easily been the most painful and terrifying of my life. Plunging through a landscape of my nightmares, surrounded by enough magic to make my teeth rattle, repeatedly pushing my body past its limits. I still ached when the weather changed because of some of those injuries.

Her eyes shone even brighter, nearly glowing in the dim light. "You can sense how much stronger it has grown, can you not? Even if you doubt me, trust what your gift tells you."

The soft sound of cursing caught my attention and I looked out of the corner of my eye to see Neffrey staring at me, a look of understanding on his dirty face. Senyr glanced nervously between the two of us.

I smirked just a little bit. I'd wondered if the master of spies had figured out my secret. Apparently not. At least not until now. I caught Senyr's gaze and he sighed.

I had bigger things to worry about. I looked at Nissa. "Why would you bring it along?"

She frowned. "It is... complicated. Perhaps we can speak in private."

I turned fully this time, pinning Senyr and Neffrey with a look. "Do you mind?"

Neffrey's face scrunched up and his gravelly voice rang through the corridor. "Course we mind. I want to hear what's going on."

Senyr put a hand on the Yellow's shoulder. "Come on, Neff. Gray is a master now, and we should trust him."

Neffrey shrugged the hand off. "Trust him? He's a lying, thieving shit."

"So am I, and you trust me."

"No I don't. I just know you better." Neffrey scowled at me and wagged his finger. "We need to have a talk, boy."

I maintained eye contact with him, but Senyr pushed him away from the apartment door.

"Later." Senyr got him moving and then turned back to look at me. "I have a job for you. Come find me for the details as soon as you're done with whatever this is." He shot a look at the elf, then grunted and pushed Neffrey down the hall ahead of him.

I took a deep breath to chase thoughts of them out of my head, and my cracked ribs sent pain racing across my chest. I clutched my side and kept all the undignified noises to myself, although my eyes watered until the pain receded.

Nissa gestured at the apartment door. "Perhaps we should go inside. I can help you with that."

I nodded and Ruena immediately darted past me to open the door. It was locked, since Deidre was out for the evening, and I had purposely not given the girl a key so she had to practice her lockpicking if she wanted to bother me. As she dug in her belt for picks, I slipped the key out of my pouch. "Hey."

She looked up and I tossed it to her.

I didn't want to stand here and wait. It'd been a long enough walk from the Lower Yard.

She opened the door and went inside first, swinging it wide for us. I shifted my gaze to Nissa and gestured with the hand not occupied with holding my ribs together. "After you."

The elf nodded her head gracefully and followed the girl inside, moving all the way to the opposite side of the heavy table before turning to watch me enter and close the door. I pushed the deadbolt home too, just to make sure we didn't have any unexpected visitors.

When the room was secure, I let my shoulders relax and took a few more steps away from the magic radiating from the elf. "Okay. We're alone. Why did you think it was a good idea to bring that thing back? Why not keep it far away from here so it can't destroy everything?"

Nissa reached into a pouch at her belt and brought out the fist-sized stone, which throbbed with a white glow to match my thudding heart. She set it gingerly on the dining table. "Because it is not the only one of its kind."

My gaze flicked up to meet hers and I tried to read those cold emerald eyes, but she just stared back impassively. Fucking elf. I narrowed my eyes. "I thought there was only one. And that's why it was so important."

"There is only one. But we stole this one from the future, and so, for the last five years, there have been two." She pointed at the stone. "This, and the one that was already somewhere in the world. This one is not supposed to be here."

The stone pulsed. The magic pressed against me, raising the hair on the back of my neck and making me want to retreat across the room, but I held my ground. "Why is it stronger?"

The stoic expression cracked a little. "It has been growing in power for five years. More power than the elders are comfortable with."

More than I was comfortable with, too. I gave in and took a few more steps away, my eyes locked on the stone. "So what are you going to do with it? Throw it into a portal when the Night of Shadows happens?"

She snorted. "No. We must ensure it is where it needs to be, so you can find it five years ago." She held up the dented tin still in her hand. "Allow me to ease your pain? This conversation is better approached with your full attention."

I hesitated, feeling as if the stone would explode here in my apartment if I looked away, but that was ridiculous. I was letting it get to me, feeding my paranoia. It was just a rock.

I took a steadying breath and nodded. "Fine. Goop me."

"Sit down. It will be easier."

I moved away from the table and to the bed, perching on the edge, though it took more effort than I cared to admit. The Warden had been true to her word about not killing or crippling me, but she knew how to

24

make it hurt. I got the feeling if Nissa hadn't returned I'd have been whining about these injuries for weeks.

The elf waited as I pulled up my shirt, then slathered ointment across my abdomen and up my lower chest. I tensed and breathed carefully for a minute, but the pain eased even as she worked and I felt the tingle of magic everywhere her fingers touched. It was weak compared to the pulsing magic that surrounded the stone. Even from a good fifteen feet across the room I could feel that pressure, vibrating in the air, waiting for some outlet.

Nissa leaned closer, smearing ointment on my jaw, cheekbones, and temples. The headache started to ease and I sighed despite myself. When she'd finished, she wiped the goop from her fingers on the hem of my shirt.

I cursed as I tugged it out of her hands and looked at the oily stain. "That isn't going to come out."

"Do you feel better?"

I stretched gingerly. "The pain is gone, but as long as that thing is in here, I don't think better is going to happen."

Nissa rose and crossed to the table, staring down at the stone. She turned it slightly, letting the lamplight bounce off the polished surface, and her face softened as her fingers slid over it. "The future must happen the way it already has, which means one of the stones must be here for the destruction of this city."

I stood and edged along the bed, keeping as much distance between myself and the stone as I could. I didn't want to destroy my city. I didn't want the future to happen the way I'd seen it. "What makes you think it's this stone? Wouldn't it make more sense if it was the other one, since it had to be here in order for us to find it? Maybe if both of them are here they'll interfere with each other."

There was a long silence and when I turned back to the elf she was staring at me. "The elders are split on this. Some believe the stones must be kept apart, while others believe they should be brought together. It has been a source of debate since I returned with it. They do not know what the best course of action is."

I grimaced. "The wisdom of elves."

"It is my task to find out what happens, why it happens, and make sure it happens. To that end, I brought the stone. Hopefully the other one finds its way here, because my people have not been able to locate it."

"Maybe it doesn't need to happen. What if we just… didn't destroy the city? Would that be so bad?" I shifted back and came up against the wall, grimacing as I realized how far I'd retreated. "Sangarie could go on being a haven of crime and commerce, and you could take that stone back home as a souvenir. Everyone wins."

She shook her head. "The future must happen, or the world breaks."

"What the fuck does that mean?"

"Terrible things happen when people try to change the future."

"Really? More terrible than the city being blasted into ruin?" I waved a hand at the ceiling. "More terrible than the streets crawling with shadowkraken and death?"

She held my gaze, her expression cold. "Yes."

I wanted to keep arguing. I was desperate to avoid what I'd seen in that vision, but something in her eyes told me she wasn't exaggerating. She'd been in the labyrinth with me, fighting alongside me, and she knew how much of a nightmare it had been. If the alternative was worse…

I dropped my gaze. It wasn't the time to argue. "Fine. What has to happen then? How are you planning to make sure the future doesn't break?"

"The city must be destroyed at sundown on the Night of Shadows, and the stone must be placed in the cavern beneath it for you to discover."

I pushed past the squirmy feeling in my gut. "I don't even know if that cavern is there. We've searched every inch of the underground looking for a passage that leads to someplace like that and found nothing."

"It is there."

"How do you know?"

"Because I found it."

I shot her a suspicious look. "When?"

"A year after we met." She reached into a satchel at her side and pulled out a rolled piece of parchment, walking around the table and pushing aside a chair.

I edged closer as she unrolled a map of the city and the surrounding land. It was beautifully drawn, and probably very expensive. She struggled to hold the curling edges, so I reached out and placed a hand on one side, pinning it down. Quality paper. Definitely expensive. The magic of the stone crawled over me and I glanced at it on the far side of the table.

"Thank you." She put a finger on the baroness's manor roughly in the center of the city. With it she traced an oblong shape across the estates toward the east, away from the river. "This is where the cavern is, but it is below any of the caves your guild uses. It is part of an underground river. There is a canyon here–" she put her finger on the foothills to the east of the city "–where a hidden crevice leads to the buried river channel. It is possible to traverse the distance to the cavern by foot, as long as you are not afraid of getting wet."

"And the cavern pillars, the white tile maze, the treasury… all of that is already there as well?"

"It is all there. When I returned, I found everything there except for the stairway leading into the manor. The site is ancient. From before humans ever thought to build a city here. After I found it, I disguised myself as a human and sought an audience with the baroness. I sold her the information, suggesting it would make an excellent secret treasury."

I chuckled. "You sold it to her? I thought you'd make a good criminal, but never pegged you as a Green Hand."

"I do not understand what you mean. She would have been suspicious if I had merely given her the information. Humans always want something in return for their favors." She shrugged. "I told her of the treasury, but not the maze or the cavern. I told her where to dig within her manor to reach the site, and even managed to get someone I knew to do the work, so she would not get curious and dig too far."

"You have a friend that digs secret stairways?"

"There is someone I know that is a builder." Her scowl deepened. "Although I have been unable to contact them since. Perhaps they were paid to disappear."

I grunted. "Knowing the paranoia of Lady Karyn, I'd say they were *made* to disappear."

"I fear you may be right."

27

I changed the subject. "Aren't you worried she'll figure out the maze and get into the cavern?"

"The maze was undisturbed when we found it, which indicates she does not."

I stared down at the map. There were always renovations and repairs going on at the baroness's manor, so it was possible–if she was keeping it hidden from the general populace–that we missed her digging the stairwell into the treasury. Especially if she used workers from outside the city.

Come to think of it, there was a report a year ago of some increased activity by the Ironguard over the course of a few nights, but nothing ever came of it. Perhaps she'd managed to move her treasury without the guild finding out. Tricky old hag.

I stared at the tiny rendition of the manor on the parchment. "So things are all set up in there." That made it seem worse. Like Sangarie itself was waiting for the hour of its death.

"Indeed." She tugged the map out from under my hand and rolled it up, stashing it back in her satchel. "The only thing I have not figured out is how the city is destroyed. I can only hope events will unfold as they should now that the stone is here."

I grimaced, the vision flashing through my memory. "Yeah. We can hope."

Her eyes narrowed and she stared at me. "Is there something I am unaware of? You are acting strange again."

"Unhappy." I gestured at the stone pulsing on the table as I took a few steps away and averted my gaze. "The word you're looking for is unhappy."

She didn't look convinced, but didn't press the issue. "There is another concern."

"Of course there is."

"I have received rumors that the human nobleman Loring seeks your death."

Ruena gasped from across the room.

I'd nearly forgotten she was here. A quick glance showed her to be tucked into the shadow of the alcove where the large bed rested. Her eyes were squinted like she stood in bright sunlight. If the stone made my skin crawl like this, I could imagine how bright it must be to her elfblood sight. I felt a little guilty for not realizing it sooner. I plucked my heavy cloak from its hook by the door and gritted my teeth as I strode down the length of the table and tossed it into a pile on top of the stone. It might help a little.

I backed off again and met Nissa's gaze. "I'd say I was surprised, but really the only surprising part is he waited this long to come after me. Do you have any details? Is he here in the city?"

"Unfortunately that is all I know. It was part of a vision I received on the eve of my journey. I recognized the human's face, and the threat to your life, but that is all."

"Well, let me know if you get anything more than vague premonitions."

She scowled. "This is a serious threat."

"Loring isn't the first person to want me dead. If I crawled under a rock every time there was a threat to my life I'd never see the sun again."

"Loring is no thug. He has power and coin."

"I doubt he has a lot of either of those since we humiliated him and destroyed his retinue. He left Sangarie in disgrace, and he's banned from the city on threat of death. The baroness wasn't happy with his part in her son's demise."

She sighed. "Just be careful. That human has harbored thoughts of revenge for five years. He should not be dismissed so easily." Her larger than usual incisors—like tiny fangs—dimpled her lip and she flicked her gaze down.

I frowned. I was good at reading people, and right now her body language told me she wasn't being entirely honest with me either. I didn't think she'd lie to me outright, but it was a pretty safe bet she wasn't telling me everything she knew.

Of course, I couldn't complain. I was holding back some key information as well. What would she do if she knew I was the one that destroyed it all? Would she blame me for this entire mess? Try to stop me? *Help me?*

I shook myself out of the morbid thoughts. "Did you find a place to stay while you're here?"

At that point, Ruena jumped up from where she'd been leaning against the side table by my bed. She jostled the table enough that the oil lamp clattered onto its side, and quickly picked it up before anything could spill. "Oh! If you don't, maybe I can help you find someplace?"

Nissa raised an eyebrow. "I have rented a room."

Rue's face fell, but she nodded. She was avoiding looking at the stone hidden on the table, or even in its direction.

Nissa turned to me. "I think it would be a good idea to leave the stone with you."

I snorted. "Ah—no. I don't want it anywhere near me." I gestured at Rue. "It makes both of us very uncomfortable."

"Very well. I shall keep it safe for now."

"Maybe don't carry it around the city, though. I have it on good authority that Sangarie is crawling with pickpockets."

She scowled back. "I will try to discover what happens leading up to the destruction. I will be in touch, as you humans say." She slid the stone out from under my crumpled cloak and stuffed it back into the pouch.

It did nothing for the tingle coursing through my body. "Lovely."

She met my gaze, her eyes narrowing. "It may be best to limit the people who know about these events for now. We need more information, and humans tend to panic when faced with the threat of destruction."

"No kidding."

She nodded, then headed for the door without another word. I let her go. As much as I considered her a friend, her magic made me uncomfortable. She could do her digging far away from me.

Rue watched from the other side of the room, looking as if she wanted to follow.

I pulled one of the chairs out from the table. "You. Sit."

She looked at me with a long-suffering dismay as the door closed behind the elf, but trudged over and dropped into the chair. She pulled her heels up to rest on the seat as well, hunching over and wrapping her arms around her knees. "Go ahead. Chew me out."

I had intended to. The lecture was bubbling to the surface, playing itself out in my head in Senyr's voice. How many times had he yelled at me for the same damn things before I learned my lesson?

If I was honest, some lessons I still hadn't learned.

I pulled out the chair beside hers and spun it around to sit backwards and lean my arms on the backrest, pleased that my ribs didn't even twinge. As much as I hated the magic, I'd missed the benefits of the elf's healing touch over the last five years. "Do you know what I'm going to say already?"

She nodded, not meeting my gaze.

"Tell me."

She heaved a sigh, blinking furiously and turning her head away from me. "I was too loud. I was careless. I should have checked for Coppers. I should have gone for help right away when they took you."

"All very good points."

"Whatever," she muttered.

She was such a mouthy little shit. I looked down at my arms. "You know all that without me screaming at you. You just need to think of it when it matters. You have to keep your head on straight, or it'll get taken off."

She dropped her forehead onto her crossed arms and mumbled in a wavering, high-pitched tone. "I'm sorry."

Six be damned. I hadn't even yelled. I stared at her bowed head and sighed as she sniffled, feeling like a total dick. She didn't have as much natural talent as I did, and though I tried to be patient with her, sometimes I forgot how young she was. She was working hard. I knew that.

I reached out and set a hand on top of her head. "Don't be sorry. Just do better next time."

She shook her head, shrugging my hand off. "No. I'm just sorry that you got hurt."

My eyebrow shot up. "So you're not sorry for all the stupid shit you did?"

She peeked at me and glowered. "If I hadn't followed you to that jail, nobody would've known where to find you."

"Ugh!" I pushed away from the chair and moved to pick up an empty glass on the counter, pouring a splash of whiskey. "You're such an ungrateful brat."

"And you're such a cocky dumbass. And you smell like death."

I pointed at her with my glass. "That's your fault too." Reaching into the top of my boot, I took out the wrapped amulet I'd pulled out of the

31

corpse in the jail. It had soaked through the handkerchief and I wasn't looking forward to washing the smell out of my boots. I tossed it onto the table in front of her. "This one counts as mine, since I had to dig it out."

She wrinkled her nose. "Not fair. I saw it."

"But you didn't steal it. The game is to steal something."

"You stole it from a corpse. That hardly takes skill." She took a corner of the handkerchief and lifted it to shake the amulet onto the table.

It was covered in congealed gore, but glimpses of its polished stone surface shone through. A corroded metal filigree surrounded it and the delicate chain had clumped and tangled into a knotted mess. It was leaving a stain on the table.

Ruena gagged and pinched her nose shut. "So gross. But also very magical. I can't quite tell what it does, though. It kind of just glows, like it's waiting." She squinted as she studied it. "So pretty."

I downed the whiskey, wishing the burn would overpower the smell of the corpse juice. A nagging foreboding hovered over me and I shot quick glances into the shadowy corners of the apartment, remembering the feeling in the jail of being watched. "Well you can take it with you. I don't want it."

She made an exaggerated gagging face as she pulled out a cloth of her own and wrapped the amulet up again.

I set the glass down and took a rag from the nearby countertop to wipe my hands the best I could, frowning at the dried blood and gore. "I think I'll clean up and turn in. It's getting late already and if I leave that gross shit on the table Deidre will tan my hide."

Rue's head snapped up as she finished slipping the amulet into a hidden pouch. "What time is it?"

I frowned at her sudden eagerness. "Probably a few hours past midnight. Why?"

"Oh, no reason. Just wondering how late it was getting."

My eyes narrowed. "What are you up to?"

She smiled widely. "Nothing. Make sure to clean up your face. It's disturbing seeing blood all over your mouth when you don't have any injuries." She made chomping motions with her fingers. "Makes it look like you eat people. See you tomorrow!"

32

"Rue!"

She hurried out the door and down the hall, her footsteps barely making a sound as the apartment door swung slowly shut again.

This was the Six getting back at me for everything I'd put Senyr through as a kid. I tossed the rag in the dirty laundry bin and wondered why I'd ever agreed to train that idiot girl. As I stared at the door I also realized she'd pocketed my key to the apartment.

Son of a—

5 – Under Suspicion

I made a quick trip to the baths first, tired of the smell clinging to me, then I had to pick the lock to my own apartment because Rue had taken my key. I was spreading fresh blankets on the bed when Deidre returned. She listened to my retelling of the visit with the Warden with a mix of concern and sympathy, wrinkling her nose at the lingering smell of corpse and dragging over the bucket of soapy water I'd set on the counter after cleaning the table to start washing it again herself.

Just when I figured she was building up to lecture me on taking such risks, I sat down at the table and told her about Nissa returning and the impending doom of Sangarie–minus the fact that I knew I was going to be the cause of it, and minus the part about Loring wanting me dead. No need to worry her with those little details.

She asked a few vague questions, but for the most part remained lost in thought, her brow wrinkled and her lips pressed so tight they wouldn't have had any color if she hadn't been wearing some. I cautioned her to secrecy with a promise that I'd tell Rigel and Senyr as soon as the opportunity presented itself. And I would. I just needed to figure out what the fuck was going on for myself first.

Once I assured her I wouldn't try to do everything alone, I got a lecture I *hadn't* expected. Apparently it was very rude of me that I didn't bother to ask Nissa anything about what she'd been doing for the last five years, how her family was, or whether she wanted to get together to catch up on old times.

I snorted. "The only old times we share are filled with nightmares and death, and I'm not keen on reliving them."

"You could have showed *some* interest. Aren't you supposed to be a master of small talk?"

"I'm *sorry*. I didn't think to inquire about her private life while she was telling me the city was going to be leveled in under two weeks."

Judging by how hard she was scrubbing the tabletop, Deidre wasn't impressed with my reasoning. "She has nobody in this city. You could have at least invited her to share a meal or two with us." She scowled at the spot where the amulet had rested. "You went through a lot together."

I leaned back in my chair, lacing my fingers behind my head and watching her clean the surface I'd already washed three times. "Just because we killed monsters together doesn't mean we're best friends."

She threw the rag back into the bucket of soapy water, splashing some onto the tabletop, then blew a lock of hair out of her face that had escaped the hasty bun at her neck. "I can still smell it! Where is it coming from?"

"I told you, I sent out the blankets and my clothes to be washed, I scrubbed the table, and I cleaned my boots. I don't know how it can still stink in here."

A brisk knock came from the door and I winced. That was probably Senyr, since I hadn't gone looking for him about the job he mentioned. "Come on in."

Sure enough, the old thief opened the door and stepped inside, looking once at Deidre and nodding respectfully before pinning his gaze on me. "Someday you'll come and find me right away like I ask and I'm going to die from the shock of it."

"I can't let that happen, now can I?"

He turned to Deidre and gave a half bow. "My apologies, dear, but I'm going to steal your miscreant away for a couple of hours."

She waved a hand distractedly while peering around the floor searching for stains. "Probably for the best. If the smell goes away with him I'll know where it's coming from."

I frowned. "That's a bit harsh. I took a bath."

"Take another one before you come home."

"Fine," I grumbled. I moved to put my boots on and remembered they were drying from having been scrubbed. With an even louder grumble I dug out the soft leather boots I wore on special occasions. They were dark and fitted, lacking the little sheath for a knife that my usual ones had, but they were comfortable.

35

When I was ready I paused to give Deidre a peck on the cheek. She raised an eyebrow meaningfully and shot a quick glance toward Senyr, but I wrinkled my nose back at her before following him out of the apartment. I'd tell him in my own time.

We walked in companionable silence for a while before I spoke in a low voice that wouldn't carry through the underground corridor. "Is this job something you couldn't speak about in front of her, or something she wouldn't approve of?"

He sighed. "Both. Let's get to the surface before we talk."

I scowled, but didn't question him. Now that I was one of the three Hands of the Master, my assigned jobs were usually sensitive, secretive, or both. I didn't have the daily duties of an enforcer, but my rounds were significantly broader. The Hands of the Master were in charge of the enforcers, settling disputes, handing out jobs, as well as taking on any hit that involved nobility. Both Senyr and the third master thief, Garion, were getting older and more willing to handle the management work and leave the actual thievery to me.

Even now, just walking through the underground I could pick up the faint whisper of my mentor's left boot scuffing on stone. He'd injured himself two years ago, and it had never quite healed. He was still quiet enough for most people to miss, but a trained ear could pick him out. I shrugged aside the feelings of worry and sadness, telling myself he was still a better thief than me. And he reminded me of it any chance he got.

We came up in Old Town, the moon on its way across the sky and the drunks happily settled at tables in the seedy bars. It wasn't the quietest place for a discrete conversation, but we were well known here and nobody would look twice at us.

It hadn't been an easy decision choosing an enforcer to replace me in Old Town. It took a special kind of thief to wrangle the unruly collection of lowlifes that worked here and I hadn't been expecting to pass along the torch so abruptly. Rigel, Senyr, and Garion had all agreed that bringing someone in from another district wouldn't work, so they'd dropped the decision in my lap and washed their hands of it.

Tekken was my choice. She was smart, inconspicuous, and most of the thieves respected her. Her son was almost five years old now, and the older thieves doted on him like he was their own grandkid. Having

36

so recently become a mother when she took up the position, she turned Old Town's Black Hands into her own extended brood.

Rigel loved to tell me she ran the district better than I ever had. I protested, of course, but it was absolutely true. And her greatest achievement so far had been to turn the wild horde of young pickpockets into her eyes and ears. Even now, deep into the quiet hours of the night, I could pick out the flash of a little figure around a corner or on a rooftop. They all knew me and within minutes Tekken would know I was around, but she would give me space for whatever I was doing.

That space was what Senyr and I were counting on for this conversation. We walked in near complete silence under the moon and occasional street lamp, and I waited for him to start.

He began with a question. "What have you heard about Lady Josyna?"

I frowned and gazed at him for a good long minute. Josyna was one of Deidre's clients. Normally I picked up a fair bit of information about the people she serviced just from her chatting about her night, whether I wanted to or not. I was a safe target for things she normally wouldn't talk about because I gave no shits about the nobility and their gossip, but this particular noblewoman had caught my attention if only because Deidre *didn't* say much about her. Over the past few months I'd grown increasingly worried Deidre was getting herself into something she shouldn't be.

I resumed my habitual sweeping gaze of the streets around us as I rattled off what I remembered from other casual conversations around Old Town. "New nobility. At least, new to Sangarie. She arrived a few years ago with a small entourage of servants and purchased an estate. She's been building her household, taking in ousted servants from other manors. Rumor has it she's sickly, so she doesn't entertain company. At least not from her peers. People joke that she can only afford second-hand servants. But she has enough money for Deidre's company, so she can't be too hard up. Deidre doesn't say much about her."

Senyr grunted. "That's all?"

"I don't pay attention to every overdressed peacock in the city. This one doesn't cast a shadow."

"Doesn't mean she isn't dangerous. Most nobles have bloodier hands than the Reds, and darker ambitions than any criminal in the underground."

"I realize that." I shoved my hands in my pockets, carefully keeping an eye out for anyone close enough to hear our lowered voices. "But I don't need to know a wolf's hobbies, as long as I understand it'd rip my throat out just for looking at it wrong."

"Well we need to know a bit more about this particular wolf."

I shifted my gaze in his direction, curiosity and worry nagging at me. "Why her? From what people say, she's harmless. Helpful even, if you're a servant on the hill. An older lady that takes in strays."

Senyr blew out in frustration, keeping his gaze on the street in front of us. I'd known him long enough to recognize that he was uncomfortable talking, and that wasn't like him when discussing a job.

My eyes narrowed. "What aren't you telling me?"

"Don't overreact."

Both eyebrows shot up. "To *what*? Spill it, old man."

"For a few years now we've been keeping an eye on Deidre. Who her clients are, how much she brings in. Her casual acquaintances."

My mouth firmed up and I scowled. When he said "keeping an eye on" that usually implied orders for the Yellows. Why would they be looking into Deidre?

He continued, "She works for a number of very high profile clients, and despite the price of her services she lives very simply."

"You're suspicious because she squirrels away her earnings and doesn't flaunt them? Does Rigel think she's cheating him?"

He sighed. "Rigel thinks it's more than that. We're aware of her altruistic side projects and look the other way because it doesn't hurt anyone, and for years we assumed that's what she did with all the money she made, but lately we've started to wonder if there's something more we've been missing."

"Like what? What are you implying and what does it have to do with this Lady Josyna?"

"We're not sure, and that's why we're looking into it. Once we started digging a little, things just weren't adding up. Where do all these smuggled servants go? How does Deidre manage to find places for them? We assumed she had an outside contact, and suspect it has something to do with Lady Josyna."

"So what? There's nothing wrong with that. Even I can't find much fault in what I've heard about Josyna."

"We know very little about her, and that worries us. Where did she come from? Why did she come to the city only to hide herself away from it? Why be so secretive, yet fill her house with gossipy servants? If she's part of Deidre's work, is it because she has a problem with the nobility? Is she here to cause trouble?

"If this noblewoman has some grand scheme to shake up Sangarie, it could be very bad for the guild. Our organization depends on the agreements with Lady Karyn, and if someone else takes her place it could mean panic in the streets. It could mean war between the guild and the guard. A return to the old way of doing things."

Until now the issue of Lady Josyna had been just uneasy stirrings in my gut, but if the guildmaster was concerned enough to be bringing in the masters, Deidre could be in more trouble than I realized.

Senyr rattled on. "She's collecting servants from all over the estates. She has money when she needs it, insider information on every household on the hill because of her rescues. We've put a Yellow Hand in her manor and they can't tell us any more than what's sent up to her room for breakfast. Only her closest servants are allowed direct access, supposedly because of the fragile state of her health. And she is very close with one of the most influential Blues in the guild. One who has intimate access to the man set to inherit the underground once Rigel's gone."

My teeth clenched at the casual mention of the guildmaster's plans for me, but I shoved it aside. "You can't think Deidre would betray the guild."

"We've asked her for information, but she refuses to talk about it. She even told Rigel to fuck off."

I grimaced. That sounded like her. She spent way too much time around me.

"She claims there's nothing going on, and if there was, she'd let us know. Rigel wasn't pleased, but Deidre's an invaluable source of information for us on the hill. She's worked closely with us before on various infiltrations and has always acted in the best interests of the guild. He has to trust her on this."

"But he doesn't."

Senyr sighed and glanced around, as cautious as I was. "Deidre is protecting that noblewoman. We intend to find out why, and whether they're working together to upset the seat of power in the city."

I shook my head, scowling at him. "Deidre wouldn't—"

He raised a hand to cut me off. "Right now we're just looking into it. But Deidre can't know."

"You want me to lie to her."

"Is that a problem?"

It was my job. Deidre and I fully understood what our duties entailed in the guild. As an escort, she had obligations and responsibilities that made intimate relationships difficult. As a high ranking thief I got into all manner of sticky situations. We didn't always handle it gracefully, but we understood sometimes our positions would be at odds with our relationship. Lying was part of both our professions, and she'd understand that. Right?

"No. Not a problem."

"Good. And we aren't going after Deidre. Not yet. We're gathering information on Lady Josyna. That may be the key."

"So I'm breaking into the estates."

"You aren't the one going in."

I scowled. "Who's going in? Only the Hands of the Master are allowed to pull hits on the hill."

"One of Neffrey's top Yellows will be infiltrating the manor. The plan is to have him impersonate one of the Lady's guards so he can walk freely in the upper level for the night. I've been assured he's a master at disguises and is fully up to the challenge. He'll look around and find out what the old lady is up to. Meanwhile, you'll be drawing everyone's attention somewhere else. We just have to decide where."

The worry edged up another notch. Rigel's eye was on Deidre, and it all hinged on what they found out in that manor. She couldn't be working against the guild. Maybe she'd gotten in over her head with something, or didn't realize what Josyna was involved in, but I couldn't imagine her actively betraying us. I'd made that mistake once, and I wouldn't do it again.

With as many servants as Josyna was rumored to have taken on, Deidre had to be smuggling them off to somewhere for her. And while Deidre took female clients, if the noblewoman was as sickly as they said, it was more likely she went there for companionship than sex. Deidre could be a pawn in all sorts of schemes and plots, and if this Yellow found something incriminating there was no telling how Rigel would react. Frankly, after the shoddy investigation into the murders five years ago, I didn't trust anyone to do a thorough job of investigating anything.

Then there was the reaction of the noblewoman herself. If the spy got caught, would blame fall on Deidre? Would Josyna think Deidre had turned on her, or that she was a liability? Would she try to protect herself by getting rid of loose ends? Too many things could go wrong and I'd be somewhere else in the city playing carrot and leading the Silvers around by the teeth.

I stopped in the middle of the street and waited for Senyr to turn and look at me. "I want to do it."

He sighed. "We already decided the beggars would be a better tool for this."

"Who decided?"

"Rigel, Neffrey, and myself."

I moved closer, lowering my voice. "Let me do this. If Deid is messed up in something, I need to know."

He shook his head. "You're too high profile."

I frowned. The worry was churning away and I tried to think of some flaw in their plan... some reason I would be a better choice.

Truthfully, I wasn't. I didn't exactly have a glowing track record when it came to the estates. I couldn't walk the streets on the hill without a dozen Silvers peeking around corners at me. I'd thumbed my nose at too many people and stepped on too many toes. Rigel was constantly telling me I needed better relations with the nobility.

Maybe that was it.

I darted forward to catch up with Senyr, who'd already started off again. "What if I had a reason to be there?"

He turned to fix me with a suspicious gaze. "What do you mean?"

"Rigel's always telling me I need to foster connections on the hill. What if I was doing that and just happened to walk past her manor a few times. And one night, after the Silvers are used to me coming and going, I can slip in for a little peek around."

Senyr frowned.

"It's better than trying to impersonate one of her guards," I scoffed. "You have to know that won't work. Once they realize what happened they'll know someone was poking around for information. At least if a thief gets caught it can be passed off as a break-in."

He stared back, chewing on the inside of his cheek. "You're willing to play nice with whoever we pick?"

That sounded suspiciously like he already had someone in mind. I wasn't sure if he'd considered this plan already, or if it was just the latest in a line of potential acquaintances he was waiting to push on me. "I'm not going to like this, am I?"

"There's a nobleman by the name of Bartholomew Henrick that's been expressing interest in getting to know the infamous Gray Raven of Vengeance."

My face went red. "The what now?"

"It's how he refers to you in his book."

"His *what*?" I took a step back. "You're joking."

"Unfortunately not. He's become obsessed with the story of how you killed the son of the baroness and got away with it. He's decided to write a book based on it. Fictional, of course, to protect the name of the baroness. But he wants to research how you did it."

My mouth opened, but the thoughts were jumbled together in my brain. How did I even respond to that?

Senyr was staring at me intently. "That's your valid reason to be in the estates. His acquaintance would open up doors that your lockpicks can't even touch. Take it, or leave it to the Yellows."

I shook my head. "Can't you find a foolish young noble for me to seduce? Or someone that likes to gamble a little too much? Does it have to be a crackpot?"

Senyr shrugged. "This fool is interested. Too interested. You'd have an invitation to the hill and a reason to keep visiting. If you want the hit, you play nice with Lord Bartholomew."

"This is insane."

"All the best plans are."

"No. You always say the best plans are the simple plans."

42

"Well what do I know?"

I scoffed and brushed past him, striding down the street in the direction of the Throat.

Senyr followed after me, his limp more pronounced as he was forced to match my pace. "Are you going to tell me what your elf friend wanted?"

Shit. I'd forgotten about Nissa. I didn't even know where to start explaining what she'd told me. She was right about people panicking, although I didn't think Senyr would. What I did think he'd do is take me off this hit to focus on helping Nissa find her answers, and I couldn't let that happen. I already knew how Sangarie ended, and who ended it. Right now it was more important to make sure this investigation into Deidre didn't go terribly wrong. Treason against the guild wasn't a slap on the wrist.

I tried to keep my voice casual. "She's doing some research."

"It seemed a bit more than that. Something about it being time. And destiny?"

"Elves are dramatic."

He grabbed my arm and pulled me to a stop to face him. "It's something bad, isn't it?"

I'd have to tell him eventually. I'd have to tell him I was fated to destroy the entire city. But right now I wanted to focus on what I could do something about. "Let me figure out what's going on first. I'll tell you when I know more."

"Don't wait too long. Neffrey's likely to send half the beggars after you."

"I assumed they were already watching me."

He sighed and nudged me into motion again. "Let's go have a drink."

6 – Rue's Friend

I got home in the wee hours of the morning and went straight to bed, curling up around Deidre and trying not to pay attention to the questions rattling around in my head. It was late afternoon by the time I woke to find her gone and a note from Senyr under my door telling me to meet him at the Running Hart for drinks at sundown, where he'd introduce me to "an interesting fellow he knew."

That was going to be Lord Bartholomew Henrick. I thought about going back to bed and apologizing later, but the more frustrating I made things for Senyr, the more difficult they ended up being for me. I couldn't get out of this meeting, but I could damn well create a contingency plan for myself.

If things got too weird, or the noble's obsession wasn't as harmless as Senyr led me to believe, I'd have someone there to watch my back. Not that I didn't trust Senyr, but he'd recently let the Warden use me like a practice dummy, and I wasn't sure how far he'd be willing to go for the job. I needed someone who'd listen to me over Senyr, and knew how to read me without verbal instructions. I needed Rue.

I dressed in my working clothes and went to get my boots, realizing they were sopping wet before I put my foot in the first one. Deidre must have cleaned them again. I cursed and grabbed my dress boots instead, then slung on a cloak and stuffed Senyr's note in my pocket as I locked up the apartment.

It was a few hours before sunset, so the most likely place to find my little apprentice would be the Devil's Throat. She'd become an invaluable help to Sans and Kash, and they'd been happy to keep her around even after she was old enough to move underground.

Technically she belonged to Old Town and answered to Tekken, but her training had remained with me when I was promoted. I had Tekken assign her the occasional hit, just to give her the experience, and I handled everything else. I gave her a lot of shit about her skills, but she was already better than many of the thieves in Sangarie. Most importantly, I trusted her.

I reached the Devil's Throat and breathed deep as I walked in, finding comfort in the scent of ale, body sweat, and polished wood. It was just hitting the busy supper hour and Kash was running around near the main bar while she glared at Basil–the server they'd hired when Sans decided to step back from being so active.

Basil was a good guy, handsome and charming, but he had a habit of getting sucked into conversations and forgetting about his other customers. Kash complained constantly. Sans, from his typical seat at a central table, had fallen into the habit of loudly clearing his throat to remind the young man to keep moving. They must have been on him pretty bad already tonight, because I could see him darting between tables and brushing aside efforts to pull him into conversations.

I slid up to the bar and waited for Kash to notice me, letting my gaze wander across the crowd. On busy nights like this, Ruena often helped out a little until I called her away, but she was nowhere in sight. Maybe she was still in bed. I hadn't talked to her since she disappeared so suddenly the evening before.

Kash set a mug of ale down next to me with a thunk and a splash of foam. "You look like trouble. Don't bring it in here."

"Blame Senyr. And I'll be taking it to the Hart. I'm just stopping to get Rue."

Kash's brow furrowed as she scanned the room. "She was here a few minutes ago. Maybe she went into the back for something."

I smiled widely. "Appreciate it. I'll stop by later when I've dusted off the trouble." I downed half the mug as she grunted and moved away. Before I could make my way to the back, I caught sight of Sans watching me from the center table. His face was grim and his brow furrowed, so if I had to hazard a guess, he'd heard about my trip to the Lower Yard.

I picked up my mug and weaved between tables, making my way to the center of the room. Sans was playing cards with a few older patrons, one of which was May. Her cane rested beside her, and she was dressed in a tasteful burgundy gown that stood out next to the workman's homespun the others wore. She rose with some difficulty from her chair and held out her arms as I approached.

I accepted the hug with grace. "You look amazing, May. Why do you gift these crotchety old men with your presence?"

Sans grunted and played a card.

May resumed her seat and picked up her cards, keeping them tightly hidden as she beamed at me. "Are you here to play? This round is nearly over."

"Sorry. I'm just here to pick up Rue." I took another long swallow from my mug. "Things must be going well with Devlen if you've left him all alone at the brothel."

May smiled. "They are. He's a calming presence and brilliant with the customers. He's everything I could have asked for in a replacement. I'll be able to retire knowing my Blues will be kept happy and safe."

I smiled back at her. "That's good. You deserve a little relaxation." I finished the mug and set it down on a different table nearby, knowing Sans would kick me out if I put an empty mug on his, and turned to the old barkeep. "You look even more grouchy than usual."

"It's because of an idiot I know."

I kept the smile plastered on for the sake of the other players at the table. It wasn't hard to guess based on his not-so-subtle glances and his scowl, that the idiot was me. "I'm sure he has his reasons."

He played a card, then adjusted what remained in his hand. "The runt blames herself, you know."

Ah. He'd been talking to Rue. In all her excitement at Nissa's return and her cheerful demeanor when she'd left my apartment, I'd forgotten how upset she'd been after my encounter with the Warden. "It wasn't her fault. These things happen."

"Did you tell her that?"

Now it was my turn to frown. "No. Not in so many words."

"Perhaps you should."

I sighed deeply, avoiding his direct gaze. "Yeah. I will."

Sans flicked another card onto the table. "See that you do. I don't want any more moping about in here, it bothers my customers."

I nodded. "If you'll excuse me, I have a kid to track down."

I gave May a quick peck on the cheek and wandered off toward the door that led to the storage room in the back. The roar of laughter and conversation lessened as I passed through the door and pushed it shut behind me. I waited a moment for my eyes to adjust to the dimness, then walked forward to look down the rows of storage shelves.

That's where I found her, although I was immediately at a loss for what to do or say. I stared down the left hand side of the room, past shelves of dried goods and spare mugs, to see Rue astride a young man's lap, kissing him passionately and giggling. He was perched on a few crates of wine, his hands firmly gripping her ass.

Anger boiled up in my chest. Half-formed thoughts surfaced and were drowned out by others. She was under my care. Was my responsibility. She was just a *kid*. How dare this beardless... horny... *asshole* put his hands all over—"*Rue!*"

She jumped and nearly fell backwards off his lap, then scrambled to her feet and stepped in front of him as he hurriedly pulled his shirtfront closed. Her face was bright red as she did her best to block my view. "What are you doing here?"

I breathed deep through my nose, glaring at the man behind her. He was fit, young, and handsome in a roguish way. I knew the type. I *was* the type. There was no way I was letting this urchin take advantage of her.

I growled and stalked forward.

Ruena intercepted me, putting her hands on my chest and pushing me back. "Gray, stop!" She was forced a few steps back, but held me long enough the young man slipped past the other end of the shelves out of immediate danger.

He looked back, glancing at me briefly with a worried expression before turning his gaze to Ruena's back. "I'll see you later."

She looked over her shoulder and flashed him a smile.

He flipped his hood over his head and ducked through the shelving and out the back door, moving quickly, without a sound.

I pushed Ruena's hands aside and started to go after him, to teach him not to touch my kid, but she put herself in front of me again. "Don't!" She pushed me backward. "What the fuck, Gray. Relax, okay?"

"Relax? Who the fuck was that? I'll show him what happens when he paws at little girls."

She gave me a hard shove, pushing me back into the shelving so I had to catch myself to avoid knocking shit off the racks. I shifted my glare to her.

She was shaking, red-faced and panting. "I'm not a little girl anymore."

I stared at her a moment, breathing almost as hard as she was. Some semblance of reason began to sneak back into my thoughts and I realized she was right. She wasn't the waifish nine-year-old I'd been assigned to watch out for. By her age I'd been doing a lot more than kissing and heavy petting.

That didn't mean I was going to let some asshole take advantage of her.

I straightened my vest and gave myself a moment to get my heart rate back to normal. I couldn't keep the tightness out of my jaw, and I imagined my eyes weren't exactly gentle, but my voice was steady. "Who was he?"

She frowned, biting her lip. "A friend."

My eye twitched, but I maintained what calm I'd managed to drag up. "A friend, huh?"

"Why are you so upset? You have all kinds of friends."

I choked back a few responses. She was right. She was almost fifteen. She'd been raised in an environment where sex was as normal as eating and sleeping. Then why did the mere thought of it instill such rage in me? All I wanted was to chase him down and scare the ever-loving shit out of him.

I pinched the bridge of my nose and closed my eyes. "I think we should talk about this later."

She grunted, crossing her arms over her chest. "There's nothing to talk about."

I forced a chuckle instead of screaming. "There are two things that can happen right now. You can go back inside and help Kash for the rest of the night, or you can come with me and be my lookout. Either way, I'm going to forget I saw this until I can look at you without wanting to murder that kid."

There was a long silence, then a sigh. "I'll go with you."

I raised my gaze to her, then blushed and looked away quickly. "Fix your shirt and let's go out the back."

I turned and strode the long way around the shelving, heading for the alley door. Behind me she stumbled along, trying to button and tuck in her shirt as she went. Thankfully I hadn't seen anything I couldn't unsee.

7 – Lord Bartholomew

We walked in silence to the Running Hart. She didn't ask where we were going, and I didn't offer it. The sun was on its way to setting, leaving long shadows cast by the buildings around us. As we crossed into the new market district we passed people heading home or to taverns for the evening.

I pushed all thoughts of that young man and what I'd seen out of my head. I needed to concentrate on my job and not worry about what was going on with her. I'd taught her to take care of herself, and I was absolutely certain she could knife the bastard in the groin before he could do anything she didn't want, but that meant I had to accept that she–

I shook my head. Not thinking about it. Concentrate on Senyr and his obsessed nobleman. I had to make this work or I couldn't get to the bottom of what was happening with Deidre and the Lady Josyna. I wouldn't just stand aside while they investigated her for whatever the equivalent was for treason to a criminal organization. The last people who'd acted against the guild itself had met gruesome ends.

My mentor loitered a few buildings down from the Hart and I pushed down the last nagging little thoughts as I crossed the cobbled street to meet him. He was dressed in an expensive-looking shirt and jacket, his pants tucked into high polished boots. He could have walked around in the estates without earning a second glance.

I smirked as I stepped up beside him. "Well, aren't you fancy. Are your normal clothes with the laundry crew?"

He looked at me, then past me to Ruena, and narrowed his eyes. "Very funny. Why'd you bring the runt?"

"Because I don't like this whole situation." I turned to face Ruena and she listened with the same serious attention she always did, which

50

made it easier to focus on the job. "So we're here because Senyr is introducing me to a nobleman that thinks I'm the Six incarnate. He wants to learn all about my most infamous deeds and write a book about them."

Her eyebrow twitched up. "He has terrible taste."

I frowned. "Just listen. This is so I can get access to the estates for a hit, so we're playing along with him. It's top level secret, so no blabbing to your–" I paused, rethought my chosen words, then pressed on. "To anyone. Not even to Deidre. Got it?"

She looked even more skeptical, but nodded slowly. "Got it. Tell nobody. Not even Deidre." Her brows creased and she crossed her arms and shifted to put her weight all on one leg. "Why specifically Deidre? What's going on?"

"Stop being smart and just keep an eye on me, okay? If things get sketchy, I want you to create a reason for us to leave."

"Sure. Are you gonna pay for my drinks? I can't just go in there and sit at a table without ordering something."

I shifted my gaze to Senyr and raised an eyebrow.

He snorted. "You wanted a lookout. You pay for her."

I grumbled, but pulled a few silver out of a pocket hidden in my vest. "Don't get fancy. You don't look like you can afford it and they'll wonder how you got the money."

"Yeah, yeah. I'll follow a few minutes behind you." She raised her gaze and met mine. There was an unspoken hesitation there. Was it because I was upset with her, or because of the encounter yesterday with the Warden?

I nodded once with as much reassurance as I could muster, reaching out to squeeze her shoulder. "I'm counting on you."

She pocketed the money and nodded back, then slipped away from us.

Senyr raised an eyebrow. "Something going on I should know about?"

I started for the door of the Hart. "No. Let's get this over with."

He joined me and we made our way into the tavern. The Running Hart wasn't as fancy as the expensive restaurants closer to the hill that catered to the rich and powerful, but it was clean, classy, and served some of the best food in Sangarie. It was more on the expensive side, so

I didn't come often, but Deidre and I tried to have dinner here every couple of months. She liked their venison, and I liked spoiling her.

One of the servers recognized me and met us at a table against the wall to the right of the door. I sat across from Senyr and ordered a mug of ale. Senyr asked for the same. She hustled off with a smile and I surveyed the room more carefully.

I spotted a few well-off craftsmen eating in groups or with partners, and a couple of merchants drinking in a corner. No nobles as far as I could tell, although I probably would've only recognized half of them anyway. It was hard to familiarize yourself with people that didn't want to visit the seedier parts of the city.

I sat in uncomfortable silence with Senyr for about twenty minutes, stubbornly brushing off his attempts at small talk. I wasn't happy about this situation, and I didn't want the conversation to turn to things I was even less happy about. Eventually he gave up and we just watched the other patrons and drank our ale.

We were on the second mug by the time Senyr straightened in his chair and waved at a man that had just entered the tavern. I didn't even try to hide my measuring stare.

He had an average build, maybe a little soft around the belly. His hair was short, black, and artfully styled to make it look ruffled. He had a large nose and ears that stuck out a little too far. His clothes were common, and the wrong size, but very clean. His skin at first glance was as dirty as if he'd been working the fields all day, then I realized his hands were clean, and it was only his face that was dirty, like someone had dabbed soot on his cheeks. He was trying to make himself look common, and it came off insulting.

I sighed as I followed Senyr's lead and rose to meet him.

The man darted over, pressing both hands down urgently. "No, no. That's not necessary. We're all friends here!"

My eyebrow went up and Senyr shot me a warning look before smiling at the man. "Of course. May I introduce Gray?" He swept a hand in my direction.

I didn't know what the best reaction would be. Should I bow? Offer to shake his hand? What was customary when meeting a nobleman in a bad disguise?

The noble reached out with both hands and grasped one of mine before I could even decide whether to offer it, and I took it back as quickly as seemed proper. I cleared my throat and sat heavily back in my chair. "Charmed."

He grinned. "You are everything I expected. Truly."

I grimaced and wiped my hand on my pants under the table. It felt slick with lotion or something. Probably whatever he used to keep his fingers that soft.

Senyr sat as well and gestured at the third chair, the one with its back to the room. The nobleman sat and leaned forward. "My name, as I'm sure you know, is Lord Bartholomew Henrick. I'm a scholar of sorts. A student of the underbelly of society. I've heard of your exploits, and they are the stuff of legend."

Senyr sighed. "Don't tell him that. His head's big enough as it is."

The nobleman chuckled, glancing from Senyr to me and back again. "Witty banter! I love it!"

I shot Senyr a look of my own. One that said: *Are you fucking kidding me?* When the nobleman turned back in my direction, I forced a smile. "So, you wanted to know a little more about me, is that right?"

The man beamed, glancing around the room furtively. "Oh yes. The more you can tell me about yourself and your lifestyle, the more real my character will seem! You see, I don't know if Mister Senyr told you, but I'm writing a book about a thief that kills a prince." He leaned in closer with a harsh whisper. "Because of course I can't mention Lady Karyn or her departed son, lest my head roll. I don't think anyone would buy *my* freedom! Ha!"

I stared at him with a carefully blank expression. Bribes and payoffs were something we didn't talk about in mixed society, and the particular payoff this noble was referencing was a sore subject with the guildmaster. He still grumbled about it whenever I did something to earn his ire.

He shifted uncomfortably. "You know, because the guild bought yours?"

Was he seriously this clueless? I glanced at Senyr and even he was grimacing at the last comment. He hid his expression with his ale mug.

The nobleman continued on. "I would love for you to come visit me at my home. There are a great many things you could teach me about the ways of those who walk in the shadows. I would compensate you, of course. Perhaps even buy you some new clothes that wouldn't be so out of place in the estates."

My eye twitched with the effort of keeping an expression of polite interest on my face despite the implications that I was dirty and impoverished. "I would love to visit your home."

He smirked back at me and socked me in the shoulder. "I bet you would!" He chuckled and glanced at Senyr, then at the table, stifling his amusement. "I can have some clothing delivered to a place of your choosing, or I could set you up with a clothier."

It was getting harder and harder to keep a civil tongue, even though he probably didn't realize how insulting he was. "I think I can manage on my own, thank you."

He looked doubtful for a moment, then moved on quickly. "We should set up a way for me to get messages to you. So you know when to come calling."

Senyr cleared his throat. "I've thought of that already, my lord. If you leave the message with the barkeep here they've been instructed on how to get it where it needs to go."

Bartholomew's eyes widened. "Perfect! Just as I expected a communication network for spies and thieves would be! Is one of the barkeeps here actually a thief too?"

Senyr's brows furrowed in a way I recognized as the end of his patience. I was glad it wasn't directed at me for once. "No. The people here are all good citizens."

"Oh." Bartholomew looked disappointed. "Well, when I know a time and date, I shall leave a message." He glanced over his shoulder at the room in general, then leaned in a little closer. "Could you do one more thing for me tonight?"

I sighed and raised my ale to hide the pointed look I tossed at Senyr. "What's that?"

The nobleman leaned even closer, using his stage whisper. "Can I watch you steal something?"

I choked on the swallow I'd just taken and started coughing. At least it was good cover for how red my face had turned.

Bartholomew thumped me on the back, voicing his apologies as I caught my breath. Meanwhile, Senyr used the noble's distraction to deftly lift the heavy purse from under his loose homespun shirt. I suppose it was as good a way as any to give the man what he wanted. I took a little more time than I needed recovering from the spell so Senyr could pass it to me under the table.

Bartholomew settled himself in his chair again, glancing nervously around the bar. "No worries. It was perhaps too forward of me to ask when we've only just met."

I tossed his purse onto the table in front of him and his eyes lit up like it was a chest of gold. "Goodness! How did you–of course! When I was distracted by your coughing. That was astonishing! I didn't even feel anything. You are truly a master of your dark craft."

I glanced at Senyr, who was smirking behind his ale mug. The old man was going to be insufferable. "Thank you. You're too kind."

The nobleman beamed and rose from his chair. "I'll send word soon. You gentlemen have a good night." He winked at me and muttered under his breath. "Just splendid!"

It was all I could do not to roll my eyes. I raised my mug to him and he turned to leave.

Senyr leaned forward once he was gone. "You handled that better than I expected."

"I feel dirty."

"Well, sometimes you have to get a little dirty on the job." He waved at Rue and she shot out of her chair on the other side of the room and hurried over, then slipped into the one Bartholomew had recently vacated.

She was grinning. "Sooooo, how did it go?"

I waved at the server and held up three fingers. "He's even more annoying than you."

She made a face and mouthed the words back at me in a silent, mocking way, then turned to Senyr. "I saw that move. Very nice. And I heard a few things about leaving messages and visiting the estates."

Senyr chuckled. "At least one of you has some respect for your elders. The messages will be passed on to a Yellow that's assigned to this district. She'll make sure they get where they need to go. It seems your boss has quite the admirer."

I took one of the mugs the server delivered and grimaced as I handed back a few gold coins to settle up for the night. "There are so many ways this could go to shit. Are you sure I can't seduce someone instead?"

Senyr took his new mug in both hands, leaning over it like an old dock worker. "I thought you were wanting a little more fun? Something about being bored now that you aren't on the streets every night."

"This isn't what I had in mind."

"We could always go back to the original plan and set you loose in the city for the Silvers to hunt. I was thinking maybe a run through the New Market and into Riverside, get close enough to the inner wall to make them nervous."

I scowled and took a long drink. "No. It's fine."

Rue was looking back and forth between the two of us, sipping at her ale.

Senyr sighed. "I told you. People get uneasy seeing you on the hill. Can't blame them for that. Lord Bartholomew is a well-respected nobleman and he has a fairly good relationship with the baroness. He may be a little eccentric, but he's got pull."

"I think you just wanted to watch me deal with Lord Barty."

Senyr's mouth twitched and he looked into his mug. "He's been asking about you for months, and I was afraid he'd try to get into the underground himself to look for you. Couldn't have a Yellow sticking a knife in him because he opened the wrong door." He took a drink and wiped the foam off his short beard. "And it's a little entertaining."

I grunted and settled into my chair, nursing the drink.

Rue fidgeted with hers for a moment, then spoke hesitantly. "Can we order food?"

Senyr and I spoke at the same time. "No."

She deflated and settled into a pout of her own.

Senyr took a deep breath, then launched into all the information he thought I'd need about Lord Bartholomew Henrick and the mysterious Lady Josyna. He described their estates, where they were located, what their neighbors thought of them, and even what a few of the servants looked like.

It was a lot of information to take in, and I was distracted with thoughts of how much trouble Deidre could be in if this went south, but I did my best to pay attention.

As he finally took a break from the hushed monologue, he finished off his ale and sighed, then held my gaze. "Don't fuck this up, Gray. I don't care how insufferable the idiot is, you need to keep him interested. This hit is too important to botch because you can't bite your tongue when something pisses you off."

I frowned, but didn't argue.

He turned to Ruena. "And you. Not a word of this to anyone, you hear me?"

She nodded quickly, her face a little pale at his sudden direct attention.

He pushed his mug away and stood. "I'm getting too old for this shit."

8 – The Talk

We left the Running Hart together, but Senyr quickly peeled off and claimed to have business elsewhere. As Ruena and I strolled back toward Old Town, I tried to think of some way to bring up what I'd seen in the storage room at the Throat.

I didn't know how to have a conversation like this. When I was a kid I figured everything out on my own and nobody cared what I did. If someone had asked me yesterday what I thought about the subject of sex I'd have said it was a basic need of life, and also a tool I was pretty good at wielding.

But now… it seemed a lot more complicated.

Rue kept glancing over at me as we walked and I ignored it. She even threw a couple of loud sighs into the evening, trying to get a response. I kept walking, heading vaguely home. She finally grabbed my arm and pulled me to a stop.

"I think we should talk."

I kept my expression flat and glanced around to make sure nobody was close enough to overhear. Habit probably, but I was as squirmy as if I held a bag full of stolen gems to my chest. "Okay. But not here."

"Where?"

I started walking again, letting her catch her pace at my side. "Let's go home. Deidre is probably there."

She grumbled and muttered, "Fine."

We walked in silence into the underground. One of those loud silences that was filled with everything we hadn't yet been able to say. I only hoped Deidre would be better at this than I was, because my only idea was to forbid Rue from associating with anyone ever again in that way, and I knew that was stupid, even if it's what my instincts screamed at me.

When I could see the apartment door ahead of us, I leaned closer to whisper. "Remember, not a word about Lord Barty or going to the estates."

She nodded.

I opened the apartment door and held it for her, glancing to where Deidre was sitting cross-legged on the bed with piles of fabric around her. No hint that anything was wrong in the world. Definitely not trying to help a disgruntled noblewoman take over the city. I shook the thoughts away to concentrate on Rue.

Deidre looked at us in surprise. "I didn't expect to see you two tonight. Are you avoiding trouble or still looking for it?"

Rue glanced over her shoulder at me as she went and sat at the table. "Already found it, I guess."

I closed the door behind my back. There was no way to start this conversation that didn't make me uncomfortable, so I figured straight to the point would be quickest. "Rue has a *friend*."

Deidre raised an eyebrow. "That's lovely?"

I scowled. Okay, less subtle. "Rue was hiding in the storeroom of the Throat, wrapped around a guy's neck like a suckerfish."

Ruena rolled her eyes.

Deidre's eyes widened and she smiled. "Oh? Who's the lucky man?" She pushed some fabric aside and patted the edge of the bed. "Come tell me everything!"

Rue hopped off her chair and darted over to join her.

I glared at them. "No. That's not how this is supposed to go."

Deidre raised an eyebrow. "What's wrong? He wasn't hurting her, was he?" She turned to Rue with a stern look, brushing the stray strands of hair away for a better look at her face and neck. "Was he? We don't put up with that."

"He wouldn't. He's very considerate."

Deidre beamed.

I stepped closer. "She's way too young to be doing that kind of thing."

Deidre laughed. "She's nearly fifteen. I was getting paid by the time I was fifteen, and I'd been experimenting before that." She squinted at me. "And I believe you were pretty well-versed at that age."

"She's fourteen. And this is different."

59

"No it's not."

"Yes it is."

"Why?"

"Because–" I had my finger pointed at her and realized my voice was raised. I dropped my hand and took a step back, trying to vocalize the feelings raging inside my gut. "Because–"

She gazed patiently back at me. "This is a normal part of her growing up." She turned to Rue and took both her hands. "Tell me about him. Is he part of the guild, or a citizen?"

Rue blushed and grinned. "He's in the guild. He got inked a year ago."

"Black?"

"Red."

Deidre blinked in surprise, her enthusiasm a little dampened. "Red? They're usually not interested in relationships."

Warning bells went off in my head. I'd been upset before, but now I was more than worried. Reds were crazy. She could be in real danger if this guy was playing at something. I cared too much about her to let this go on. "Absolutely not. You can't get involved with a Red."

Ruena glared at me and pulled her hands out of Deidre's. "You don't even know him."

"I don't need to. He's an assassin. You realize they have to make a kill to earn their ink, don't you? You can't get involved with a killer."

She stood up, her hands clenched into fists at her sides and her voice full of indignation. "Like you're so innocent?"

I stepped closer, poking the air between us. "Everyone I've killed has been to protect the people I care about. I don't kill on command like a dog."

"A *dog*?"

Deidre stood up and put a restraining hand on Rue's shoulder, extending the other in my direction. "Let's not say something we regret."

My words came out clipped. "I'm worried she'll *DO* something she regrets."

Rue was shaking, her eyes blazing as she raised her head high and stared back at me. "I already *DID* do something. Actually, we've done it more than once! How do you like that?"

60

My face flushed even darker. Worry, embarrassment, and rage vied for dominance. "Not anymore. You're forbidden from seeing him."

"You can't do that!"

"I just did."

Ruena screamed back at me. "Fuck off! *You aren't my father!*"

The words echoed through the sudden silence in the apartment.

My chest knotted up and I forced myself to swallow, holding in the churning mass of anger and sudden hurt.

Hurt?

Deidre bit her lip and put a hand on Ruena's arm, glancing at me.

I shook my head and backed up a shaky step. She was right, I wasn't her father, but why did it bother me so much to hear her say it?

Ruena covered her face with her hands and started to cry. Deidre looked between us, seemingly at a loss for what to do, then wrapped an arm around Ruena's shoulders. Ruena turned into her chest and sobbed even louder.

I only wanted to protect her. I took a deep breath and reached out. "Rue, I–"

"*Go away!*"

I flinched and took a couple of steps back. The ball in my chest was turning hollow, eating away at the rage and leaving just pain in its wake. What had I been I thinking?

Deidre met my gaze and sighed, then she nodded her head gently toward the door. She mouthed: *Let me.*

Right.

I walked to the door, trying to ignore the sobbing and Deidre's gentle hush as she stroked Ruena's hair. I looked back as my hand touched the knob, trying to think of something I could say. The problem was that I still wanted to keep her away from this guy–I still wanted to protect her–but I felt like a wall had been put up between us.

I dropped my gaze to the floor. "I'm sorry."

Ruena's sobbing got louder and I grimaced, then slipped out the door and down the corridor.

I trudged through the underground to the surface, not paying any attention to the Yellow stationed at the trapdoor. The night breeze hit me and a shiver went down my back.

The streets were too cheerful. It wasn't even midnight yet, but drunken laughter and song drifted from the taverns and brothels of Old Town. I ignored the first few greetings tossed in my direction, then decided to take to the rooftops to avoid the rest.

I jumped and climbed and balanced my way to the flat roof of the Throat, to the shadow of a chimney where heat radiated from the fire within. The otherwise rough surface was worn smooth there, the bricks scratched by years of idle hands. Mostly mine. I sat and leaned into the heated clay.

The muted sounds of the bar drifted around me, rising and falling with the excitement of the crowd. I crossed my arms over my chest, staring at my drawn up knees. My breath was shaky, so I concentrated on it for a few moments, just trying to even it out.

Flashes of thought and emotion rose in my mind and sank back down again. Anger that Ruena wasn't listening to me. Worry that this Red would hurt her. Shame that I *had* hurt her. Pain that she had pushed me away. Fear that I was losing her.

I winced at that one.

I'd never thought about it before... that I thought of her like a daughter.

I was her teacher and her boss. Reluctantly, at that. But somehow in the middle of everything she'd become more. We... her, Deidre, and I... had become a family.

I was so fucking stupid.

I dropped my head onto my raised knees, wrapping my arms around them. I just wasn't sure what was more stupid... that I thought I could ever be someone's father, or that I was failing so miserably at it.

I got it now. I understood why I'd been so upset about the Red. Why I'd been so protective. I still didn't know what to do about it, or how to let it go.

My thoughts drifted again, calmed somehow by the acceptance. I rubbed the heel of my hand over my cheeks where the chimney smoke must have been making my eyes water, and listened to the sounds of the Throat below me.

In eight days it wouldn't matter anyway. In eight days I was going to destroy the entire fucking city. Deidre, Rue, Senyr, Sans, May... The building I sat on would be rubble. There wouldn't even be bodies left.

Shadowbeasts would prowl the streets and the monstrous shadowkraken would pulverize what was left. Echoes of the destruction would rip backwards through time itself to haunt the city.

Time was running out, and I'd just fucked up what was left of it with Rue.

9 – Shadows and Sleep

"*Come closer.*"

I most definitely did *not* want to get closer.

Where was I? Everything was dark. I felt like I was floating somehow, but without even the sense of water pressing in around me. It was like I didn't have a body at all.

The voice came again, not really closer, or louder, but somehow having grown. It was smooth, and trailed across my thoughts like the touch of a lover's gentle finger. "*I know you.*"

An unreasonable panic flooded through me and I thought about running. I wasn't sure how I could run, not having a body, but I yearned for it. If my mind could have run away, it would have.

Then I did feel something. A presence, behind me, looming over me.

Yes. Behind was a thing that existed now. I focused on that, forcing my mind to realize that if something was behind me, it meant I had a physical form. A head. Shoulders. A back that was vulnerable.

I turned around and staggered away from the presence, looked down at my hands, my arms, my chest. I was real. I could see myself clearly, but nothing else. There wasn't a floor, although something felt firm beneath my boots. There was no light, even though I could somehow see myself, just more darkness extending forever.

"*You are part of the shadows.*"

The voice came from all around me now, and I spun slowly, trying to find a source for it, trying to peer through the blackness for some sign of movement. My heart was thudding against my ribs. My hands shaking. "Who are you?"

An answer came back to me in my own voice, twisted and amplified. "*Shadows are a thief's friend.*"

64

The sound of crumbling stone echoed sharply from my left and my head swiveled to see, but it was still all blackness. I stepped away from the noise. What else was in here with me? What was this place? Was I still on the rooftop of the Throat, or somewhere else?

A low, rumbling growl came out of the darkness and I froze as it vibrated through my chest. My heart began to race and a shiver ran through me.

Where was it coming from?

I waited, and the growl came again, right on top of me. Hot, dry air puffed against the back of my neck.

I flung myself forward, spinning to look and seeing nothing. My feet tangled and I reached out to break my fall but the surface that had been solid under my feet was nowhere to be found. Panic overtook me and I flailed my arms as I started to fall into the darkness all around me.

***

I woke with a start, flinging my arms out and knocking my elbow against the chimney with a numbing *thwack*. I gasped for breath and curled up around the pain in my elbow, my eyes darting across the dark rooftop.

It was just as it had been before. The noises from the Throat below were going strong, and the moon above had reached its high point. I set a hand on the tar-covered gravel beneath me, feeling the roughness and the wear from decades of exposure to the elements.

It was a dream. I sighed and bowed my head, leaning shakily back against the chimney. I must have dozed off.

It couldn't have been for long, judging by the position of the moon above and the noise beneath me. Maybe an hour? I looked around at the shadows that formed naturally along the edges of the roof. Just shadows.

My breath smoothed out and my heart settled into a normal rhythm. Regrets and images of the labyrinth kept me company the rest of the night, holding back any sleep I might have gotten, and eventually the sun rose high enough to burn my eyes across the rooftops. I was exhausted, and grunted as I dragged myself up the side of the chimney. Ruena hadn't come back to the Throat, at least that I'd noticed, so she was probably still at the apartment with Deidre. Which meant I couldn't go home.

I also couldn't sleep at the Throat, because I didn't want her to come back and find me. I'd done enough damage already. There had to be someplace I could crash for the—

A shadow at the edge of the rooftop bulged and stretched, moving as if it was alive, then stilled.

The breath hitched in my throat and I stumbled away from it, sliding my hand over the rough bricks of the chimney to keep my balance as I stared unblinking at the patch of darkness. Was it deeper than the morning light warranted? Did it extend just a bit too far to be cast naturally? I wasn't sure.

Thirty seconds passed. Then a minute. Then two. My eyes watered and I still hadn't seen anything move again. Had I imagined it in my exhaustion and stress? Maybe a large bird had flown overhead and cast a brief moving shadow and I just hadn't noticed.

I crept forward, scolding myself for how twitchy I was being just walking across an empty roof. There was nothing there. I could see the whole roof, even the parts in shadow, and there was nothing. I stopped just at the edge of the shadow cast by the low wall that made up the roof parapet, then deliberately slid my boot through it, scraping the rough tar.

I felt like a fool. Of course nothing happened. My breath came out in a shaky laugh and I rubbed both hands over my face and up through my hair. "I need to get some sleep."

If I couldn't go home, and I couldn't stay at the Throat, maybe a brothel would do the trick. Vin kept late hours, and while I wasn't in the mood for sex, her room was quiet and she had a big enough bed I might convince her to share it. I swung myself down from the roof and headed for Tanji's.

Not many people were up yet, but the food shops were well into their daily baking and it made my stomach growl. I stopped and bought a pair of sweet rolls fresh out of the oven, eating one on the way to the brothel.

When I walked in, the front room was empty except for an older man sweeping the floor. He glanced up at me and raised an eyebrow. "You're out late."

"Why not early?"

"Only honest folk are up this early. Who are you looking for? Most of them have gone to bed."

I glanced at the stairs leading to the second floor. "Vin?"

He grunted softly and resumed his sweeping. "She's in her room. Alone at the moment."

"Thanks." I took the stairs slowly, not just because of my tiredness, but to avoid disturbing anyone after a long night of work. Vin's room was the third on the left, and I knocked softly on the door, hoping she was still up.

My sharp hearing picked up the sound of her getting out of bed and padding to the door. It opened a crack, and she squinted at me, her hair tied up and a blanket around her shoulders. "Gray? Bit late, even for you."

"I need a favor."

"I've had a full night, sorry." She yawned and started closing the door.

I stopped it with my boot. "I don't suppose I could pay you *not* to have sex with me?"

She frowned and opened the door further. "You're gonna have to explain that a little better, hun."

I sighed and ran a hand through my hair. "I'm very tired, and I can't go home right now. Can I sleep here?"

"Seriously?"

"I brought you a sweet roll. Freshly baked." I waved the pastry in front of her.

She pursed her lips, tilting her head to stare at me a moment longer, then pulled the door open fully and took the roll before stepping aside.

I entered gratefully and looked around for a place to lay my cloak.

She crossed to the bed and climbed on, crawling to the far side and crossing her legs to sit and pick at the roll. "You have a fight with Deidre?"

I sat in a chair to pull off my boots, using it as an excuse not to look at her. "No." Once they were both off, and my cloak and vest were hanging over the back of the chair, I started to unbuckle the harness that held my knives at the small of my back. "With Ruena, actually."

"You wanna talk about it?"

I dropped my coin purse next to the knives and crossed to the bed. "Not really."

She made room and I stretched out on top of the blankets, her scent all around me like spicy wine and cinnamon. The room was pleasantly warm and familiar.

She paused between bites, giving me a mischievous smirk. "Just to warn you, I kick in my sleep."

I snorted and glanced at her. "Do I get a discount if I wake up bruised?"

"You pay extra for that." She leaned over and kissed me on the cheek, then popped the last of the roll into her mouth and squirmed under the blankets so her back was to me.

It was strange, trying to fall asleep in this room. It was topside, for one thing, and the morning sun already filtered through the cracks in the curtains despite the heavy fabric. But it was also a place I normally did more energetic things. Tonight—well, this morning, really—that was the last thing I wanted.

I lay still for a few minutes, my fingers laced over my stomach, staring at the shadows on the ceiling. Just plain old shadows. Eventually the soft sound of snoring reached my ears and I smiled despite myself.

This was my city. These were my people. Everything I'd ever known was here, and I'd be damned if I was going to let some magic rock make me destroy it all. There had to be a way out, and I was going to find it. Nissa might bow to destiny, but I definitely fucking wouldn't.

I'd patch things up with Rue, figure out what was going on with Deidre and Lady Josyna, and find a way to save the city from... myself.

I didn't know how, but the how didn't seem all that important right now. Just having decided to do something made the chaotic thoughts settle down. I rolled onto my side to let sleep claim me.

***

I woke when a pillow smacked into my face. I flinched and reached from reflex toward the small of my back, but of course there were no knives there and I was in bed and tangled in a blanket. I sat up instead, squinting in the light when Vin flung her curtains wide.

"Time's up, sleepyhead. Have to keep this space available for paying customers."

I rubbed my palms over my cheeks, blinking away the last of the sleep from my eyes. "What time is it?"

"A few hours to sunset." Vin tossed my knives and purse onto the bed and pulled her chair, still draped in my cloak and vest, over to a dresser with a large mirror on a swivel. She sat and began touching up the coal over her eyes. "I went to see Deidre."

"That was nosy."

"Can I give you some advice, hun?"

I buckled the harness with my knives, shifting to settle them a little more comfortably. "You're going to anyway, whether I want it or not."

She ignored the comment, gazing at me through the reflection in the mirror. "Trust Ruena. You taught her well, didn't you?"

"I think so."

"Then trust she can take care of herself, and when she can't, she'll come to you." She wiped a smudge of lip color from the corner of her mouth with her fingertip, then made a kissing face to the mirror. "And don't take what she said personally. I can't tell you how many times I've told my father I hate him, and I love the old coot dearly."

Her father, huh? Except I wasn't Rue's father. I crossed to where she sat and slipped my vest out from behind her back, trying to ignore the knot in my chest. "Deidre talks too much."

Vin twisted to grip my forearm, looking up at me. "What are friends for?"

I grunted and slung my vest on, then picked up my cloak and draped it over my arm. "What are you charging me for not having sex with you?"

"First one's free, hun."

I smiled and turned to go, but as I opened the door I paused and looked over my shoulder.

Over the years Vin had become more than just a source of fun. She'd been one of the few people to fully support me when the majority of the guild thought I was murdering people five years ago. And she wasn't interested in relationship games, which made things much easier for Deidre and I as we navigated whatever it was we'd become. Maybe the impending doom of the Night of Shadows was making me brood too much.

I cleared my throat. "Thanks."

She winked. "Don't mention it."

10 – Apples

I didn't know what to do with myself, so I walked my old enforcer route. The Old Market square was thick with shoppers and workers just getting done for the evening, and it felt good to be swept up in the crowd as I passed through.

Then I started getting the itch on the back of my neck that meant someone was watching me. It was a feeling I depended on in my profession, so I slipped under the shade of a vendor's stall and lowered my head like I was browsing, using the opportunity to glance at the people around me.

The source of my discomfort was rather obvious at that point. An older woman dressed like a farmer's wife, a cloak thrown over her shoulder, was pushing awkwardly through the crowd in my direction. Her hair was auburn, streaked with gray, and was tied at the nape of her neck, and her cheeks were wrinkled. People kept stepping in her path, and she was getting irritated.

Interesting. I gave up the pretense of browsing the stall, since she wasn't trying to hide her intent, and watched her come. When she reached my side the hair rose on my arms from the creeping tingle of magic. I casually slipped a hand behind my back to my knives, but didn't draw one. "Good evening, missus."

She glared at me. "I hate this city."

My eyes widened. That was Nissa's voice. Things suddenly made a lot more sense and I released the knife and relaxed my shoulders. "Well, it won't be here a whole lot longer, will it?"

She raised an eyebrow, but didn't answer.

I squinted, trying to see any flaws in her human-like face. "How do you look like this?"

She huffed and glanced at the crowd around us. "Magic, of course."

I sighed at the dismissive answer and gestured at the square. "Shall we walk and talk? I assume you wanted to speak with me."

"Very well." She fell into step beside me. "I have been thinking about our problems. My meditations are not providing any useful information on either the stone or the Night of Shadows."

"Your meditations?"

"Yes. Elves are connected to the world in a way humans are not. We can sometimes use that connection to touch the world and find the answers we seek within ourselves."

"Kinky." I wasn't thrilled to talk about our *problems*, as she put it. I'd been thinking about it too much as it was, and right now it only reminded me I needed to make it up to Rue sooner rather than later. I didn't want us all to die while she was still mad at me.

She continued in a lowered voice. "At first, I thought the city was too loud. It is a distracting place. But I was finally able to sink into a trace, and try as I might the issue of the stone's destiny did not come up."

"Maybe it's not as fixed as you think? Maybe destiny can change."

"Not this destiny. It has already happened."

I scowled and edged a little closer, mindful of the crowd around us and lowering my voice even more. "Are you such an expert in magic and time? What if the labyrinth is a place out of time because of the portals. What if it doesn't have to exist as a real place. Have you thought about that? Maybe they disappear at dawn because the labyrinth disappears at dawn."

Nissa frowned and stared at the street passing beneath us, biting her lip.

I was rather proud of that theory. It fit everything I wanted to happen. It could all be a long nightmare and when the sun came up everything would be fine. The city would be back to normal, I wouldn't have killed tens of thousands of people, and my life could continue with little to no magical bullshit.

But she had to pick it apart.

"What you suggest is possible, but pocket worlds are small and contained. There were stars and clouds and a moon in the labyrinth, so the city was real. Therefore, the destruction was real and a power as strong as the destructive force would be necessary to reverse it. We saw no evidence that such a power was in use. Without someone to reverse the destruction, it would remain. The only thing we can be sure about is that the portals closed."

"But it's possible."

"We know the labyrinth is there. We know the city is destroyed. I suppose it is possible it does not remain so."

"Then we find a way to fix it. Mediate on that." I was wondering how I could get the elf to stop talking about impending disaster when my casual glance landed on a woman arguing with a merchant. The late afternoon sun caught on a bit of silver in her artfully styled hair and my eye was drawn to the hairpin that held it up. The game Ruena and I played came to mind.

The rules were simple. Steal something small and unique. And of course I was limited to Old Town, because she technically couldn't be working outside her district. The corpse necklace had been stretching the rules in more ways than one.

My fingers were itching to actually do something, and a little casual pilfering might calm my nerves. Besides, that hairpin would be a nice ice-breaker for when I did try to speak to Ruena again. But how–

My eyes darted around the crowded square and landed on a mostly dead potted bush next to an apple vendor. Perfect.

I touched Nissa's elbow and led her in that direction as I hummed an interested affirmative to what she was saying about her inability to focus in her meditations on the destruction of the city. I flicked up the hood of my cloak, combed my hair forward, and took a more hunched and meek posture.

She changed direction without complaint, staying close and keeping quiet enough her words didn't carry far. "So I focused on what the meditation *was* giving me, hoping if I played it to its conclusion, I could move on to the things I wanted to ponder. Many of my thoughts turned to you. To our past together. To your child."

I scowled as we neared the apple stall. "She's not my child."

Nissa waved dismissively. "There is much tension here. There needs to be more focus."

I picked up an apple and rubbed my thumb over it to test for firmness. As I picked through the fruit, I snapped a twig that was about the size of the hairpin from the dead bush, sliding it up my sleeve with a twist of my wrist. I pitched my voice low enough not to carry to the vender. "Seems to me you're the one lacking focus. Why is your chaotic brain my problem?" I pulled out a silver coin and handed it to the vendor, then loaded my arms up with apples.

The vendor watched me skeptically. "Do you want a bag?"

I smiled beneath the hood, careful to keep most of my features hidden, and slipped into a rural drawl. "No, thank ye. Me ole ma here is in a hurry."

Nissa frowned, but didn't say anything. She really was the perfect grumpy accomplice.

I mumbled my thanks, nodded politely, then turned to scan the crowd for my real target. She was just leaving a fabric stall, so I headed in that direction, speaking in my normal voice over my shoulder to keep the elf tagging along. "I'm listening. Tension. Focus."

Nissa took a breath and started in again, talking about how the things happening in our lives might be overshadowing the more subtle whisperings of destiny, and how that could be affecting what was getting through the meditation. About how *her* mind *was* focused, and she'd practiced this art for centuries, and how humans were the emotional ones.

I juggled the apples enough to slide the stick out of my sleeve, along with a tiny, razor-sharp blade I used for slitting purses. I bit my lip as I struggled to shave the bark from one end and sharpen it into a point while not dropping the armful of apples, then slipped the blade back in its place and palmed the stick. "Oh yes. We humans are so emotional."

We came up behind the woman and I glanced around to make sure nobody was watching too closely, even though I was about to draw everyone's attention. When we were right behind her, I sighed loudly, angling myself to not quite pass her, and grumbled back at Nissa with the rural accent. "Fine, fine! We're goin! I dunno why ye–"

I hit the woman's shoulder hard enough to stumble us both, but not to knock her over, and let the apples tumble from my arms onto the street. While we were both bent over to catch our balance, I raised the stick behind her, slipped it into her hair next to the pin, and plucked out the real one, all in one deft motion. The pin went into my sleeve and I touched her back to steady her with the same hand.

"So sorry, missus!" I put on an exaggerated grimace and set my other hand on her forearm to catch her gaze. "Was all my fault. Ye ain't hurt, are ye?" I didn't wait for her to answer, just ducked my head nervously and started picking up apples. "I shoulda been paying more attention. We were arguing and–well, anyway I'm awful sorry."

The woman was brushing herself off and watching me scramble around on the street. She scowled and humphed, checking her purse—which I hadn't bothered with—and rearranging the two packages on her arm. "Watch where you're going next time."

I plucked the last apple off the cobbles and stood in front of her, trying to look sheepish instead of cocky, making sure my hood shadowed my face. "Ah–yes. I will. Would ye like a–" I held an apple out, then frowned and pulled it back. "No. Of course ye wouldn't. Again, so sorry." I bowed awkwardly and made a show of almost dropping the apples again, then shuffled away at an angle.

Nissa was standing in the street, staring at me in shock.

I jerked my head at her, motioning her to follow, and she fell in behind me. From there it was easy enough to duck onto a side street and out of sight of anyone that had been watching in the square. Once we were inconspicuous again, I straightened into my normal posture and shuffled the apples into the crook of one arm so I could slide the pin out of my sleeve.

It wasn't silver, but a very polished nickel probably. That was fine. The point of the game wasn't the value, but how much skill it took to steal. Really, the lower the value the better, since it was less likely someone would report it and ruin our fun. The pin was rather simple, with a stylized leaf on the head, although not a master craftsman's work. It would do.

I tucked it inside my vest and met Nissa's grumpy, disguised stare. "What?"

"You just stole that."

"It's kind of what I do, remember?"

"Were you even listening?"

"Of course. We need to take care of all the chaos in our fates so you can see the stone. At any rate, this," I patted the side of my vest over the hairpin, "will help with that."

"How exactly will petty theft help our cause?"

A group of four young kids darted around the corner and caught sight of us, grinning as they came forward. I picked out one of the apples and tossed it to the first child. "There's a lot going on in my life right now, and if that's interfering with your disturbing little bonding-with-the-world ritual, you're just going to have to let me sort it out."

I quickly handed out the rest of the fruit, keeping two back. The kids giggled and winked at me, then scampered off. I held a shiny red apple out to Nissa, a small bruise already forming where it had hit the street earlier. "I'm sure the answer will come to us by the time we need it."

She narrowed her eyes, but took the apple from my hand. "We do not have *time*. You can not just expect it all to work out. The shadow that covers my visions—"

My brow creased and I paused with the apple halfway to my mouth. "Shadow?"

"Everything is hazy, shadowed. Nothing can be seen clearly since I arrived in this cursed human city."

I gestured with the apple. "So you don't mean real shadows then? Creepy moving ones?"

She scowled. "No. Why?"

I felt foolish just mentioning it, so I shrugged and flashed her a false smile. "We have a bit of a history with shadow things. Just clarifying."

I was getting that prickling feeling again, and made sure to keep the smile on as I glanced out of the corners of my eyes and flicked my hair back into place after my impromptu disguise. A figure at the edge of a building shifted and was still. Someone was watching. An actual physical someone, thank the Six.

I raised the last apple and took a bite, gesturing at Nissa to walk down the street in the direction I'd seen the figure. "You just keep doing whatever it is you're doing, and leave sorting out the chaos to me."

She frowned. "Have you told the leader of your people?"

"Rigel?" Guilt blossomed in my gut.

"Both your criminal leader and the baroness of this city should be informed. They may have some insight into events. At the very least they can help deter the nobleman that hunts you."

"I thought you said we should keep things to ourselves?"

"That is obviously not working. We need answers more than we need secrecy."

"Not yet. I will." And I would. But Rigel would turn it into an opportunity to foist even more responsibility on me. He was continually dumping things into my lap to see how I dealt with them and asking for input on decisions that affected the entire guild. Part of grooming me for my future. And he might take me off the hit on Lady Josyna, which I absolutely didn't want.

The space between the buildings where the figure had gone was a dead end. I knew that already. So when I walked past it I looked up instead of at the street level, and just caught the flutter of a cloak disappearing over the edge of the roof.

That meant it was a guild member. Nobody else walked around on the rooftops.

I stopped at the mouth of the alley. "Why don't you keep trying your meditations and talk to me again soon. I have another conversation I need to have."

She gripped the collar of my shirt and pulled me around until we were face to face, glaring at me through her disguise. "You dismiss me so easily?"

"Look. I don't know anything about all this mystic bullshit, and I don't want to. You do what you need to do, and if you need something from me, just ask. Until then I'm going to keep taking care of the things I *do* know something about." I shrugged her grip off.

The muddy brown eyes of her disguise swirled into green and back again. The wrinkled lines of the human face tightened so drastically I wasn't sure if it was a slip of the magic or just the severity of her expression. "He comes for you."

A shudder went up my back. "Who?"

"Loring. A darkness follows him. I can feel his hate, seeping through the visions."

Damn elves. I shook myself and let the panic slide away, glancing once more at the nearby rooftop. "That's something I can handle on my own. You just worry about the shiny rock."

She threw her hands up and turned around, heading back toward the square. "Fine. I have warned you the best I can. If you die it is your own fault."

I snorted under my breath and turned into the alley, moving to the series of handholds on the side of the building that made climbing easier. I had to hold the apple with my teeth as I climbed, but was relatively sure I didn't need to hurry. I still had the feeling of being watched creeping across my neck.

Sure enough, when I swung onto the roof a figure was standing nearby. I wasn't sure if I should be worried about an attack, so I was tense, but I avoided going for my knives and took another bite from the apple, then spoke around it. "Why are you following me?"

The figure lowered its hood to reveal the bronzed skin and dirty blonde hair of Ruena's friend.

My eyes narrowed as I swallowed, but I didn't move. If I wanted to patch things up with Rue, I needed to at least try to hold a civil conversation with this young Red. "What do you want?"

He spoke quietly, with a gentle rolling timbre and a hint of an accent. No wonder she found him attractive. "I wanted to apologize for how we met."

"Is that so."

His face reddened. "It wasn't how we wanted to tell you."

I gripped the apple and imagined it was the handle of a knife, just so I wouldn't feel the need to draw one. "Apology accepted. Was there anything else?"

He hesitated, and for a moment his youth was all too apparent. He couldn't have been more than a few years older than Rue. He stood with an eerie stillness, letting the silence grow for a moment, then cleared his throat. "I won't hurt her, you know. We aren't all monsters."

"That remains to be seen."

He scowled, still not moving. "All I want is a chance to prove it to you."

"Why?"

"Because she loves you."

That caught me off guard. There was an immediate flaring of guilt in my chest, and a flicker of hope, which I shoved back. This Red could be lying to put me at ease, but why would he bother? Ruena was obviously sharing quite a bit of herself in their private moments, which meant she trusted him.

My eyes hardened. My track record with Reds was pointedly the opposite. I worked with them in the barest sense of the word, but I only trusted them to put a blade in my back at the earliest opportunity. Now this kid stood in front of me, wanting what? My blessing?

My fingers dimpled the surface of the apple. "We'll see."

He nodded, breaking the unnatural stillness. Then he turned and silently swung himself over the edge of the roof and down to the street below. I heard the muffled thump and scrape of gravel as he landed, then nothing.

A dozen or so breaths later, I finally let my shoulders drop.

11 – Barty Time

I figured it was time for a drink, and to finally settle down for a few hours and let my head straighten itself out. Best way I knew to do that—apart from sex—was playing dice or cards at the Throat. Sans would appreciate the company and I knew he'd have some words of wisdom that might calm my scattered thoughts. Maybe I'd even run into Ruena and have a chance to apologize properly for being such an asshole.

The sun was deep orange and barely visible between buildings by the time I wound my way through the Old Market. The square was still pretty full, but I didn't get any curious glances from people who may have remembered my clumsy encounter earlier. It was amazing what a change of bearing and mannerisms did to people's memories.

I pushed open the door to the Throat and strolled in, covering the room in a quick glance. It was starting to fill up, but nothing crazy yet. Kash was behind the bar, Sans was eating at his usual table, and Basil was carrying a small cask in from the back room. No sign of Ruena.

A woman stood up from a table as I got closer and turned around to face me, blocking my progress through the common room. I paused and lowered my brow, trying to remember where I'd seen her before. Plain features, brown hair braided close to her head disappearing beneath the collar of her cloak. Clothes simple but well cared for. The picture of ordinary. A thief?

What finally sparked a memory was when she looked up, nearly a full head shorter than I was, and smirked. It transformed her face, turning her from unremarkable to impish. She was one of the high ranking Yellows from the central districts that I'd passed information to a few times, but we'd never spoken more than a phrase or two.

I smiled back. "Long way from home, aren't you?"

She held a folded piece of paper up between us, her fingers almost covering the red wax seal.

It suddenly felt like there was a rock in my stomach. There was currently only one reason I would get a sealed message from the central districts, and I was dreading it. I took the paper and broke the seal, glancing down to scan the short letter.

My dear Mister Gray.

I grimaced at the honorific. It had always bothered me and felt like a cheap attempt at respect. This was already going so well.

Please accept this invitation to supper at my home at sunset tonight. Bring a bottle of good wine. With kind regards, Lord Bartholomew Henrick.

Below it was a quick sketch of the estates and a black dot where the manor was located. Not that I needed the directions. Senyr had described the location already, along with the home of the mysterious Lady Josyna.

I muttered a curse under my breath and met the Yellow's gaze, then slid mine past her to see Sans visiting with a regular sitting next to him. So much for a nice calm evening. It was almost sunset now.

The Yellow stepped closer, her voice artfully lowered not to carry further than my ears. "I'll bring you to find something more appropriate to wear."

I grimaced. "Let me grab a bottle of wine first."

I got a bottle from Kash, sidestepping her curious questions about who it was for. She knew I didn't care for wine, and it took one glance at the stoic Yellow beside me to guess something was going on. When she sighed and tossed out a "be careful," I faked a smile and winked, promising nothing.

I followed the Yellow out of the bar. We took Market Street most of the way, then cut onto a side street to reach the alley that circled the inner wall around the estates. Generations ago it had been a wide buffer zone between the wall and the rest of Sangarie, but as space became hard to find it turned into a staging area, then storage. Eventually buildings started going up to protect the goods there and it became a narrow, twisted alley that snaked its way around the wall.

Halfway between two of the four main streets that led to the gates in the wall was a ramshackle building that belonged to the guild. We went into the rickety building, then through a trapdoor to the underground storage area that had been carved out to keep an assortment of clothes for just these types of occasions. It was usually the Yellows that made use of them, but I was a Hand of the Master, so they'd agreed to outfit me.

Within minutes I was dressed in black pants, a white shirt, a dark gray jacket that was open at the front and hung to my thighs, and tall black boots polished to reflect the light of the lamps. A black half-cloak was slung over it all, reaching almost to the back of my knees, the high collar on it brushing the bottom of my hair in the back. The boots were tight, but not uncomfortably so. The jacket sleeves pulled at my shoulders a little, but at least they were straight instead of poofy or frilly. As I looked into a full length mirror of polished silver, I cringed at how easily this outfit would get dirty. If I so much as looked at a stone wall, I'd probably walk away with dust on me.

The Yellow walked back into the small room where I'd been sent to change and looked at me critically. "It'll do." She handed me back the letter and the bottle of wine. "You're late."

I followed her to the door of the building and she peeked out to look both ways.

"Circle back to Market Street and enter through the gate. The guard will question you, but should let you through with that letter. When you come back later, go out the gate first and then circle around here to change clothes. You need to be seen going both in *and* out. Got it?"

"Things were so much simpler when I could just sneak in."

She grunted and stepped aside to let me leave.

It took a few blocks to get the hang of walking without making the boots squeak, but I made it to Market Street and straightened my back as I approached the massive gate and the Silvers stationed there.

They watched me approach and the looks of vague boredom changed to suspicion once I was close enough to recognize. One stepped forward and his spear came down to block my way. "Where do you think you're going?"

Easy now. They had no reason to suspect me of anything. I held the letter up between two fingers, turning it so the red wax seal caught the light. "Supper, of course. And I'm already late."

81

"You're that thief. Gray. You don't think I'm going to let you walk into the estates with that lame excuse, do you?"

There was a time I could walk this city as just another face in the crowd, but after I snuck in and killed Lord Firmin five years ago, then became a Hand of the Master, it seemed like more and more of the Silvers recognized me. I wouldn't be surprised if they handed out sketches of my face when they assigned gate duty.

"I'm flattered to have an admirer of my work. I assure you I wouldn't try such an obvious ruse." Mainly because it would never have worked. I waved the letter again like a little parchment flag. "I have an invitation."

The guard's eyes narrowed and he snatched the letter out of my hand, staring at me while he unfolded it and looked down briefly to read. His face grew even more troubled, and he glanced at the bottle of wine I carried. "How did you manage this?"

Of course he'd question it. I didn't blame him. Even though the letter was completely real I was still ultimately up to no good. "Caught the right attention at the right time, I guess." The corner of my smile quirked up even higher. "I made a friend. I'd hate for Lord Bartholomew to be cross with you for detaining his supper guest."

I made to walk past him, but he leaned his spear in front of me again. "Not so fast. How do I know you didn't forge that letter?"

"Good point." I flicked a finger at the point of his spear so it gave off a metallic ring and flashed him a grin. "You don't. I suppose you could hop on over to the Henrick estate and verify it, and I'll just wait here with your partner. Tell Lord Bartholomew to keep the food warm while you sort it all out, since you won't take his seal at face value."

The other Silver shifted uncomfortably and cleared his throat. "Lord Bartholomew did come out earlier today dressed in his—"

The one in front of me waved him back. "That doesn't mean anything."

I raised an eyebrow. "Are you sure? Sure enough to risk getting on the bad side of a nobleman?"

The guard's eyes narrowed and he pulled his spear back. "Very well, but we'll be patrolling, so supper better be the only thing *you* take in there."

I bowed my head graciously and plucked the letter out of his hand as I walked past. "Have a good shift, soldier."

I walked into the estates, head held high. I could tell they were staring at me the entire time I was in view by the itch between my shoulder blades, but I ignored it. They needed to see me. This was part of the plan.

To be honest, I was pleasantly surprised at how well it had worked. They didn't even question that Lord Barty would have someone like me as a supper guest. His reputation really did precede him.

I turned immediately to the right on the outermost concentric street. Barty's manor was in the middle ring, but if I went this way and cut through at the next main straightway, I could walk past Lady Josyna's first. I liked to be at least a little familiar with a place before I had to sneak in, and I wasn't sure how often I'd be able to stroll through here.

The manors in the outermost ring were typically of lesser nobility, since the closer someone was to the baroness on top of the hill, the more favor they were seen to hold. Even so, the nobles here put a lot of money into their manors trying to make themselves appear rich and powerful to their neighbors.

Most of them had gardens in the back with high stone walls or ivy-covered iron bars, and yards in the front with half-walls of stone, iron, or hedges. The manors were two or three stories, often with towers sticking up at the corners. There were different styles, as each tried to stand out.

Behind the outermost row where Lady Josyna's manor was located was the area commonly called the back passage, a stretch of patchy grass between the backyards of the rich and the massive inner wall. It allowed troops to move between gates without disturbing the streets of the estates. A few narrow, alley-like paths between manors linked this area to the street in places. Small buildings clung to the wall inside the passage, used for troop barracks, maintenance, or storage. Some of these also played host to the handful of secret entrances under the wall that were guarded by the Yellows.

Lady Josyna's manor was large compared to its neighbors, but in need of repair. The garden was the only thing that seemed to be well cared for. Considering the large number of servants she was said to take in, it was surprising anything went undone.

There was speculation that most of these servants had left their previous posts because they were lazy and wouldn't work, and now they took advantage of the lady's kindness. I suspected it was more because they were only being housed before Deidre could find another place for them. Whether that was by the design of the noblewoman or a favor for Deidre, I wasn't sure. It was part of what I hoped to find out.

Even though it was after sunset now, I saw a great deal of lights on in the manor, so a large number of people had to be moving about in there. It would make things difficult.

The wall in front was a green hedge with a free-standing wooden gate. The wall in back was stone, just over chest high and covered in moss and climbing vines. The building was three stories, and while most of the first and second story was lit up, the third only had a few lights shining. That would be the Lady's private area, off limits to all but her closest servants.

I continued down the street, pretending not to show that particular house any more mind than the ones around it. It'd be tricky to make my way through all those lit rooms. I'd come back this way after my supper at Barty's and see if things calmed down as the evening progressed.

I turned up the next street and strolled into the second ring, then doubled back three houses to the one I knew belonged to Lord Bartholomew Henrick. The best way to describe it was "aggressively quaint." The roof tiles were blue, and peaked high. The walls were made to look like a forest cottage, but on a much larger scale. The front garden was enclosed with iron bars I could have stepped over, and contained a scattering of ornamental trees, flowering bushes, and cobbled walkways. I could barely see the back garden wall through the landscaping, but it seemed to be vine-covered iron as well, taller than a man.

I walked up the cobbled pathway to the set of double doors and pulled the bell string. I'd had very few opportunities to enter a house like this from the front door, and they'd all ended rather badly, but I tried to put that out of my mind. I needed to endear myself to this nobleman, or at least hold his interest. I could be civil.

An elderly man with fluffy gray hair answered almost immediately. His gaze measured me and the slightest hint of a frown showed through his otherwise strictly professional bearing, then he stepped aside to hold the door for me to enter.

The front room was richly appointed with a staircase winding to the second level. Carved woodwork lined the corridors leaving to either side. A pair of paneled doors were closed straight ahead that probably led to a gathering hall of some kind. The floor was wood with thick rugs, and a modest chandelier hung above me.

The butler closed the door and sniffed. "I will inform his lordship you've arrived. Please wait here." Then he tottered off.

I didn't know whether to be frustrated at having to stand in the entry and wait, or amused that they'd left a master thief alone in the house.

Within minutes the nobleman himself bustled in, beaming. "Mister Gray! How marvelous to see you! I was afraid my message hadn't reached you."

My teeth grated together and I forced myself to relax. Charm. Charm and mystery, that's what I had to portray. I held out the bottle of wine. "Just running a little late."

Bartholomew blinked down at the offered bottle for a moment, then motioned his butler forward to take it. "I'm sure you're quite busy. But you did come, so how about a tour of my grand house?"

"You realize I'm a thief, right?" I raised an eyebrow. Was this stupidity on his part, or naivety? It was getting harder and harder to tell.

The noble chuckled. "It does seem like a bad decision, but I assure you I have an ulterior motive. You see, I want you to tell me all the weak points and all the things you'd take advantage of. It will help me be authentic when writing my story."

I glanced at the butler, who still stood nearby with the bottle of wine cradled in his arms. His mouth was drawn into a grim line of disapproval, but he didn't speak. I wondered how many of the servants weren't keen on their master's academic interest in crime.

I cleared my throat, conscious of the gaze of the butler on me. "I'm not sure that's a good idea."

Bartholomew's face fell, but he nodded. "Trade secrets, I suppose." He drew himself up and straightened the lapels of his jacket. "But I shall give you the tour, nonetheless, and hope for some comment or guidance that would steer my pen."

By the Six, it was amazing someone hadn't already taken this fool for every coin he owned. What kind of nobleman invites a known thief into his house and gives him a tour? I followed behind him, avoiding most of his questions as we walked and answering with noncommittal noises when I couldn't ignore them. Of course I did pay attention to the layout of the manor, because I was still a thief, but I tried not to seem too interested.

There were three floors. It was one of the larger manors, and still appointed well enough to show he wasn't hurting for coin. Some nobles had to sell off possessions if they incurred enough debt, but these rooms were full. There was a grand hall, a main and secondary dining hall, a library stuffed with books and several study rooms. We passed a scattering of various color-themed sitting rooms, a great many bedrooms–most of which were unoccupied–and two complete kitchens. There were suites on the third level, which I only vaguely got to view, as the man finally seemed to show some reservations at taking me into his private living spaces.

By the time we returned to the smaller of the dining rooms, food was already laid out for us. I was deposited at a chair in front of a plate overflowing with slices of roasted pig, baked game bird, tiny buttered potatoes, baked squash, boiled greens, and some kind of cheese pastry. A servant filled the wine goblet in front of me, then stepped back to hover at my shoulder.

I frowned at the wine. Why did nobles think they had to have wine all the time? I doubted there was any ale in this manor, but maybe... "Lord Bartholomew–"

"Oh please, just call me Bartholomew. We're friends now."

I left that alone. "I was wondering if you had anything else to drink? Maybe something a little simpler? Or stronger? Either would work, really."

He chuckled and raised his glass. "I'm afraid not. I'm not fond of stronger liquors, and I didn't think to have ale available, but we have a large selection of wines. If the ones I have aren't to your liking, we can enjoy the excellent vintage you brought for us. I promise that when we next meet I will have something more suited to your taste."

I grimaced. "Right. I think this will be fine."

Bartholomew started talking again, telling me how his family had first come to Sangarie, that his father and grandfather had been in property management, then about how he'd decided to go into the literary arts, to the disappointment of his mother.

I ate quietly, nodding when it seemed appropriate and trying not to look bored. I drank as little as I could. Ale or liquor would have been fine, but a few glasses of wine would have me giggling like a Blue and giving things away I really shouldn't. Unfortunately I was a nervous drinker, and it was hard to tell how much I was drinking, because whenever the level in the goblet started going down a servant would come up behind me and top it off.

It made me jumpy, having someone hover behind me as I ate. Only Barty and I were sitting at the big table, but at least half a dozen servants were in the room at any given time. They rotated out, bringing new dishes and taking away others that had barely been touched, and two of them were always behind the lord, waiting to fill his goblet or his plate, or hand him his napkin.

The food tasted excellent, but it sat heavy in my stomach so I picked at it and moved it around on my plate to make it look like I was eating more. Watching my hand move, I realized I was already buzzing from the wine. Everything was a little fuzzy and warm at the edges.

Bartholomew finally pushed his plate to the side and one of the servants took it away. He folded his fingers together and propped his elbows on the table. "Are you sure there's nothing you can tell me about my manor that a thief could take advantage of?"

I sighed and dropped the chunk of bread I'd been nibbling on back to my plate. "It's not really about weaknesses in the house. It's about exploiting the weaknesses in people."

"Are you saying I should have some guards? Or my servants aren't trained well enough?"

The wine was making me speak before I could think, and I frowned as I pushed the goblet away. "Your servants are fine. A thief just finds the cracks."

Bartholomew's face lit up and he searched the tabletop, shifting plates aside. "That's a great line. Where's my notebook? Carmine!"

Ugh. I needed to stop talking before I said something to insult him or get myself in trouble. Next time I visited I'd bring a bottle of whiskey instead of wine.

The white-haired butler stepped forward, presenting the lord a small bundle of parchment loosely stitched together.

Bartholomew beamed. "Thank you." He took the stack and paged through it for a moment, muttering to himself, then accepted an ink pen and began scribbling. "So, can you expand on this whole idea of exploiting cracks?"

My face grew hot and I looked down and ran a hand through my hair to hide the flush. "Uh... Not really. It's more of a spur of the moment thing."

He gazed up from the notebook, his brow furrowing. "Well, if you had to do it right now, how would you break into my house? We can go outside if you want, and you can show me."

I squirmed in the chair. The servants were staring at me, a few of them frowning. This all felt very wrong. A thief hid in the dark, kept to the shadows, was silent and left no trace. They didn't explain to someone exactly how they'd steal from them. "I don't think I can do that."

Bartholomew's brow crinkled and for a moment he looked like a toddler who'd just been told he couldn't have a sweet bun. Then he sighed and nodded. "I understand. Secrets. Don't want to get in trouble with the King of Thieves."

I cut off the snort that came automatically, changing it to a more neutral sniffle. The King of Thieves? I assumed he meant Rigel, and wondered what kinds of rumors floated around in the estates about the guildmaster.

Bartholomew closed the notebook and pushed it a few inches away. "Perhaps another time, when I've earned more of your trust."

There was no way I'd ever trust a nobleman, no matter how harmlessly naive he made himself seem. "I thank you for the delicious meal, Lord Bartholomew. I should probably be getting back to where I belong or the Silvers will get twitchy." As I got to my feet, the room swayed a little bit, but quickly righted itself.

He stood as well and motioned at a servant, who left the room immediately. "I have one more request for you tonight, Mister Gray."

"What would that be, my lord?"

"I would be honored if you'd pick a lock for me."

My eyebrow went up. "Are you serious?"

The nobleman hurried around the table and ushered me toward the door. "Yes! I need to be able to describe it properly in the story, and I'd love to see you do it."

I frowned and brushed his hands away from my chest. "Ah. No."

Bartholomew deflated. "Mister Senyr assured me you'd be a great help to my research, but I feel as if I'm imposing on you."

Shit. If I screwed this up and Barty didn't ask me to come back, my entire excuse for handling this investigation into Deidre and Josyna would be blown. Not to mention Senyr would be furious. As much as I'd prefer to do this the sneaky way, after getting a look at the lady's manor I didn't think I should. Not entirely. I needed some legitimacy, at least for being in the area and studying the target.

Six be damned.

"No imposition." I plastered on a smile and slipped a pair of lockpicks from a groove in my belt. "I only meant that I needed some room."

Bartholomew chuckled. "Of course! All the room you need, as long as I can see what you're doing."

He took my arm and led me forward again, and I let him. Every instinct I had was telling me this was stupid, but I didn't have any other ideas to encourage him to have me come back.

We stopped at a closed door and he wiggled the knob to show it was locked and gestured grandly as he backed away.

I grimaced and sank to one knee to get a better angle and let him see what was going on. The wine was still making me a little fuzzy, and one of the lockpicks twisted in my fingers before I even started. I'd just have to be deliberate and careful. No way did I want to fumble this in front of an audience.

I slipped them both in and felt around for the shape of the lock, immediately realizing I needn't have worried. Rue could have picked this lock when she was nine. I'd have to make it look good, though, or he'd just ask to see it again.

What should have taken seconds, I dragged out into a full minute while I put on a very serious working face and cringed at the amount of eyes trained on me. It made my neck itch and left a bad taste in my mouth. When the lock finally clicked and I pushed the door open, Bartholomew started clapping.

"Amazing! It's like watching a master craftsman at work."

I hid the grimace and tucked my lockpicks away. "Thank you. Now if you don't mind, I should be getting back. I look forward to our next meeting, my lord."

He was smiling, but his gaze was now trained on the doorknob as if he could intimidate it into giving up its secrets. "Yes, of course! Carmine will see you out, and I'll contact you soon."

12 – Back to the Throat

I took the same route back to the gate, pleased to see there weren't nearly as many lights in Lady Josyna's manor now that it was well and truly night. I even walked along the front hedges, peering into the yard and getting a better look at the back garden wall. I paid attention to the neighbors as well, and which gardens might be used as cover, or which houses were still lit up at this hour that could witness anything that happened.

I didn't linger. There was too much of a chance someone would get suspicious. The Silver at the gate narrowed his eyes when I came into sight, but didn't stop me from leaving. I did notice there were four of them standing there, which was becoming more and more common these days once night fell. They kept watch on both sides of the gate.

I passed through, walked a few blocks down Market Street, then slipped to the side and doubled back to the ramshackle building where the Yellow waited for me. All she had was a nod to greet me, and I appreciated the silence. I was feeling a little dirty at having picked a stupid lock for Barty like some kind of street performer, and I didn't really want to talk about it. When I was once again in my own comfortable clothes, I left without a word.

By now the effects of the wine were nearly worn off, and I wanted a real drink. I meandered toward Old Town, taking note of the beggars on street corners and the citizens finding their way either to their homes or their next source of entertainment. After a couple of districts, I sensed I was being followed and sighed, stopping in the middle of the street to turn around.

"It's been quite the night already, so why don't you just come out?"

I waited, not even sure at this point who to expect. Senyr, come to check on me? The Red, stalking me? Belatedly, I realized it could be

91

someone sent by Loring to kill me. I'd forgotten about him with everything else happening.

Rue stepped out from behind a building, walking slowly toward me.

That probably should have been higher on the list. I kept my expression blank, unsure where this was going and how to handle it. "Hey kid."

She stopped half a dozen paces away, her gaze on the street, digging the toe of her boot into the crack between two cobbles. "I picked something up."

"Did you now?"

She reached into her pocket and tossed a small, shiny object my way.

I snatched it out of the air and held it up between my fingers to look. A thimble? I turned it, raising an eyebrow as I realized it had been cast to look like the head and comically puckered mouth of a fish. It was well-used, covered in tiny scratches from the impact of the needle. "Does this belong to–"

"Charlotte, the mender."

I snorted. She was getting better at this game. "I picked something up too." I slipped the hairpin out of a pocket and strolled forward, twirling it in my fingers so the nearby lamp reflected off the polished nickel.

Rue closed the distance and flung her arms around my waist, laying her head on my chest.

I froze. As a little kid she'd always been doing this, but in the last couple of years it had stopped. I figured she'd either outgrown it, or she'd finally started listening to my half-hearted protests. Whatever it was, the hugs had been replaced with teenage sarcasm. I hadn't realized how much I missed them.

I sighed and wrapped my arms around her shoulders, setting my chin on top of her head. "I'm sorry, kid. I acted like an ass."

She chuckled, following it with a sniffle. "More than usual, yeah."

"You don't have to agree so quickly."

She pulled away from my chest, but stayed tucked under my arm. "So what did you pick up?"

I held out the hairpin. "Plucked it out of a woman's hair in the Old Market."

She took it and held it to the light, squinting. "You sure you didn't just buy it?"

I scowled and pulled her into motion down the street, keeping my arm over her shoulders. "I'll let you buy me a drink to apologize for that question."

She chuckled and stuck the pin inside her pouch. "I think mine was better."

"It was. You win this round."

She beamed and matched my steps as we walked. My gait was naturally soft, but she had to work for her sneakiness and she apparently didn't care right now. I left it alone, since we were only going to the Throat and I didn't feel like ruining the moment.

After we crossed into Old Town she looked up at me. "Elias said he talked to you."

"Who?"

"My friend that you hate."

So that was his name. "I don't hate him. I strongly dislike the idea of him."

She sighed and pulled out from under my arm, putting a few feet between us and staring at the street as we walked.

I was still worried this Red was taking advantage of her somehow, or using her as a cover, or just pretending to be a normal human being for the novelty of it... but Vin was right. I'd rather Ruena knew I was on her side than have her think of me as an enemy. I'd rather she felt safe coming to me for help if she ended up needing it.

I took a steadying breath. "I'll make you a deal."

She gazed up at me with narrowed eyes. "I'm listening."

"I'll give him a chance, and even try to play nice, if you promise me you'll keep both eyes open and come to me if anything seems even a little bit off."

"What if it's a sex question?"

I grimaced at the blush rising to my cheeks. "May the Six take me."

She laughed, the sound ringing down the street. "Don't worry. I'll talk to Deidre about that."

"It would be appreciated. By the way," I held out my hand, "I'll have my key back."

Her face screwed up into a pout and she dug through her pouch for a moment, then pulled it out and slapped it into my hand. "Don't you think I get enough practice in Old Town? What if I need to get inside in a hurry?"

"Pick it faster."

She huffed in exasperation, but stuck her hands in her pockets and swayed happily as she kept pace with me. "So how did your date go with Lord Bartholomew?"

I rolled my eyes and gave her a dirty look. "He kept asking me how I'd break into his house, and then he asked me to pick a lock while he watched."

"That's a little weird. Did you do it?"

"I didn't want to, but Senyr is determined to use this as a cover, and I couldn't brush him off the entire evening." I shuddered. "I'd rather not talk about it."

We came up to the front door of the Throat and I pushed it open and held it for her, then followed behind. "Why don't you join me at the table with Sans."

She nodded, grinning widely.

I wound my way through the bar to the center table. Sans was there, along with May and three other older patrons. They were drinking and chatting, and as we neared the table I caught the end of a joke and the round of laughter that followed. It sparked a wistful feeling in my chest, and I would have done just about anything to be that carefree again.

I set my hand on Sans' shoulder. "Hey old man, enjoying your night?"

He raised an eyebrow. "I was. I noticed you left in a hurry earlier. Everything all right?"

"Of course. Nothing I couldn't handle."

He peered closely at me, squinting a little in the low light of the common room. "You look shaken."

Did I? I was trying to appear nonchalant, but I definitely didn't feel that way. I'd need to do better. My job depended on being able to portray myself in a certain way, and while Sans had put up with enough of my bullshit over the years to be able to pick up on my fake smiles, he didn't normally comment on it.

He narrowed his eyes and tossed his cards into the center of the table. "I'm out gentlemen." Then glancing at May he added, "And lady." He heaved himself out of the chair and gestured at the stairs that led up to the second level. "Why don't we catch up? I have a wonderful bottle of whiskey I've been saving for a quiet night."

As good as that sounded, I didn't want the conversation that would go along with it. "I don't know if—"

Ruena shoved herself into my side, pushing me off half a step and smiling at Sans. "He'd love to. He could use a good long talk."

I glared at her. "Don't meddle."

Sans clapped a hand on my shoulder and turned me toward the stairs. "It's settled then. Let's see the evening out somewhere a little more quiet."

May rose from her chair as well and took up the cane beside it. "I think I'll join you."

Sans offered his arm and together they made their way through the crowd to the stairs. The old barkeep's voice rose over the noise around us. "Coming, Gray?"

I blew out in exasperation.

Ruena walked ahead of me, glancing back over her shoulder with her eyebrow quirked up and an impudent smirk on her face.

What a little shit. I scowled back at her and followed.

I'd been upstairs at the Throat many times, having lived there for a few years myself as a kid, but rarely had I been in Sans' private room. It was decently sized, sparsely furnished, and smelled of cedar chips. A large bed—big enough for two people—was against the far wall, and I wondered if there had ever been someone to share it with.

My eyes went to the table and four chairs in the middle of the room where Sans was helping May into a seat. An earthen bottle was already in his hand and he set it on the table and squeezed her shoulder gently before moving to pick up four small glasses from a shelf nearby and returning to his seat.

I slipped into a chair between Ruena and May.

Sans began to pour, giving Ruena only a finger width in her glass. "So. What's weighing so heavily on your mind, boy?"

"Like I said, it's nothing I can't handle." I took the offered glass and sipped appreciatively. Anything Sans kept back for his private use was usually excellent. "No reason to worry."

Sans sighed and leaned on his elbow to rub his temple. "Does it have to do with that elf friend of yours coming back to town?"

95

I shot a disgusted glance at Ruena, but she stared determinedly at the glass in her hands. "How much did she blab?"

"Just that. But I know you, and I know when you've gotten yourself in over your head. You look as if you haven't slept in a week and your worst nightmares have come to life again." He reached out and took May's wrinkled hand in his. "We care about you, boy. Tell us what's going on."

How did I begin? How did you tell someone you were about to destroy the city? Sans knew most of the story I'd told Neffrey five years ago, since he'd been standing nearby at the bar when I gave my report, and I hoped I could fill May in as needed, because I didn't want to start at the beginning.

It turned out May knew most of what had happened too. Between Sans, Deidre, and Rigel, she'd pieced together everything important at least. So I started by confirming the elf had returned, and repeated what she'd said about needing to ensure the destruction of the city. It felt good to tell them, to say out loud the things that had been rattling around in my brain.

I wanted to tell them about the vision I'd had. It was eating away at me, sitting like a weight in the pit of my stomach. But whenever I got up the courage to start, I changed my mind and said something else. I felt like maybe if I didn't say anything–didn't acknowledge it–then it wouldn't happen. I could find a way to stop it, as long as I didn't give it voice.

I answered the questions they had the best I could, hoping it might spark some idea about what to do next. Details about the labyrinth and the treasury, about the extent of the destruction, about the theories of the elves. May was mostly quiet and thoughtful, her troubled gaze focused on me. Sans was scowling and grumbling to himself.

He finally peered out from under his bushy white eyebrows at me. "How many people have you told about this?"

I cringed, remembering my promise to tell Rigel and Senyr. "Only Deidre and Ruena know. And now the two of you."

His eyebrows wrinkled together. "Rigel doesn't know?"

"I was going to tell him, but I just haven't had the chance."

"And the other masters? Senyr?"

"I've been busy."

He grunted and shook his head.

I glanced at Ruena and spoke in a subdued tone. "Hey kid, can you go get us a round of ale?"

She nodded and slipped out of the chair, quietly leaving the room.

Once she'd gone I set my elbows on the table and put my head in my hands, trying to keep my voice from shaking. "What do I do?"

May leaned forward to squeeze my forearm gently. "You'll do whatever you can."

"What if it makes things worse?"

Sans grunted from where he was slouched in his chair with his arms crossed. "Not a lot worse it could be."

I dropped my arms to the table, raising my gaze to his. "I didn't see any bodies in the labyrinth." I grimaced and shook my head. "I mean, I saw fresh bodies of people that were being killed by the shadows, but nothing that looked like it had died during the blast. Where were all the bodies? Had they all been turned to ash as well?" I rubbed a hand over my eyes. "Is everyone I know going to explode into dust?"

Sans huffed and shook his head. "Would be better if they all ran away first."

I stared at him. "If they all ran–" Why hadn't I thought of that? It wasn't like the city was the whole world, so they could just... leave. Hope flickered in my chest and I leaned forward. "You all need to get out before the Night of Shadows. If you aren't here, maybe you won't be killed."

Sans wrinkled his nose. "I haven't closed the Throat since the day I opened the doors."

I slammed a hand on the table. "When the sun sets on that day, there will *be* no more Throat. Please..."

May put a hand over mine. "When the time comes, if you haven't found a way to stop it, we'll go."

Relief bubbled up and I didn't know if I wanted to laugh or cry. Things still looked really bad, but maybe there was something that could be salvaged. I just had to convince tens of thousands of people to leave the city in time.

Without telling most of them what was going on.

If I started screaming from the rooftops about the destruction of the city, people would think I was one of those crazy mystics. They'd laugh me into a locked room for my own safety. I snorted as I rubbed a hand over my face.

The door opened behind me and I turned to see Ruena standing there with a tray and four mugs of ale, but she was biting her lip and glancing behind her. "I wasn't sure if I should bring her up."

I scowled. "Who?"

A hooded and cloaked figure entered, and I recognized the small stature and the scratched armor peeking behind the edges of the cloak just before she pulled the hood away. Nissa stood there, her expression as cold as ever.

I made introductions and the elf took the chair beside me while Rue leaned against the wall nearby. Nissa was hesitant to talk with Sans and May in the room, but when I assured her again that they already knew everything I did, she finally just ignored them and turned to face me.

"I have been trying to find you. I visited one of your human mystics that claimed to be able to see the future."

My nose wrinkled. "You went to a fortune teller?"

She frowned. "They were… less than impressive."

"I can imagine. Not many of them could hold a candle to the insight and wisdom of the great elfish leaders."

"Are you mocking me?"

"Yes." I took a long drink of my ale and sighed. "But I'm listening. What did this mystic tell you?"

"That the other stone is already here."

I set the mug down. "How do you mean? Where?"

"Someone has it and they are here, or very close to here. That is all they were able to tell me. I still have not been able to meditate on the stone. I have not been able to contact the elders." She growled and stared at the table. "I am no closer to learning what is meant to happen, and the days are passing too quickly. Now the other stone is here and I do not know if that will make things better or worse."

"Worse. The answer is definitely worse."

She looked away, wringing her hands in her lap.

I was pretty good at reading people, and what I saw in Nissa was worry and things left unsaid. Either she had more information from her elders she hadn't told me about, or that mystic had said something the

98

elf didn't want to repeat. I was in no place to judge her for keeping secrets, but at the same time I couldn't just let it go once I realized it.

"Whatever you're holding back, you need to tell me."

She raised her gaze to mine. "The mystic told me a man was in danger. A man touched by shadows and marked by the stone. I think that man is you."

I frowned. "I've been called a lot of things, but that's my new least favorite."

She heaved a sigh, rolling her eyes away from me again. "Can you not be serious, even now?"

"Did they tell you what the danger was?"

Her gaze was turned away from me, but I caught the tightening of her jaw and the way she continued to clench her fingers over her thighs.

I lowered my voice. "What do you know?"

Her voice softened as well. So quiet I had to focus to catch everything because of the muted background noise from the common room below. "Have you been seeing shadows?"

The hair rose on the back of my neck. "What—exactly—do you mean by that?"

"The mystic was in a trance of sorts. She was not aware of most of the things she said, and could not recall them afterward when I asked about them. But…" She blushed, which turned her green skin a ruddy brown color. "She trailed off during her reading, then muttered about shadows clinging to the man, and when I tried to ask for more information she only said one name."

I waited, watching her discomfort for longer than I had the patience for. "What name?"

She raised her gaze to meet mine. "Dakara."

I stared back. That name meant nothing to me, and by the look on her face, it should have. I hated feeling like I was out of the loop. It was a dangerous place to be in my line of work. "Who is that?"

Her eyebrow raised. "You do not know?"

Sans broke in. "I do."

His brow was furrowed and his expression was a mix of suspicion and shock. He glanced from me to Nissa, licking his lips and adjusting his grip on May's hand on the table between them. "Dakara was one of the Six."

99

13 – The Six

My eyes narrowed and I leaned back from the table. "Are you fucking with me?"

Sans shook his head. "I remember it from when I was a boy. I was raised outside of Sangarie, in a village called Iyesgarth. They had a strong temple presence, and the priests clung to the old stories."

Nissa looked at him with interest. "What did your priests say?"

He gave a loud, drawn-out sigh, staring off into the distance. "It was a long time ago, and I was very young. They told stories of how the Six were once individual gods, and through greed for magic they were cursed into one entity. I remember Dakara was a god of darkness. There was a goddess of light named Luxali as well, and the other four were the elements.

"There was a big tile mosaic in the temple that depicted the goddess of light and the god of shadow opposing each other in the middle, and the elemental gods surrounding them. It was very colorful, and caught the attention of a little kid who was otherwise bored out of his mind when he had to go to the temple.

"I think the priests in the village favored Luxali in secret, and their stories were cautionary tales that always ended in Dakara punishing the bad children. I don't even remember the names of the other gods."

Nissa sighed. "Humans have always forgotten history so quickly."

Sans scrunched his bushy brow at her. "Your people would too, if they only lived a fraction of a century."

She nodded graciously, then turned to face me. "The gods that make up the Six were neither male nor female. They were divinity, and therefore could become whatever they wished when they took form. They had domains, much like your friend describes.

"Luxali was the god of light, including the sun, moon, and stars. Dakara was the god of shadow and the night. Mera was the god of water and the seas. Matzee was the god of earth and all the green things that grow upon it. Aurel was the god of the sky and weather. Hone was the god of fire and the live-giving hearth. These six gods ruled over the early times.

"They bickered among themselves, like most family does. Their followers took up these quarrels and the peoples of the land became divided, waging wars and killing each other in the names of their gods. The gods themselves fed off this turmoil, becoming what their followers believed them to be.

"Night and day were no longer constant as Dakara and Luxali opposed one another. The seas of Mera swelled and battered the earth of Matzee, which shook and split with quakes, and the skies of Aurel flung storms across the land, while the fires of Hone grew unpredictable and dangerous.

"The more the people fought, the more the gods fought. The more the gods fought, the more the people fought. Eventually the gods met in one place and a battle raged so violently that the earth split and the First Stone was forced to the surface.

"The gods all sensed the power of the stone, and they all wanted it for themselves. They began to fight even more recklessly. The power they flung about was absorbed into the stone, causing it to become unstable. They did not notice.

"At the height of their battle the stone exploded with power and the gods were caught by the blast. They were reduced to their essential being, existing as raw magic, struggling to escape the pull of the stone as power turned and rushed back to it. They were not strong enough on their own, so they merged into one. With their combined magic they ripped free of the stone's pull and fled the land, drawing all the remaining spent magic with them. The stone flickered and went dark.

"They became the Six. Forever bound together, forever tied to the stone. They remained far away to resist the pull, but a thread of each god's power exists within the stone, and it holds the power of creation and destruction."

The elf's voice trailed off.

I'd never questioned the origin of the Six. It was portrayed as a Six-in-one deity, observing from afar. Most people believed it was something made up to control the populace through fear or guilt. Worship was hollow at best in Sangarie. The temple was a place of community, but it was all the doing of the priests and mystics.

I leaned back in my chair, staring at the edge of the table in front of me. "That's an interesting story. I don't see what it has to do with me."

Nissa's eyes darkened. "The Six are connected to the stone. Most think it is an anchor, but what if it is a window? Or a door?"

I shifted my gaze to meet hers, not moving. "And me?"

She frowned. "I cannot be sure. Perhaps Loring has the stone and his hatred focuses it on you. I do not see what other connection you would have with it."

Her words sent a shiver up my spine. She didn't know about the vision. Had touching the stone back in that cavern linked me to it somehow like it was linked to the Six?

I shook my head, forcing the thoughts away. I wasn't a god. I was a thief.

Nissa spoke up again, her voice tight with worry. "Five years ago in the labyrinth we fought creatures of shadow. If the stone has a connection to the gods, perhaps Loring has found a way to connect to Dakara. There are stories of the powers of the original gods. Dakara created all sorts of shadows that served them in the war."

"Like the shadowkraken?"

She nodded. "The shadowkraken, the shadowbeasts, and the watchers."

A cold pit was forming in my stomach. That morning on the roof of the Throat I'd been sure I was having a dream brought on by stress. Later, I could have sworn I saw a shadow move. Had it been more? "What's a watcher?"

"It is said the watchers are formless shadow. They are Dakara's eyes and ears in the world."

"Could Loring command them?"

Nissa frowned. "They are part of Dakara. No single human could command even part of a god, but the god could willingly grant the use of its power."

"Are you saying Loring recruited a god?"

She cursed in elfish under her breath. "You have seen one."

"Maybe. Maybe I just imagined it. But we both saw what was in the labyrinth."

"Only Dakara himself could grant the use of their creations. It seems that Loring uses Dakara's power in the near future to create the labyrinth with the stone he carries."

Maybe I should tell her about the vision now. Would that make a difference in her theory? In my vision the city had seemed to be on fire, guards were readying for a fight, but I was still the one who raised up the stone in my hand before everything exploded. Loring and his pet god may have started it… but I think I ended it.

I bowed my head. "Can we get the people out of Sangarie?"

"What?"

"Can we evacuate the city?"

She scowled. "Are you asking me if it can be done, or if it will break the future?"

"Both."

She pursed her lips and thought. "We saw no people in the labyrinth other than those who came through portals, and I've seen nothing of them in visions, so if they leave I do not think it will have an impact on events. However, I am unsure how you intend to convince an entire city to leave their homes."

"I don't know either. But it's an option at least."

"Right now we need to determine if Loring has the stone, what his intentions are with it, and where it is." She pinned me with a grim stare. "And you need to be careful."

"I appreciate the warning." I glanced at Sans and May, both of which were staring at us worriedly and tight-lipped.

I didn't want them to know. I'd rather they remembered me fighting to save the city than as the one who brought it down. I'd tell Nissa, but not here. Not now.

Nissa stood and gazed down at me. "Somehow you are connected to the stone, and you may have a larger part to play in this before the end. I will keep investigating. Rest well."

I leaned forward in the chair and rested my arms on the table, the vision screaming in my head. I definitely had a larger part to play. "You too."

14 – Riverman Festival

Deidre woke me the next evening with a kiss.

Well, technically I woke when she entered the apartment, but I pretended I hadn't until she leaned in and kissed me. At that point I decided kissing was better than sleeping and wrapped my arms around her to pull her over me and into the bed.

She giggled and threw a leg over mine, nuzzling my neck as I hugged her to my chest. I hummed and relaxed into the blankets, hoping I'd be lucky enough to get both kissing *and* sleeping.

Her whisper tickled my ear. "Gray, time to get up."

I gave a low rumbling chuckle and slid a hand along her thigh. "If you insist."

She laughed and caught my hand before I could grab her ass. "Not like *that*. It's time to get dressed and go topside."

I sighed and flopped back. "What for?"

"You promised you'd take me to the Riverman Festival."

"That's weeks away."

"Not this year. It starts today."

I squinted at her, my brow wrinkling. "Since when?"

"Since a month ago. Surely Rigel mentioned it in his briefings over the last couple of weeks?"

"I don't know. I don't usually go to them."

"It's amazing he tolerates you, or that Senyr hasn't choked you in frustration yet."

"Senyr says the same thing."

She squished both of my cheeks in her hands, leaning over me. "Get moving, dearest. You're going to dance with me, and buy me candied apples and wine, and take me home when I'm too drunk to walk straight."

I groaned and the pressure of her hands on my cheeks made my words come out slurred. "Alright. I'm getting up."

I dressed under her impatient gaze. The last few days had set me on edge, what with imminent destruction, vague threats on my life, and worrying about what Rigel was planning to do with Deidre. I'd barely seen her, not wanting to give away anything about Rigel's suspicions and the investigation into her private affairs with Lady Josyna. It would be nice to forget about it for an evening. Maybe a night of drinking and fun would give my mind a rest from the worries of the future, because the Six knew—

I frowned at the automatic turn of phrase. I'd never been a religious person. To me the Six were an outlet for frustration or a convenient scapegoat when things went wrong. Nobody really expected a response out of them. This Dakara was something else entirely, and I didn't know what to think of it.

I made sure my knives were secure and hidden, both because of the normal dangers of a large festival and because of the threat of Loring's revenge, although I didn't think they'd have any effect against shapeless shadows. I glanced at the wardrobe in the back of the apartment where the black-handled magic knife was packed away, but before I could decide whether it was worth the discomfort of carrying with me, Deidre dragged me out of the apartment.

The Riverman Festival took place mainly in the New Market district, but it spilled down Market Street and into Old Town. It was a once-a-year party that lasted three days, and it coincided with the arrival of a merchant caravan that traveled the length of the river throughout the year. According to Deidre, they had shifted their route this year to avoid a cluster of villages involved in a border dispute, and it set them three weeks ahead of schedule.

The festival drew people from the surrounding farmland that wanted to sell their goods or buy something they couldn't normally get in the city. The days were filled with crowds. The visiting merchants and farmers set up temporary stalls wherever they could find space along Market Street and it became a clogged mess. The nights were filled with eating, drinking, and dancing in the New Market square.

What it used to mean for me as an enforcer in Old Town, was a whole bunch of pickpockets trying their *very* best to have a little restraint, and failing miserably. It had been three days of hardly any sleep while I tried to keep the thieving and fighting to a minimum, so as not to drive off business or let anyone get hung. Visiting merchants and farmers were tempting targets because they weren't technically part of the agreement the guild had with the baroness.

But I wasn't an enforcer anymore, and while I'd helped Tekken out the first couple of years after she took over Old Town, the only duties I had now were negotiating if something went truly wrong, and making myself visible on the streets to remind the other Black Hands to behave. And because my negotiating prowess with the Warden was severely lacking, Senyr and Garion had quickly relieved me of that portion of the duties.

Which meant I was supposed to be as visible and present as possible, and if I noticed something getting out of hand I had to back up the enforcer in the district.

We went through Old Town so I could make sure Tekken had everything under control, but I shouldn't have worried. Her half-pint pickpocket army were running wild in the streets with their mouths sticky from candy and clutching streamers or wooden swords. I was pretty sure she was bribing them to be good, or distracting them with sweets, but it was working.

I was confused about why I wasn't seeing many of the older thieves on the streets, but when I stopped one I recognized to ask about it he said they were mostly gathered at the docks, where Tekken had purchased a few casks and set up some tables for gambling.

"She's great." He hiccupped, already swaying a bit. "I mean, you're great too, but Tekken is great."

I smiled, trying to ignore the little spike of jealousy and disappointment at not being directly involved with the district anymore. I'd chosen Tekken specifically because I'd hoped something like this might happen. I just didn't expect to feel so replaced. "I'm glad she's taking care of you good-for-nothings."

He threw an arm over the back of my neck, pulling me off balance and laughing. "Come join us, boss! I mean... bigger boss. Is that how that works?"

I extracted myself, glancing at Deidre. "Sorry, but I have a date."

He gazed slyly at her and gave me a knowing wink. "I'll have an ale for you then."

I snorted and patted his back. "You do that. Tell Tekken I'm headed to the New Market."

He nodded and walked off. "Sure thing!"

Deidre slipped her arm under mine as the thief wandered away. "Do you miss them?"

I watched him head toward the docks, swaying back and forth across the street and greeting everyone in his path. "Yeah. At times."

She tugged me up Market Street. "I don't know why you accepted the Hand of the Master. At least you enjoyed being an enforcer, even if you complained about it constantly."

"I enjoy being a master, too."

"You say that, but we both know you don't like the responsibility. You miss Old Town. You don't—"

I squeezed her hand. "Let's forget about it for tonight. All I have to do right now is dance with the most beautiful woman in the city, get her drunk, and take her home. Those are responsibilities I can handle."

She laughed and leaned her head on my shoulder as we walked.

Tonight I was going to forget all about that damn magic stone and its visions, and I was going to pretend everything was perfectly normal with Deidre and the guild. I was letting it get to me and it was dulling my brain. I needed all the skill I had for sneaking around in the estates in a few days. If I screwed up during a hit on the hill, the Warden would be within her rights to arrest me and she wouldn't let go of me this time. It didn't matter what shadow god was stalking me if I got myself hung.

The best thing for it was to enjoy myself now, let off a little steam, get a little drunk, and maybe spend some quality time with Deidre back at our apartment. I could do that. Besides, I couldn't very well let her think something else was wrong and have her start asking where I was going these next few days.

I pulled my arm out from under hers and instead draped it over her shoulders and planted a kiss on the side of her head. "Let's get you some wine, lover."

The New Market square was ablaze with lanterns, giving everything a reddish-orange glow. Food stalls lined the edges of the square and a troupe of musicians had set up around the fountain in the center. They played quick-paced songs that kept the crowd moving and laughing–and donating coins to the cups at their feet.

I made sure my own purse was tucked under my vest. While a Black Hand would be crazy to steal from one of the Hands of the Master, some of them still tried, and these events always carried their own thieves from the caravans with them as well. I'd never live it down if I let some outside cutpurse pull one over on me.

Deidre tugged me to a food stall and I got her a cup of wine and one of those baked apples on a stick, while I got a mug of ale. I had to pay a bit extra for her wine cup and my ale mug since we hadn't thought to bring our own and the stalls were selling it out of casks by the pour. The cups were stamped with the vendor's symbol of a boar's head with a disturbing grin showing oversized teeth and bristly whiskers. Deidre thought it was cute.

As we strolled around the edge of the festival we waved at people we recognized. Deidre drifted from person to person like a flower caught up in the wind, and I tried to keep up with her as I got pulled into my own conversations. Between the music, the soft glow of the lanterns, the cheap ale, and the feeling of Diedre's fingers entwined with mine as we laughed and joked with criminals and citizens alike, I was finally starting to relax.

When a familiar dancing tune started up, Deidre pulled my mug out of my hand despite my protests and set it down beside her cup on top of a nearby barrel. She took my hand and led me into the square, a mischievous smirk on her face. "Dance with me?"

I grinned back and adjusted my grip on her hand as the music picked up, spinning her as I drew her into my chest.

One of the benefits of living with an escort for so many years was exposure to a variety of social skills. With my thief's dexterity, and the practice I'd already had at defensive brawling, dancing came naturally. Deidre had taken full advantage of that and conscripted me as her practice partner early on. I realized pretty quickly that I actually enjoyed it.

We spun across the cobbles, finding our rhythm in the beat of the drum and the notes from the flute and fiddle. Deidre's skirt brushed my knees as she twirled, and I turned with her, guiding her around my back and into a coiled embrace, then spinning her away again, catching and holding her gaze when I could.

The square opened up around the dancers, and the surrounding crowd laughed and clapped along with the music. Everything else disappeared. The music and the crowd were all I could hear and Deidre's shining, laughing face was all I saw. The entire world was the feel of her hands in mine and her body brushing past me.

We carried the dance into the next song, and the next, but when the music trailed off and the crowd booed in protest, I wrapped my arms around her from behind as I caught my breath and whispered in her ear. "I love you."

She cuddled back into my chest and giggled. "I love you too, scoundrel."

A new tune started, a little more folksy than the last one, but I glanced at the crowd and saw Ruena smiling at us from the edges of the square. A little twinge of disappointment rose, but I pointed in her direction without releasing my hold around Deidre. "I think someone is looking for us."

She twisted and craned her head back to kiss my cheek. "Maybe a short rest."

I sidestepped, taking Deidre's hand and leading her from the center of the square where the dancers were starting in on the next round. We pushed away from the crowded edge of the dancing space and I looked for the cups she had set down earlier, but they were nowhere in sight. Damn it anyway.

Ruena pushed through the crowd around us, coming to a stop in front of me with her Red at her shoulder. She bit her lip as she looked up at me and fidgeted. "Hey."

I took a deep breath and smiled back. I'd promised her I'd try, and I was in the best mood I'd probably manage in a while, so… "Hey kid." My gaze lifted to the Red's. "Elias, wasn't it?"

He looked uneasy, but I wasn't sure if it was because of me or because he was missing his long cloak and dark clothing. He looked more like a farmer's son than an assassin. "Yes, sir."

I grimaced. "Don't do that."

Deidre bumped into me from behind, leaning against my shoulder and clinging to my arm. "Is this your friend, Rue?"

Ruena nodded and blushed. "This is Elias."

Deidre reached her hand out from behind me, and the Red glanced at me before taking it, his expression nervous and on edge. "It's a pleasure to meet you, miss."

Deidre laughed. "I'm afraid I'll have to agree with Gray on this one. Please just call me Deidre. Miss sounds so formal."

An itch crawled up the back of my neck, and I made sure to maintain my relaxed expression as I raised my eyes to the crowd. Deidre, Rue, and the Red continued to exchange pleasantries and I pretended to be listening as I covertly scanned the crowd for the source of this feeling of being watched.

There were so many people, and the lantern lights swayed in the gentle breeze and made the shadows shift and twist so they caught my gaze. I didn't know if they were naturally shifting or if they were part of a god's wiggly lookout system. I didn't see anyone suspicious, but that didn't mean much. With Nissa's warnings about Loring and Dakara fresh in my head, I couldn't ignore my instincts. It would be easy for someone to get close to me in this crowd.

Deidre squeezed my arm. "Gray?"

"Hmm?"

"Should we all get something to drink?"

I smiled. "Of course!" I pulled my coin purse from inside my vest. "Why don't you and Rue go get them, and Elias and I will find some benches to sit at for a while. Right, Elias?" I turned my gaze fully on him.

He hesitated, then nodded.

Ruena looked a little unsure about the situation, but gave me a stern warning glance and let Deidre drag her off. I watched them go, letting them get out of the immediate vicinity, then gestured at the Red to follow me toward the outer edges of the square. I spoke low, and hoped he'd be able to pick out the words.

"Someone's paying us quite a bit of attention."

"I noticed."

I raised an eyebrow. The kid was good, even as young as he was. I couldn't believe I was thinking it, but I hoped he was just as good at a fight if it came down to it. I pointed at a pair of empty benches just past the crowd and we walked that way. "You wanted a chance to prove yourself, right?"

He merely nodded in response.

I risked a quick scan of the crowd, still not seeing anything that stood out. "When they get back, I want you to sit with Deidre. Talk with her. Distract her." I caught and held his gaze. "And keep her safe."

His face was back to the impassive mask he'd worn on the rooftops in Old Town. "Do you think someone is targeting her?"

"No. But I've been wrong before." Loring probably had just as much of a bone to pick with her as he did with me. And while I hadn't yet made a move on Lady Josyna's manor, I couldn't help but worry Deidre would suffer the backlash of what I was planning if anyone found out. If I was wrong and I wasn't the target, at least she'd have protection.

"What about you?"

"I'm going to take Ruena and figure out what's going on."

His eyes flashed–just enough to show me he had some objections to the plan–but eventually he nodded again. "I'll make sure she's safe."

It went against my better judgment leaving Deidre in the hands of a Red, but I didn't know what else to do. I glanced in the direction of the ale stalls, seeing the ladies accepting drinks from the vendor and looking around for us. I stepped closer to the Red and pitched my voice very low. "I have a less than glowing history with the Red Hands, and I'm very protective of my–" I scowled as my brain unhelpfully supplied the word *daughter* and my mouth refused to say it, searching for another word. "Apprentice." Not the best choice, but it would have to do. "I don't like you, and I'm hoping you prove me wrong."

I held his gaze a moment longer, then looked at Deidre and Ruena with a smile. "About time!"

Deidre held out my new stamped mug and I took it with a sigh. How many mugs was I going to have to buy tonight? I set a hand on Ruena's shoulder as she handed a mug to the Red. "Let's talk."

Her eyes narrowed and she glanced back at Elias. "Now?"

"Just for a minute. I need to get a few things off my chest."

She looked down at Deidre, who shifted her gaze between us and smiled back encouragingly. "Don't worry, Elias and I can visit until you come back."

"Okay." She followed after me, mug in hand, as I walked around the outer edge of the square.

I still felt eyes on me, but too many people were here. If I found someplace more private maybe I could deal with it without getting anyone else involved. Making myself a tempting target should draw them out. I stopped and turned to face Ruena, keeping a pleasant expression on my face as I spoke.

"Something's off, and we're being watched. I think it might be Loring and his peeping shadows, so I told your friend to look after Deid while we handled it."

Ruena exhaled in relief and her shoulders relaxed. "Thank the Six."

I raised an eyebrow. "Really? Having an ancient god's pet shadows after me is better than fielding complaints about your personal life?"

She shrugged.

I sighed. "Just pay attention. I'm going to head into the alley beside that jewelry shop and act like I'm taking a piss. I want you to get yourself on the roof and have your throwing knives ready."

"To throw at shadows?"

"Just get up there and keep your eyes open. Don't do anything unless it starts looking bad. If it's creepy shadows you can't help me anyway, and if it's a person then I want to talk to them. You start raining steel down too soon and he'll bolt and I can't do that. Got it?"

She scoffed. "He's not bolting if he has a knife behind each knee."

I scowled. "Too far."

"It's a knife. How else am I supposed to keep someone from leaving? It's not like I can pin his boots to the cobbles."

"I should have had you learn to use a sling or something instead."

She rolled her eyes.

I waved my hand off to the side. "Just go."

With a massive sigh, she carried her mug of ale off toward the other side of the block containing the jewelry shop.

I turned and watched the crowd, trying to look like I was enjoying myself as I drank the cheap ale. I could just make out Deidre and the Red where they sat off to one side, but still no sign of anyone watching me, shadow or otherwise. A couple of minutes passed and I downed the last of the ale and turned to search the buildings, pretending to be

112

looking for a good spot to relieve myself, then walked determinedly for the entrance to the alley.

The alleys in this district tended to intersect each other, and this one was no different. A short way in I had the option of keeping straight or turning to the left or right. I kept to the block that had the jeweler's shop and turned right, blocking my view of the crowded festival. The noise dropped considerably once I rounded the corner and I went a few more feet and turned to face the side of the building.

Before I could do more than glance at the wall in front of me, I caught the scuff of a boot and looked deeper into the alley. A man was walking toward me, his face hidden in the dark, but obviously intent. He must have circled around to come at me from the other side. At least it was just a man.

I stepped into the middle of the alley to wait for him, glancing down at the mug in my hand and sighing as I tossed it out of the way with a clattering noise.

The man strode forward without pause, and when he was only a few paces away he growled out. "Gray…"

I tilted my head. "Who's asking?"

He reached to his belt for a long knife. "Gray."

Something was wrong. The hair rose on the back of my neck and I took an involuntary step back. He was too intent. Too focused.

From the corner of the alley where I'd just come from I heard the chipper, self-important tone of Lord Bartholomew Henrick. "Mister Gray! I've been looking for–oh!"

Shit.

That's when the attacker chose to rush forward, knife extended at my stomach. I slapped a hand onto his wrist and twisted to push it past me, then whipped my other fist at his face.

It connected with a crack and I jumped back two steps as I shook my hand out and glanced over at the nobleman. What in the name of the Six was he doing here? He was dressed in his commoner disguise again and was fumbling out a fancy silver dagger while he gaped at us.

The attacker pushed away from the wall where he'd stumbled, turning to pin me with that intense look.

Barty rushed up beside me, facing the man. "Don't worry! There's two of us now!"

113

If I let this idiot get hurt, all my efforts would have been for nothing. I put an arm out in front of him. "No! Get back."

"Really, Mister Gray, I can—"

The man leaped for me again and I shoved Barty aside. I twisted to avoid the forward thrust of the knife, but the man pulled it back with a vicious sweep and opened a slice across my ribs under my arm.

I hissed and covered it with my hand, hunching over as I backed away.

The attacker was ignoring Barty completely, staring at me with eyes that were glazed and shining with a disturbing light, his face screwed up in rage, muttering. "Gray. Gray. Gray."

I drew one of my own knives, taking a final step that put my back to the alley wall. At the edge of my vision I could see Barty with his knife held out, staring pale-faced between the attacker and me, looking torn.

The man in front of me had blood running down his chin from where I'd split his lip, but he hadn't seemed to notice. He continued to mutter my name and raised the knife.

As he rushed to attack I yelled, "Rue!" and caught his wrist, slowing the downward arc of the knife, but he was stronger than he looked and I quickly brought my other arm up and braced my forearm against his so I didn't drop my knife.

That meant I couldn't *use* my knife, either, as long as I was holding up his arm.

The whistle of Ruena's compact throwing knives warned me just before they thunked one after the other between the man's shoulders. He twitched, but otherwise didn't react. I was both surprised that she'd taken a potentially killing shot, and disturbed that it hadn't done anything.

My back was pressed to the wall and I strained to keep the tip of the knife a few inches away from my face. The man was a little taller and bulkier than me, but he didn't look this strong. Something was giving him an unnatural advantage.

The man's face contorted as he whispered my name even faster, and his free hand shot up to grip my throat.

I choked as he shoved my head back and cut off my air. The knife was still poised above me, but it had slipped a little and the tip quivered an inch from my cheek as my arms shook. I tried to croak out for Rue to attack again, but couldn't get the breath for it.

Barty came up beside the man and thrust forward with his dagger as he shouted, "Back, you cur!"

The man twitched when the dagger went into his side and the pressure of the knife bearing down lessened somewhat. I heaved at the man's arm to push it away from my face and divert it to slam into the stone wall beside my head, then stabbed my own knife in the side of his neck.

The expression on his face slowly went slack and his death grip on my neck let up, his hand dropping away and his body collapsing in a heap against the wall.

I sucked in air and the breath caught in my throat, making me cough and gasp like a beached fish. I braced myself on the wall beside me while I found a rhythm to my breathing again.

"Oh dear." Barty stood staring at his bloody knife. "That was–"

A clatter across the alley reached my ears and I looked to see Rue staggering from where she'd dropped the last few feet to the street. She steadied herself and ran to my side. "*Gray!*"

I held her off. "I–" The words stuck in my throat and I coughed again, bending over and holding my hand over the cut on my ribs. It was sticky and warm. I swallowed thickly and tried again. "I'm okay."

"I'm sorry. I should have been faster, but I was worried I'd hit you."

"It's fine."

Barty let out a manic little giggle and I lifted my gaze to see him still staring at his bloody knife.

"Lord Bartholomew?"

He looked at me and lifted it like he was trying to show me. "I just stabbed a man. That was–" He shook his head. "Well, it was rather frightening, to be honest, but so *real!* He was attacking, and then you were fighting, and then I feared he was going to get the best of you, and so I–" His empty hand shot to his mouth and he looked like he was going to vomit.

"Oh my." He gagged, then closed his eyes briefly to regain control. "Very enlightening. I think I'll go home now and process this."

I met Rue's confused expression before straightening to face the nobleman and giving him my best threatening enforcer look. "Don't tell anyone about this. Do you hear?"

Barty's lips quivered trying to hold a smile and he was a little green in the cheeks, but he nodded. "Of course not. Crime and all that. We're like brothers now, aren't we?"

My cheek twitched. "Right." I didn't want the Coppers getting involved here. I didn't want this traced back to the nobleman at all, because an investigation by the Warden would make my work in the estates nearly impossible. This had to remain just another random knifing in the city.

The nobleman backed away, his gaze darting to the body and the blood that was pooling around it. "I think I'll go home now. I look forward to seeing you again, Mister Gray." He stumbled on a loose cobble and caught himself, waving his hand over the scene. "Maybe without all the blood."

I stood with Rue and watched him scurry away. When we were alone again she looked at me and frowned, her face a lot more pale than usual.

"You're bleeding."

"I'm aware."

"Is it bad?"

"I don't think so." I stepped carefully to the body and wiped my knife on the man's clothes, then put it away. "Get your knives."

I checked his pockets while Ruena awkwardly pulled her throwing knives out of the man's back and cleaned them with trembling hands. I studied her face as she did, worried about how she was handling it. She'd never used her knives on people before, despite her bravado. While I'd technically been the one to end him, she was part of the effort.

She looked serious–grim even–but not hysterical like the nobleman had sounded. She worked quickly and efficiently even if she was a little shaky, then stepped back and waited for me to straighten up. Maybe she was still pushing away the reality of it for now.

The man's pockets were empty and I winced as I staggered to my feet with my bloody hand over the cut on my side. I couldn't shake the wrongness of this attack. It was obvious he'd been targeting me specifically, so I was guessing it had to do with Loring. The man had been repeating my name like a chant. His strength and obsession felt like something brought on by drugs… or–

I narrowed my eyes. "Rue?"

Her voice was soft and uncertain. "Yeah?"

"Did you see any magic?"

There was no immediate answer. Her forehead was wrinkled as she thought, and her arms were crossed tightly in front of her chest. She was definitely having trouble, but managing to hold it together for now. "There was something, but I'm not sure what. Almost like an echo or a cloud. It floated around his head."

"Is it gone now?"

She nodded.

I sighed and walked away from the body. "Let's get out of here before someone finds us."

She fell into step beside me. "Are you going home?"

"Deidre will be upset about not getting to enjoy the festival."

"She'll be upset because you're hurt."

"That too. I'll have to add it to the list of things to make up for. Try to block the view of my side, would you? Don't really want to advertise what we've been up to."

She nodded and edged closer as we entered the square.

15 – Telling Nissa

Deidre saw us first, since the Red had his back to us. Her expression quickly went from relieved to concerned, and she stood as the Red turned to search us out. His expression landed on me briefly with a tightening of his mouth, then darted to Ruena with a more thorough gaze and a deeper worry.

Deidre ran up and stopped us. "You look pale. Is something wrong?"

"Just a scuffle, lover, but I think I'm done dancing for the night."

She frowned and lifted the edge of my vest where my hand was pressed against my side. Her breath caught and she raised her gaze, her face probably as white as mine was. "How bad? What happened?" She glanced at Rue and looked her up and down. "Are you okay?"

Ruena brushed off her concern and avoided the Red's gaze as he joined us. "I'm not hurt."

Deidre frowned and turned back to me. "Well?"

"It's just a cut. Let's get out of the crowd, shall we?"

Ruena tugged on my sleeve and I stopped again, looking down at her. She was starting to look a little wild around the eyes.

"I think I'll go home."

The Red spoke up, setting a hand on her shoulder. "I'll go with you."

She shook her head and pulled away from him. "No. I'm okay. I just want to go home and rest."

His face twitched into a frown for a moment, then smoothed out again. He nodded and backed off. "I'll see you tomorrow then." His eyes drifted to mine and stayed for a moment, although I wasn't sure if he was judging or pleading. Then he turned and walked away.

I set my free hand on top of Rue's head. "You did good, kid. Get some sleep, and if you need me I'll be at home."

She nodded and spun away, but not before I caught the tears welling up in her eyes. I watched her hurry off in the direction of Old Town.

Deidre gazed after her with concern, but tugged on my arm. "Let's go. People are starting to look at us."

I followed her around the edge of the square and to the nearest entrance to the underground. Climbing the steep steps into the caverns below the city was a little painful, but at least it wasn't a ladder. Once we were underground I relaxed some, since no Coppers or curious citizens would be looking my way.

Once we were home, Deidre shut the door and tossed my coin purse on the table, then pointed at a kitchen chair. "Sit."

I did so gratefully, shrugging out of my vest before she could ask.

She pulled the bottom of my shirt out of my pants and lifted it up to look, and I flinched as the blood-soaked cloth—half dried now—tugged at the edges of the cut. She poked gently, sighing.

"It's deeper than you made it sound. It'll need to be stitched up."

I leaned back in the chair. "I'm sorry your night was ruined."

She didn't look at me, just went to fill a basin with water from the pitcher on the counter and dug some clean towels out of a drawer. "What happened? You owe me that at least."

I opened my mouth to answer, but caught the sound of footsteps outside our door and paused, waiting to see if they'd pass by. Instead a sharp knock sounded.

I caught Deidre's worried stare and waved her back. "Attackers wouldn't knock."

She didn't look convinced, but nodded as she picked up the bundle she'd gathered and moved to where I sat. She called out as she did so. "Come in. It's not locked."

The door opened and Nissa stood there, pulling away her hood to gaze in with concern and anger.

She closed the door behind her and stopped halfway to the table, taking in my bloody clothes and what I hoped was an irritated expression on my face. It might not have come across very well, because I was tired and in pain.

Her eyes narrowed. "What did you do?"

"Really? That's your question? I'm bleeding over here."

"You are obviously alive. Were you fighting?"

119

"Yes. If you must know, a man followed me and jumped me in an alley. Do you have any goop with you?" I looked at Deidre as she knelt at my side, holding up my shirt and raising a wet towel in her other hand. "As much as I love you, dearest, I don't want you sewing up my skin again."

She started washing the blood away. "Then stop getting sliced open."

Nissa dug in a bag at her hip and brought out the tin, setting it on the table near Deidre and stepping a little farther away. "Loring?"

"No. Could have been sent by him though."

Deidre looked up sharply, frowned, and went back to cleaning the wound. I'd forgotten I hadn't mentioned him. Her expression told me she'd have a few words for me about that later.

Nissa scowled. "Tell me more."

"There's not much more to tell. What are you doing here so conveniently anyway?"

"I was looking for you at the bar you favor. I saw Ruena come in. She directed me here and mentioned you had been badly injured."

"I'm touched at your concern."

She glanced at Diedre, biting her lip in hesitation, then sighed. "Your child also mentioned the encounter was… strange. I feared something darker was at work."

"I see. Six inches of steel slicing me open isn't dark enough for you."

"Keep making light of our situation. I can leave you to navigate your enemies alone and focus on my own goals. I have yet to discover how the Night of Shadows is brought about, and dealing with your pageantry is exhausting."

I grimaced, partially from the pain in my side as Deidre worked and partially because this was the time to speak up. Even knowing I needed to say it, my mind was trying to convince me otherwise. I shifted my gaze to the floor. "I didn't tell you everything when we parted five years ago."

Deidre stopped cleaning away the blood, her hand pulling back.

Nissa's voice was cold. "What did you *not* say?"

I took a deep breath, making sure to keep my gaze on the floor. "When I first picked up the stone, something happened. I had some kind of vision."

Both women were silent. Waiting.

I rushed ahead. "I saw the future, from the stone's perspective. I saw myself carrying the stone through the baroness's manor, up to the battlements. Guards were all around, yelling and running, but I couldn't hear anything. Then I saw you and Ruena, as you are now, waiting for me at the top of the manor. It was sunset, and the city looked like it was on fire. You came to me, and I raised up the stone and everything exploded and went dark. That's it."

I waited, but all I heard was breathing in the room. Then Nissa spoke in a quiet, angry tone. "You did not think to tell me this before?"

I could feel the heat on my face and kept my gaze averted. "I didn't want it to be true. Would you want to be the one that destroyed everyone and everything you cared about? I was hoping I could find another explanation for what I saw."

Deidre gripped my knee, but I refused to look at her.

Eventually Nissa sighed. "At least we know where we will be."

That was no consolation for me. I'd hoped she would tell me I understood it wrong, and I wasn't going to be the one to do this. I'd hoped she would come up with a way to prevent it.

Fuck.

I just wanted to be done with this. I clenched my fist as Deidre started smearing ointment on the cut over my ribs. Nobody said anything for a long moment, and eventually the pain just faded away from my side.

"Is there anything else you have yet to tell me?"

I closed my eyes. "No." The attack in the alley popped into my head. "Wait. There is one thing from the attack tonight."

"What is that?"

"The man who attacked me was saying my name. Over and over."

"Why?"

I sighed. "I don't know. He looked strange, though. Like he was drugged or sleep-walking. He didn't seem to feel pain, and he wouldn't stop saying my name once he saw me. Ruena said she saw a cloud or an echo of magic around his head, but it disappeared when he died."

Deidre's hand on my knee clenched, then she pulled it away.

I looked down at her and she was staring at me with her brow wrinkled up in worry. "You killed him then?"

"It was a joint effort. I really didn't have a choice, since he was trying to stab and choke me at the same time."

She bit her lip. "No wonder Rue is upset. I should go and talk to her."

I put a hand on her shoulder to keep her from standing up. "Leave her be for now. She'll come to us if she wants to talk."

Nissa's face was thoughtful. After a few moments she turned toward the door.

I frowned and called after her. "Care to fill us humans in?"

"I will investigate. I do not wish to speak out of turn."

Deidre grabbed the tin and rose to extend it, but Nissa shook her head.

"Keep it. He will likely need it again."

I grunted.

She left without further comment.

Deidre looked at the tin in her hand, rolling it around in her fingers as she bit her lip. "Loring?"

I'd hoped to avoid telling her about that. She was sure to worry, and I didn't need her trying to keep track of where I went when I was investigating her. "Yeah. Nissa got word that he's still sore about what happened five years ago, and he blames me for it."

"So he's trying to kill you? Is he in town?"

"I'm not sure. He seems to have some connection to the stone, so he's all tied up with what's going on. Nissa has this theory about the stone being a window to the Six or something. One of the Six is all about shadows, and Loring might be using them to spy on me."

She scrunched up her face. "Are you serious? That sounds like big magic."

"It sounds like bullshit." I feigned nonchalance, hoping she wouldn't push the issue. From everything Nissa had said, the shadows were eyes and ears. Eyes and ears were meant for spying, not killing, right? As long as I found a way to stop the labyrinth I wouldn't have to deal with the really dangerous shadows.

"When were you going to tell me about it?"

I pulled my ruined shirt off over my head and wiped the last of the blood from my stomach with the damp cloth she'd left on the table. "I didn't want you to worry."

"We're in this together. I'm sure he isn't happy with me either, and I'd rather know if he's back."

"You're right. I'm sorry."

She tossed the tin on the table and it clinked and slid a few inches before stopping. "No more secrets."

My jaw tightened and guilt roiled in my gut, but I couldn't tell her what was happening. I had to clear her name first or Rigel would pull me off it entirely and do it his way. I didn't think Deidre would do anything to endanger the guild, but she had her own goals. I just had to prove they didn't conflict with the guild. That she wasn't plotting or scheming.

I swallowed and nodded. "No more secrets."

16 – The Baroness

A loud, insistent knock woke me from a restless sleep. Deidre sat up in bed beside me, rubbing her eyes and mumbling. "Who is it?"

Senyr's irritated voice came from outside. "Gray! Get up and open the door."

I flung the blankets off and padded across the room, sliding the bolt and opening the door partway, then leaning on the frame. A breeze from further down the underground corridor raised goosebumps on my bare chest and I shivered. "What do you want?"

He flicked his eyes down at my loose cotton pants and bare feet. "I want a single day where I don't question all my life choices, but that's not going to happen."

I yawned. "And in lieu of that?"

"I want you to get your ass into your very best clothes and find your grownup manners in whatever drawer you stuffed them in, then join me in Rigel's quarters."

"What time is it?"

He wiped a hand over his face. "Not late enough. Now hurry up or you'll be wearing my foot up your ass." He turned and stormed down the corridor.

I watched him until he turned a corner, then I closed the door.

Deidre was sitting on the edge of the bed. "What was that all about?"

"I have no idea, but I'm guessing it's at least partially my fault."

***

Twenty minutes later I was standing before the two Reds that guarded Rigel's door, trying not to squirm under their watchful eyes. I pulled at the neckline of the tunic Deidre had chosen for me, wishing I could release a couple of buttons. The undershirt was itchy against the freshly healed skin at my side, and the sleeves bunched up at my wrists and made me feel like an idiot. The pants tucked into my dress boots, but any amount of walking made them puff out at the tops and caused swishing noises as I moved.

By the time Rigel called from inside and bade me enter I was eager to get away from the gaze of the Reds. I braced myself for the faint buzz of magic that always permeated his private quarters and strolled in, determined to defend myself for whatever I'd done to get a weirdly formal summons from the guildmaster.

Three people—Rigel, Senyr, and a woman I didn't recognize—waited inside, lounging on separate couches. Senyr had changed since I saw him last and now wore the outfit I'd seen the other day at the Hart. His long dark cloak had been switched out for a short cape, which was a fluttery and useless thing for a thief. He was avoiding my gaze, scowling at the rug.

Rigel's eyes, however, followed me as I entered. He always dressed like a nobleman, but today he looked more like royalty, crisp and clean and full of egotistical bullshit. His short graying beard was neatly trimmed and oiled, and I think he even had makeup on. It did nothing to mask the disapproval on his face. His finger tapped the cushioned arm of the couch, making a very faint rhythmic noise that made the relative silence in the room even more noticeable.

The woman sat stiffly, impatiently if I had to hazard a guess. Her hair was a glossy black and done up in intricate braids, her skin a light tan, and her eyes black. She wore a dress of blue and gold, simple yet elegant. Noble? Something about her put me off. Perhaps the arrogant arch of her eyebrow, the exaggerated care with which she moved, or the familiarity in her gaze.

The soft drumming of Rigel's fingers stopped and he sighed. "I'm going to give you the opportunity to tell me a few things you seem to have kept to yourself."

My gut dropped. I shot a glance at Senyr, but he was staying out of it apparently. Had someone told Rigel why Nissa—

Oh. Of course. I couldn't feel the magic of her disguise because of the general buzz in the guildmaster's room, but I recognized the posture and mannerisms now. Nissa seemed to have gotten impatient and taken a few things upon herself. I took a deep breath and nodded.

"Right. Well, you already know the labyrinth is Sangarie's future. Apparently it's coming due. On the Night of Shadows the entire city will be destroyed by the stone we brought back five years ago."

Rigel raised an eyebrow and turned to look at Senyr, who had finally raised his head. While they didn't look surprised, they definitely looked taken off guard.

I grimaced. "That wasn't what you expected me to come clean about."

Senyr rubbed his forehead and muttered a curse under his breath, and Rigel leaned more comfortably into the couch.

"No. But by all means, continue."

Sure. Why not dig myself in deeper? I sighed. "Honestly we don't know much." I glanced at Nissa in her fancy clothes and dark hair, but she didn't seem inclined to jump in. Fair enough. "The city will be destroyed. That future is already written. We've been trying to discover how, and we suspect it has something to do with Loring and with the Six."

I filled them in on everything I knew, carefully leaving out the vision from five years ago. Each time I tried to mention that my mouth would get dry and I'd veer off to a different topic and glance at Nissa to see her frown. Rigel listened calmly after his initial surprise, fingers steepled and a thoughtful expression on his face.

By the time I'd finished I was pacing between the couches and tables, frowning back at him. "How can you be so calm about this? It's taking all my effort not to lock myself away in my apartment until it's over."

"Because that's exactly what I shall do."

"Lock yourself away? I doubt that will help." I stopped behind one of the couches, putting both hands on the back and trying to put all my anxiety and worry into my next words. "We don't have to die here. Nobody does. There's no reason we can't evacuate the city."

He chuckled and crossed his legs as he leaned back. "Have you ever tried to move that many people?"

I glared back. "That's why I'm asking you. You must know what we can do. I don't want—" I dropped my gaze. I didn't want to give voice to it, but I had to make him see. I needed his help. "I don't want the entire city to be destroyed."

126

"Tell me something, Gray. When you were in the labyrinth, did you go underground?"

My brow creased. "No."

"I was curious, after you came back. So I sent a volunteer into the labyrinth the following year."

"You're kidding."

"I'm not. I wanted a corroborating report. Not that I don't trust you, but you left out a great many details."

"I was kind of running for my life."

"Understandable. Without going into too many dreadful specifics, let's just say that the underground survives."

I edged around and dropped onto the couch, taking the ramifications of that into account. I hadn't bothered to check, being so concerned with getting through the ruins. The underground has never been a shortcut anyway, and I'd assumed it was ruined or collapsed. If the underground was intact, and the people there had survived…

I cringed at the thought of spending the whole night below ground, hearing the screams that sounded through the city, knowing death walked the streets above. "All of it? You're sure?"

"Fairly certain. There were too many people down there to allow my scout to move freely."

"Too many people… then—"

"It seems at least a portion of the city fled—or will flee—to the underground for shelter."

I nodded, feeling a rush of relief in my chest as I realized not everyone had died.

Rigel sighed. "Which means I must have opened it to the general populace. There's no way so many citizens could have decided to come down here at the spur of the moment." He rose from the couch and walked a few steps away, his hands behind his back. "There are, of course, some finer details that will need to be worked out, but some of the city may well survive that night."

So there was hope. I raised a shaking hand to pinch the bridge of my nose and give myself time to settle into a more neutral expression.

A knock came at the door. A series of taps that I recognized as the indication that a master requested admittance. Who else was supposed to be here? For that matter, why were we all dressed up?

Rigel called out for whoever it was to enter and I stood as two figures joined us. At first I didn't recognize either of them, then one gave a rasping cough that was all too familiar. My eyes widened. "Neffrey?"

His pale pink cheeks flushed an even darker red. He looked as if he'd been scrubbed top to bottom. He wore a fancy, if slightly outdated, nobleman's outfit that flared at the knees and the elbows. His hair was a golden yellow and fell past his shoulders, curling slightly at the ends. Even his fingernails had been scrubbed clean of dirt.

I choked down the laugh, but couldn't prevent the grin. "By the ever-fickle whims of the Six. How much skin did you take off when you peeled away all the dirt?"

Neffrey ignored my jibe and gestured at the other man. "You remember Rohgart?"

My humor was immediately squashed. A towering figure I *should* have recognized immediately, despite the fancy clothes that were stretched tight over bulging muscles and the slicked back hair. Rohgart the Butcher. One of the three highest ranked Red Hands, the Blades of the Master.

Rohgart was a relic from the times before Rigel came to power and he'd pledged his life and loyalty to the guildmaster, helping him take over from the previous leader. He'd earned the name of Butcher when he swept through a pocket of criminals who resisted the transfer of power, leaving nothing but body parts in his wake.

As much as Rigel worked to gloss over the violence and chaos required to raise the guild to what it now was, there were always things like the Butcher here to remind us we weren't as civil as we pretended to be.

And pretend was a good word for what Rohgart was doing, as his clothes looked even more out of place on his bulky frame than any of the rest of us. They were red, pulled almost to bursting across his chest and forearms. His hair was combed down close to his scalp and tied at the nape of his neck instead of hanging in oily tendrils around his face like it usually did, and his wild beard had been trimmed and combed.

Despite the rather tamed appearance, the look he gave me said his hands could rip my face from my skull without much effort. Even at his age, he was one of the deadliest men in Sangarie.

Now I was really suspicious. The guildmaster would never dress us all fancy to come and meet with him in his rooms, which meant we were going someplace. Someplace I probably didn't want to go.

Rigel's intensity had returned and he straightened his expensive-looking jacket. "Welcome, gentlemen. It seems that Master Gray's elf friend has taken it upon herself to visit Lady Karyn and whip her into a paranoid frenzy about an outcast nobleman that's after her treasury." He scowled and gestured at Nissa in her human-guise and finery. "Well? Tell these fine gentlemen what you told me."

She raised an eyebrow, then stood and clasped her hands in front of her stomach as she explained with cold efficiency how she had visited the baroness, told her some rumors about Loring coming to the city to look for a treasure said to be in her own vault, and how he was even now sending his underlings to determine how best to infiltrate her manor.

I listened to it all with growing understanding, cringing at each new phrase. This was what Rigel had expected me to tell him... that an old enemy had come to collect a debt, and that Nissa had decided the baroness would be a deterrent for him. I wasn't surprised the guildmaster was angry. He'd cultivated the guild's relationship with the city's leading authority very carefully.

After a long pause, Rigel capped it by turning to me and saying, "At which point, our Lady Karyn bid her go to the Court of Thieves and summon their king to the hill." He shot a glare at her. "How did she put it? To discuss events that endanger our shared peace?" His anger returned to me. "The destiny you two are chasing here is putting the political wellbeing of the undercity at risk."

Nissa's nose wrinkled up and she muttered under her breath. "There will not be a city here in five days. Your treaty with the leader of this place will not protect you from that."

I glanced at Rohgart and Neffrey. They weren't reacting to her statement, which I hoped meant they hadn't heard it. Let Rigel fill them in as he thought was needed.

Rigel turned to me again. "I have been *bidden* to bring my most trusted advisors to this meeting, specifically including you. At first I wanted to refuse. I didn't think it would be a good idea to put you in the same room as the baroness after your adventure five years ago."

Neffrey choked off a laugh and Senyr snorted.

I glared at them both.

Rigel continued, "Then I realized you may be just the distraction we need. The baroness will be consumed by her own issues with you, and less focused on what we're doing."

I frowned. "I'm a decoy?"

"Exactly."

"From what... *exactly*?"

"From a great many things our dear Lady Karyn is skirting the edges of. She has spies of her own, and keeping them fed with a careful mix of truth and fabrication eats up nearly a quarter of our Yellows' resources. I don't have the time or patience to be at her beck and call."

"And what if she decides I'm a problem? This isn't distracting some guard during a hit, it's dropping a mouse into a cat's food bowl."

"Then you'd better be on your best behavior, little mouse."

I glanced at Senyr, but he looked away. Some help he was.

Rigel straightened his tailored coat and brushed off some non-existent dust. "That said, you are to be *agreeable*. Turn on that infuriating charm and don't fuck this up."

I ground my teeth. "Yes, sir."

He looked at Nissa. "Have a good day, madam."

She smiled sweetly back at him. "You as well, false king."

I sucked in a breath, but Rigel merely glared at her as she gathered her skirt and walked toward the door. It would bring her right past me. I avoided her gaze and she paused briefly next to me.

"Do be careful. The Lady Karyn had no love for her son, but she has not forgotten the slight against her lineage."

I winced as she continued past me. Of course she hadn't. That would be too easy.

***

It was disconcerting to walk through the city behind Rigel and the Butcher. For one thing, all of us except Rigel looked like a troupe of actors about to put on a comedy about the nobility. I figured someone would have to be drunk or stupid to think we belonged on the hill.

Which led to the second thing. We were creating quite a stir as we made our way through the city. The Riverman Festival was still going on so we'd come topside near Craftsmans Row and were taking that to the inner wall, but people were spilling in from the south as word spread

130

about the spectacle. By the time we reached the north gate it was a fucking parade.

I kept my head down, wishing I'd brought a hooded cloak. It went against everything I'd learned as a thief to attract so much attention to myself, and I noticed Senyr was just as uncomfortable walking beside me.

I got the feeling Rigel had done it on purpose. There were much closer exits from the underground we could have taken, avoiding the crowds and the whispers. He wanted people spreading word of us, maybe to the hill itself.

Needless to say, none of us looked comfortable with this except Rigel. He strode with his head high, nodding at people and smiling. People—criminals mostly—occasionally called out to him or whooped in delight, and he ate it up. Rohgart strode beside him like a bodyguard, so nobody approached us, and I was thankful for that at least.

We walked through the gate in the inner wall without issue. The Silvers didn't even try to stop us. The streets in the estates were much quieter. I caught sight of servants or guards peering from the windows of manors as we went, but nobody came out to get a closer look. We walked right up to the main gate and Rigel spoke briefly with the Ironguard stationed there.

In the five years since I'd fought my way through the labyrinth I'd been to the estates many times. It had been eerie at first, with the memory of the blasted inner city so fresh in my mind, but there weren't reminders everywhere of what it had looked like. The manor of the baroness was a different matter.

I'd only ever been inside it twice. Once to kill her son, and once while navigating the labyrinth. Walking through the gate now, in the brightness of noon, I started to feel the first fingers of panic and shoved them back. I could look up at the towers and pick out which windows would be shattered by the writhing mass of tentacles, and picture the crenulations being broken and falling to shatter on the courtyard below. I braced myself for what I'd see inside.

Rigel followed the Ironguard through the front doors and Rohgart, Neffrey, and Senyr entered on his heels. I could sense the Irons behind me, making sure nobody "got lost" on the way to their audience, and it kept me going long enough to get through the doors. Then I stuttered to a stop.

It wasn't as dark as the labyrinth had been, since the sun poured through a multitude of high windows, and there was a feeling of being occupied that hadn't been there in the ruined version. Even so, I remembered what it had looked like, and recognized a vase that would soon be broken, and a tapestry that was yet to be coated in dust and ash. I glanced in the direction of the library with its secret staircase to the treasury, but the doors leading there were closed.

My chest was tight, I was sweating, and the collar of the tunic was choking me. I lifted a shaking hand to undo the first three buttons. Five days. Five days and the shadowkraken would be here, shaking the building, shattering the glass...

"Gray?"

I snapped my gaze to Senyr, who stood halfway between me and the far double doors that the others were just disappearing into. He frowned and glanced across the upper balconies where I'd been looking. "Don't fall behind."

I clenched my jaw and nodded, willing my legs to move and shuffling to meet him. It got a little easier as I went, and he fell into step beside me as we followed the others into the main audience hall. It was better there, because I hadn't seen it broken before.

Senyr edged closer and spoke low. "Hold it together, boy."

I didn't respond. I needed to pay attention. There were no shadow monsters here, only the human ones. Senyr must think I was scared out of my wits to face the baroness, and the thought of that dredged up even more anxiety.

The hall was massive, even bigger than Rigel's. Courtiers lounged at the edges and guards were stationed throughout, so it was almost like walking through a town square. Columns held up the decorated ceiling and wood paneled doors broke up the walls to either side. Tables and chairs were scattered at the edges for the people who attended at the pleasure of Lady Karyn.

At the far end was a raised platform and a large table, behind which a high-backed chair sat, flanked by four smaller versions on each side. They were all unoccupied, and the table was clear.

The Irons led us to the right side of the platform, through a decorated pair of doors, into a large sitting room. Tapestries hung on all the walls here and padded chairs were scattered around with small tables next to them, leaving an aisle cleared to the other side. Ironguard lined the walls, standing at attention, but no courtiers were present.

At the far end was a huge chair cushioned in burgundy, the wood inlaid with gold flaking. An older woman sat there, perched angrily on the edge with her hands clutching the padded armrests. Her hair was gray and coiled on top of her head with gold combs to hold it, and her dress was burgundy and gold, spreading around her in layer upon layer of rich fabric, making her frail figure look bigger. Jewelry glittered from her ears, her neck, her wrists, and her fingers.

I'd never seen the baroness in person, but I'd assumed a few things, like arrogance and self-importance, gaudiness and over-indulgence, but I hadn't expected the strength of presence she broadcasted through the entire room. She was not playing at being noble, she was as comfortable with it as Rigel.

Movement drew my attention beyond Lady Karyn's left shoulder and I realized with a start that the Warden stood there. I'd been so focused on the baroness I hadn't even noticed her, but she had certainly noticed me.

Her expression hovered between a sneer and a grimace, her eyes blazing as she locked her gaze on mine. She didn't seem to care that the guildmaster himself stood there performing a gentlemanly bow, or that the Butcher was cracking his knuckles one at a time at his side, or that the best thief and the best spy in the city were giving the room little glances. All she cared about was that I was standing in front of her and did not have chains around my wrists.

Surprisingly, the thought steadied me. I pulled my shoulders back and found my charming smile, taking comfort in the glare she cast my way.

Lady Karyn spoke in a commanding and condescending tone. "Who have you brought with you, Rigel?"

I couldn't see the guildmaster's face, but I could see the tension in his shoulders at the lack of respectful address. However, when he answered, his voice was clear and friendly. He extended a hand to his side. "This is my Blade of the Master, Rohgart." Then he made a quarter turn and gestured at each of us. "My Eye of the Master, Neffrey. And two Hands of the Master, Senyr and Gray."

Silence descended on the room. The baroness's eyes met mine and narrowed just enough for me to notice, her jaw tightening.

I broke eye contact and glanced at Rigel, who merely waited patiently with his arms crossed over his chest. Beyond him I saw one of the Ironguard, his gloved hand flexing on the shaft of his spear and his eyes moving across our group. It raised the hackles on my neck. I could feel the eyes of every Iron in the room trained on us, and the hatred from these two powerful women bearing down on me in particular.

I should have stayed in the underground. I was *way* too far out of my comfort zone with these people.

Rigel cleared his throat. "I don't think this needs to take very long. A certain young woman came to me with your invitation and explained the circumstances. Though I don't see how it has anything to do with the guild, in the spirit of good faith I have come to see how we may be of help to you."

Lady Karyn turned her sharp gaze back to Rigel, frowning. "So you deny having any knowledge of this outcast nobleman's return and his plans to steal from me?"

"My dear lady, no member of my guild would ever be part of a plot against you. My anger would be all-consuming and my punishment swift."

"Is that so?" Her gaze flicked to me briefly, then settled back on Rigel. "I cannot help but wonder if he is receiving assistance from someone under your protection. Perhaps even without your knowledge."

His voice rose, and the anger was artfully apparent in his response. He really was good at these political games. "Lady Karyn, I assure you we would never threaten the peace of this city. It is to our benefit that the truce remains intact. We have no knowledge of this nobleman's whereabouts, and as a show of our continued cooperation I offer you the assistance of Master Neffrey, our most esteemed gatherer of information, in discovering where he may be hiding."

Lady Karyn pulled her shoulders back and ran her gaze over each of us, finally resting on me where I'd attempted to escape her line of sight by stepping behind Senyr. "I would rather you offer the assistance of your top thief, to catch a thief."

Rigel chuckled. "Of course, if that is your wish. Master Senyr–"

"No. I want your Master Gray to represent the guild on this hunt. He shall work closely with my Warden to root out the exile."

Fuck.

My face flushed and I looked at the Warden, whose grimace had suddenly turned into a grin. This was not good.

I started to chuckle and it caught in my throat, but I cleared it and pushed on, trying to keep all the Irons and the Warden in my field of vision at the same time. "Investigations are not my strength."

Investigation was how all of this started five years ago. Back then it had ended with me killing Lady Karyn's son, so I could only imagine how wonderfully this one would go.

She settled back into her chair, smiling like a cat. "I'm sure you are eager to prove your usefulness to me, and your loyalty to the peace of our beloved city. Besides, you are rumored to have a history with the target, and surely it would be in your favor to apprehend him as well."

Rigel turned to look at me, his face impassive but his eyes sharp. He didn't say anything, merely waited for my reaction.

I didn't know what to do. He'd warned me to be agreeable and charming, but I was fairly certain he hadn't intended this. The last thing I wanted was quality time with the Warden. She'd be waiting for an excuse to hang me. And my plan so far had been just to stay as far away from Loring as possible, which was at odds with helping to track him down.

Had this been Nissa's doing? Had she planted the idea in the baroness's obsessed little head in order to get help finding Loring and the other stone? I'd need to have words with her about the value of my life at some point.

I glanced at Senyr, but he was facing the baroness, his shoulders curled forward, ignoring me. I looked at Neffrey, who was peering over his shoulder at me, and caught the briefest hint of a nod.

It felt like a death sentence. I drew myself up and raised my eyes to meet those of the baroness. "I would be honored to help you catch this thief."

17 – Summons

Shit. Shit. Shit.

I followed the others out of the manor and through the estates, ignoring the glances Senyr shot me as we walked and keeping my eyes trained on Rigel's heels.

How was I supposed to work with the Warden? I usually did my best to avoid her so she wasn't tempted to accidentally stick a sword in my chest. This was obviously a setup. The baroness wasn't looking for answers from me, only from Rigel. This was revenge, or hatred, or entertainment.

"Gray."

Senyr had fallen back to walk at my side. I took a deep breath and chased the thoughts from my head. They were just circling uselessly anyway. "What?"

He started to speak, then frowned and grunted, glancing at the guildmaster and the other two masters ahead of us. His brow furrowed and he tried again, his words so quiet I could barely hear them. "The world is going to shit around us."

"You noticed."

He growled and continued. "It has you off balance, and that's going to get you killed. If you don't think you can do this job in the estates I want you to say so."

I scowled. "I can handle it."

"Don't be stubborn. You have a lot going on, and I can have someone else do it."

I looked straight at him. "This is about Deidre. You and I both know she would never betray the guild. I can't let anyone else handle this."

"I could do it myself."

"You?" I laughed.

Neffrey glanced back at us and we both glared at him until he turned around again. I stepped closer to Senyr to be able to lower my voice even further.

"You can't do this and you know it. You're better than me at a lot of things, old man, but I'd like to see you jump out a window or outrun the guards if things go sideways."

"I won't let them go sideways."

I snorted and shook my head. "I said I can handle it."

"Then you'd better get your head on straight. Don't go in there unless you're on your game. Do you hear?"

"Yes, *master*."

"You're such an ass," Senyr muttered under his breath.

I ignored the comment. It was pretty accurate anyway. And he was right about me needing to get my head on straight before I fucked something up. This meeting with the baroness had me rattled.

Rigel stopped us at an entrance to the underground, glancing around before speaking in a low, authoritative tone. "Here is where we part. Neffrey, please find out everything you can about Loring and what he's up to. Rohgart, have your people scour the streets for unregistered assassins or spies." He looked at me and Senyr. "I fear we must move up the timeline for our investigation into the reclusive Lady Josyna. There are things about the baroness–"

His brow furrowed and he clenched his jaw over what he'd been about to say, then switched back into his usual no-nonsense tone. "If plans are truly being made against her, we need to know. Lady Karyn is roused, and if this is part of a larger ploy, we are unprepared to counter it. She is a crucial part of the operation here and her rule must be maintained."

I shot a look at Senyr, but he only nodded.

Rigel pulled open the cellar door, but paused before entering and turned back to us. "Gray, I will remind the baroness you are under my protection, but I cannot dictate the actions of every individual under her command. Mind yourself. And know that if things go wrong I'll do what I can, but I will choose the survival of the guild over any one member."

I straightened my shoulders and nodded. "Yes, sir."

He ducked into the cellar and I stood next to Senyr and watched him go, unsure what I should be doing, but positive I didn't want to go down there after him and give him a chance to upend anything else.

After a minute Senyr sighed and turned to me. "Want to get a drink?"

"Desperately. But I need to change out of these clothes even more."

"It's lunchtime, so I'll grab us some food and join you at your place."

I nodded and looked at the cellar door. "He should be well away by now. I think I'll take the less conspicuous route."

It was still a long walk to my apartment, but at least underground I was out of the crowds and could stick to the shadows. The normal shadows I trusted. When I got home Deidre was gone and I wasted no time in stripping off the costume to return to my familiar shirt and vest, comfortable pants, and well-worn boots.

I pulled two clean glasses out and poured one for myself, leaving the other next to the bottle on the table so I could collapse into a chair and put my feet up on the one next to it.

Senyr arrived not long after, still in his good clothes but carrying a package that smelled like roasted meat and fresh bread. We shared the contents without a word, letting the silence settle into the room and ease the tension.

Senyr had never been one for a lot of talking—unless he was lecturing me—and during my training over the years we'd often spent hours just sitting in each other's company. Usually it was to observe a target, or wait for an opportunity to practice some skill. Either way, there was nothing uncomfortable in it, and right now it was familiar and calming.

When we'd finished our meal and I was nearly to the bottom of my second glass, a knock came at the door. I stared at it, wondering if I could just ignore it and hope they went away.

Neffrey's voice came from the other side. "I know you're in there. Open the damn door."

I looked at Senyr and sighed, then swallowed the last of the whiskey before setting the glass on the table. "Come in. It's open."

Neffrey entered, glancing up and down the corridor outside before closing the door behind him. He was back in his beggar's clothes, but his face was still pink and his pale blonde hair wisped around the rags that covered most of his head. "You have a busy night ahead of you, Gray."

"I thought that might be the case."

He pulled a folded piece of parchment from under his rags and tossed it to the table. It bore the seal of Lord Bartholomew.

I grimaced. "Lovely."

"You'll bring your little apprentice this time. Apparently he was quite taken with the pair of you and wants to talk to her."

I shook my head. "No. I don't want her involved in this."

"Too bad, because it's her he wants to meet. You need to be in the estates tonight and that's your ticket. Afterward, my Yellow will meet you an hour before midnight in the back garden of Lady Josyna's manor and provide you a way in."

I frowned. "Already? I've barely had time to scuff my boots on the street outside. I've learned nothing about the schedule of the house, the people inside, the defenses."

"That's what my spy is for. He'll tell you all you need to know."

"What's the point of dragging Rue to the hill then? Why bother going to another dinner? I could just sneak in and we could dispense with the obsessed noble altogether."

Neffrey groaned and turned his gaze on Senyr. "Why couldn't you have taught him not to argue?"

Senyr shrugged and poured another splash of whiskey.

Neffrey grumbled and stepped forward to snatch the glass from his hand.

"Hey!"

The old beggar sat heavily on one of the chairs, draining half the whiskey in a gulp as Senyr went to get another. "Here's the thing, boy. Bartholomew is an alibi, yes, but he's also the beginning of your network of contacts on the hill. Your effort to make nice with Bartholomew is the only reason Rigel's letting you handle the investigation into Deidre."

I frowned and crossed my arms over my chest, leaning back against the countertop. I didn't like where this conversation was leading. It was getting perilously close to talk about my future. "I don't need a network of egotistical asshats."

"You will as guildmaster."

I barked out a short laugh and shook my head, but my palms had started sweating and my heartrate had jumped. "I'm not going to be guildmaster."

"Every triple bar in the guild knows Rigel's been grooming you to take over for him. The Six as my witness we've tried to argue his choice, but in the end we accepted it."

"Why? Even I know it's a terrible idea."

"Because you're young, well-liked, and too fucking clever for your own good. He sees something in you most of the rest of us don't. Maybe he's gone soft and domestic." He swirled the whiskey in his glass. "However you spin it, at the end of the day we all know you'd choose this city and its people over yourself, and not many of us would do that. Rigel thinks you'll outgrow the rebelliousness."

"Rebelliousness?" I snorted. "I have all I need already. Why would I want every beggar, thief, and spy looking at me to tell them what to do, fawning at my feet like they do for Rigel?"

Neffrey's voice rose and he poked a finger at me as he responded. "Without Rigel and what he did for the guild, you'd be cutting purses to pay for shots on the dock. Or selling yourself for coin to gamble with."

"And I appreciate that!" I flung my hand in the general direction of the door. "I follow him, just like everyone else does. I play his game and live in his ideal little underworld. That doesn't mean I want to be him. Let him pick someone who wants to be important and beloved and surrounded by nonsense."

Neffrey shook his head and grunted. "I assumed you were being obstinate, not stupid."

My eyes blazed and I pushed away from the counter. "Stupid? You gossipy little–"

Senyr stepped between us, setting an arm against my chest. "That's enough. You have a job to do tonight, don't you?"

I ground my teeth and glared past him at Neffrey. "Get out of my home."

The beggar grunted and shot back the rest of the whiskey, then rose and made his way to the door, calling over his shoulder. "Come to peace with things, Gray. It'll be much easier for you. Otherwise you're going to fail Rigel, you're going to fail the guild, and every one of us will be fucked."

I flinched when he slammed the door behind him.

Senyr cursed under his breath and rubbed his eyes. "Ignore him. He's all worked up because he can't figure out what's going on with Deidre."

"He's right." I turned to face the counter, putting my shaking hands on the edge. "I'm just a thief, Senyr. I can't lead anyone. I can't even keep myself out of trouble. Why would Rigel want me to take over for him?"

Senyr didn't answer.

I chuckled ruefully and squeezed my eyes shut. "I don't want it. I don't want to run this guild. I don't want to be responsible for the lives of everyone around me."

He sighed. "You aren't. At least not right now."

I snorted, trying to keep thoughts of the stone's vision out of my head. Of the destruction of Sangarie and my part in it.

Senyr put a hand on my shoulder. "Tell me honestly, are you good to do this hit tonight?"

"I will be."

"Don't die for it. Deidre will never forgive me."

I smiled at that. "Do me a favor and find Rue? Tell her to meet me at the little disguise shop the Yellows run next to the wall."

"She'll be there." He slapped me on the back and moved to the door. "By the way, I'll make sure Deidre is distracted most of the night. I don't want her trying to figure out where you are, or showing up at Josyna's. But you might want to send Rue back here to pin her down after the meeting at Lord Bartholomew's."

"Thanks."

He opened the door and looked back. "Be careful."

18 – Thieves Tools

I spent the rest of the day avoiding everything I could. There was a tavern in Crafthold called the Three Barrels that was dimly lit and not frequented by anyone that would recognize me by sight, so I spent the time glowering into an ale mug in the corner, trying to reset my head. By the time I dragged myself out of the chair and got to the little shack along the inner wall, it was past sunset. I knocked and the Yellow I'd met before answered and scowled at me.

"You're late."

I shrugged.

She ushered me inside and led me to the basement where my clothes from last time were laid out. Rue already stood there, turning to see herself in the long silver mirror.

She wore a light green dress, simply cut with a scooped neck and sleeves pulled off the shoulders. A darker corset hugged her chest and shaped her figure so she looked more feminine than usual. I hadn't noticed how much she'd grown, and it didn't make me very happy. I thought of the young Red and frowned.

Her hair was gathered above her head in a style Deidre liked to use, and curled at the ends. It would have made them look very much like mother and daughter. I stepped up behind her and reached for the hairpin she'd used to secure it.

It was the one I'd stolen in the Old Market square. I chuckled and adjusted it so the silver leaf was less visible. "Careful where you use that. It's not a common piece."

"Of course. I'm not stupid."

I squeezed her shoulders and whispered in her ear. "You're very pretty. Now go away so I can change my clothes."

She blushed and followed the Yellow out. I changed quickly, making sure my knives were secure and putting my own belt back on so I had all my tools available. I wouldn't have a chance to change into my normal clothes before going into Josyna's manor, so I'd have to bring what I needed with me. Sadly, I'd have to put up with the dressier boots. I'd be down a knife and an extra set of picks I kept in my own boots, but if that much was going wrong I was in big trouble.

I finished and joined the women upstairs. The Yellow sent us on our way after one last tug on Rue's corset. I offered Rue my arm as we circled around to come at the gate head on. The guard there was the same as last time, and he scowled at me and snatched my letter away.

"This is for the female associate of Mister Gray." He glanced at Rue. "I assume that's you?" Then he returned his glare to me. "You aren't listed on it at all."

I smiled and made a show of sighing. "He was eager to meet her, but my daughter is too young to be walking the streets alone after dark. Besides, Lord Bartholomew is a man of few words in his correspondence. Are you implying he'd invite a young girl to his home by herself? Think of the scandal."

Rue had stiffened at the word daughter, but I was proud of how quickly she recovered and leaned into me, just like a shy young lady would do.

The guard frowned, but unless he turned both of us away he couldn't send her in on her own now.

He looked to his partner—who shrugged and stepped aside—then glared back at me. "Perhaps next time Lord Bartholomew can be more clear with his invitation."

My smile curled wider. "I'll tell him you said as much. I'm sure he'll take the criticism with grace."

The guard paled a little, then stepped aside as well. "No criticism."

I led Rue past him without another word. That was easier than I'd expected. I'd never admit it to Senyr, but perhaps there was something to be said for having a legitimate cover.

I pulled Rue onto the first concentric street in order to walk past Lady Josyna's manor on the way. It was still relatively lit up, and I hoped things quieted down before it was time to meet our spy.

I leaned in closer to whisper. "That's the house I'll be breaking into later. Did Senyr brief you?"

She nodded. "He said I was supposed to get out on my own and head back to your place to keep Deidre company."

"Get rid of these ridiculous clothes first so she doesn't ask questions, and make sure you aren't seen doubling back."

She swirled her skirt beside her as we walked, putting a little hitch in her step. "I like the clothes."

I sighed. "You would." I caught the brief glimmer of steel strapped to her calf as her dress lifted during the swirl. That would be her throwing knives. My mouth quirked up at the corner. Good kid.

We reached Barty's manor and I walked Rue up the cobbles and rang the bell. "Careful what you say."

"I know."

The old butler answered and blinked at me a moment in uncertainty, then ushered us both in. "I'll have the kitchen prepare an extra place setting for you, sir."

I tried to keep the smile from turning into a sneer. "So good of you."

It took only a few minutes for Barty to find us in the front hall and he, at least, looked delighted to see me.

"Mister Gray! I'm so glad you came along as well." He stepped forward and took both Ruena's hands in his, holding them out and looking her over. "You look beautiful, my dear. Please, what shall I call you?"

Her gaze darted to catch mine, and I stepped forward. "This is Ruena. She's my apprentice."

"Apprentice thief! How delightful. I didn't realize you learned the trade like any other." He bowed at the waist. "It's lovely to meet you Miss Ruena. Shall we retire to a sitting room while we wait for our food to be set out?"

She blushed and took his offered arm. "Uhm… Of course, Lord Bartholomew."

I rolled my eyes as they headed toward a door, but followed close behind. I wasn't about to leave Rue alone in here. As harmless as Barty seemed to be, he was still a nobleman, and I had no respect for a nobleman's morals.

The sitting room was cozy and had a multitude of padded chairs surrounding a low table. Barty led Ruena to one and seated her, then moved to the largest and most opulent. A small table rested beside it with a notebook and an ink pen.

I found a seat across from Ruena so he had to split his gaze.

"So, Miss Ruena, how long have you been a thief?"

She looked at me for guidance, and I made a facial expression that told her to go ahead as she wished. She turned back to the noble and started answering his multitude of questions about how she'd become a thief, how she liked it, and how she'd met me. I was proud of how little information she gave him, though she talked quite a bit. Half of what she said was outright lies, and the other half was painted with exaggerations.

As I listened, I began to realize exactly how much of a gift she had for subterfuge. There hadn't been much call for it in her training so far, but she was quite believable and endearing. Even I would have believed most of what she said if I hadn't known better.

She would have made a better spy than a thief. Maybe I should have Neffrey give her some lessons too.

Barty's face wrinkled up and he leaned even closer, peering at her carefully. "Those eyes. Tell me, child, are you of mixed blood?"

Rue's eyes widened and her fingers tightened on her skirt.

I laughed before she could try to stammer through a response. I'd been ready for this particular observation. When I had Barty's attention I answered for her. "I can see why you'd wonder, but no. It was an accident a few years ago. We were pilfering some rare goods and a bag of powders exploded as we made our escape. She was blind for days, and while her vision eventually returned, her eyes had been badly scarred. The healers were dumbfounded."

He frowned and peered closer. "Fascinating."

The butler interrupted then and announced our meal was ready. Barty led the way and I put an arm around Rue's shoulders as we followed and leaned close to whisper. "You're doing great."

She nodded, brushing off the anxiety that had settled over her when he asked about elfish blood.

We filed into the dining room and sat at the oversized table. This time there was ale in addition to the wine, and I thanked the Six I wouldn't have to go dry to keep myself ready for the after dinner entertainment.

Though I still had to put up with the discomfort of having people stand around watching me eat. To make things worse, Barty turned his questions to me again.

"How did you like my disguise at the festival, Mister Gray?"

I picked at the roasted pork and struggled to remember what exactly he'd been wearing. "It was very... common, my lord. You blended in quite well."

"Yes, well I study the common folk when I go out, to see how they act and what they wear and eat. I must attempt to inject some realism into my story."

What an ass. He spoke of common folk like they weren't the same kind of human. I pushed the food around on my plate.

"But one thing I don't quite have a handle on is how to look the part of a thief. What do you wear when you work? Something to blend into the shadows? Something to help you remain silent? Please tell me how you prepare yourself."

It was too much of a temptation. I couldn't let Rue have all the fun of lying to him. I schooled my expression into one of suspicion and wariness, looking at the servants around us. "How safe is it to talk here about these things?"

Barty quivered and waved at the servants. "Please, leave us for a few moments."

They filed out and he leaned over his plate and listened eagerly.

I matched his posture. "There are some things, actually, that help us in our work."

He bounced in his chair like a delighted child. "I knew it! Enlighten me, if you would?"

"Well, first of all, the best thieves have cloaks soaked in mystic power to let us blend into the shadows if we stop moving."

His draw dropped. "I knew the guild employed mystics, but I hadn't realized that was what they were for. Fascinating." He scrambled for his notebook, spilling his wine and completely ignoring it.

He didn't need to know the mystics in the guild were mostly cons. Sure there were real practitioners of magic here and there, but the ranks of the White Hands were full of fortune tellers, ex-priests, and doomsayers.

I took a quick drink of ale to hide the smile, then continued. "And we have a special suit of clothes we wear sometimes. It's all black, tight-fitting, and covers the entire body so only the mouth, eyes, and ears are exposed. In this way we're very hard to spot."

Rue snorted and I glanced at her in time to see her hide the laughter with her napkin. "So sorry. Just shocked that you're giving away all our secrets, *Master* Gray."

I waved a hand in the air, thoroughly enjoying myself at this point despite her cheekiness. "Nonsense. After the other night, Lord Bartholomew is a trusted friend. I'm sure he'll be most discrete in his use of the information." I leaned in again. "Now then, we also have special shoes that have wool on the bottom to help us step without any sound. And we have gloves with hooks sewn into the fingers that allow us to climb vertical walls."

I took another drink of my ale, trying to think of anything else I could make up that didn't sound too far-fetched. "And of course there are special powders that render a victim senseless or let us disappear without a trace. Paints that make our faces look like someone else."

Rue coughed to cover her laughter.

I grinned conspiratorially. "And of course the fabled master key that opens any lock. I haven't found that one yet, but I have some leads on it."

Barty was scribbling as fast as he could, not even looking at us. "Amazing! Where do you think this master key could be located?"

I chuckled. "Well I can't tell you that, my lord. Not until I've had a go at getting it for myself."

He laughed and tapped a finger against his temple. "Of course not. You will tell me all about it if you manage to capture one?"

"You'll be the first to hear about it." I leaned back in my chair with my mug. "After the guildmaster of course."

"Of course." He flipped through his current scribbles, adding notes here and there.

I gazed at Rue and she met my eyes briefly before biting her lip and looking away to keep from laughing.

After a few minutes, he looked up from his book again. "I wonder if you could tell me a few phrases my character might use to sound more realistic? What kind of things do you say when you're in the thick of it all?"

I shrugged my shoulders, making a show of thinking about the question. "Well, there is a secret language all thieves know. We can communicate with each other without anyone else understanding."

His eyes widened. "Can you show me?"

I glanced at Rue and cleared my throat, then made some nonsense hand signals at her and said, "The glow of the moon is lovely tonight."

Barty looked eagerly at Rue, who blushed and looked between the two of us.

I leaned back in my chair and picked up my mug. "Go ahead, tell him what I said."

Her eyes narrowed briefly at having been put on the spot, then she smiled. "He told me to steal some of the silverware while the servants are out of the room, and we'd split the loot later."

Barty stared at each of us in awe. "That's remarkable. Could you teach me this language?"

I shook my head and darkened my expression. "Never. We'd be killed if another thief ever found out we were teaching the secret language to an outsider."

His face fell. "Of course. That makes sense." He scribbled in his book some more. "I shall just have to fake it for the book then, shall I?"

"Probably for the best, my lord."

After another brief pause, Barty set his pen on the table and looked up at us both. "It's getting late and I have so many ideas to get down." He turned his head and shouted, "Carmine!"

The butler entered so quickly he had to have been standing just beyond the door.

Barty rose and went to kiss Rue's hastily outstretched hand. "Carmine will see you out. It has been most educational. I can't wait to see what you have for me the next time we meet!"

I rose and steered Ruena toward the door. "I look forward to it, my lord."

I didn't look forward to it, and I hoped there wouldn't *be* a next time if all went well at Lady Josyna's tonight, but I had to play the part.

The butler saw us out and I gave him a deep bow and a smirk just to make him uncomfortable, then guided Rue toward the street.

She waited until we were out of earshot before commenting. "You're so full of shit. Senyr will be furious."

"Probably. Lord Barty was eating it up though."

"Paint that changes your face to look like someone else? Like anyone would believe that."

"People are willing to believe a lot when they don't want to accept they're just careless. If they believe it was magical abilities that resulted in the loss of their valuables, they think couldn't have prevented it. That it wasn't their own fault."

She snorted. "You just wanted to fuck with him."

I grinned. "So badly."

"Now what?"

"Now you get yourself out of the estates and go to my place to make sure Deidre is there and kept busy. I'm going to have a look around that other manor."

"Won't the guard think something's wrong if I leave without you?"

"That's why you're going through a different gate. Take the south gate, and be careful not to be seen crossing Market Street to get back to the Yellow's shack."

"What should I tell Deidre? You know she'll ask where you are."

I thought for a minute. "I haven't seen her since early this morning, before I got called to meet with the baroness. Tell her I've been wandering around the city, meeting with people and squaring things up."

"Pouting then."

I scowled at her. "I don't pout."

She snorted. "Whatever. Be careful, okay?" She broke away from me and started back the other way to the south gate.

I grumbled in her general direction, then put her impertinence out of my mind. I had other things to worry about right now. The biggest thing on that list was sneaking into what was still a somewhat lit up manor.

I gazed at it from down the street and sighed. It wasn't as full of light as earlier in the night, but servants were definitely still up. The third floor was nearly dark, so that was encouraging. I continued on the street until the first little alley that connected to the back passage along the wall, then casually checked behind me and ducked inside it.

If I was going to meet the Yellow in the back garden, it made the most sense to approach from the back. The going here was more dangerous, since it was primarily used by the Silvers that guarded the estates, but it was shadowed and out of view of curious servants or nobles looking out of windows.

I paused at the end of the alley, using the stone wall of the garden beside me to shield me from sight as I surveyed the area. Luckily, Lady Josyna's manor was roughly centered between the west and south gates, so the natural curve of the row of houses hid this area from sight of either.

I didn't see any Silvers, and waited another minute just to be sure. There was plenty of time until I was supposed to meet the Yellow and my best option would be to work my way into Josyna's garden and hide myself until then.

I slipped into the back passage and stayed close to the garden walls, edging around any large weeds. When I reached the crumbling wall of Josyna's manor I stood on my toes to peer over the top.

It was shorter than most of the back walls, and vines would make it even easier to climb, so I wasn't concerned with how or where I'd get over. I surveyed the garden itself for how best to cover my entry.

The area was filled with ornamental trees, flowering bushes, winding paths, marble benches, a pair of fountains, various statuary, and carefully designed flowerbeds. A couple of posts held oil lamps that lit the benches or statuary with a soft glow. While the manor itself looked weathered, the garden was thriving and lovingly maintained. There were plenty of places I could hide.

I also didn't see anyone in the garden, although plenty of windows faced it from the house. If I stepped under one of those lamps I'd be visible to anyone happening to glance out, so I'd have to plot a winding path to stay in the shadows.

I chose a spot sheltered from the view of the house by the upper branches of a tree and hoisted myself to crouch on top of the wall. It was about a foot thick, and my added weight caused some of the loose mortar to skitter down. I couldn't see what was in the shadows at the base of the wall inside the garden, so I lowered myself down as quietly as I could instead of jumping, my feet crunching lightly on gravel when I reached the bottom.

I crouched and froze in place, listening for any movement from the garden, the opening of doors, or alerts from the back passage I'd just left. Deep in the shadows my eyesight adjusted as well, and I could make out the trunk of the nearby tree and dark blobs that were bushes surrounding it. I even took the time to make sure those blobby shadows didn't move with a god's will before allowing myself to relax a little.

When I was comfortably sure I hadn't been seen, I crept forward to get out of the gravel. If I was going to hide in here, I needed to find someplace where I could keep eyes on the entrances to the house. I kept to the shadows and moved around the garden, counting three doors that led inside.

One was large and surrounded by windows, and was probably the main entrance from some kind of sitting room or hall. The one close to the right hand side of the house had a cleared area of stone in front of it but not a lot in the way of plantings, so probably a kitchen or work entrance. The one close to the left hand side of the building had no windows, but there were planters with flowers around the stone paving and it was taken care of, so either a side entrance or a servant entrance.

I found a spot in the garden where I'd be hidden, comfortable, and could keep both side doors in sight, since I didn't know which one my contact would be coming out of. Then I settled in to wait.

19 – Josyna's Manor

I watched a few of the lights go out in the windows, then some come on briefly and go out again. Things were definitely quieting down in there as people finished up their duties and got ready for bed. It was maybe two hours later when the more dreary-looking door opened and a man peeked out to peer around the garden.

I waited a moment longer, watching him step outside, walk to the edge of the stone paving, and pull out a bright yellow handkerchief to mop the sweat from his forehead. The yellow handkerchief was a recognition tool of the beggar spies, and while it was entirely possible for someone who wasn't affiliated with the guild to have one, it was unlikely I'd encounter one exactly where I was expecting it to be.

I crept from my hiding place and made my way to the door, avoiding the pools of lamplight until I had to step out in front of the door itself.

The Yellow jumped and cursed under his breath. He whispered, "Could have warned me!"

I didn't bother to reply, just raised my eyebrow with as much sarcasm as I could insinuate.

He grumbled and waved me through the door.

Inside was a small storage room. It looked like a staging room between the garden and the rest of the working part of the manor, and was filled with baskets of recently harvested fruits and vegetables, a few pairs of work boots and gloves, stacks of empty baskets, and other such things. The Yellow picked up a bundle and stuffed it into my arms.

"I grabbed something big so you could slip it on over your clothes."

I slung off the short cloak I wore and draped it over the Yellow's arm, then shook out a homespun tunic that was closer to burlap than cotton. It seemed to have permanent wrinkles, and there were stains that smelled like food grease. I wrinkled my nose, but pulled it over my head, sparing a brief thought for the fancy noble clothes I was probably ruining.

It was definitely made for a much larger man, with the sleeves hanging well past my wrists and the hem nearly hitting my knees. I felt like a child as I did my best to cinch up the neck ties. The Yellow held out a rope belt and I wrapped it loosely around my waist so it didn't interfere if I had to lift it all up to reach my knives or picks.

He wrinkled his nose at me and sighed, staring at the shiny black boots. "It'll have to do. Stay behind me, but don't cower. The other servants will try to make friends and help you if you look too miserable."

"How nice of them."

"Apparently Lady Josyna's kindness inspires them."

I grunted and followed the Yellow to the door. "What's the plan?"

"I can get you to the second level easily enough, and show you to the servant's stairs that lead to the third, but we aren't allowed any further. You're on your own at that point. I've found nothing of interest on the lower levels, so what you're looking for must be up there."

What I was looking for, huh? I wondered how much this spy knew. If he was placed in the estates he was high ranked, but Neffrey was a secretive bastard. Someone who dealt in the currency of information only told his people what they needed to know.

I, on the other hand, was here to push my luck. I needed to find out what the Lady's plan was, who she was in league with, and what she had at her disposal, as well as how much Deidre was involved. I'd be shocked if Deidre wasn't at least acting as a go-between to get people out of the city, but I was beginning to fear it went deeper than that. She wouldn't try to keep things from me unless she knew I wouldn't like it.

I bent my head and fell into step behind the Yellow as he picked up a hand lamp, opened the door, and slipped into the kitchen. It was empty this close to midnight. Most of the evening's work had been finished and the morning's work wouldn't start for a few more hours, so the fires were banked and the bread was rising next to the hearth.

He led me into the connecting corridors and then to a side staircase. At the top of the stairs a young woman came toward us and I followed the Yellow's lead as he moved to one side and slipped past her. She didn't even look our way. I glanced back and watched her, just to be sure, but she rounded a corner and was gone. The next staircase going up was deeper in the house, and when we reached the bottom I paused to listen.

The Yellow glanced up it nervously, then up and down the corridor we stood in. He pulled a more compact version of his hand lamp from a pocket and slipped it to me. "There you are. I assume you can find your way out."

I nodded silently, then grabbed his arm as he started to walk away. "Tell me how to get to the main staircase leading to the third level."

"It's rarely used. Only by the escort that stops by once in a while."

I glanced up the stairs again, listening for any sign of someone coming. "If I need to use it to get out, I want to know where I'll end up."

He frowned, but nodded. "It's the main staircase that covers all three floors. It's near the front of the house. If you follow this corridor through, you'll eventually end up there."

"And the way to the garden from there?"

"Through the hall behind the grand stairs, then through another sitting room. The opposite wing is set up similar to this."

I nodded, looking up the stairs. "You might want to tuck yourself into bed or something."

He huffed and wandered off, my short nobleman's cloak rolled up under his arm.

I fumbled with the miniature lamp for a moment. It was a model used by the guild quite often, as it had its own striker to light the oil wick, and a clever hood that only allowed a targeted glow to escape. It was perfect for sneaky work. I hit the striker a few times until the wick caught, then narrowed the light to barely shine in front of me.

I started up the stairs, taking my time and pausing to listen every few steps. Getting here had been the easy part, even if there were more people about. If anyone saw me now, it'd be clear I didn't belong. I also had no intel on the third level layout, so I'd have to poke my nose in everywhere until I found something.

When I reached the top I listened before peeking out to see the empty corridor. The oversized tunic was making noise as I brushed against the wall, so I paused to shuck it over my head. The common servants didn't belong up here anyway, so it would do me no good to remain disguised.

At the first room I came across, I listened for a moment at the door, then opened it as slowly as I could. It was empty. A bedroom that wasn't in use. I ditched the tunic and closed the door again, marking it in my memory. I'd need to remember what I found so I could get back out, and so I could draw a rough layout when I got home.

I made my way slowly down the hall, checking every room. Eventually I came across one where I heard gentle snoring on the other side of the door, and quietly passed it by. After that I listened extra long at each of them, and if I didn't hear anything I opened it even more carefully. Sure enough, a section of the rooms past this one seemed to be in use, although only one of them didn't have anyone currently sleeping in it.

That meant it was possible at least one person was still up and about somewhere.

I kept moving as logically as I could in order to keep track of it all, and soon came to larger empty suites. These were guest rooms most likely, which meant I was getting closer to the family suites.

At one point I heard the faint sound of footsteps and slipped inside an empty suite and closed the door. I flicked the lamp entirely closed and leaned against the door frame to listen as the person walked from the direction I'd been going to the areas I'd already searched. Maybe heading for bed if I was lucky.

I waited until I was sure they'd left, then waited a little longer to make sure they weren't coming back. I had all night, and better safe than caught. When I figured the person was out of range, I turned the lamp up just a bit and cracked the door open to look.

Empty.

I continued on my way.

A few rooms later I opened one that looked to be in use. It was a suite, and the door opened into a sitting room. It was dark, but there wasn't the smell of disuse the others had. I crept forward and made sure my light didn't shine into any connecting doors that may have been left open.

I needn't have worried. At each door I listened for noise and then opened it to find it lived in, but empty. Even the bedchamber was empty.

Was this a guest room for when Diedre visited? They'd said Lady Josyna was sickly, and nothing here indicated that. Besides, where would the lady of the house be in the middle of the night except her bedchamber?

It must be a guest room. I moved between the side rooms again, searching more thoroughly. The bedchamber seemed to be rarely used, which strengthened my theory that it was a guest room, however there was a study opposite it that was full of interesting things.

A shelf was stacked with books about nobility and history, a map hung across the wall depicting the city itself, and a small table with a few recorked bottles of wine and some glasses sat next to a comfy looking armchair. A large desk dominated the center of the room.

I went to the bookshelves first. I pulled each book out and methodically fanned through them before putting them back in place, making sure to glance behind the books and under the shelves. Nothing was hidden or loose. I stared at it in mild frustration before stepping to the enormous map and carefully lifting it away from the wall enough to make sure nothing was hidden there either.

I turned to the big desk next. A short stack of letters was under a smooth rock being used as a paperweight and I scanned through them briefly, just to get the gist of the contents. Correspondence between Josyna and some contacts within the city, mostly dealing with servants she was trying to bring on from other estates, some to nobles themselves discussing various things that really didn't interest me. I put them back in order and placed the rock on them.

I searched inside the desk and found a host of normal desk things: paper, ink wells, pens, wax, a stylized seal like the one on the letters under the paperweight. A few drawers contained detailed logbooks and financial records, which all seemed rather boring when I paged through them. It seemed the Lady Josyna had some business ventures outside the city. Things like inns, taverns, and various shops, all managed by a few other people. Nothing I didn't expect a noblewoman to be involved in, and quite possibly part of how they extracted people from the city. I even pulled out the drawers and checked for inexplicable dead spaces that would indicate a secret compartment or a false bottom. Nothing.

I leaned back in the chair, the leather creaking beneath me. This couldn't be everything. My gaze swept the room and I racked my brain for anything I might have overlooked. The partial decanters of wine caught my attention and I glanced down to the table they rested on, a small accent piece with a short wooden apron just beneath the tabletop surface.

I pushed myself out of the desk chair—which had been rather comfortable, truth be told—and dropped to one knee beside the table to look beneath it. I'd learned years ago never to blindly put my hands in places like that.

There was a bundle strapped to the underside. I grinned and worked the straps free, standing up with a heavy envelope full of letters. They were from outside the city, from a different contact than the rest of the correspondence. As I began to scan the contents I sat down heavily in the armchair next to the table.

They were reports on the location of Loring. According to these, Josyna had people checking on him, and they went back years.

I knew that after the incident five years ago he'd fled the city, and I'd assumed that was the end of it. His excuse for being here was gone, his sister was dead, and the baroness had sent out a notice that he was no longer welcome after she realized his part in things.

According to these letters, he'd gone home for a few years, then suddenly he was sending out people in search of some rare item. Probably trying to find out what had happened to the stone he'd wanted so badly.

Is that how he'd found it? Nissa had wondered if they were connected, and this made it seem like he was at least looking for it, although it never mentioned him finding anything.

I shuffled quickly through a bunch of them stating roughly the same things, until they started reporting that an elf had visited him at his home and not left. By the date on the letters, that was about a year ago.

Only a few letters followed, and they all said the same thing. Everything was quiet. The elf hadn't been seen leaving, so they suspected he was still there in the nobleman's home. The last one was dated about a month ago.

If this was a guest room, why was there a hidden sachet full of what essentially read like spy reports? Why was Lady Josyna keeping an eye on Loring? What was her connection to the nobleman? She'd come to Sangarie after he left, so she wouldn't know him unless she knew him from beyond Sangarie. Was she in league with him? An enemy? Could the correspondence have stopped because they reconnected here?

The letters weren't addressed to anyone and there was no seal on them, so maybe these didn't belong to the lady at all. Maybe someone else used this room, and used it often enough to secret away their reports because they knew it wouldn't be searched. I'm not sure which theory I liked less. The only person I could think of that would be here was Deidre, and she'd acted surprised to hear Loring was back in the picture. Could that surprise have been fake, or was it a reaction to knowing where he was after the reports trailed off?

I briefly thought about taking them with me, but then someone would know they'd been found out, so I put everything back how I'd found it and closed the door to the study.

Searching the rest of the rooms in this suite turned up nothing but a good deal of clothing, jewelry, and personal items. It was all feminine, and of high quality. As I poked through the jewelry I sighed at how little temptation I felt to take any of it. There was a time even a few years ago when I would have plucked a few pieces out to sell for myself or give to Deidre, but it just didn't have the same appeal. Maybe I was too comfortable in my position. Maybe it was just too easy for me to get such things now.

I looked around the dressing chamber one last time and my gaze landed on a woman's cloak, dark blue with a deep hood. It was simple, yet obviously richly made. I plucked it down and slung it over my shoulders, then gathered it around myself and held it closed at the front. The scent of moonflower clung to the cloth, reminding me of Deidre. Maybe she'd left it here the last time she called on the Lady.

It hung down far enough my boots were in shadow, and if I held it shut from the inside there was no way to tell from the bulge at my chest if I had breasts or it was just my arms. There were thieves that could change their entire demeanor to appear more female, but I'd never mastered that skill. Even so, this should be enough at a distance to suggest I was a woman if I pulled the hood down low, and maybe if someone saw me they'd assume I was the lady herself, or Deidre coming to call. At any rate, the hood would prevent them from identifying me.

I slipped through the sitting room and paused at the door to make sure nobody was in the corridor before leaving the room exactly how I'd found it, minus the fancy cloak. There were three more suites left to check, all of which turned out to be empty, and still I'd found no sign of the sickly noblewoman.

I stood in the last empty suite, grumbling to myself and running over the layout in my mind for something I might have missed. Senyr had told me there were half a dozen of the loyal servants that were allowed to see the lady, and I'd accounted for exactly that many people up here, once I added in the one I'd heard walking around earlier. But no lady of the house.

The only room that looked as if it might belong to her had been the one I believed to be a guest room. But if the lady was sickly, where were all the odds and ends sickrooms tended to accumulate? Bed pans, washing cloths, medical instruments, the pungent smell of teas and herbs, and the too-sweet smell of illness. None of that had been in evidence.

Unless the lady was not actually sickly. Maybe it was a cover, and her being here was part of whatever this thing was with Loring. Even so, where was she? That room had been empty, and while it wasn't totally unused, it didn't seem to be set up for daily living.

Deidre's name hadn't been on anything in that guest room, though the scent on the cloak I wore suggested she'd been there. The financials had mentioned escort services, but no names. Where was the lady of the house?

Maybe I'd missed something.

I decided to go back through the level and make sure I checked every door and every room, and that I accounted for all the servants. It was possible the lady was in one of the rooms I had assumed would be for the servants. Maybe for ease of caring for her?

I moved quickly, but silently, through the empty rooms, slowing down once I reached those that were inhabited. At each one I paused to listen and when I heard snoring I quietly cracked open the door and peered inside. Each time I thought my heart would beat out of my chest and that the servant inside could probably hear it, but I managed to shine a tiny pinpoint from my lamp around enough to verify the room did not contain a noblewoman, sick or otherwise. The rooms containing sleeping servants were well appointed, but definitely more for cherished employees rather than the owner of the house.

I approached the room that had been in use, but empty, the first time around. That meant my unseen wanderer was probably in there. I listened at the door, heard nothing, and was just about to crack it open when a foot scuffed on the floorboards inside, mere feet from the door.

My heart jumped into my chest and I backpedaled to the opposite side of the corridor, one hand clutching the tiny lantern and the other touching the wall behind me. I hadn't made a sound, but the blood pounded in my ears. I had two choices. Freeze and hope the person was just getting ready for bed and would settle down, or run now before they left their room and saw me.

If this was the missing Lady Josyna herself, I should wait it out. It's what I came for. If this was truly just the sixth servant, they could be awake on purpose this late as a personal guard or caretaker, and that meant they could leave that room at any moment.

I clenched my teeth and tried to calm my heart as I crept closer to the door, trying to listen for sounds from within. Hopefully I'd have a moment of warning before they tried to leave, so I could make my escape.

I pulled the hood up while I listened, tensed and ready to bolt. Every sense I had was focused. I could hear faint footsteps inside the room, then they abruptly began to move toward the door with purpose.

Shit. I held the hood with one hand and the lantern with the other as I fled down the corridor as silently as possible. If I was quiet, they might not notice me moving in the dark when they opened the door. A quarter of the building still separated me from the service stairs, but at least it wasn't a straight shot. I'd have corners to hide my retreat.

I took one turn and neared another corner, but skidded to a stop before I reached it as the dim light of a lamp shone across the wall. Someone was walking this way.

Fuck. Fuck. Fuck.

My heart was pounding in my chest and it was all I could do to keep my breathing from becoming audible as I panicked. I glanced back at the corridor I'd come from. Not the best option, but maybe the first servant had gone the other way.

I started back, then froze as the faint brightening of the wall warned me a light source was nearing from that direction as well. I was trapped between the two. The only doors in this stretch of corridor were the last two occupied rooms, so ducking into one would be risky, and might pin me down, but it was better than trying to bull my way past either of these people.

I darted to the closest room and did my best to open the door quietly. My hands were shaking with adrenaline and I was trying to listen at the door and down both ends of the corridor all at once. Just as a hand extended with a lamp from the direction I wanted to be going, I opened the door and ducked inside, then pushed it nearly shut, just short of the latch clicking. With a little more care, I eased it the rest of the way closed so that no noise gave me away and crouched behind it trying to calm myself.

Snoring rose and fell behind me in the room, uninterrupted. It made my back itch to know someone slept there and I was in full sight of them if they woke up and turned on a lamp. At the base of the door, the light from the approaching lampholder slowly brightened and the shadows slid from one side to the other, then started to dim again. They had passed by.

At that moment the person in bed behind me gave a stuttering snort and I nearly jumped out of my skin. I caught myself against the door and it shifted in the frame, knocking sharply before I stilled it with my hand.

The light from the corridor stopped moving.

The bed creaked behind me.

The single most common downfall of a thief, and the thing that ultimately leads to their end, is making the wrong snap decision in times of stress. That's why Senyr had mercilessly drilled it into my head to always keep thinking when I was working. Always be paying attention to every possible outcome. Never allow panic to make my choices for me.

There was no light in this room. That meant the person in the bed couldn't see me. If I stayed quiet, they might go back to sleep, and the person in the hall would go away when they didn't see anyone outside.

I readied myself to run, but didn't move.

The bed creaked again, and the blankets slithered. Were they tossing and turning as they tried to go back to sleep, or were they rousing themselves? The light still hadn't moved in the corridor, and now I heard a muffled voice from below the door as the two servants encountered each other outside.

They spoke in whispers, but I was listening with desperation and managed to catch about half of it. One had woken unsettled earlier and gone down to get something to drink. Something about a maid asking if there had been a new rescue. Then some lower whispers that I couldn't make out.

They were suspicious. That wasn't good. That meant they wouldn't be going back to bed any time soon.

The bed creaked behind me and I heard the servant's feet hit the floor, then a scraping noise as something was pulled across a side table. If this one saw me and shouted for help, the ones outside would be here in moments. My only chance was to surprise them and get past them quickly on the way out.

I twisted the doorknob and shifted my weight, said a quick prayer to the Six and a quick curse to Lady Josyna and her uncharacteristically attentive servants, and made my choice.

Speed would be more important now than stealth.

I held my hood so my face would remain covered, then shoved open the door and darted down the corridor. The cloak billowed out behind me, blocking most of the light from their lamps. There was about three seconds of delay before all three started shouting and moved to follow. I skidded around corners, careened off walls, and struggled the entire time to keep my face hidden and use my tiny lamp at the same time.

I barreled down the flight of stairs to the second level, and when I reached the bottom I chanced a look back to see two men just starting down, one of which was fully dressed and carried a loaded crossbow.

What the fuck? Had he been patrolling the house with that?

I ran, retracing the path I'd taken earlier with the Yellow. Hopefully the beggar was safely tucked in bed like I'd suggested so he wasn't caught up in any of this. Although I was a little irritated he hadn't mentioned the servant with the crossbow that walked the halls in the middle of the night.

It was a straight run across the length of this wing to the top of the stairs leading to the ground floor, and I took it at a full sprint. Even so, my pursuers shouted when they came into view and I heard the zing as the crossbow released. I ducked my head and it flew high, ricocheting off the wall with a spray of plaster. Then I was on the stairs.

I jumped the last five or so, landing hard and touching the floor to steady myself as I stumbled into a run again, breathing heavily. More winding corridors, then the kitchen was ahead. I ducked inside and slowed long enough to slam the door shut behind me. I darted around the big tables in the center of the room, shoving a startled baker out of my way, then through the next door into the small storage area just as the kitchen door opened.

I slammed into the door leading outside and realized it was locked. *Damn it!*

I spun and shoved the door shut between me and the kitchen, and it closed just as the crossbow went off again. The bolt embedded itself in the door and the tip splintered out the back of a joint between two planks.

I fumbled with the exterior door lock, then saw the sliding bolt and shoved that open as well. This fucking noblewoman was more paranoid than any criminal.

I slipped out and slammed the door shut behind me as I took off for the back of the garden. No time to duck and weave between the pools of light now. The lighted areas were actually more helpful, as I didn't have to worry about tripping over plants in the dark.

The door to the manor opened and two men shouted at me to stop.

I was almost there. I dodged around bushes and gauged my jump to vault over the wall. If I used that tree trunk ahead as a launching pad, I could do it in one smooth motion and not worry about trying to scramble my way over.

I dug in for a final burst of speed, then leaped and planted my foot on the trunk, twisted, and pushed off. My hands gripped the top of the wall and I lifted my feet to vault over, the cloak rising above me like dark wings.

I didn't hear the crossbow release, but I felt the impact as it pierced my side and threw me off balance. I gasped and one hand slipped from the stone. My entire body clenched and I forgot I still needed to land.

20 – Wounded

Momentum carried me over and I fell beyond the thin verge of grass at the base of the wall and slammed onto my back in the dirt, knocking the breath from my lungs in a violent huff and sending stabbing pain into my side. Luckily I didn't have the breath to scream. I clenched my teeth and writhed in pain.

I struggled to catch my breath as I rolled to my knees and tried to listen for signs of pursuit. I couldn't stop. Not now. I was in the back passage, and from here I could search out a secret entrance through the wall, then disappear into the city.

I reached for the garden wall beside me and used it to pull myself to my feet, then stumbled a few steps with a groan, my hand going to the bolt still sticking out of my side under the cloak. When I tried to straighten up, it felt like the embedded metal tip was slicing at my insides.

This wasn't good. It had sunk in deep. If I pulled it out, I'd probably bleed to death before I got to anyone that could help me. If I left it in, it would keep cutting into me and the damage would get worse.

I chuckled breathlessly and grabbed for the wall again as I wavered on my feet. I'd be damned if I was going to die in the estates. I pulled the cloak off and rolled it up, then carefully tucked it around the bolt and put as much pressure on it as I could with one arm.

Still no sign of pursuit from the manor. Either they were trying to mobilize, or they were happy with just chasing me off. I didn't want to wait around and see which it was so I shuffled across the back passage and toward the nearest small building along the inner wall with a secret tunnel. Normally I'd be checking the wall itself for patrolling Silvers, or looking around for anyone watching, but it was all I could do to walk in a straight line and not drop to my knees.

I reached the little building and rattled the door, cursing and resting my forehead against it when I realized it was locked. I pulled out a couple of picks and leaned against the door as I worked on it. My hands were shaking and slick with blood. I dropped one pick and didn't even try to bend over to get it, just pulled out another and kept working. Eventually the lock clicked and I dropped the picks into my pocket and went inside.

It was pitch black in the building, and I'd lost my tiny lamp while I was fleeing the manor. Usually there was something inside that could be used as a light source. I felt around the door frame, looking for a shelf or cabinet of some kind, and my hand eventually bumped into what felt like a bookcase. On a shelf at about head height was a regular oil lamp and a striker.

I fumbled with it a moment, trying to lean against the wall for support to use both hands. When it flared up and I could see, I moved around the stored goods to find the trapdoor under a rug in the back.

After pulling the rug aside and lifting the door, I had to stop and breathe for a few moments to let the pain recede again, then I smothered the lamp and pushed it aside. There was no way I could use a ladder and carry it with me. The dark was absolute as I made my way down the ladder, through the short tunnel, and back up the other side. This side was closed as well, but there should be a Yellow stationed there. I pounded on the door, nearly losing my hold on the ladder and having to squeeze my eyes shut and count my breath.

When it opened, I looked up into the face of a man I didn't recognize.

He squinted at me and scowled. "Aren't you supposed to be going out through the gate?"

"Give me your hand." I held mine up, balancing on the ladder and keeping my other arm pressed against the cloak at my side.

The Yellow clasped my forearm and tugged, and I groaned as I pushed through the pain to get the rest of the way up the ladder. Maybe the gate would have been easier. I dropped to sit on a nearby crate and hunched over to get my breathing back to normal.

He stared at my middle and I looked down as well, alarmed by how much blood had soaked through the cloak. I needed to find help. Now.

"Should I fetch a healer?"

I wanted to say yes. Mainly because I didn't want to even stand again, let alone walk. But the guild didn't have any healers that could fix this. I needed Nissa, and I could only hope she had the magic to mend me.

Where had she been staying? Ruena knew, but by now she was probably settled into my apartment with Deidre, waiting for me to get back.

I absolutely couldn't let Deidre see me like this. Lady Josyna was sure to tell her about the break-in, and it wouldn't be hard to piece together who'd done it if I showed up with a crossbow bolt in my side. Maybe I could get someone to bring Rue here.

The door to the building opened and a cloaked figure slipped inside. The Yellow stepped away from me, and I wasn't sure if he was preparing to run or fight. Maybe both.

The figure swept his hood down and I scowled as I recognized Rue's Red. "What are you doing here?"

His gaze dropped to my side and his eyes narrowed. "I was watching from the wall and saw you drop into the back passage. You looked injured, so I thought I would see if you needed any help."

"Why were you watching me? Did Rue tell you where I'd be?"

He nodded. "She was worried."

I grunted, then cringed at the pain it caused.

He was still staring at my side, which was covered by the wadded up, blood-stained cloak. "How bad is it?"

That was a question I didn't want to answer. "Do you know where my friend Nissa is staying?"

He nodded.

I couldn't believe I was asking this, but... "Can you help me get there?"

He merely nodded again and moved toward me.

Before I took his offered arm I looked over at the Yellow. "Not a word to anyone about this except for Neffrey. That's an order from the Hand of the Master."

The Yellow nodded and stepped farther away, clearly not wanting anything to do with whatever was happening.

The Red lifted my arm on the side opposite the wound and helped me stand. I did my best not to make any noise, but a small groan of pain still escaped me and I tightened my arm across his shoulders until I could support my weight. My other arm remained locked against the balled up cloak.

Even gravely injured, hanging on the shoulder of an assassin, I made very little noise moving through the city streets, but every step hurt. The Red told me Nissa was renting a room in Copperton at one of the more affordable inns, and I was glad I wouldn't have to walk all the way to Old Town. Copperton was about half the distance.

By the time we'd crossed a district and a half, I was staggering and breathing fast and shallow. My heart rate was up, and I was starting to feel very cold. I hung my head, relying on the Red to watch where we were going. I had to concentrate on keeping my feet moving.

When he suddenly stopped I wasn't ready for it and my wobbling legs couldn't compensate for the change in momentum. I sagged to my knees, dragging him down until he flung an arm in front of my chest to hold me up.

"This is the staircase. Can you make it?"

I raised my head and looked at the stairs in front of me, leading up the back of the building to a second level balcony that ran the entire length. At least I wouldn't have to go through a crowded common room.

I was so tired. I knew how bad that was, and how little time I had left, so I clenched my jaw and nodded. "Let's go."

The Red helped me start up, and within three steps I had to let go of the cloak at my side and clutch the railing. The cloak fell away, hitting the steps with a wet thwap. I looked down at the blood covering the borrowed fancy clothes, soaking my entire side and down my pants almost to the knee.

My vision narrowed and I swayed.

The Red lifted my shoulder. "Keep moving."

I didn't answer, but I did start climbing again. Between the support of the Red and my hand gripping the railing like a lifeline, leaving a trail of blood on the smooth wood, we made it to the balcony and he pulled me to the second door on the left.

The Red pounded on it a couple of times, then steadied me with his free arm. He was supporting nearly all my weight at this point, and I think I would have been more embarrassed or upset if I could think clearly.

It seemed like a long time before Nissa answered the door. Her voice was loud on the dark balcony. "What did he do now?"

The Red answered for me, "It happened on a job. He said you could help."

She sighed and stepped aside, holding the door. "Bring him in. Put him on the bed."

I tried to walk inside. I really did.

Nissa caught my other side when I started to fall and I cried out in pain. They dragged me into the small room and onto the single bed against one wall.

Laying down hurt almost as much as standing upright, and I rolled to curl onto my uninjured side. I was panting. Sweating. My whole body was tingling.

The Red's voice sounded far away. "Can you heal him?"

"I do not have any potions, but I can stop the bleeding and knit the flesh back together. We will have to remove the bolt first."

The bed shook as the Red moved to kneel over me, a knee on either side of my legs, and gripped the bolt in one hand and my shoulder with the other. Nissa walked up and lifted my chin, then put a strip of leather in my mouth. It tasted like grass.

"Bite."

I did. And closed my eyes.

The Red was quick. A horrible rending tug pulled at my side and it felt like he'd tried to pull out half my insides with it. I screamed around the leather in my mouth and tried to move, but his knees held my legs still and his weight on my shoulder kept me from trying to rise.

I shuddered and the room darkened at the edges. The sounds of Nissa and the Red talking became mostly just noise. It didn't even hurt anymore. The only thing I felt was a tingle all over my body.

Probably magic, right?

I hoped it was magic.

***

I opened my eyes and stared at the ceiling of a small room. Orange sunlight streamed in from the window. Was it sunrise, or sunset? My hand moved to my side and touched smooth skin.

I frowned and glanced down at myself. My shirt and tunic were gone, and my skin was stained with dried blood, but there was no sign of a

168

wound. I pressed a little harder, then took a deep breath to fill my chest. It ached, but there was no stabbing pain. There was, however, a strong tingling sensation, and I wondered if it was the stone. Where had she hidden it?

Nissa's voice broke the silence. "You are whole again." She stood up from her chair and crossed to the bed, standing over me. I was struck again by the short cropped white hair against her greenish tinged skin, and the thin scar that outlined her jaw on the right side. What had she been doing for the last five years to look so rough?

I pushed myself up and swung my legs over the side, but even that change in position made me dizzy. "I still feel off."

"I could not return the blood you lost, so you are weakened. Food should help, and water."

I nodded and frowned at the stiffness of the dried blood on my pants.

She continued, "Red meat or fish would be best, and try not to drink alcohol until you are feeling back to normal."

"Where's the Red?"

"Who?"

"The Red that brought me here."

"He left once you had been healed. He said he was going to talk to Ruena."

I winced. I hoped he hadn't let Deidre in on what had happened. Rue should know better, but...

I set my elbows on my knees and my head in my hands. I was still so tired, and the tingle of magic was a constant irritation. "What time is it?"

"Just after sunrise."

"Do me a favor. Don't mention any of this to Deidre."

"If that is what you wish."

I looked up at her. "I found something tonight that worries me."

One of her eyebrows shot up. "Was it worth almost bleeding to death on my doorstep?"

"Maybe. A noblewoman in the estates has been keeping tabs on Loring. I broke into her manor last night and found a bunch of letters describing what he'd been doing since he left the city. He's been looking for something, and I think it's the stone."

She chewed at her bottom lip, then glanced at the window. "What else did they say?"

169

"The letters mentioned an elf that had entered his home, but not left. Would you know anything about that?"

Herr brow furrowed and she thought a moment, then sighed. "There are some rumors, but none of us wanted to give them credit."

"What rumors?"

"There is an elf known to humans as Ailred. He is something of an embarrassment to the elders, and they sent him away because he has an obsession with magic that is… unhealthy. Rumors say that he allied himself with humans in his search for relics, but we did not look into them. If I had known the human was Loring, I would have mentioned it."

"Even so, it seems like a power-hungry elf would be important enough to keep a handle on. Especially when you're holding an ancient magical artifact and can't find the other one just like it."

Her eyes narrowed and I glimpsed the small fangs as her lip curled. "It is humans who crave power. Ailred was said to be searching for great magics."

I snorted. "What do you think magic is?"

She grumbled and turned away.

I rubbed at my side where the bolt had been embedded, trying to see if any twinges remained. "Look. I'm sorry. The Six know I've bungled this in more ways than a beggar attracts fleas, but if we're going to figure out anything we need to work together. Maybe if you came with me to see Rigel again we could—"

"I do not wish to see your leader."

"Neither do I most of the time, but he's better at dealing with these things than we are."

She turned away, but I saw how her face screwed up with even more contempt than when she'd been talking about petty human ambitions and the tips of her ears darkened.

Now that I thought about it, she seemed to have nothing *but* contempt for the guildmaster. Even five years ago she'd avoided him when we returned after the labyrinth. What little interaction I'd witnessed between them had been filled with tension on both their parts. If I didn't know better I'd think she had something against him personally.

"Nissa."

"We can deal with this on our own."

"Did you know Rigel before he came to Sangarie?"

She shot me a piercing look, her mouth tight and the scar on her face appearing pale against the darkening of her greenish skin. "Who or what I know does not concern—"

"Then what's the problem? Why the eye daggers? Don't tell me a human can get under your skin so easily."

"You do not know him. None of you do. This charade he puts on, how he acts so important and wise, it is all to soothe his damaged ego."

"How is Rigel connected to the elves?" I tried not to look too eager, but this mystery was one that had burned through my brain for years. If Nissa had the pieces...

She stared at me a moment longer, then sighed. "That story is not mine to tell."

"Why not? In a few days we're going to stand on top of a wall and usher in the shadows of a god, so why not ease my curiosity a bit?"

"If I tell you, will you be more cooperative?"

I thought I *had* been being cooperative. Mostly. I wasn't telling her to fuck off like I really wanted to. "Absolutely. Focused and ready to meet destiny."

She narrowed her eyes, but sat slowly on the wooden chair by the small table. She bit her lip and looked at the floor, thought a moment, then began to speak in a tone that reminded me of a White Hand reciting old stories.

"Rigelian Orionis was sent to the elves as a small child. His grandfather had been the product of violence between elves and humans, and left decades earlier to pursue a calling he felt for that darker half of his parentage. Most halfbloods never return, and any offspring are lost to the churning of human civilization. Somehow Rigel's human mother knew where to send him."

Shit... It was like windows were opening in my head. Tiny details were linking themselves together and questions I'd long ago forgotten suddenly now had answers. Rigel was an elfblood. No wonder he'd tried to protect me. And Rue. Is this why he was so stuck on me as a successor?

"He grew to manhood among the elves, quicker than any of us mature. He studied alongside us, trained for war alongside us, and dreamed of the future. But what he dreamed was not within his reach.

"He saw what he wanted in a young elfish woman. A daughter of one of the elders. They spent many nights in long conversation and contemplation."

I snorted and covered it with a cough when Nissa broke out of the near trance she'd adapted to tell her story. She scowled at me and continued.

"Rigel asked the elder for his blessing, but for a highborn elf to marry one so removed from our blood was unthinkable. The answer was no. Rigel studied harder, fought fiercer, and asked again. Still the answer was no. For many years this went on, until one day the pair were caught in each other's embrace and the elder petitioned for his removal.

"He was offered a gift to ease his passage into human lands, and he accepted it and went away."

"The coins. The dragonoak chests of coins." I rubbed a hand up through my hair. "That was how he got them. And why you looked at them so strangely when we found them in the treasury."

She grimaced. "I recognized them, yes."

"So you did know him." A thought popped into my head and I asked without really thinking about it. "You weren't the elfish woman, were you?"

Her lip curled into a snarl and she all but growled at me. "No." She dropped her gaze to the floor and her face took on a pained look. "But I know her. She is a friend."

"So he loved her. Did she love him back?"

"She did, at one time. After they were discovered, he asked her to run away with him. She refused and there was an argument. She lied and told him that she hated him and it was all a game she had played with the poor elfblood boy. He left heartbroken. She has regretted it every day since."

I didn't know what to say. Never in all my bored fantasies had I dreamed up a story like that for Rigel. It was like a tragic bard's tale. I'd expected something daring and brash, befitting a king of thieves.

Nissa twisted her fingers where they rested on her lap. "I did not know he was in this city when I first came here. I never expected to meet him again."

"Did he ask you about her?"

"No." She stood and turned her back to me, crossing her arms over her chest. "It is the past. There can be nothing gained by dragging it back into the light, and we have more important things to be doing. I suggest you not speak of this with Rigel."

"Yeah. No kidding."

She just stood there quietly, staring at the other side of the room. As much as she'd talked about not dragging up the past again, it was obviously weighing heavily on her. I didn't know what kind of relationship she'd had with Rigel back then, but her story explained the animosity I'd witnessed in their interactions.

The silence stretched on for a few more moments, then she turned and her face was once again dismissive and arrogant. "If Ailred and Loring are both outside the city we need to be on our guard. Ailred has access to magic of his own, as evidenced by his control of these assassins you have encountered. We will need to be vigilant and discover what their plans are."

I raised an eyebrow. "What I don't understand is why you involved the baroness. Wouldn't it be easier investigating Loring without the guards lurking around too?"

"Most likely. But it will also be much harder for Loring to enter the city and move about on his own now. I am hoping this hunt for him will keep him outside the city for the time being and take some pressure off you."

"It could keep him at bay until the Night of Shadows at least. But now I have to somehow work with the Warden to track down a thief that isn't here. Maybe I should tell her we know he's outside the city and let them send out guards to scour the countryside."

Nissa shook her head. "If they found him, they would bring him here. You must keep them looking inside the city."

"You want me to play the Warden."

"For as long as you can. Keep her focusing on Loring and away from the stone."

"Any ideas how to do that?"

Her brows creased, but she didn't look at me. "I will meditate on it. For now, try to stay alive."

I couldn't keep the contempt out of my voice. "So I can destroy Sangarie."

"If that is what needs to happen, yes."

"Do you realize how infuriating you are?"

She finally looked down at me and scowled, but as she held my gaze the irritation faded. "I am doing the best I can with the information available to me."

I snorted and looked down at the dried blood. I supposed I was being a little unfair. It wasn't like I'd been entirely forthcoming with her, or done anything to try to figure out what was going on. Pieces of the puzzle were just falling into my lap, whether I wanted them or not. "Thank you, for saving my life again."

"Your clothes are on the table. I am going out."

She snatched up her satchel, slung on her heavy cloak and raised the hood, and left without another word or even a look in my direction.

I found a pile of my own clothes on the table. Someone must have fetched them from the Yellows. At least I didn't have to go home looking like I'd bathed in blood. It'd be hard to explain that to Deidre.

There was a basin of water and some rags on the table as well, and I cleaned myself up and changed as quickly as I could, eager to be away from the ever-present tingle of the stone. As curious as I was about where she'd hidden it, I didn't want to get too close.

21 – Home

I was guessing Deidre would be worried sick without any explanation about why I hadn't come home, so I planned to go there first, but when I walked onto the balcony I saw Ruena waiting for me.

She'd been sitting on the bottom step, holding a small, paper-wrapped bundle and a waterskin. When she heard the door and looked up to see me, she hopped to her feet and watched intently as I trudged down the stairs. Nissa had been right about feeling weak. My legs wobbled and I did my best not to look like I was swaying. I glanced once at the railing, surprised to see it had been scrubbed clean of the blood I remembered leaving on it.

Ruena called up, her voice shaky. "Are you okay?"

"Course I am. What's that?"

As soon as I stepped onto street level she darted forward and flung her arms around me in a tight hug.

I flinched, expecting some residual pain, but there was none. The scent of grilled beef and fried fish rose up around us, making my stomach growl, and I patted her shoulder.

She continued to hold me with her head tucked under my throat. I waited a few more seconds for her to pull away herself, but that didn't seem to be happening. I shifted my weight and cleared my throat. "Okay that's enough."

She sniffed and wiped the back of her hand over her cheek as she looked up at me. "What happened? Elias said you almost bled to death."

"He's exaggerating."

"I doubt it. Who shot you?"

I looked around the alley, making sure nobody was within hearing distance, and lowered my voice. "Just some servant-looking guard of Lady Josyna's. It was a lucky shot."

She still looked doubtful, and worried.

I sat on the bottom of the steps and pointed at the bundle she held. "Is that for me? Because it smells really good."

"Yeah. He said you should replenish your strength. And that fluids would help too." She held out the waterskin first.

I took it and raised an eyebrow. "You didn't fill it from the river, did you?"

"I should have," she grumbled.

I opened it and sniffed, smelling cider. It wasn't ale, but it was better than water, and I was suddenly very thirsty. I tipped it back and drank deeply as she unwrapped the bundle and revealed a hollowed out loaf of bread filled with meat.

I handed back the waterskin and took the loaf, using my fingers to eat. The beef was cubed and charred on the outside, but pink in the middle. The fish was coated in a light golden breading and fried crispy. Both tasted amazing.

She sat next to me, extending her legs and rocking her feet back and forth as she held the waterskin. "Just so you know, Elias didn't give anything away to Deidre. We talked after we left."

I sighed in relief and mumbled around a mouthful of food. "What did you tell her about where I was?"

"He said he ran into you, and you were going to be out late. He was supposed to make himself useful and pass on the message."

I chuckled and popped another chunk of beef into my mouth. "Sounds like me."

"I thought so too." She scowled at me. "Then he brought me home and told me what happened. Are you sure you're okay?"

"I'm fine. Just a little tired."

She nodded, ducking her head and avoiding my gaze. "Well I'm going home again to get some sleep. Elias said he'd wait for me there."

I'd been about to swallow, and the insinuation that the Red would be joining Rue in her bed made me choke on it. I coughed and thumped my chest, then grabbed the offered waterskin and drank deeply to get it all to go down. My eyes were watering and I glared at her, but didn't say anything.

It wasn't my place.

I was making the effort. And the Six could go fuck themselves. I could be a good... mentor.

She sighed and twisted her hands together. "Be careful, okay?"

I could tell she was worried. Scared maybe. It cooled my own anxiety about her and the Red enough that I could at least respond gracefully. "Tell him thank you. For his help."

I stood and wrapped up the last of the loaf, taking the waterskin with me as well. A quick glance showed Rue smiling up at me and I rolled my eyes and walked away. I hoped she didn't think she could just do whatever she wanted with him now and I wouldn't complain. I still needed to look out for her.

I quickly found an entrance to the underground and went below. The morning sun was too bright, and the people were too cheerful for my rattled brain. As much as I'd brushed it off with Rue, that crossbow should have ended me. If Nissa hadn't been here, it would have. Now I'd have to face Deidre and pretend like nothing interesting had happened.

I arrived at my apartment and found the door unlocked, so I had a moment to put on a grumpy face that had nothing to do with almost dying–I hoped–then I opened it.

Deidre was in bed, but the lamp was on, and when the door opened she sat up. "Gray?"

"Expecting someone else?" I kicked my boots off and crossed to the table, sitting down to open my food again. I might as well finish it, or I'd have to throw it away. And it was really good.

Deidre rose and pulled a blanket with her to join me.

I pushed out a chair so she didn't have to let go of the blanket she'd wrapped around herself.

"Thanks. Is everything okay? It has to be morning by now."

"It is morning. And everything is fine."

"Did you have some trouble last night?" She poked an arm out of the blanket and stole a chunk of beef from my bread loaf.

I moved it closer so she wouldn't have to stretch so far. "Just a bunch of things that piled up. More irritating than anything." I didn't like lying to her, and she could read me better than anyone, so I kept it simple and mostly truthful. Let Senyr feed her the story and I'd just play along.

"You look like death."

My face flush at her comment and I forced myself not to duck away. That would only make me look more guilty. "I'm tired. Haven't been sleeping well because of the whole Night of Shadows and destroying the city thing. Nissa doesn't help matters when she keeps popping up and reminding me of it."

"You stopped to see her then?"

"Yeah. We talked a bit."

She stole another bite. "Anything new that could help?"

"No." I couldn't tell her anything about Loring and the letters or she'd know I was snooping in the estates. And I most certainly couldn't tell her all the history I'd learned about Rigel. If any of that got out he'd know exactly where it came from, since Nissa was the only one that knew it.

"Are you sure you're okay? Something seems wrong."

I took a deep breath and smiled, although I was careful to keep it small. "Tired. Do you want to go to bed?"

"I can sleep for a few more hours." She popped the last piece of beef in her mouth and rose, heading back to the bed.

I left the empty loaf on the table and quickly changed into something more comfortable, hoping she didn't notice the dizziness or the wobble. I left my pants on these days unless we were having sex, mainly because Rue had gotten into the habit of barging in unannounced, but my chest was bare. See... no gaping hole here. Everything is fine. It wasn't me your client's servants were shooting at.

I hoped I'd gotten all the dried blood off.

I slid under the blanket and she wrapped her arms around me and laid her head on my shoulder. I expected her to talk more, ask questions about what had been so irritating, but I underestimated how tired I still was. The last thing I remembered was her settling against my side, and thinking it felt much better than being shot.

***

She was gone when I woke up. That was probably for the best, because I wouldn't need to explain anything or worry about whether my face was giving me away.

I went to find Senyr, and after an hour of asking around I tracked him to the private baths. Most of the hot springs in the underground were open to anyone, but there was one large pool sectioned off that only the

178

highest ranking masters were allowed to use. It was a little ways from the rest of the baths, and down a long sloping corridor. A Yellow was always stationed at the beginning of the corridor to keep people from going in who had no business being there.

He didn't even look twice at me as I passed him. I didn't use the private baths often, but it was his job to recognize those who had access. The length of the corridor was hung at intervals with simple wool rugs and curtains to catch the sound before it reached the top, making it an ideal place to discuss private business.

When I reached the bottom it opened into a large cavern with a low ceiling and a steaming pool in the middle. Benches were placed around the outside, and Senyr and Neffrey were both soaking in the pool. They turned to look at me as I entered.

I stopped and raised an eyebrow. "Glad to see you're lounging around while I'm out risking life and limb."

Senyr sighed and eased back against the side of the pool again. "Glad to see the elf was able to patch you up."

"Did none of your intel mention guards? Not many household servants carry crossbows around in the middle of the night."

"No. It didn't. We've hardly discovered anything from inside the manor since our plant isn't able to get up to the third floor without compromising himself."

Neffrey moved closer, creating ripples in the pool as he peered up at me. "What did you find out?"

I gave them the most detailed report I could, about the layout, the record books, the letters, the lack of an actual noblewoman, and what I could remember about the glimpses I'd had of the servants. I left out any speculations, because they liked to jump to their own conclusions.

It was a little uncomfortable, standing there and droning on while two naked old men floated in the pool. Not to mention the heat was making me a little dizzy. Sleep had done wonders for my general weakness, but it apparently was still affecting me.

When I finished, I waited and listened as the two discussed the information. They bounced ideas off each other and argued in lowered voices, but by the end of it they came to roughly the same conclusion I had.

The Lady Josyna was not there.

Whether she was just away from home or the illness was all a lie was still something they weren't sure about. They were also unclear what purpose this farce served. Why move into Sangarie or create such a persona only to gather intelligence from outside the city? Something was still missing.

Then there was the question of why Deidre visited the manor. Senyr reminded Neffrey that Deidre had always worked to remove the servants of the nobility from abusive or dangerous situations, using her high status as an escort and her favor with the nobility. It could be she'd found a kindred soul in those pursuits and was being used as a pawn.

Neffrey reminded Senyr the coin didn't add up, and where the coin was sour, the criminal was up to no good. I growled a little at his accusatory tone and stepped forward, but Senyr threw a hand back and warned me off as they continued talking.

Finally Neffrey pinned me with a narrow stare. "Do you think you can get back inside?"

Senyr sliced his hand through the air above the water. "No. He's not going back in."

I raised an eyebrow, but kept my mouth shut. He'd actually sounded worried about me.

Neffrey turned his glare to the old thief. "We need more information."

"They'll be on high alert now. We need to let things settle down and see what they do in response."

Neffrey grumbled, but didn't argue.

Senyr looked up at me. "You're going to be busy for the next week anyway. The Warden has been ordered to work with you to search the city for Loring and his associates. We've been informed they have a lead."

Apparently not so worried about me that he wouldn't shove me in front of the Warden or the oncoming assassins. I narrowed my gaze and stared back at him. "Can I go teach Lord Barty to be a thief instead?"

Senyr ignored the sarcasm. "Go and meet with her now, since you slept so late. You should be able to find her at her office."

"Lucky me."

Senyr glared up at me, although the effect was lessened since he was naked and pruning in the water. "Cooperate with her. This is important."

I blew out in a huff. "Fine. At least make a good toast for me when I'm dead." I turned around and stomped back up the sloped corridor.

Childish? Maybe. But I was pretty sure I was at the top of some kind of wish list for the Warden, and it wasn't going to be easy working with her and *not* implicating myself in a great many things. I'd be lucky to make it to the Night of Shadows alive at this rate.

22 – Warden's Call

I wound my way through the tunnels, up a rickety stairway, and stalked out of the little storage room that hid the underground entrance onto the street. Then I headed south toward Tinkers Row. I was more familiar with Market Street, which led straight to the western gate of the estates, but Tinkers Row would cut through the southern districts until it met up with Old Keep Road and then I could take that north to Varinston.

The Warden's jail was in Varinston, which was just south of the estates. There were also a lot of official buildings and places for outsiders to do business in that district. There was a massive healer presence so the area was full of White Hands, and a number of moneylenders which made it lousy with Green Hands as well. And of course the main headquarters for the city guard was there.

I felt sorry for the enforcer in Varinston, having to manage thievery in a district full of Greens and guards. It was another place that technically I had oversight in as a Hand of the Master, but avoided like the plague. In my defense, Senyr avoided it as well. Garion was the only master thief that did anything there, and that's only because he'd cultivated a good relationship with the guard over the years.

As I strode onto Tinkers Row, I caught someone following me out of the corner of my eye. I acted like I hadn't seen anything and continued to walk with purpose, weaving in and out of workers when I needed to. Tinkers Row was never as busy as Market Street, but it was getting close to the time of day when people would be thinking about going home to their families, or trying to get that last bit of work done. I nodded at people and glanced at the buildings as I went, using it as a reason to check over my shoulder.

The figure was definitely following, and as we got closer to Old Keep Road they started closing the distance.

The encounter during the festival came to mind, along with the strangely intense way the man had repeated my name, like he was compelled or hyper focused. Could this be another attacker? Loring was an obsessed man, and I'd be shocked if he gave up trying to kill me after one failed attempt. It might be best to stop and face it here in the open.

If the figure kept advancing, it'd catch up to me anyway. I picked a spot at an intersection ahead so if I needed to run I had more options, trying to calm myself in preparation to act as I approached it. When I reached the spot, I stopped and spun around, letting my momentum naturally swing my arm behind me where my knives were sheathed. I curled my fingers around one, but didn't pull it free yet.

The figure was only a couple of paces away, and as soon as I tensed and zeroed in on him, I realized it was that Red of Rue's. His hood was up, but not pulled so far forward I couldn't see his tanned face and the dirty blonde hair framing it. He blinked and rocked to a stop, waiting for me to make the first move.

I frowned. "What are you doing?"

"Following you."

Between Ruena and this kid... Six be damned, I felt bad for how much I'd put Senyr through at that age. I settled my knife back into the sheath and sighed as my shoulders relaxed. "*Why* are you following me?"

"Ruena worries about you. When I saw you, I thought I'd make sure you didn't need any help."

I raised an eyebrow. "I'm gonna be honest here. The last thing I'd expect a Red to do is help. Unless it was to help relieve me of the burden my life had become."

He tilted his head, standing in that eerie motionless way he had. "You're a Hand of the Master. No Red would try to kill you unless the guildmaster himself ordered it."

I knew it was technically true. I was probably safer with the assassins than the city guard. But after that farce of an investigation five years ago when I was their number one murder suspect, and the strangely free rein Loring's outcast Red had enjoyed, I couldn't help but suspect those rules were flexible.

Short of asking this Red to show me his ink I had no way of knowing if he was playing some kind of game. Although, to be fair, Rue would have seen–

I squeezed my eyes shut and forced the train of thought from my head. "Okay. I don't need any help. Enjoy the rest of your evening." I turned to go.

He called after me. "I'll follow you anyway."

I paused and took a deep breath. "Don't you have real work to be doing?"

"Not tonight."

"Did it ever occur to you that I don't want you around?"

"Yes."

I pinched the bridge of my nose. Fucking kids. Why did she have to find someone so damned stubborn? I glanced over my shoulder. "Fine. I'm on my way to visit the Warden. You can trail along–*out of sight*–and give a detailed report to Rigel if she guts me like a fish."

He nodded.

I swore an oath to the Six that I'd never give Senyr a hard time again, then started forward.

As I walked down Tinkers Row I could sense him following me, but I had to admit it made me a little less nervous to be walking into the Warden's lair. At least someone would be there as a witness if I got in too deep. And I hated to admit it, but I was getting strangely tired already. Almost dying the night before had taken a lot out of me. Blood specifically. A lot of blood.

I reached the large intersection where the Old Keep Road crossed Tinkers Row and turned onto it heading north. The Warden's jail was part of a large complex of buildings that included barracks, training grounds, and the armory. Her office was attached to the jail itself, and I walked up to the main doors with as much nonchalance as I could muster while feeling like I was walking to my own trial.

A pair of Silvers stopped me at the door.

"What's your business here?"

"Reporting to the Warden. I'm here to help her do her job."

He scowled back at me, sneering down past a fluffy mustache. "Wait here. I'll tell her that."

I bit my lip as I inclined my head and stepped back a few paces to wait. I really should have said something less confrontational, but I was on edge and the sarcasm had just slipped out. I was pretty sure I was going to pay for it. Somehow.

The other Silver was glaring at me and his hand rested on the hilt of the sword at his hip. After a couple of minutes passed with no returning mustache man, I spoke to him. "If she's busy, I can come back later."

He stretched himself taller, looking down at me without a word.

I sighed and looked away. "Right."

By now the sun was beginning to set, painting the little courtyard in front of the building with an orange glow while purple shadows stretched near the buildings. Another few minutes went by and I was seriously considering just walking away when the door opened.

The Warden herself walked out. She looked as severe and unyielding as ever, pausing on the threshold to glare down at me. "I didn't think you'd show up, thief."

I smirked and called back. "And miss this golden opportunity to stand at your side?"

Her lip curled in a sneer. "Like you could ever." She stepped down onto the street, her armor jangling and her sword sheath clinking against her thigh.

As she approached, my mouth went dry and my gut dropped. I managed to keep the jaunty expression on my face, but I'm sure it wavered. Every instinct told me to run. Instead I stood my ground and raised my chin.

She stopped within arm's reach and I had to look up to meet her gaze. If she was going for intimidating, it was working. I found myself suddenly thinking about the Red nearby and was torn between relief he was there and embarrassment he was watching this. It wasn't going to be my proudest moment.

The Warden's armor creaked as her shoulders flexed. "You heal fast. I didn't even see a hint of a bruise when you stood before the baroness."

I swallowed past the lump that had formed in my throat. The whole district was full of guards, and this courtyard in particular was lined with them now. There were even guards without armor that had wandered out of the nearby barracks and stood watching the scene. I felt more like a sacrificial lamb than ever. I just kept hearing Senyr's words in my head. *Cooperate. This is important.*

She eased closer so she was towering over me, and a scent of onion wafted down from whatever she'd had for supper. "What do you know about Loring?"

"No more than you."

"You're lying."

I snorted nervously. "Of course I'm lying. I know a lot more than you do, but none of it has anything to do with the baroness or her treasury."

She got even closer, her chest bumping mine. I leaned back, but refused to take that step. My heart was pounding and I was starting to feel a little light-headed. I wasn't sure if it was from the lingering effects of blood loss or from the tension of facing down the Warden.

"Do you know where he is?"

I glared back. "No."

"Do you know what he's after?"

I clenched my jaw. I absolutely did know that, but the last thing I needed was to alert the Warden—and by extension the baroness—to the existence of a powerful and ancient magical artifact hidden in a cheap rented room down in Copperton. "No."

She narrowed her eyes. "What use are you then?"

"Not much. Maybe you should just send me on my way and tell the baroness you can do it yourself."

She stepped into me and I was forced to stagger back to keep my balance. "I would dearly love to do that. Even better, I'd love to take you into the building behind me and do unpleasant things to you until you answer my questions."

I backed up another step as she advanced. "Then why don't you?" Standing my ground was one thing, but letting her knock me down because I was too stubborn to move was another.

"Because I'm an extension of the law. And the word of Lady Karyn is the law. She wants to cooperate with your silly king of fools, so I'm left with little choice but to follow orders. So as long as you cooperate, you walk free."

I flashed her a smile. "I'd be glad to share any pertinent information we have. Just ask away." How was I supposed to feed her false information? She'd take anything I gave her and follow up on it, then realize I was lying.

"Do you know anything about a body found in an alley outside the New Market square the night before yesterday?"

The shock must have shown on my face, because her eyes narrowed and a sneer wrinkled her lips. "I'll take that as a yes."

"I don't see what a body in an alley has to do with anything."

"Neither did I, until we found the merchants he'd traveled with to reach Sangarie. The Silvers returned his body to them, and they told an interesting story about meeting an eloquent traveler on the road, and their friend not acting quite right after that."

I wanted very badly to back away another step, but she'd interpret it as an admission of guilt, so I stood firm. "Is that so?"

"Judging from the stab wounds, there was more than one killer. What can you tell me about that?"

My smile was more of a grimace. "People die all the time in this city. Maybe he crossed the wrong group of party-goers."

"His companions mentioned he'd been muttering to himself a lot those last few days. The same thing, over and over. Just mentioning the color gray."

I snorted with what I hoped came across as amusement. "I think you're obsessed with me, Warden."

She grabbed the front of my shirt and wound her fist into the cloth.

As I started to bring my hand up to push her away, she jerked me close and it was suddenly pressed between my belly and hers, where my knuckles hit a hard lump of coins inside soft leather.

A coin purse.

The Warden's coin purse.

I swallowed the mix of anger and anxiety, then flashed her a roguish smile, squirming just a bit in a way that would seem like I was merely uncomfortable in her grasp. Which was true.

I absolutely shouldn't do it. She was in the middle of threatening my life and limb, and just my toes were touching the cobbles at my feet. If she caught me I'd be dragged into the jail for sure and probably never come back out. Adrenaline was coursing through my body and making me giddy.

The knot was easy to loosen.

"What do you know about it?" she hissed.

"Well." I stalled, squirming again as I pulled the purse free. "I know what you just told me. Which tells me I should watch out for visiting merchants in alleys. Unfortunately I don't know the dirty bastards that jumped him, although I hope their night was profitable."

Her cheek twitched with anger. "So help me Six... if you cross me I'll drag you through the streets behind my horse and hang your broken body on my wall as a trophy."

"A little gruesome, don't you think?"

She shoved me back, but not before I had her purse securely in hand.

I spun as I stumbled and made a show of catching my balance, slipping the coin purse inside my vest before anyone could see it. Then I brushed the wrinkles out of my shirt and tugged it back into place, facing her from a safer distance.

"Someday your mouth will get you killed, thief."

"So I've been told."

"Go. And stay away until I summon you again."

My eyes narrowed. Summon me? What a self-important, arrogant—

Cooperate.

I bent at the waist and swept my arm out in a mocking bow, keeping the thought of my prize firmly in my mind to soothe the insult. "I await your pleasure, Warden."

She growled low in her throat.

I very deliberately turned my back on her and strolled away, doing my best to ignore the guards lining the road.

23 – Stabby Farmer

By the time I was out of sight of the barracks the sun had set. Old Keep Road was a main street, and it was well-lit by lamps and thick with citizens making their way through the city. Since I was in Varinston, and it was the best time of the day for the White Hands to peddle their mystic bullshit, I was shouted at occasionally from doorways or alcoves. Some offered salvation by the Six, some asked for coin for the teeming masses, and others were selling glimpses of fortune. I ignored them all and kept walking, letting my adrenaline seep away.

Once I was well beyond the Varinston district and turning onto Tinkers Row the traffic was starting to thin a bit. The Red stepped into line beside me and matched my pace, looking straight ahead as we walked. "Did that go well?"

"Did it look like it went well?"

"I'm not sure what you wanted to happen, so I don't know."

I sighed and glared at the cobbles in front of me as I walked. "It wasn't one of my proudest moments, but we're both still alive."

The Red glanced sideways at me. "I could've put a crossbow bolt in her forehead. It would've been easy from where I was."

"As sad as I am to admit it, it's probably best you didn't."

The fear and paranoia I'd always felt when it came to the Warden was quickly being replaced with anger and frustration. I was still worried about getting caught and executed in some horrific way, but the last couple of meetings had turned her into less of a boogeyman and more of a dangerous thorn in my side. The weight of the pouch under my vest was my only consolation.

Eventually I turned onto a side street to cut up toward Old Town and the Red followed. Speaking of thorns... why wasn't he slipping off into the shadows? Was he planning on keeping me company all evening? Was this his idea or Rue's?

We crossed into Old Town, and the street was fairly empty this late in the evening since the buildings in this part were mostly small shops or storehouses. It was part of my old route as an enforcer, and my pace adjusted automatically to something more distance-eating. The outlines of the buildings in the dark, while not as brightly lit as on Tinkers Row, were familiar, along with the sounds and smells that drifted out from the docks to the west.

It had to have been a thief's luck that drew my eyes to the alley we were passing just as a figure rushed forward. Lamplight glinted off the edge of the dagger in his hand, and instinct took over as I pushed it away, then punched him in the nose.

His head snapped back and I expected a screech of pain and a few moments of reaction, but instead he immediately swung the blade sideways, as if he hadn't felt the punch at all.

I managed to jump back and dodge it, frowning at the blood coming from the guy's nose and the pain in my knuckles. I'd connected pretty good, and it should have made his eyes water at least.

The Red attempted to slip past me, but I flung an arm out and pushed him back. "No! Don't kill him." If this was another of Loring's assassins I wanted to talk to him and get some information about his boss.

The attacker lunged forward, totally ignoring the Red and focusing on me. I side-stepped and grabbed his wrist as he staggered past me, bending the arm back until the elbow popped and the dagger fell with a clatter to the street. Then I shoved him between the shoulders to send him further away.

He caught his balance and turned, his eyes locking onto me once more and his voice pushing out between clenched teeth. "Gray. *Gray.*"

A chill went up my spine and I backed away. "Who sent you?"

"Gray…" He rushed forward, faster than I was expecting, and his fingers caught the side of my vest as I tried to dance away. He pulled with an inhuman strength and flung me to the cobbles.

I had enough time to turn onto my back and then he was on top of me, reaching for my throat. I pushed the hands away, trying to wriggle free, but he planted a knee on either side of my ribs and pressed a hand onto my chest.

I wound my arm around his, dislodging the hand that pinned me down and trying to push myself up, but his other hand thrust out for my throat again and gripped just under my jaw, slamming my head back to the street. He squeezed and cut off my air.

I hit his elbow, but it held. I choked at the pressure against my throat and tried to buck him off, but he was too high up on my chest for me to get enough leverage. My fingers dug into the muscles of his arm and drew blood with my nails, with no reaction other than a tightening of the hand on my throat. My chest burned with the lack of air.

Off to the side I caught a glimpse of movement and shifted my gaze to see the shadows of the alley where he'd come from twist and extend onto the street a few feet further than they should have been able to, as if they were eagerly watching the attack. Chills went down my spine and I squirmed harder.

The Red shifted into my narrowing field of vision and brought the butt of his crossbow down on the back of the man's head.

The man went limp and the hand fell away from my throat as I pushed his body to one side. I scrambled to my feet, coughing and rubbing at my throat, sucking in gulps of air and staring at the mouth of the alley where the shadows once again looked perfectly normal. I backed away and glanced at the Red. "Is he dead?"

"No." He squatted at the man's side, lifting one of his eyelids. "What do you want to do with him?"

"Let's take him to Nissa. Maybe she can tell us what's wrong with him." I coughed again and settled into a normal breathing rate as my body was no longer panicking. No matter how hard I stared into the alley, nothing was moving. Maybe my panicked mind had been playing tricks on me.

The Red helped me lift the man up and we each ducked under an arm and walked him back out of Old Town toward Copperton district, like a trio of drunks heading home way too early in the evening. It was a long trek, and by the time we reached the inn she was staying at and stopped at the bottom of the stairs leading up to the second floor, I was huffing and sweating.

I glared up the steps, wishing she'd been able to get a room at ground level. "Ready?"

The Red shifted his grip, then nodded.

We dragged him up the stairs, having to stop a couple of times to adjust our hold. The stairs weren't very wide and we couldn't go up side by side, so one of us was dragging and the other was shoving from the back. We reached the balcony, pulled him to the elf's door, and I pounded on it with a closed fist.

Nissa's voice came through a moment later. "Who is it?"

"It's me. Open the damn door before someone reports us to the Coppers."

The door unbolted and opened. Nissa stood there in the shadows and frowned at me, then her gaze dropped to the figure hanging between us. "Who is *that*?"

We dragged the man forward and dropped him to the floor, then I crouched next to him and began rummaging through his pockets. "He just tried to kill me, and he was acting very odd, like the one from the festival. Repeating my name, and stronger than he should be. Can you tell what's wrong with him?"

She raised an eyebrow as she watched me turn out the man's pockets. "What are you doing?"

I patted his shirt. "It's easier to roll someone when they're unconscious." Paper crunched under my hand and I reached in to take it out and kept looking.

She grunted and crouched at the man's side, running her hand above him as she examined him.

I was exhausted, a little dizzy, and a tingle of magic was raising the hair on the back of my neck. It was probably the stone. Did she have it under the floorboards or something? I finished my search and pushed myself to my feet, then retreated to sit on the bed.

The Red stood nearby and spoke in an undertone. "You look very pale."

"I'll be fine."

Nissa glanced up at us from her squatting position, her emerald eyes gleaming in the lamplight. "I am going to heal him, then we can question him."

I nodded. The paper in my hands was a folded letter. No seal, and no name on the outside. I unfolded it to find a few lines of text, scrawled in fancy cursive but from a shaky hand.

G,
I'm coming for you.
Kindest regards,
L.

A chill went through me and I swallowed past the dryness in my throat.

Nissa stood from where she'd been crouching next to the man, brushing her hands off. "That should do it."

The man's eyes fluttered open and he gazed dimly around the room until he saw me, then lurched to his knees, reaching for me.

I slipped off the bed and stepped into the corner of the room as Nissa placed herself between us. She slapped a hand on the man's forehead and spoke words I couldn't understand in a commanding, piercing tone that made my ears ring.

The man paused and rocked back on his heels, then his eyes cleared and his face screwed up in confusion. "Where am I?" He recoiled from Nissa's elfish form. "And what are you?"

Nissa grimaced and stepped aside. "*What* am I?" She grumbled to herself. "Why do I bother with humans?"

I stepped cautiously out of the corner. "Do you know who I am?"

The man focused on me and frowned as he backed out of Nissa's reach. "No. Should I?" He looked at each of us with growing fear. "Why am I here?"

"That's what we'd like to know. Who do you work for?" I had a nagging feeling he wouldn't be able to answer. His confusion didn't seem like an act.

"I'm a farmer. I work for myself. Look–how did I get here? If this is some kind of kidnapping, I'll have you know my brothers will come looking for me."

I glanced at Nissa. "Did your magic scramble his brain?"

She snorted. "Says the human that hit him in the head. But no, his brain is fine. I removed the compulsion he was under, and whoever created it must have done so without his knowledge."

"Compulsion? So he was being controlled?"

"In a way. Magic was flooding his mind, driving him to a single purpose. Which, apparently, was killing you."

193

The man's face had paled, and he looked back and forth between us. "What are you talking about?"

I crumpled the note in my hand. "Could Loring have done this?"

Nissa glanced at me sharply. "Not alone."

The man edged toward the door. "Who's Loring? Who are you people?"

The Red stepped between him and the door, just standing there with his hood pulled down to hide his features. His posture and the shadows hiding his face made him look menacing, as befitted an assassin.

The man looked back at me nervously. "Let me go."

I pinned him with my enforcer stare, hoping it looked more intimidating than I felt right now. "Did Loring send you?"

"I don't know who that is. I was minding my own business in the barn, putting the horse up for the evening, and next thing I know I woke up here. I think you people have more explaining to do than me."

Nissa spoke from where she stood on the far side of the room, staring at the floor with a deep crease on her brow. "You will not get any answers from him. He was merely a tool."

I waved at the Red and he stepped aside. "Fine. You can leave, but don't say anything about this to anyone or my scary friend here will track you down and kill your whole family, then burn your house and barn to the ground."

The man nodded quickly, slipped out the door, and clattered down the stairs outside. The Red sighed and turned his gaze to me. "Was that a good idea? Letting him go?"

"I'm not killing some random farmer that got snatched up." I held the note out to Nissa. "What kind of help would Loring need?"

She read the note, then handed it back. Her expression was darker than I'd seen it yet, and she refused to meet my eyes. "Only an elf can do this kind of magic."

I sat heavily on the bed beside me. "So he still has his visitor with him. I thought the elves were working on our side?"

"We are not mindless slaves to our elders. Do all the humans in this city follow the will of the baroness?" She frowned even deeper. "Although it is degrading to allow our magic to be used for petty human vengeance. So I am surprised any of us would stoop so low as to willingly be a pawn."

"Can we convince this elf to fuck off?"

"You would have to find him first, and talk to him."

I set my elbows on my knees and hung my head. I couldn't think in here with the magic of the stone constantly washing over me. "What's Loring after?"

"Apart from killing you?"

I rolled my eyes. "Yes. Apart from that."

"The stone is powerful, and Loring wanted to rule. If he truly has the other one he may be here to conquer Sangarie."

I shook my head. "If that's all he wanted, he wouldn't be sitting outside the city sending farmers after me. He'd have gone straight for the baroness. Then he'd have all her resources at his disposal to kill me at his leisure."

"Humans are an emotional species. Perhaps he wants you first."

"Great."

"There is another possibility."

I raised my gaze to hers. "That would be?"

"He may be waiting for the Night of Shadows as well. If he is indeed channeling Dakara from the stone, it is possible he intends to make his final move at a time that would give him the most power."

A chill went up my back. "You think Dakara will get some kind of power from the labyrinth?"

She frowned. "I think the power of Dakara will create the labyrinth. Loring may not have realized it yet."

"Fuck." I rubbed a hand over my face and sighed. "How can we do anything about that?"

She tilted her head, staring at me with an unblinking intensity. "Why do you *still* think we are trying to prevent it?"

I wanted to shout back at her that preventing it was exactly what I wanted to do, but I bit my tongue. I knew she'd said the future needed to happen, but all those warnings were vague and cryptic. What was absolutely staring me in the face—racing closer with each passing hour—was the destruction of the entire city. She wanted me to let that happen to prevent some even bigger disaster that her elders *thought* would happen.

I still wasn't convinced. There had to be a way to stop it. I pushed myself wearily back to my feet and walked to the door without another glance at her. "If you find anything else, let me know. I'm done for the night."

24 – Drinks

I sent the Red on his way once we'd left Nissa's rooms. I didn't ask where he was going because I didn't really want to know if he was going to see Ruena. Then I headed for Crafthold.

In the district of Crafthold, smack dab in the middle of a block containing blacksmiths and other metal workers, was a bar called the Wolf and Bear. It was a favorite of Senyr's, and I was hoping I'd find him there tonight. I kept my eyes out as I walked, avoiding the shadows when I could, and trying not to hold my breath when I couldn't. Truth be told, I should have been more concerned about another mind-controlled farmer. At least the shadows were only watching me for now and not trying to knife me.

I breathed a little easier as I neared the Wolf and Bear, comforted by the uproarious laughter and the sound of a fist pounding on a heavy table. Even if Senyr wasn't there, I could do with a drink or two, and tonight the Warden was buying. I patted the heavy purse under my vest.

The Wolf and Bear wasn't a dive, but it wasn't exactly welcoming either. It was full of metalsmiths and laborers, big men and women that could have split me in two if they got a good grip on me. The Blues didn't frequent it much, because the patrons that came here were only interested in washing the dust out of their throats and letting off steam in the form of good-natured fist fights and contests of strength. Lionel–the enforcer of Crafthold–discouraged his thieves from hanging about, since getting caught picking a pocket in here would result in heads being bashed in.

I'd asked Senyr once why he favored this place, and he said it was because he liked the atmosphere. I think he'd been trying to intimidate me, but I'd suffered from a powerful case of invincibility as a kid, so it hadn't worked. I'd figured out on my own that Senyr had made quite a few friends in here, and it was never a bad idea to have a crowd like this at your back.

Tonight I walked in and at least half a dozen men–and one muscular woman–roared out greetings as I made my way to the bar. One of them slapped my back so hard I stumbled. I took it in stride, knowing damn well they did it on purpose because it amused them how scrawny I was compared to them. But they liked me, and that was the important thing.

The smell of steel and coal hung in the air, mixing with ale and whatever meat was roasting on the hearth on the other side of the room. Something was always roasting over that fire, and patrons usually just meandered up and sliced bits off it with their belt knives and wandered back to their tables. The furniture was heavy, and repaired with metal straps in places, a testament to the frequent friendly bar fights.

I sat myself at the bar and waited for the barkeep to amble over. He was as muscular as the patrons and sometimes I wondered how he didn't crush the mugs in his hands as he scrubbed them. A thick mustache covered his upper lip and draped down his chin, and his head was bald. He leaned on the bar in front of me until it creaked.

"What'll it be, Gray?"

"Ale. You seen Senyr?"

The barkeep moved to fill a clean mug at the barrel on the wall behind him. "He's around here somewhere. Might've went to take a piss."

I grinned. "Perfect." Keeping my hands below the level of the bar, I dumped the contents of the Warden's purse into my palm. There were more gold coins than silver, and I grinned even wider. The silver went into my own pouch, and the gold I slapped on top of the bar. "Why don't you pour one for everybody. It's a good night for drinking."

The barkeep's eyebrow went up and he lifted his head and bellowed: "Next round's on Gray!"

I winced as the words rang in my ears from this close in front of him, and the patrons that filled the bar roared in response. A couple of meaty hands slapped my back. When I decided it was finally safe to pick up my own mug without having it knocked out of my hand, Senyr slipped into the seat beside me.

He glanced at the gold the barkeep was sweeping off the counter. "Feeling generous?"

I leaned in and spoke low enough it wouldn't carry. "The Warden dropped it."

He frowned at me. "You didn't."

"I did."

He chuckled and wiped a wrinkled hand over his face. "You're fucking crazy."

The barkeep slapped a mug in front of him as well, and Senyr took a long drink.

Over the next hour, in between greeting people that came up to claim their drinks, I told Senyr all about the meeting with the Warden and the attack in Old Town. I even slipped him the note I'd found on the poor farmer, which made him scowl into his mug for a full ten minutes while we discussed the outcast nobleman's possible plans.

Eventually I claimed my fourth mug from the barkeep and realized my vision was getting a little hazy at the edges. The buzz of the alcohol was nice, and sitting among these smiths and heavy workers I felt as safe as if I was in my own apartment. I turned the conversation to lighter things… harmless rumors, old stories, and jokes.

I wasn't sure how long we sat there, laughing and drinking, even singing a few times when some worker broke into a rowdy song. It was good to let everything slide into the back of my brain for a few hours. Eventually I stood up from the stool and swayed, grabbing the bar to keep from stumbling.

Senyr eased off his stool as well and pushed his mug away with a chuckle. "Let's get you home."

"Good idea." I checked that my purse was secure and patted the shoulder of the big man with his head down on the bar next to me. "G'night, Beryl." He was already out cold.

Senyr took my shoulders and guided me toward the front of the bar. We got stopped at nearly every table, either to catch our balance as someone gave us a friendly pat, or to pause while a drunk patron engulfed one or both of us in a bear hug. These people really appreciated free ale. When we finally stumbled onto the street and the quiet pressed in on my ears everything was spinning gently and the lamps were fuzzy.

I put my arm around Senyr's shoulders and we walked together toward Old Town. The cool night air cleared my head a little, but I was still more drunk than I'd been in a long while. I was guessing part of it had to do with all the blood loss from the day before.

We reached a good place to go underground that had a set of stairs instead of a ladder, and clattered our way down. Well, I clattered, and Senyr went somewhat more gracefully. Normally at this point we'd separate, since his apartment was in one direction and mine was in the other, but when I tried to pull away he held my arm in place over his shoulders.

"I think it's better if I see you all the way home."

I scoffed and swayed as he started us forward again. "I'm fine. Really."

"You worry me, boy."

I rolled my eyes and the room rolled with them, so I gripped his shoulder a little harder until it settled back down. "What are you so worried about?"

"How many times have you almost died in the last week?"

"Three? No…" I swung my free hand around with four fingers raised, tensing my arm around his shoulders to keep from overbalancing. "Four if you count the Warden hitting on me." My mouth quirked and I snorted at the innuendo.

"You realize that's a lot, right?"

"We're thieves. Everything is trying to kill us."

He sighed and shifted my weight to make it a little easier to support me as I staggered. I tried to tell if his limp was bothering him, but I couldn't keep my eyes focused enough.

"I think you're dealing with a little more than most."

"Aww come on, old man. The city's gonna be destroyed in a week anyway, and I haf a be–" I blinked and brought my slurred words back into line. "Have to be there for that. I can't die."

"Idiot. You don't know that."

I frowned and set a hand on his chest, pushing away from his support. The cavern wall tilted and I staggered back until I was leaning against the cool stone, then I slid down the wall and rested my arm on my raised knee as I swallowed back the dizziness. "I do. I saw it, you know."

He stood, staring down at me. "Saw what?"

"Everything. That fucking stone showed me the end. And I was there. It was in my hand." I raised my hand, as if holding an invisible stone. "And I did it."

He just watched me. And waited.

I didn't know why he wasn't saying anything. Did he not believe me? Had he not heard me? The seconds dragged on and I lowered my hand and tried to focus on him standing there. "Don't you get it? It's all my fault. And everybody's gonna die." I closed my eyes against the spinning walls. "I destroy the city. Me."

I heard the scrape of stone as he lowered himself to sit beside me. "What are you talking about?"

I snorted, letting my head loll to one side. I was really tired all of a sudden.

He shifted beside me and a sharp pain flared in the tip of my ear as he flicked it. I flinched and raised a hand to the side of my head.

"Ow! The fuck?"

"What are you talking about? The stone showed you?"

"Five years ago. The first time I picked it up I had a vision. It showed me how I made the city explode."

"And you didn't tell anybody."

"Would you?" I looked at him, my vision fading on the edges. "I hoped it wouldn't happen."

"Do you think you *can't* die because of that... or are you hoping you will so it doesn't happen?"

My brow creased. "I don't know."

He sighed and pushed himself to his feet with a groan, then dragged me up and waited as I caught my balance. When I was supporting myself, he curled both fists into the collar of my shirt and pressed me back against the wall.

"You listen to me, boy. I didn't raise you to roll over and accept whatever happened. It would've been much easier for me if I did, but I wanted you to question things. To push at things."

I snorted. "You hate that."

He shook his head. "It's what you need to do. And yes, you've been a pain in the ass, but I'm glad for it. So don't give up on being a pain in the ass now. You do what you think is right, not what you think you're supposed to do because some rock stuck a vision in your head."

I tried to focus on his eyes, but they kept splitting and turning into four, then eight. "Does that mean I should tell you to fuck off next time I have to play with the Warden?"

He scowled. "No. You still have to do what I tell you."

I groaned and leaned my head back, my mind drifting a little into the black hole that was trying to drag me down into sleep.

Senyr shook me. "If you pass out here, I'll leave you in the tunnel for the pickpockets."

I grumbled something about rudeness and tightened my arm over his shoulder as he ducked under it. It must have been a short distance to my apartment, because we arrived very quickly after that. Senyr pounded on the door and a sweet, feminine voice came from within.

Deidre opened the door and raised her eyebrow at us. "You reek of ale."

Warmth filled my chest and I smiled back at her. "Better than blood."

She frowned and shot a look at Senyr. "What?"

He pulled me forward. "Nothing. He's drunk."

"I see that." She went to my other side after shutting the door and helped get me to the alcove with the bed in it.

I was so happy to see her. The last few days I'd felt like we were in two different worlds, even when we were here together. I just wanted to hold her. I wanted to protect her and keep the rest of the world away.

I pulled her closer and she stumbled, cursed, and sighed deeply as she helped Senyr sit me down on the edge of the bed. She worked on getting my boots off while he held me upright.

"This isn't like him. Why is he this drunk?"

I vaguely remembered she wasn't supposed to know about my injury from the night before, and I was glad I wasn't the one expected to come up with some reasonable explanation. I chuckled at the thought of Senyr having to cover for me and decided it served him right for sending me into that manor in the first place. Fucking crossbow carrying butlers or whatever.

The room dimmed and tilted and Deidre hugged me.

No. Caught me. I think.

I raised a hand to her cheek and rubbed my thumb lightly over her bottom lip, her face very close to mine. "I miss you."

202

She sighed and pushed me back on the bed. For a brief moment the thought rose in my mind about her joining me, but then it dissolved away as the blackness finally washed over everything.

25 – Too Early

A heavy pounding noise woke me from a deep, drunken sleep. I gazed into the darkness of my room in confusion, wiping a bit of drool from the corner of my mouth. Deidre was curled up behind me, her arm flung over my waist, but she woke at the noise as well and rolled onto her back with an incoherent mumble.

Bang. Bang. Bang.

I winced as the sound rattled my skull, and with a groan in reply I pulled my pillow over my head. I was way too hungover to deal with this right now. I needed at least another four or five hours of sleep.

Bang. Bang. Bang. "Gray! Get up." The voice was vaguely familiar. Female and a little scratchy.

Deidre prodded me in the lower back. "Go see what they want."

I grunted and flung the blankets off, realizing I was still fully dressed and wondering what time it was. The room spun a little as I sat on the edge of the bed, just enough to warn me about the nausea and pounding headache as they hit. Definitely too hungover for this.

I set my elbows on my knees and cradled my head, deciding it'd be easier to call out from here. "What do you want?" Easier yes, but unmercifully loud.

"The Warden wants to see you. Says you've been summoned."

By the Six... I fell back into the still warm indent where I'd been sleeping. "Tell her to go fuck herself."

"The guildmaster sent me to fetch you. Should I tell him to go fuck himself too?"

I groaned. I was tempted to say yes, but I didn't think Rigel would be amused.

Deidre pushed a hand against my arm. "Just go, so I can go back to sleep."

"Thanks a lot." I hauled myself to sitting and reached for the lamp on the side table. I kept the hood down so it only let a small amount of light filter out to show me what I was doing as I went to the dresser to look for a clean set of clothing.

The pounding came at the door again and I barked back at it. "I'm coming! For fucks sake."

I dressed, made sure my knives were secure, then took a sip of whiskey straight from the bottle to swish around in my mouth and try to get rid of the cotton feeling. There was no food in here, but maybe there'd be a stall open on the way to the Warden's jail. I returned the lamp to the side table, snuffed it out, and made my way in the pitch dark to the door.

Waiting for me in the tunnel was the Yellow that had been acting as messenger for the meetings with Barty. She stood with her arms crossed over her chest, looking as grumpy as I probably did. "About time."

I closed the door behind me. "What time is it?"

"Just after sunrise."

I looked sideways at her, not moving out of the space in front of my door. "Are you kidding me? Who the fuck–"

"The Warden. Obviously." She held out a folded piece of paper. "Look, I just deliver the message and make sure you're up and moving. Now I'm going back to bed myself, and I'm going to dream about the days when your work didn't disrupt my life so much."

I huffed as she walked away. Disrupt *her* life? She's lucky *she* didn't have to go out and meet with the people whose messages she delivered.

What would happen if I just went back into my room and went to sleep? I could say I got sidetracked on the way. Surely nothing was so important that the Warden needed me by her side at the ass crack of dawn.

I flipped open the paper.

Gray. You're to meet the Warden at the Devil's Throat immediately. Lyra will tell me what time she gave this to you, so don't think you can pretend you didn't know. Rigel.

I let out a groan and crumpled the paper, then shoved it into a pocket as I stalked in the opposite direction *Lyra* had taken.

Lyra, huh? Finally a name for the face I should avoid.

The throbbing in my head was a nuisance as I made my way through the underground and along the familiar route that took me topside close to the Devil's Throat, but after I climbed a set of cellar stairs and opened the door to the shack that contained them, the sun pierced straight through my eyelids like daggers. I cursed and shaded my face with my arm. It felt like a string connected my eyelids and the back of my skull, and every time I blinked it was pulling too tight. I should have grabbed my cloak with the deep hood.

There were a few food stalls in the Old Market and I wandered up to one that offered flaky bread with eggs and sausage stuffed inside, along with a rich cream sauce. I paid the man, then stood in the shadow of his stall and ate it as I scanned the other side of the square where the Throat was.

Even a casual glance revealed the Silvers stationed outside. They weren't being subtle about it. I counted half a dozen, two of which stood to either side of the door. The others were scattered close by, either scanning the few early morning shoppers and storefronts or staring off into space as if none of it existed. The Warden herself must be in the Throat.

I bet Sans had smoke coming out of his ears by now. He had no love for the Warden, and he hated having guards in his bar. Even off duty guards weren't particularly welcome, as it tended to scare off the majority of his patrons.

I swallowed the last bite of the bread and licked the sauce off my fingers, then took a deep breath. Might as well get this over with so I could go back home and crawl into bed for a few more hours.

As I slipped back into view and strolled across the square, a Silver caught sight of me and nudged her companions. By the time I reached the Throat they were formed up in a vaguely threatening funnel leading to the door. I ignored them the best I could.

The Throat was empty other than Sans, Kash, and the Warden with another half dozen of her accompanying guards. She must have chased out the pre-work crowd and the overnight drinkers. Even Basil was nowhere to be seen and I wondered if they'd sent him away too. Sans and Kash stood behind the bar. They both looked grumpy. Sans had his arms crossed over his chest. Kash was leaning against the counter behind the bar.

My eyes flicked to the door that led upstairs where Ruena's room was. Was she still asleep up there? Had she been sent away too?

The Warden rose from the chair she'd been using, gaze locked on me. "I had hoped I was going to need to send the Silvers after you, thief. It would have brightened my morning to see you dragged before me in chains."

I was keenly aware of the stares of the Silvers in attendance, and from Kash and Sans. "Sorry to disappoint you."

She stopped two paces away, her eyes running down the length of me and then back up. I'd been measured like that many times before, but having the Warden do it was a special kind of uncomfortable. She seemed to linger around my belt and general waist area, and her eyes tightened as she did.

I smiled past my clenched jaw. She must have figured out her coin purse was gone by now, and maybe she was suspicious. Even if she searched me, she wouldn't find anything. I'd ditched the purse in a gutter, and the few silver that remained of the coins wouldn't look out of place in my own pockets.

"What did you want, Warden? I can't imagine you've been missing my company."

Her sneer didn't change, but she finally met my gaze and held it. "My Silvers have been asking around about the exiled nobleman with no luck. Everywhere they go they're met with indifference or amusement."

I didn't need to fake the smile that came at her words. If Silvers were asking around about anything in the common districts of Sangarie they'd be met like that. The Warden and her Silvers couldn't get directions to the nearest dock from the street people of the city. She was "other" and unless she tried threatening their livelihoods or families, she could investigate in circles and get nowhere. "Is that so?"

"Maybe I'd have better luck if I played it your way." She took one step closer, putting her within arm's reach.

I swallowed against the fluttering in my stomach and held my position. Normally I'd meet brashness with brashness, bravado with bravado. Rank aside, you held your position in the guild because of how well you handled the people around you. But I'd spent my entire life running from the Warden, and the warning bells in my head were at odds with my instinct to posture. "What's playing it my way?"

Her gloved hand was resting on her sword hilt. I was pretty sure it was a habit and not intentional, but I was aware of it. Her entire demeanor was that of someone who knew she had the upper hand, and whether she did or not, the confidence was enough to give me pause.

"I'm going to have you do the talking."

I scowled. "What do you expect me–"

She grabbed the front of my shirt and twisted her gloved fist in the cloth, then leaned in. Her breath was warm in my face and still smelled like onion. With the hangover I was nursing, it was enough to make my stomach turn. Was that all she ate?

"You're going to come along with us, and you're going to ask people if they've seen or heard about Loring. If they won't talk to the guard, maybe they'll talk to the guild."

My heart thudded against my ribs, a combination of anxiety and anger. With all the Silvers in here if I drew a knife we'd both be bleeding on the floor of the Throat before Sans could complain about it, so I simply glared back at her. "You have a very bad habit of putting your hands on me."

"You're lucky that's the only thing I put on you."

I lowered my voice, trying to keep the anger out of it. "And you're lucky the guildmaster told me to cooperate. Otherwise this conversation would be very different."

Her voice lowered as well, making our conversation as intimate as it could be in a room full of guards. "Lady Karyn is focused on the goal, not the means. She thinks you're connected to this somehow. That you'll prove... useful." She lifted, making me shift my weight to my toes. "But go ahead and keep running your mouth. I'll explain to her how you outlived that usefulness."

I took a deep breath, swallowing the petty insults and false bravado I wanted to come back with. "If you want me to be useful, maybe treat me with a little respect."

"You don't deserve any respect from me. You're a lying, murdering thief."

I curled my lip in a sneer of my own. "Except that's *exactly* what you need from me, isn't it? My criminal connections. My reputation."

She snorted and shoved me away.

I caught myself on the edge of a table and it scraped a few inches across the floor. The Warden just glared, not saying a word as I brushed the wrinkles out of the front of my shirt.

My eyes shifted to Sans and Kash, and I was surprised to see the old barkeep looking pale and worried. He met my gaze and crinkled his eyebrow, then made a slight shake of his head, as if to dissuade me from doing anything stupid. His eyes darted to the Warden and back to mine, and he twisted a dirty rag in his hands.

Much of my anger drained away. I knew Sans cared, but I'd never seen it written so clearly on his face. He usually only heard about things after the fact, when it was easy to brush off the danger and laugh about it. Maybe it was different seeing it happen in front of him.

The Warden snapped her fingers and the Silvers all stiffened with the creak of leather and the clink of breastplates. She pointed at two of them and then at me, then promptly started walking toward the door. "Let's go, thief. We're wasting daylight."

I glanced at Sans again and gave him what I hoped was a reassuring wink, then stepped in front of the two guards who had hung back, letting them take up positions behind me as I followed the Warden out the door.

26 – Interrogation

The sun was blinding, and it made the pain in my forehead and temples jump back to distracting levels. I should have asked Sans for some water while I was in the Throat. It didn't look like I was getting back to bed anytime soon, and with only a couple hours of sleep I had a long way to go before this hangover worked itself out.

I followed the Warden and her dozen guards through Old Town, trying to ignore the curious stares of guildmembers and citizens alike. Occasionally she would stop at a shop or home and motion me forward, and I'd trudge up with my two Silvers and half-heartedly ask questions on her behalf. After the first couple of stops I knew what questions she wanted to ask and didn't bother waiting for her to give them to me to repeat. Yes, it felt uncomfortably like cooperating, but it would make things go faster.

I managed to snag a cup of water at a bar closer to the dock, though it tasted like the river and left a gritty feeling on my teeth. At least it would help with the hangover.

We worked our way through Old Town and then went north to the next district. The Warden didn't seem put off by the fact that nobody had any information, and I wondered if she expected to find something or if she was just doing this to punish me. I wouldn't put it past her.

By midafternoon we'd reached the North Gate into the city and the streets were teeming with people. I now had four Silvers behind me, and it amused me to think the Warden was worried about me slipping away. To be fair, I could have done so even with the four guards, but I knew it'd be more hassle than it was worth when she found me again.

A Silver came trotting up from the gate itself, looking excited and pleased. He spoke briefly with the Warden in a voice low enough I couldn't hear it, and she glanced over her shoulder at me and narrowed her eyes.

Great. What had I done now?

The Silver trotted ahead and we followed him to the guard tower next to the gate, out of the way of the people being questioned coming and going from the city. The guards must have been given orders to talk to everyone, because there wasn't normally an interview process to get through here.

I stepped inside the guardhouse with a mixture of relief at getting out of the bright sunlight, and anxiety at the surroundings. Most of the Warden's entourage waited outside, although my four shadows stationed themselves in front of the door just inside, and there were at least half a dozen already there. As we entered, they stepped aside and I caught a glimpse of the reason for our detour.

A man sat on a chair near a table, dressed like a farmer, looking confused and frightened. And familiar. It was the man who'd attacked me the night before in Old Town. The one we'd taken to Nissa's room and questioned, then released. My gut dropped and I slipped out of the man's line of sight, standing behind a Silver and turning my face away.

The Warden walked up to him and glared down. "My men tell me you have some information about a man named Loring."

The farmer fidgeted on his chair, started to stand, and was pressed back down by a Silver beside him. He glanced at the guard and swallowed before answering. "I told them I don't know anyone by that name... but I *have* heard it."

Shit. Maybe I should have made sure he left town instead of just letting him go. I needed to keep the Warden looking, but not let her get too close, and this man knew enough to fuck that plan to pieces if he said the wrong things. The Warden would know for sure I had more than I was letting on.

The Warden crossed her arms over her chest and her armor creaked as her muscles bulged beneath it. "Tell me what you know."

The man paled and glanced at the guards around him. "I already told them. It was just mentioned in passing. I wasn't listening to what was being said. I only recognized the name."

The Warden sighed and motioned for me to come forward.

Damn it.

A Silver nudged my shoulder and I stepped up. The reaction from the farmer was instant and obvious when he recognized me. His eyes went wide, his face paled, and he jumped up from his chair and tried to leave, but the Silver behind him grabbed his shoulder and pressed him down again. The farmer looked from me to the Warden and back to me.

I kept my face carefully neutral. If I looked the least bit threatening he might think this was a continuation of last night and start blabbering again. My only hope was that he'd pick up on my cues and keep things to himself. If the Warden figured out Loring was sending people to kill me, she'd know for sure that I had more information than I was letting on. She might decide to interrogate me next.

I started with the first question on the list I'd been asking all morning. "Have you heard of or seen a man named Loring?"

The Warden growled. "He obviously has. We already established that."

The farmer looked back and forth between us, licking his lips nervously.

I took a breath and abandoned that line of questioning. If I didn't at least attempt to do this right, the Warden would do it herself and I wouldn't have any control over what she asked him. Maybe I could lead the conversation and give the man an opportunity to keep his mouth shut. "Do you know who Loring is?"

The farmer was trying to figure out what was going on. That much was obvious. He wasn't sure if he should be more afraid of me or the authorities, and he didn't understand why we were here together. He wrung his hands in his lap. "No. I don't know who he is."

I nodded. "Have you seen him yourself?"

"No."

"Do you know what he's planning?"

"No."

The Warden cut in. "You said you overheard someone talking about him. Who were they?"

I narrowed my eyes at the man, putting as much threat as I could into it.

He noticed. He shifted on the chair, still pinned by the Silver's hand on his shoulder, and dropped his gaze. "I don't really know. I didn't get a good look at them."

212

She stepped closer, towering over him. "What did they say?"

He glanced up at me, then down at the floor again. "Uhm. I don't really remember."

Her hand shot out and gripped the man's shirt, much like she'd done to me in the Devil's Throat, and she lifted him to his feet. "You dare lie to the Warden of Sangarie?"

He gripped her forearm and whimpered. "Please. I don't remember. I was–I was drinking! Very drunk."

"What did they say?" She tightened her grip, lifting him to his toes.

He glanced in my direction again.

The Warden noticed and slowly looked over her shoulder, her eyes narrowing.

It was about to go to shit. There was nowhere I could go. There was nothing I could say that wouldn't make it worse. I'd leaned on enough people in my career to know this farmer was one threat away from breaking and telling her everything.

The only thing I was still asking myself was whether this would be enough for the Warden to end our uncomfortable truce. I was trapped in here, surrounded by Silvers and stone walls. If I made the first move it would be done and they'd cut me down, but maybe, if I didn't fight her, she'd feel the need to continue following her orders.

She grunted and turned back to the farmer. "This thief can't protect you from my wrath if you don't tell me what I need to know."

I snorted softly and looked down. She'd misread the situation, but it wouldn't matter. The farmer didn't think I was protecting him. He'd been afraid of what I'd do to him, and it was the only thing keeping his mouth shut. But faced with something scarier than I was…

He whined, a last apologetic appeal before he focused on her and the words tumbled from his mouth. "It was him." He pointed at me. "He was the one talking about someone named Loring. Him and another man and some green-skinned elf. They called me a tool and said this Loring person had done magic on me so I would come here to kill them."

I should have let Rue's Red take him outside the city.

The Warden looked over her shoulder again, her eyes hard and her mouth in a tight sneer. "Anything else?"

The farmer stammered a moment, his hands still wrapped around the Warden's forearm as she held him up on his toes. "Oh! I think they said

213

the Loring person had help. That's all. Then they threatened my family and told me to leave." He glanced at me, then away. "That's all. Please just let me go now, and keep him from coming after my family."

She released him, shaking off his hands as he sank back into the chair. "Take him down for further questioning."

The man panicked, pushing himself out of the chair, but the Silvers grabbed him and dragged him deeper into the guard tower. He yelled the entire way, about how he'd told her what she wanted to know and how he hadn't done anything wrong. The shouting was quickly muffled when one of the guards closed the heavy door between them and us.

I looked up at the Warden, tight-lipped, forcing myself to remain still. My heart was pounding and my hands were already sweating.

She stared back at me for a few moments, then slowly approached, holding my gaze.

Each step she took made my heartrate jump a little higher, until she was standing in front of me and I was sure she could hear it racing. My hands shook and the temptation to run was nearly overpowering. My eyes flicked in the direction of the door.

She thrust her palm at my chest and shoved me into the wall, startling the Silvers nearby as much as me. The back of my head smacked against stone, new pain blossoming alongside my hangover headache, and I squeezed my eyes shut as I leaned on the wall and waited for the stars to die down enough to be able to see again.

She grabbed my shirt in both hands, pinning me to the wall. The leather of her gloves creaked, and I could see the outline of hardened plates on the knuckles. "Should I ask you again?"

I blinked past the pain in my head. "Loring's problem with me has nothing to do with the baroness or her gold."

"That's for me to decide."

I chuckled, and it sounded a little hysterical even to my own ears. "Fine. You want to know why he's after me? Because I made a fool of him five years ago. I'm sure you can sympathize."

She growled and flung me away from the wall. The momentum carried me across the room, into the chair the farmer had been sitting in, and it went flying. I landed hard against the far wall.

I shouldn't have added that last bit. I was panicking and letting my mouth run. Senyr had always told me it'd get me killed, and maybe we'd

214

find out today if he was right. I winced at the fresh pain of what would definitely be bruises by tonight, pushing myself to my feet using the wall.

The Warden kicked the chair out of her way as she approached. "Where is he?"

She was going to grab me again. I could try to dodge and make her work for it, knowing I couldn't evade her forever, or I could go along with it and hope she showed a little restraint.

"I don't know where he is."

She took hold of my shirt and slammed me against the wall. "Liar."

"Look, if I knew where he was, would I let him keep sending people to kill me?"

She hit me in the jaw with a right hook. It snapped my head to the side, but she was still holding me up with one hand so I just faced her again and flexed my jaw. It didn't feel broken, but it stung like a bitch and the ache went all the way to my ear.

"How do you know it was him? You must've had contact with him, or someone working for him."

"Can we talk without the punching?"

"Answer my questions and I won't hit you."

I closed my eyes and sighed.

She shook me and pressed me against the wall again. "Tell me about the elf. Is it the same one that was here five years ago with Loring?"

I clenched my jaw, despite the pain. How much could I tell her that wouldn't put Nissa in danger? I couldn't say anything about the stone, or the baroness might try to take it. Then everything we were trying to do would be ruined.

She pulled her arm back, preparing to strike again. "Is it the same elf?"

"Yes. Fuck. It's the same elf. She came here to warn me about him. That's how I know it's him."

"Where is she?"

I glared back. "She left."

"I doubt that. The guards have been searching everyone at the gates. You're hiding her somewhere."

"She's an elf. You don't think she can get through the guards with her magic?"

215

She leaned closer. "I think she *hasn't*. I don't think she's done here, is she?"

I frowned and squirmed to ease the pressure of her fist against my chest. "She has nothing to do with this. She's just a friend, and came to deliver a warning."

"Tell me exactly what she said."

"Just that Loring was trying to kill me because he was bent out of shape about what happened. That's all."

She narrowed her eyes and studied mine.

If she started guessing at things and came to the wrong conclusions, it could make this a lot more difficult for us. Somehow we needed to be in the baroness's manor on the Night of Shadows in three days, and I didn't know how to make that happen. Maybe I should give the Warden more. Enough that she could help. Maybe stretch things just a little. I took a deep breath and hoped it was the right choice.

"He's here to kill me, then he's going to take Sangarie. On the Night of Shadows he'll make his move and everyone in the city will be in danger. He's wielding powerful magic. We're trying to stop him."

The Warden's mouth tightened and she shook her head. "Now you're mocking me?"

I snorted. "What? No, I–"

I saw the gut punch coming, but with her fist holding me against the wall there wasn't anything I could do about it except tense my stomach. It still hit hard enough to force the breath out of me and I wheezed and pressed my arms over my abdomen as she let go.

I dropped to my knees and then to my side, trying to get my breath back. "I'm not... lying."

She paced in front of me, her armor clinking and her footsteps clomping as she moved. "I'll tell you what I'm going to do, thief. I'm going to let you go today, and at dawn tomorrow I expect to see you standing at my door with your elf friend beside you, ready to give me all the information you have about Loring and his whereabouts."

I scowled back. How was I supposed to convince Nissa of that? She'd realize as quickly as I had that she wouldn't be walking back out of that jail. I averted my gaze. "Fine."

She grunted. "Good." Then she walked toward the door leading further into the tower where they'd taken the farmer and called over her shoulder. "Throw him out."

27 – Pains and Plans

My head was throbbing, the entire left side of my jaw ached, and my gut felt bruised from my ribs to my waist. I figured the best place to go right now would be the Throat. I'd have to talk to Nissa eventually, but I was pretty sure Sans would be pacing the length of the bar until he heard how things had gone. Besides, I wanted to check on Rue.

It was a long walk and I was grumbling when I stepped inside the Throat and looked around. The patrons were back, and there wasn't a Silver in sight. Thank the Six. Kash was behind the bar, Basil was serving tables, and Sans was sitting at the end of the bar talking to Rue.

They noticed almost immediately when I stepped inside. The worried look on Sans's face melted into relief and he bowed his head as Ruena hopped off her chair and rushed to my side. She frowned and poked a finger under my chin so I lifted my head.

"You're bleeding. Again."

I wiped my fingers along my aching jaw, feeling the roughness of dried blood over a small cut. "The Warden has hardened knuckles on her gloves."

"I'll get a bowl of water and some rags." She leaned in and lowered her voice. "Sans has been really worried."

I glanced at him. He was laughing with Kash about something as she set a mug in front of him, and not looking at me. I sighed and walked up to sit on the stool next to him, not able to keep from letting out a pained grunt and holding my gut. Kash slid a mug in front of me.

We sat in an uncomfortable silence for a minute, then he bowed his head and spoke. "Did you mouth off?"

"You know me. Can't keep a keen observation about someone's inadequacies to myself."

He grunted and took a long pull from his ale. "Bad habit."

218

"Yeah, well people wouldn't know what to do if I suddenly became diplomatic."

He still wouldn't look at me. "This was the Warden. You could be a little more careful. I don't want–" He grumbled and took another drink.

I waited.

When he finally spoke again, he turned to face me. He looked tired, in the way older people grew weary of the world's bullshit. "I don't want to see you die for something as stupid as not being able to keep your mouth shut. The Warden isn't someone to fuck with. She answers to nobody, and she'd love nothing more than to see you hanged."

"I know."

"Then why do you–" He blew out in exasperation again and hunched over his drink. "I know you don't need me telling you what to do, but I can't just sit here and watch you throw your life away."

I turned the mug between my hands, widening the wet ring under it on the bar, staring at the scratches and dents on the surface.

He added, "All I want is for you to be careful, boy."

"I will." As much as I could while still doing what I needed to do.

Rue cleared her throat and we both looked behind us. She stood with a basin of water in her hands, a couple of rags floating in it. Her mouth was set in a tight line and her eyes were wet, but she looked irritated. "You want help with this or not?"

I sighed and pushed my mug away. Sans scooted his stool to one side to give her room to stand between us.

She set the basin on the bar and wrung out one of the rags. As she started cleaning the cut on my jaw, I noticed the amulet around her neck and tapped it with a finger, feeling the buzz of magic. "Isn't that the one I plucked out of a corpse?"

"Yes it is."

"You're actually wearing it?"

"Yes I am."

She was definitely upset about something. I couldn't think of anything I'd done recently, and I was even trying my best to make nice with her boyfriend. Maybe she was upset with him?

She took my chin in her fingers to crank my neck up, and I winced. "Careful. That's sore."

"Then quit hurting yourself."

Ah. Not irritation then, but worry. I glanced at Sans to see him finish his mug and lean over the bar with his own thoughts. Unfortunately, no matter how careful I promised to be, the end was coming.

Rue finished up and dropped the bloody rag in the basin, scowling at my chin. "It's bleeding again, but it's not deep." She pulled a clean rag out of her pocket and pressed it over the cut.

I winced and took the cloth to hold it myself. "It'll be fine. You want to go see Nissa with me?"

She nodded.

I stood, groaning a little, and clapped Sans on the shoulder. "I'll try not to be too stupid."

"Thank you." He stared down at the bartop.

I nodded to myself and ruffled Rue's hair. "Let's go, kid."

***

I waited a full minute at Nissa's door, knocking multiple times, before I gave up and picked the lock. Her room was empty, but the faint buzz of magic told me the stone was still hidden there. Her traveling pack was still there as well, so she was probably just out somewhere. As I turned back to the door, I noticed the paper pinned to the inside and ripped it down.

Gone to guildmaster.

I sighed. The guildmaster was one of the last people I wanted to see right now, especially if Nissa was there as well. I'd have to be very careful not to give away that I knew anything. Besides, the last time Nissa had visited him I'd ended up being dragged along to see the baroness and conscripted by the Warden.

Rue peeked over my arm to read the note. "Are we going to see Rigel then?"

I crumpled it and shoved it into a pocket. "It's that or wait for her to come back."

She moved for the door. "Let's go then. I have a date tonight."

"A date? With the Red?"

"His name is Elias."

I scowled and followed her onto the balcony, then locked the door behind me. There were a number of things I could have said at that point, but most of them were rude, and none of them would be well received. I swallowed it all back.

Rue clomped her way down the steps and I grimaced at the noise she was making. I held my aching gut and followed silently behind her, using the railing when the steps proved painful to navigate.

I let Ruena lead the way into the underground and to the guildmaster's chambers. I was glad for the reprieve from the bright sunlight, and even though it was still a few hours until dark I was going to bed after this conversation. The pain in my gut made me want to throw up, and I kept shifting my jaw trying to make the ache go away.

Ruena asked the two Reds guarding Rigel's door for entrance, and they glanced at me and waited for my brief nod before one of them sighed and rapped a series of knocks on the door. The guildmaster called out from inside.

"Let them in."

I knew as uncomfortable as the collection of magical knickknacks in Rigel's suite was for me, it was likely blinding for Ruena. I shot her a glance and watched her take a deep breath to prepare herself, then push open the door ahead of me. She went in first, then stepped to the side to let me pass. It wasn't often she was on her best behavior, and I was proud she still remembered her manners.

Rigel was seated on a couch with a teapot and a plate of little cakes on the table in front of him. He set the cup he'd been holding on the table as I walked forward.

"To what do I owe this rare visit? Hopefully nothing that requires my intervention."

I'd have been more insulted, but it was true I only came when I needed something. I didn't like giving him the opportunity to find projects for me. I glanced around the room for Nissa. "Did my elfish friend stop by?"

He raised an eyebrow. "No. Is she planning to?"

"I thought she was." I glanced at Rue. "Maybe I was wrong."

"Hmm. Well, did you have something you wanted to talk to me about other than your friend?"

I gingerly took a seat across from him on a fluffy couch that was more comfortable than my bed, then leaned back into it with a sigh. "We could discuss evacuating Sangarie."

He sighed. "I am the leader of a band of beggars and thieves, not a general. This isn't the kind of thing I have experience in."

"And I do? You must have some ideas."

"A few, but I'm still not entirely sure how the underground was spared from the destruction. A force like that should have collapsed the tunnels and destroyed the entrances."

"The destruction was caused by magic. Maybe it just didn't reach underground?"

Rigel grunted and stared at the cup of tea on the table in front of him, his brow creased.

I watched him for a moment, trying to reconcile the image of the most important man in the underworld of Sangarie with that of a heartbroken elfblood. What had led him from there to here? What had driven him to undertake such a massive campaign and seize control of an entire city of criminals?

He steepled his fingers and raised his gaze once more. "What is certain, is we need a better story for why everyone needs to leave so quickly. I'm afraid urban legend won't be enough to convince the masses to uproot themselves, even for a few nights. It would be better if there was some threat they could see coming."

I thought of the burning sky in my vision, and wondered what had been causing it. I had assumed it was Loring, but rumor had it he only kept a handful of people with him, and that was destruction on the scale of a small army. Had some other element been in play that I didn't yet understand?

I played the memory of the vision over and over in my head, trying to find something I'd missed. Something to cause the sky to be burning and people to be screaming. It hadn't been sunset yet, so the Night of Shadows hadn't started, not until I raised the stone…

"Something on your mind, Gray?"

I took a steadying breath and shifted my aching body. "Secrets."

"Care to share the burden?"

I rubbed a hand over my face and flinched at the pain in my jaw. Why not? It was only a few more days now and none of it would matter. "I had a vision five years ago that showed me bits and pieces of what happens. Not much, but enough to know what does it."

"And what did it show you?"

I sighed, a little surprised at how casual I felt about it all. Had I just thought about it so much it no longer had the impact? "The manor of the

222

baroness. I was there with the stone, alongside Nissa and Ruena. The city was full of fire and smoke and the sun was setting. Then I raised up the stone and everything exploded."

Rigel nodded and eased back in his chair, looking deep in thought. Not shocked or afraid, only contemplative. The silence stretched on. With each passing moment my aches and pains settled in more, and I dreaded the soreness of waking up the next morning. At one point Ruena leaned over the back of the couch and put her hand on my shoulder, and I realized I'd started to nod off.

Finally Rigel spoke. "We're worried the people won't believe the truth, so maybe we give them a falsehood they will believe."

"Like what?"

"Something we already know the baroness is afraid of. Loring."

I frowned.

He stood and began to pace between the chairs and small tables, his fingers stroking his neatly trimmed beard. "We'll have to spread the word about the outcast nobleman and his quest for vengeance. Tell people he's raising an army and they intend to take advantage of the Night of Shadows to attack the city. It would raise panic, or incite drastic action from the baroness. I'm sure she will want to deny the danger to the populace."

I nodded. "It wouldn't surprise me. She'd feel like she's losing control."

He raised a finger in my direction. "Exactly. Very good."

I frowned at his eager praise, but pushed on. "There isn't time for rumormongering though, and if we're direct and start spreading the word in public the Warden will have time to shut us down. This has to be kept somewhat under the beggar's robes."

"Indeed. I think we'll spread word through the guild tonight, letting them fortify their spaces against the topside refugees, and on the day of the Night of Shadows we will start to inform the city."

I thought about Sans and his reluctance to leave the Throat. I'd already heard from Ruena that he was planning to lock it down tight while he was gone. "That's not a lot of time for them to prepare."

Rigel pursed his lips and his eyes narrowed in thought. "Perhaps we can spread the word to those loyal to the guild first, let them plant the seeds. The rumors may not have time to spread completely, but they can start. We tell them to keep it to themselves to limit the involvement of the guard, and when the guild supporters disappear into the underground early that day it will give credence to the warnings we send out."

I nodded, but frowned and looked at the floor. "What about your concerns with the underground holding up?"

He continued pacing. "It does hold up, so either my fears are unfounded or I discover a solution to my worries. I suggest you continue playing with the Warden. It will keep her busy so she isn't looking too closely into what we're doing, and you can reinforce the rumors behind her back as you get the chance."

I sighed and rubbed my sore stomach. "Much more time with her and I won't be alive to destroy the city."

"I'm impressed she hasn't imprisoned you already if I'm honest."

"So am I. I think she enjoys torturing me, or she might have."

He chuckled. "The appeal isn't lost on me."

Ruena snorted and I shot her a dirty look. She was leaning against the back of a chair, her eyes averted from the majority of the collected knickknacks.

A knock came from the door in a series different from what they'd rapped out for us. Rigel's head tilted as he listened and deciphered it, his smile slipping. "Let her in."

I looked to the door in time to see it open for Nissa to enter. She raised an eyebrow at me and hesitated, but quickly regained her poise.

"Greetings, king of thieves."

Rigel inclined his head gracefully. "Greetings to you, mistress of the woods. Please, join us."

She started forward, but paused in front of Ruena and reached for the amulet resting on her chest. "Where did you get this?"

Ruena glanced at the guildmaster and then at me, shifting uncomfortably. "Well… Gray found it actually."

Nissa looked at me expectantly.

I shrugged. "Picked it up off a dead guy in jail."

Rigel snorted softly as he retrieved a second teacup and returned to his couch.

Nissa frowned even deeper. "In jail? Who was this dead guy?"

I shrugged. "It was dark. He'd been dead for a while in the abandoned Lower Yard jail and I stumbled upon him while I was…" I glanced at Ruena. "While I was waiting to see the Warden. He must have swallowed it, because it was inside him. Wouldn't have known about it except the kid saw the magic."

Rigel finished pouring the second cup and held it out to Nissa. "Magic you say?"

Nissa hesitated, then joined us and accepted the tea.

He hadn't offered *me* any tea.

She sat on the couch beside me. "It belonged to an acquaintance of mine. I lost touch and have been trying to reach him."

I grimaced. "I'm sorry. I didn't know you had other friends in town."

"He was the builder hired by the baroness to construct the stairs to her new treasury. When she put out the call I made sure someone I could trust got the job."

Rigel sighed. "I'm guessing she had him killed to keep the place secret. She's become obsessed with the thought that someone is after her fortune."

I lounged back on the couch, turning enough that I could see both Nissa and Rigel. "So you know what it does? Is it dangerous?"

Nissa glanced at the amulet around Ruena's neck again. "It is a piece of motherstone."

My brow furrowed. "A *piece* of motherstone? Like the stone we found in the labyrinth?"

"The Enhali Voga Surai is a one of a kind specimen, ancient and powerful, erupted whole from a place deep within the earth. In your language it would translate to First Among Stones. That amulet," she pointed one green-skinned finger at Ruena's chest, "holds a tiny shard of ore, but is still worth a small fortune in human coin, and would be coveted by all human mystics as it represents true magical potential. It is a power source."

Rigel motioned Ruena forward. "Let me see it, child."

She glanced at me and frowned, but came forward as bidden and pulled the chain over her head. "Are you taking it away?"

Rigel accepted it and answered without looking. "I'm asking to borrow it. I think it may help with a hole in our plan."

Her face scrunched up, but she nodded and glanced at me again, looking disappointed.

I was pretty sure she'd never see it again, but maybe Rigel would surprise me.

He held it a moment, then tucked it into a pocket and picked up his tea. "Where were we? Ah yes, what brings you to my quarters, Miss Silvertree?"

Nissa tore her eyes from Rigel's pocket and shot me a look that asked for privacy. Maybe she'd decided to close up some holes in her own past, and since I wasn't supposed to know anything about that I shouldn't stick around for it. I groaned and clutched my gut as I pulled myself out of the couch.

"As fascinating as this is, I need to get some rest if I'm going to be meeting with the Warden at dawn again." I glanced at Nissa. "Speaking of which, she wants to question you as well."

Rigel shook his head. "Stall her. She can't find out too much about things this soon or she'll try to contain it. Tell her the elf will be available the day after tomorrow, because she is entertaining me tomorrow."

Nissa shot Rigel a startled look which she quickly smoothed back into her usual haughtiness.

I grimaced. "She's not going to be happy with me."

"I'll write you a note. She can be unhappy with me."

I sighed, but waited as he fetched paper and ink. She'd still take it out on me somehow, but maybe it wouldn't be a beating or an arrest. I'd be glad when all this bullshit with the Warden was finished and I could go back to avoiding her like my life depended on it.

Note in hand, I steered Ruena ahead of me and made my way to the door. Rigel and Nissa barely noticed, and were staring at each other intently as we walked out. Once we were well out of hearing distance from the Reds guarding the door, I set a hand on Rue's shoulder.

"I'd like you to spread the word to a few people in the morning."

She nodded. "Just tell me who."

28 – Ailred

Before I passed out back at my apartment, I pulled out the crumpled note in my pocket from Nissa's door and scratched a message on the back for Deidre to wake me before dawn. So at the Six-cursed hour of too early for anything, she did.

I blinked at her in confusion for a moment and she plucked the note off the side table and dropped it onto my chest. I groaned and crushed it in my fist before rolling over to go back to sleep, but she lightly slapped my bare back.

"Get up. You can't keep the Warden waiting."

I mumbled into the pillow. "How do you know that's what I'm doing?"

"A little weed told me."

Ruena. I groaned and rolled onto my back again. "Any ideas for getting out of it?"

She sat on the bed next to me, idly tracing a line on my side. A line that came very close to the spot where that crossbow bolt had been buried.

I knew there was no mark. I'd checked pretty thoroughly. Her touch still dredged up anxiety and guilt, and I was glad I already looked bedraggled so I didn't have to worry about schooling my expression too much. The urge to brush her hand away was strong, but it would only make her suspicious.

She sighed. "Why do you have to play these games?"

My stomach dropped and a lump formed in my throat. Had she figured it out? Had someone seen my face at Josyna's manor and told their mistress?

227

The movement of her fingers stopped and she focused fully on me, frowning. "Is everything okay? You suddenly look like a new pickpocket who just got his fingers caught in my purse."

I swallowed thickly and lifted her hand from my side.

Damn. I was jumping to conclusions and making her question things. This is why I didn't like keeping shit from her. I was off my guard around her, and she knew how to read me too well. Think, idiot. "Did Rue tell you about the evacuation?"

She narrowed her eyes, but joined me in the change of topic. "A little. I thought I'd visit our dear guildmaster later this morning and get a better feel for what he's planning."

That should go over well. Hopefully Rigel still trusted her enough to involve her in this. "I told her to warn the crew at the Throat and a few others. Give them plenty of time to prepare."

"Good idea." She watched me closely. "Are you sure there's nothing else?"

I pulled away and sat up, avoiding her gaze. "Just nervous. Feel like I've been staring down the edge of a blade for too long and it's getting to me. Somehow I have to stall the Warden so she doesn't find out about the evacuation too soon."

"Alright."

I could feel her eyes on me as I went to get dressed. I did my best to ignore it, reassuring myself there was no way she could know it had been me in that manor. Lady Josyna wasn't even there, so Deidre had no reason to visit to find anything out.

She crossed the room and set a hand on my arm, pulling me down a fraction to be able to kiss my temple. "Best behavior. I don't want to see you hanging in the square because you mouthed off to the Warden." Her finger came up to stroke along my jaw where the cut was.

I grimaced. "I'll do my best."

She cast one more narrowed gaze at me as she picked up her cloak and walked out of the apartment.

Now she was suspicious. She accepted my excuses for now, but she knew I was hiding something. Hopefully I could get through the next couple of days and destroy the city before I had to face her about it.

***

It was still dark when I went topside, but it wouldn't be for long. The sky was already getting a gray tint to it and the shopkeepers were putting out their merchandise. Smells of baked goods almost covered up the normal smells of Old Town. I had a long walk to Varinston where the Warden's jail was located, so I stuck my hands in my pockets, put my head down, and settled into a block-eating stride.

I lost myself in thoughts of who else I might want to warn ahead of time and Varinston came up much sooner than I expected. I shrugged off my mental list, plastered a smile on my face, and made sure to nod at a few Silvers as they glared at me from the front of their barracks. Maybe politeness would help.

When I stopped in front of the Warden's jail, the Silvers standing outside narrowed their eyes and stepped briskly to either side of the door, waiting for me to enter. Neither of them looked thrilled about it, but they didn't say anything.

I *really* didn't want to go in there.

I took a deep breath and pulled the note from Rigel out of my vest. Hopefully it would get me off the hook. With a nod in their direction, I stepped between them and pushed the door open.

The Warden's jail was a stone building with the windows barred by iron. Inside was a long hallway with heavy doors spaced evenly on both sides and a smaller hallway that branched in both directions in the middle of the building. There were no Silvers in here, and I hesitated as the door swung shut behind me on its own.

I was a master thief, and one of the highest ranked in the guild, so I knew the layout of this building from maps. Senyr was obsessed with being prepared, and the Hands of the Master were tasked with interfacing with the Warden, so he'd made sure I knew what to expect if I was ever called in here. It was one area of my training I'd never complained about. I'd known someday I'd be standing here, desperately wanting to leave, and the knowledge could come in handy. I just hadn't expected to be trying to find my way further in.

The Warden's office was at the end of the hallway. As I passed the intersecting corridors I couldn't resist looking down them. They both ended in a heavy door after about twenty-five feet and beyond those doors would be the jail cells that ran the length of both sides of the building. At least the ones at ground level. There was another level below this one. No guard was stationed at the door on this side, and no guards seemed to be walking the halls. She was pretty confident that her prisoners were secure.

At the Warden's office door, I took another deep breath and rapped my knuckles on the thick wood.

Her voice came from inside, gruff and already sounding cranky. "Come in."

I opened the door and caught her gaze as she looked up from behind her desk. Her expression cycled through a handful of emotions in just a few seconds. The first was surprise, then eagerness, followed by a look of disapproval when she realized I was alone, and culminating in anger. She deliberately set her ink pen back in the holder.

"I thought I told you to bring your elf friend."

"Unfortunately, the guildmaster has her otherwise occupied today." I held the folded note up between two fingers. "He figured you wouldn't believe me, so he sent you a love letter." Snarky? Yes. But it was hard to choke back *all* the snide comments that came to mind when I was this nervous, and she'd be more suspicious if I wasn't at least a little mouthy. Right?

She scowled and held out her hand expectantly.

I kept the smirk on as I stepped deeper into the viper's nest and placed the letter in her hand. I even managed to hold my position on the other side of her desk as she read it.

Her face only got more disgusted and she tossed the letter onto the desk when she'd finished and muttered under her breath. "What is that conniving bastard up to."

"I'm sure I don't know." I took half a step back. "If that's all, I'll just be getting out of your way."

She raised her eyes and shook her head. "Oh no. We still have half a city to search."

Fuck. I'd hoped she'd given up on that. Nobody was going to know anything about Loring, and even if they did, they wouldn't tell her. Not even if I was there and asked them nicely. I still smiled and gave her a bit of a mocking bow of the head.

"As you wish, ma'am."

She glared.

I raised an eyebrow. "Too much?"

"Tell me, thief," she held up a piece of paper from the top of the pile on her desk, "do you know anything about a mystic fortuneteller running down the street before dawn this morning, babbling in terror until she ran headfirst into the side of a building and cracked her skull open?"

I blinked and frowned. That wasn't at all the response I'd been bracing for. "That's a disturbingly vivid question, but no."

"The guild cleaned up everything before my Silvers could get there. All they heard were whispered rumors about what had happened. The old woman had been screaming about shadows watching her, moving in the corners."

A shiver crawled up my spine and raised the hair on the back of my neck.

The Warden's eyes narrowed. "What do you know?"

I swallowed, thinking of the shadows I'd seen, and of Sans and Nissa telling stories about Dakara, god of darkness. "Nothing. This is the first I'm hearing about it."

"I don't believe you. The guilt is all over your face."

I raised both eyebrows and snorted, bringing my thoughts back in line and leaning into the sarcasm. "You mean the reaction of being told the beginning of a horror story? And first thing in the morning, no less? I'm not sure what kind of circles you run in during your off time, but that was some creepy shit."

She growled under her breath.

"Really, Warden, do you think I did more than crawl out of bed half an hour ago and drag myself here? Do you think the entire guild reports to me?"

"Go wait outside the building."

I spun on my heel before my mask of bravado could slip and made my way back out.

The two Silvers stationed outside didn't say a word, even when I stopped a couple of paces away and just stuck my hands in my pockets and stood there, watching the nearby guards going about their morning chores.

If that story was true, could it have been the fortuneteller Nissa spoke to? Had Ailred gotten to her? Shadows watching and lurking around sounded suspiciously like what I'd seen, and what Nissa had described.

Had they killed the woman, or had her crazy mystic brain finally snapped?

I'd have to talk to Nissa as soon as possible and ask her what those shadows were capable of. I shuddered to think of them leeching their way into my brain.

The Warden made me wait for nearly half an hour, but I didn't dare wander off. When she finally did come out, I gave her another courtly head nod. She grumbled and began walking as a whole troop of guards formed up around me.

"Let's go, thief."

I sighed and followed after her, surrounded by Silvers.

We did a repeat of the day before, except in the landward side of the city, stopping at whichever shops or homes the Warden picked out, asking about Loring, and moving on when they had no answers. The one difference in today's search was that a few places seemed to be packing up or muttering to each other when nobody was in earshot. The districts we covered weren't as familiar to me as Old Town, but I'd wager these particular shops and homes were connected to the guild somehow and were preparing to evacuate.

It did wonders for my mood seeing something done to protect at least some of these people. I even quit bowing mockingly to the Warden every chance I got and just walked along and chatted with the people she pointed out. Whenever I could manage it without the Warden or the Silvers noticing, I added rumors about Loring's plans to attack the city on the Night of Shadows, how people were already packing up to be gone that night, and about how the underground would be open to people fleeing the attacks. The more obvious I made it that I was trying not to let the Warden and the Silvers overhear, the more truth it gave my words.

Later in the morning, when the food places were just starting to send tempting scents out of their stalls and windows to entice the lunch crowds, I asked the Warden for a break so I could take a piss. We'd been walking all morning and even my rounds as an enforcer hadn't involved covering so many streets.

She was grumpy and growing suspicious of the odd behavior of some of the shops, but she waved me off and stepped into a cobbler's on her own. A Silver followed me to an alley, came a few paces inside after

232

me, then stood and stared at me. They were obviously not trusting me to stick around.

I sighed and walked deeper in before facing a grimy sidewall to do my business under his watchful gaze. My thoughts turned to the preparing citizens and I wondered if Rue had talked to Sans and his crew yet. I expected him to be on the guildmaster's list anyway, but I'd also told Rue to warn a few of the shopkeepers in Old Town that had always been understanding and kind to me or my people in the past. Some of them I knew wouldn't have been included otherwise.

As I finished up and turned back toward the mouth of the alley I stopped and stared at the unmoving body of the guard on the cobbles just out of sight of the street. I hadn't heard a thing, and a man falling to the ground in a breastplate made a lot of noise.

My gaze darted around the alley and I turned to look behind me as well. A figure stood a little ways off, concealed by a cloak with a deep hood. From what I could see below the clasped cloak, he wore sturdy leggings and tight leather boots like a forester, along with fitted gloves. My first thought was it could be Rue's Red, but the clothing beneath was wrong.

I scowled and took a step backward, toward the fallen body of the guard. "Who the fuck are you?"

A melodious chuckle came from under the hood. "I could have killed you just as easily, but I wanted to ask you something first."

If I called out, the Silvers would come running. Assuming they were still alive out there. But the real question was whether they'd get here in time to stop whatever this person was planning to do. My instincts told me I was in more danger than it looked, and I tried not to ignore those hunches. I took another step away. "A lot of people seem to have questions for me lately."

"Where is the stone?"

My expression tightened, but I tried to look casual as I edged closer to the downed Silver. Definitely more dangerous. It had to be someone connected to Loring, and this one wasn't mindlessly brainwashed. "You don't expect me to answer that, do you?"

The head lifted enough to give me a brief glimpse under the concealing hood, revealing a green-toned, angular chin with a nearly lipless smirk dimpled by an elf's long incisors.

A shiver went up my back and I stumbled over the guard's outstretched arm, keeping my gaze locked on the figure before me. He was an elf. Probably the elf mentioned in those letters. The one who'd magicked Loring's would-be assassins. There was no telling what power he had.

His voice was smooth and haunting, sliding into my head. "You will show me."

Fuck this. I spun and shouted at the same time, only a few yards from view of the street. "*Guards*!"

The plan was to dart around the corner where it was a dozen feet at most to the wide street and the Silvers waiting there. Hopefully once I rounded the corner I'd be somewhat protected from any ranged attack the elf might have.

I reached the corner and a bright green light overtook me, then solidified into the elf directly in front of me. I was going too fast to stop and barreled into the figure, sending both of us crashing to the cobbles.

I lifted myself off him and prepared to launch into motion again, but he gripped my arm and pulled me back down, slapping his other hand against my forehead as he spoke a sharp word of command.

Everything became muted and I froze in place. I recognized the shouting of the guards and the sound of armored boots, but it seemed far away, smothered in shadow. A whispering noise hung in the air, just quiet enough for me to hear the sound but not the words. My eyes met the glowing emerald eyes of the elf and I couldn't look away.

His slithery voice was the only thing I could hear clearly. "You will bring it to me."

It was like the world around me had slowed down. I stared back at him, and for the first time since this whole fiasco started I knew what I had to do. There was no worry, no doubt. I was no longer afraid of what was coming, or troubled by what I was going to do about it. I had a goal. A direction.

An arm wrapped around my chest and flung me to one side, breaking my contact with the elf. The shouting and chaos of the guards swarming us rushed back in a deafening wave and I shook my head as I picked myself up off the ground. Two Silvers gripped me by the arms and dragged me away from the elf as I tried to get my bearings.

The elf, held down by guards and seeming amused more than anything, barked a short word and shrank into nothing in a flash of green light, which shot up the side of the nearest building only to expand and solidify back into the figure of the elf on the edge of the roof. His laugh rang through the alley and he quickly darted out of sight across the rooftops above.

I stared after him, ignoring the shouting as the Warden ordered her people to track him down. He'd probably be headed back to Loring. I wasn't too worried about it, though. I had a feeling I'd be able to find him when I needed to.

After I retrieved the stone.

The guards dragged me forward, forcing me to my knees in front of the furious Warden. She didn't seem all that intimidating anymore and I smirked up at her.

She glared back. "Who was that? Your elf friend?"

"That was *Loring's* elf friend. Good luck tailing him."

"He seemed very interested in you."

I couldn't very well have her arresting me. I wouldn't be able to get the stone away if I couldn't move freely. "I'm glad your guards were so quick to respond or he might have managed to kill me. Too bad they weren't fast enough to catch him too."

Her face got even more red. "Mind your tongue, thief, or next time I'll let you die."

I scowled back, but kept my mouth shut.

29 – Magic Haze

They held me for nearly half an hour, until the Warden dismissed me with a disgusted grunt and told me to report to her office again at sunrise with my elf friend or she'd track me down and have me dragged through the streets behind her horse. It wasn't hard to notice the man who peeled off to follow me as I started back toward Old Town. Did she really think I couldn't shake one of her men? He was nowhere near the level of a Yellow or a Red.

I ignored him for now, thinking about my options as I strolled along. I needed to get into Nissa's room and get the stone without her knowing, because I was pretty sure she wouldn't understand what I was doing. Then I needed to find the elf and give it to him. I didn't know exactly where the elf was, but I knew he was outside the city to the east.

Getting outside the city would be tricky with the Warden having locked down the gates, but not impossible, especially if I waited until after dark. There was a tunnel from the underground that led through the east wall and came up in a ditch nearby. I'd just have to make sure nobody saw me climb out.

It was still early afternoon, so I had a lot of time to kill until dark and I didn't want to carry the stone around with me. I wasn't looking forward to touching it at all. At any rate, it'd be best to swing by and take it after dark if I could get Nissa called away. Maybe I could tell Rue to take her somewhere.

In the meantime, I figured I'd lead my trailing Silver to the bar and make him think I was settling in for a night of gambling and drinking. Later on I could slip out and he'd be left watching the bar while I did what I needed to do.

I headed for the Throat, making sure not to lose my new friend in the crowd prematurely. As I went, I found myself smiling at people who recognized me, pausing to chat and give a few words of encouragement. I was in a great mood now that I knew what I had to do, and even if I hadn't wanted to waste the Silver's time I'd have gone to the Throat. I could finally relax a little.

All throughout the city people were whispering behind their hands and boarding up their homes. Rigel's notices must have gone out with every Yellow he could find. In Old Town especially I saw evidence of people preparing for the worst. When I walked into the Throat hardly anyone was there.

Sans looked up from his place behind the bar and breathed a heavy sigh of relief before limping over. "Glad to see you, boy."

I grinned and seated myself at the bar. "Glad to be here. It's been a long week."

"You can say that again. I've got Kash and Basil in the back trying to secure everything they can. Word is spreading, so not many people have been coming in this afternoon."

I glanced over my shoulder at the tables. "I noticed. I'd been hoping to play some cards or dice, but I guess I'll have to settle for just the drinking."

Sans frowned, but obliged with a mug which he filled before speaking again. "Not many people in the mood for gaming today. I'm kind of surprised you are."

I shrugged and took a long pull from the mug, then sighed in appreciation. "I've been worrying too much. Today everything kind of came to a head and I realized I only needed to concern myself with one thing."

Sans had his brows furrowed and leaned on the bar from his side. "And what is that?"

Maybe I was being a little *too* nonchalant about things. I couldn't very well tell him about the stone. One of the first things you learned as a thief was not to count your gold until you were clear of your mark. I smiled back at him with my most charming expression. "Just the next thing in front of me. I was thinking too far ahead."

One of his shaggy eyebrows shot up. "I suppose that's good advice."

"Maybe I'm getting wiser in my golden years?"

He snorted and started packing mugs into a crate I hadn't seen on the floor. He must have been worried someone would break in while the

237

Throat was shut down for the Night of Shadows. He'd said Kash and Basil were securing things, so maybe they were packing away their stores someplace safer.

I shook my head, but kept the grimace off my face. There wasn't anything to worry about anymore. If I took the stone to the elf, the Night of Shadows wouldn't happen. I couldn't destroy something with it if I didn't have it. Nissa had to be wrong about things getting broken from not happening the way they were supposed to.

I took another long drink, my thoughts struggling with the idea that things weren't adding up. She'd never really explained what would happen if Sangarie wasn't destroyed. I'd taken her at her word that it would be horrible, but this other elf seemed to think differently. Maybe she was wrong and it wasn't as dire as she made it out to be. Maybe I could escape that vision after all. If so, the city wouldn't be destroyed and it was a good thing Sans was protecting his property.

I pushed the line of thinking aside. It was giving me a headache. Instead I focused on making small talk with Sans as he worked, enjoying the luxury of not having to worry constantly about how to stop the future from coming to pass. I even regaled him with a few of the stories and jokes I remembered from my evening at the Wolf and Bear. It was good to hear his rolling laughter again.

A few hours later the door opened and I turned as Ruena jogged inside. Her face lit up when she spotted me, then her expression tightened. She looked uncomfortable and dropped her gaze to the floor.

What was that all about? "Hey kid. Come have a drink with me."

Her eyes darted up to mine, then down again, and she fidgeted in the doorway. "No. I'm good. What are you doing?"

My eyebrow shot up. "Having a mug of ale. Why are you so jumpy?"

She glanced at Sans, and I followed her gaze to see him frowning back at her. Was I missing something? I wasn't bleeding at the moment, and I hadn't threatened her Red lately, so I didn't know what could be bothering her so much. "Everything okay?"

She nodded and reached behind her back for the door. "Yeah. I just remembered something I forgot to do. I'll be back in a little bit."

With that, she spun and darted out the door, letting it swing shut on its own.

I glanced at Sans, but he shrugged and focused on the crate at his feet. "Don't look at me. You raised her."

***

I was nearly finished with another mug of ale by the time the door opened again and Ruena entered with a hooded figure at her heels. After the door closed, gloved hands came up to pull back the hood and reveal Nissa's scowling face.

My chest immediately tightened and I had the urge to get up and leave, but instead I plastered on a smile and tipped my mug in her direction. This was probably a good thing. This way I knew where she was and I could figure out how to get her somewhere else later on when I needed to break into her room.

She walked straight up to me and peered into my eyes, looking as disappointed as I'd ever seen her. Her gaze was intense enough that I squirmed on my seat and cleared my throat.

Ruena stood nearby, wringing her hands.

I rose from the chair, intending to put some space between us. "What in the Six are you–"

Nissa's hand shot out and slapped against my forehead, her fingertips curling into the skin with a grip that felt like it was going to leave bruises.

I dropped the mug of ale and tried to break away as she shouted something I didn't catch. A force of some kind slammed into my mind, brushing clean through and scattering everything. My sight went entirely to white and all I could hear was the thump of my own startled heartbeat.

***

I staggered back, catching myself out of pure instinct on the surface of the bar beside me.

The bar?

I glanced around quickly and recognized the familiar common room of the Throat. Sans was staring wide-eyed at me. Nissa was glaring, lowering her hand beneath her cloak. Ruena–

Ruena jumped forward and flung her arms around my middle, hugging me and pressing her face into my chest with a muffled sob. I froze, raising my gaze to meet Nissa's.

239

I was so confused. I was just in an alley with that elf of Loring's, who had somehow appeared out of thin air in front of me, and now I was standing in the Throat. The Warden was gonna be so pissed that I'd disappeared right in front of her eyes. "Care to tell me what's going on?"

Nissa sighed, but before she could say anything Ruena looked up at me from where she was clinging to my chest. "Someone messed with your head. I walked in and saw that same hazy cloud around you that the guy in the alley had."

I frowned and wedged a hand between us, pushing her back, then caught Nissa's gaze. "Is that true?"

"Indeed. You seem to have been under some kind of compulsion."

My brow furrowed and I dropped my gaze as I ran over the last few things I remembered, trying to make a connection. The elf had appeared in front of me. I'd smacked right into him and toppled us both. I'd tried to get up...

Had he grabbed me? I remembered his eyes and his smirk, but that was it.

Ruena spoke from a few feet off, clutching her arms around herself. "Are you feeling okay now?"

"I have a nasty headache, and I can't remember anything past encountering that elf, but otherwise yeah."

Sans leaned over the bar, his voice pitched low. "People are staring."

I looked across the room. There weren't many people in the Throat, and only one that I didn't recognize, but sure enough they were all staring at our group. That could have been because Nissa didn't have her hood up and was very obviously an elf. Or it could have been because she'd just shoved me hard enough to knock the magic out of me.

I cleared my throat and tipped my head toward the back storage room. "Let's talk."

Ruena walked on my heels all the way to the back room, then hovered over me as I sat on a barrel against shelves that seemed to have been half emptied already. Kash set down the box she'd been moving and scowled at the four of us, then looked at Sans.

He tipped his head back the way we'd come. "Go watch the bar, would you?"

She narrowed her eyes, but didn't protest. With a last muttered comment to Basil, which sent him scurrying out the back door, she nodded at me and left.

I sighed as I leaned my throbbing head against the shelf. As if I didn't have enough to worry about with all that was going on, now I had an elf trying to control my brain. I tried to sense whether something was wrong in my head, or figure out if my thoughts were my own now, but I wasn't even sure how you'd know.

Nissa looked down at me. "Do you know what the compulsion was trying to get you to do?"

My brow creased as I struggled to remember anything from the alley to here. I didn't even know how long I'd been brainwashed. Had I lost hours? *Days*? I looked down at myself and the grime from tussling in the alley with the elf, still very evident on my clothes. Not days then. "I have no idea. I can't even remember how I got here."

Sans groaned as he eased himself onto another barrel, rubbing his bum knee. "I thought you seemed a little more cheerful than you've been lately. More like your old self. Not a care in the world."

Nissa turned her emerald gaze to him. "Did he say anything that might tell us what he was doing or thinking about?"

Sans shrugged. "Just wanted to gamble and drink."

I snorted. "I'm a thief and a liar, You may not have picked up anything important if I was hiding it."

Ruena tore her gaze off me to look at Nissa. "Can you get in his head and find out?"

I narrowed my eyes at her and my "no" was in chorus with the elf's. I continued, "Nobody's digging around in my head again."

Nissa crossed her arms over her chest. "I do not understand why Loring shifted from trying to kill you to trying to get you to do something for him."

"Could he have ordered me to kill myself?"

She shook her head. "Not directly. He could have ordered you to do something that would indirectly cause your death, but self-preservation remains despite the strongest compulsion spell."

"To get me out of the way? Maybe he ordered me to go drink and play cards instead of fucking around with his plans?"

"I doubt it. The risk of getting to you would suggest a stronger move."

"Will he know you broke the spell?"

She shook her head. "Not until you fail to do whatever he ordered."

"Then let's not worry about it. As long as you're sure it's gone, we'll just have to watch out for the elf showing up again."

She finally met my gaze, her eyes narrowed in thought. "You may not see him coming. He can utilize disguises the same way I can."

Just the possibility that any random person on the street could be this elf waiting to kill or control me was enough to make me shiver. If I gave into that paranoia I'd never leave my apartment. "He probably doesn't know yet, right?"

She shook her head. "Not until you fail to follow through."

"Which could be days."

"Or hours."

I sighed and leaned my head against the shelf again. "It doesn't matter. I can't hide away."

Ruena was twisting the hem of her shirt into a knot and looked over at Nissa. "Isn't there some kind of magic protection you could do?"

She scowled back, then stared at me. "There are things I can do to protect myself, but nothing for someone else. I can only remove it once it has been placed."

I waved Ruena off. "It's fine. You'll just have to watch for magic clouds around me, yeah?"

She frowned, but nodded.

"Let's get out of this storeroom and let Kash and Basil work. I think it's time I was headed home anyway."

Sans sighed and creaked to his feet. "It must be nearing midnight by now. Things have been slow all day, so they'll either get very busy soon as people try to soothe their nerves, or it's going to be a long quiet night." He offered me a hand.

I stared at it for a moment, realizing how tired I must look if the old barkeep was offering to help me up, but in the end I accepted. The headache had started to fade, but the weariness was settling in. I was also buzzing just a little, and wondered how much I'd had to drink during the hours I couldn't remember.

30 – Exposing Josyna

It took a little effort to convince Ruena I could walk home by myself, but she finally relented after making me promise to go straight there.

The fresh air did wonders for the haze that had been mucking up my thoughts, and I didn't go underground until I absolutely had to, finishing the short jaunt to my room and trying to think of what I was going to tell Deidre about my day if she asked.

I needn't have worried, because the apartment was empty. Deidre's fancy cloak was still hanging by the door, so maybe she'd gone to the baths or to visit a friend. I bent to take off my boots and my gaze lit on a piece of quality parchment paper under the table.

I picked it up and unfolded it. In a fancy looping script was written a simple message.

Lady Midnight, please come to my manor tonight. I have news you'll be dying to hear. J.

I scowled at the words and read them a second time. Lady Midnight was Deidre's alias with the nobility. It was hard to tell from the handwriting alone, but I was guessing "J" was the elusive Lady Josyna.

I fought down the instinctive panic, trying not to imagine in too much detail what could be happening on the hill right now. If Josyna had returned, her servants would have told her about the break-in. What if she suspected Deidre was to blame? What if she thought someone was onto her and wanted to eliminate any loose threads?

Dying to hear…

Maybe the noblewoman was working with Loring and he was trying a new tactic. Deidre could be walking into a trap. Loring had used her before, and I had no doubt he'd use her again to get to me if he had the opportunity. If he knew his elf's compulsion had failed, he could have opted for a more direct approach.

243

Dying to hear...

I crumpled the note in my fist and glanced at the door. Walking into the estates would be risky with everything else going on. The Silvers were on edge because of the Warden's frantic searching, and that elf could still be out there waiting to jump me again. We also hadn't figured out what Josyna was up to, and whether it was in the guild's favor or not.

My gaze settled on Deidre's cloak. It had been a gift from one of the wealthier nobles. I personally thought it was gaudy and tasteless, dark blue velvet trimmed in white fur, a scattering of stars on the hem done in real silver thread.

But it was *recognizable.*

She usually wore it when going to the estates for business, and the Silvers would be familiar with it. I stuffed the note into a pocket just in case I needed more proof. On the way out I picked up the cloak and slung it over my arm.

***

Walking through the city set my teeth on edge. I was looking into every shadow and glancing into every alley hoping I didn't run into the crazy elf or more of Loring's brainwashed assassins. It occurred to me that I hadn't seen any of the strange moving shadows in days, and the thought made me pause and look about nervously. Was I just not seeing them, or had they stopped watching me? I wasn't sure which option worried me more. I had to stop myself from breaking into a jog multiple times.

The Silvers at the gate turned me away. They only snorted at the note I held and rightly concluded it didn't give me access to the hill. One of them even had the gall to make shooing motions with his hand and I glared at him as I spun on my heel and walked back the way I'd come.

I had to get through that wall.

After a few blocks I glanced over my shoulder to make sure I wasn't being watched, then ducked onto a side street to the south and doubled back. I made my way to the same rickety building I'd used to cross the wall after my disastrous break-in at Josyna's, growling at the Yellow there about guild business before yanking open the trap door and making my way to the other side.

I took a little more time at the back passage, making sure I wouldn't be spotted by any guards that happened to be walking on top of the wall or straying from the gates. Josyna's manor was across the dusty expanse of the passage, and as I hurried to a nearby alley so I could come at it by the front door I glanced at the splash of blood on the garden wall and shuddered.

It was only a few days ago that the Lady's servants had tried to kill me, and though I was certain they hadn't seen my face and I'd been dressed in richer clothes, I knew better than to think it was impossible to be recognized. Those servants had been skilled guard-types, and I hadn't tried to hide my build or change my movements.

By the time I was striding up to the front door I was tense and jumpy. I swallowed my misgivings and rang the bell, straightening my vest and holding the cloak over my arm in front of me like a shield.

The door opened and I almost sighed in relief that I didn't recognize the person behind it. He was an older man, dressed in a slightly worn jacket that was immaculately clean and unwrinkled. The shirt beneath was crisp and clean as well, and his boots were even shiny.

He glanced down at the cloak I held and his eyes narrowed. "Can I help you?"

"I hope so. My friend is here visiting the lady of the house and she forgot to bring her cloak with her. It gets very cold at night, and I don't want to see her catch a chill." It was a stupid excuse, but it was all I could come up with when I didn't know the specifics of Deidre's visits here. I couldn't think of any real reason for them to admit me, so I was relying on improvisation to figure out how to get inside. I expected him to try to take the cloak and shut the door in my face.

The man glanced at it again, then nodded. "Come with me."

I stared after him a moment.

That had worked surprisingly well. Too well. This was probably a trap, and I could either leave Deidre here and walk away from it, or fall into it. Son of a bitch.

I stepped inside and closed the door behind myself, following the man through the expansive entry hall. It was dimly lit this late at night. We went up the main staircase I hadn't gotten a chance to use the last time I was here, but the man stopped at the base of the stairs leading to the third floor.

He moved to one side, turning to look at me with a piercing stare and waving a hand up the stairs and toward a door on the right that could just barely be seen on the next level. "Lady Midnight went that way."

The door he indicated led to the corridors full of suites. I remembered peeking out of it onto the landing during my last visit, so I knew where Deidre was most likely to be, but I couldn't let on or they'd get suspicious. "Where do I go?"

The man gestured again. "One of the third floor servants will be waiting."

Great. Hopefully it wasn't one of the ones that had chased me through the building last time. I took a steadying breath and turned my back on the man as he trudged down the stairs.

Sure enough, as soon as I reached the third floor and opened the door a man inside pushed away from the wall where he'd been leaning and looked me up and down. I didn't recognize him, but I hadn't gotten a good look at the faces of all the people chasing me that night.

This man was fit, wore clothes befitting a traveling sword for hire, and had a crossbow hanging from his belt. I swallowed thickly as I tore my eyes away from it and smiled. "I'm here to talk to Deid–Lady Midnight."

"Follow me."

The man led me through the familiar corridor to the suite where I'd found all the letters. He paused at the door and knocked with the back of his knuckles. "Your visitor."

A feminine voice muttered from inside and I was certain it was Deidre's. Relief washed through me and I moved forward as the man stepped aside and opened the door for me. The sitting room of the suite was empty, but the doors that led further in were open, and light was coming from the study. The main door closed softly behind me.

The rugs muffled my already quiet footsteps, and I tossed the cloak over the back of a couch on my way to the study, not sure what I'd find. I certainly didn't expect to see Deidre sitting at the desk in her finery with half a glass of wine at her side and a scattering of papers before her. She was leaning back in the chair with one leg crossed over the other and her hands folded demurely on her knee. Her mouth quirked a little at the corner when I came into view.

A quick scan of the room told me we were alone. I glanced over my shoulder at the door that led to the unlit bedroom. Was the Lady Josyna in there?

"It's just us, my love."

I frowned. "Didn't you come here to meet with the noblewoman?" As soon as I said it, I knew it wasn't true. I looked at her again, taking note of the casual ease with which she sat at the desk and the scattered papers before her. The quiet confidence in her posture, so different from her work persona. My jaw tightened. "You *are* the noblewoman."

She grimaced. "Are you angry?"

"Angry?" I was trying to rearrange the pieces in my head. Weirdly, this made a lot more sense than the story Senyr and Neffrey had told me about Lady Josyna. All the little inconsistencies were lining up, and I was disgusted that I hadn't put it together sooner. I blamed the impending destruction of the city for distracting me. "No. A little embarrassed maybe."

She rose from the chair, taking a few steps toward me and smoothing her skirts. "I'm sorry I couldn't tell you. I didn't want you getting mixed up in it if I messed up."

"You mean if you got caught."

"Well… yes. Or if I tugged on the wrong strings. These are dangerous people."

I glanced at the map of the city on the wall, the shelves of books on nobility and politics, and the desk of papers. Surely she couldn't be working against the guild after all… "What are you trying to do?"

She followed my gaze, then looked back at me. "It started out as a way to help the workers on the hill. I've seen so many things up here that turned my stomach in my years as an escort. People that don't have the protection of the guild."

"It's not enough to smuggle them out and find work for them elsewhere?"

"I can only do so much as an escort. At the end of the day I'm still just a prostitute to the nobility. But if I were a noblewoman myself I'd have the power to influence change. So I used the gifts meant to curry my favors and bought all this." She gazed at the study around her.

"Neffrey and Senyr are very concerned with the doings of Lady Josyna and what it means for the guild."

"I know. There's a Yellow spy on the floors below." She met and held my gaze. "And they sent someone to snoop around up here a few days ago."

There was no longer a reason to keep my break-in from her now that I knew about her ruse. She was telling me what had been going on, laying her cards on the table, and there was nothing to gain by holding onto my own secrets. I sighed and opened my mouth to tell her, but she narrowed her eyes and interrupted me.

"It *was* you."

I gave a little shrug and a sheepish smile.

Her face flushed. "They told me the person was probably dead. They'd shot him in the gut with a crossbow, and there was blood all over behind my garden wall."

"Yeah. They did."

Her eyes dropped down my chest to my abdomen and her brow wrinkled. "You weren't injured, though."

I raised an eyebrow. "Oh I was. Your hired swords are pretty good. If it hadn't been for Rue's friend and Nissa's magic I would have been the Six's problem."

Her face paled and she moved forward to tug on the bottom of my shirt with shaking hands. "Show me."

Now it was my turn to blush. The tickle of her fingers on bare skin, the sweet scent of the wine on her breath, and the hint of adrenaline from being in one of the estates of the rich when I was definitely not supposed to be there was working me up. I glanced back at the sitting room behind us, listening for any sign that her hired guards were around. "I'm not sure this is the most appropriate place for that."

She paused, her face tilting up so she could meet my eyes. Hers widened as she caught my shift in mood. The scent of moonflower hit me and her skirt brushed against my legs.

How long had it been? Our duties kept us busy, and our sleep times barely overlapped anymore. Every moment we got alone was ruined by injury or impending disaster. I missed her touch. I looked away and sighed.

She shifted closer and her forearms came to rest on my shoulders, her fingers sliding through the hair at the back of my head. Her voice was low and raspy, like the feel of velvet. "This is the perfect place."

I snorted softly. "The manor of a fake noblewoman, with her guards probably walking the corridor outside?"

"Fake or not, I bought this house. And I pay those guards." She slipped her hands down my chest and around my waist. "Besides, haven't you ever thought about having a noble lady in her own bed?"

The corner of my mouth twitched a little. "I'm not really into noble ladies."

Her eyes shone and she smirked. "Oh really?"

"Really."

She tightened her arms around my waist, pulling our hips together. I'm sure it was fairly obvious to her I was lying, considering the bulge between us. Although it was *her* in her noble finery I thought about and not any of the rich court ladies on the hill. The thought of stripping her out of the silk and satin, of freeing her hair from the artful tresses until it fell around us, that was on my mind every time I saw her dressed up to impress her clients.

I gripped her arms just below the shoulders, figuring that was the safest place, and she breathed on my neck as she whispered, "Do you want to feel what it's like to have everything?"

Her scent and the press of her body had my blood racing. I ducked my head and nuzzled her ear, whispering back. "I already have everything. I have you."

I saw her ear turn red even if I couldn't see her cheeks, and bent to kiss it softly, then added, "But I wouldn't mind having you here."

She gave a little laughing hum and turned her head to kiss me fully, clinging to my waist and pressing hard against my hips. I could taste the wine now and closed my arms around her shoulders.

There was an urgency in her kiss that perfectly matched mine, building up the need I'd been neglecting for so long. I tried to pull away to shrug out of my vest. Deidre moved her hands to my head, holding my jaw and the back of my neck to keep me close enough to kiss as I tugged the fabric off my arms, then worked on getting the belt off that held my knives. Her palm pressed against the cut on my jaw, but I ignored it.

I dropped the knives in the same general area as the vest, barely registering the dull thunk as they hit the floor, and moved back into her.

Fuck the Night of Shadows. Fuck Loring and his pet elf. Tonight we were far away from all of that and I meant to enjoy it.

31 – Morning After

I didn't know what time it was.

We had started in the study, but after a wine glass shattered on the floor and prompted the guard outside to ask if everything was alright, we retreated giggling to the bedchamber. The first time was urgent and exhilarating, then Deidre insisted on examining me for any sign of bolt holes. Her expert hands wandered and we built up to a second time.

We fell asleep in each other's arms, buried in fluffy pillows and thick blankets. It was the best sleep I'd had in months. When I woke, I curled up tighter around her and sighed, setting my cheek against the top of her head.

The opening of the outer door brought me to full wakefulness and I tensed to roll out of bed, but Deidre clutched my arm to her chest and hushed me, then whispered. "They won't come in here. Just be quiet."

I relaxed around her the best I could, my ears pricked in the direction of the half-open door leading to the sitting room. I couldn't see anything, but I could hear footsteps, then what sounded like a tray being set down with the clinking of dishes.

"Lady Josyna, your lunch." The voice was deep and a little rough, but respectful.

Deidre called out in return. "Thank you, Rylan."

The footsteps moved to the outer door and once I heard the latch swing closed I finally let the remaining tension out of my muscles. "Lunch?"

Deidre shifted in my arms and raised herself to her elbow, glancing at the shuttered window. "It would seem so."

I stretched and watched her climb off the bed, pull on a silk robe over her nakedness, and pad out to the sitting room.

It occurred to me that I was probably the only outsider other than Deidre to be allowed onto this floor of the manor, and I'd been here for a very long time. It was a little shocking someone hadn't interrupted us sooner. I frowned and eased myself out of the bed as well.

I didn't have a robe near to hand, so I searched the floor in the dim light coming from the sitting room until I found my pants. The rest could wait. I finished tying the front laces as I stepped into the other room. "Deid?"

She was on a couch, blowing into a steaming cup of tea. "Yes dear?"

Someone really should have been questioning my presence. I had a sneaking suspicion… "How did you know I was coming here last night?"

She had the decency to blush. "I thought it was time to tell you what was going on, so I left a few suggestive clues. I wasn't sure you'd figure it out."

I scowled as I remembered the note. "I was worried about you."

"Would you have come if you weren't?"

"You could have just asked outright."

She pushed a small plate from the tray closer to me. It held a couple of artfully stacked sandwiches. "I didn't know if you'd be the one to find the note."

I picked up a sandwich before joining her on the couch. A glance at the rest of the tray revealed various types of cut fruit and vegetables, some tiny bread rolls with the butter glaze still dripping, little cubes of cheese and slices of cold sausage, two glasses of juice, and a second teacup. They'd prepared enough for us both.

The sandwich was some kind of thinly sliced meat and cheese, with crisp cucumbers and a tangy sauce. It tasted okay and the ingredients were all high quality and fresh, but as I chewed I thought about how I would have preferred something from the bakery in Old Town, or the little restaurant by the docks that specialized in fish and fried potatoes.

Deidre sighed and leaned back on the couch with her teacup in both hands. "I was planning on telling you what I'd found here, but since you've already broken in to steal all my secrets, maybe you should just ask me questions?"

I stuffed the last big bite of sandwich into my mouth, chewing as I tried to think of what to say to that, then washed it all down with juice. I still didn't know what her purpose was in doing this. I didn't believe she was a traitor, but what was she up to? I glanced at the study, then back to her. "First off, why are you tracking Loring?"

She dropped her gaze to her lap and gave a little inaudible snort. "I wasn't as willing to move on as you were. I knew he'd come back eventually, and I wanted to be ready."

"How many people are working for you?"

"Not as many as you might think." She looked across at the door to the corridor. "I mean, there are quite a few servants in the manor, but most of them are sheltering here and working for their bed and board rather than permanently employed. I've learned a few good people are better than a host of mediocre ones. There are less than a dozen that I employ myself. Six stationed here, one whose job is to track Loring, and a few others working in the interests of Lady Josyna in other parts of the kingdom, mainly managing properties I've acquired over the years. I have to keep up the pretense of nobility. The servants downstairs only work in exchange for shelter until they can find someplace else."

"How much money did you–" I frowned and looked down. I knew she was given lots of gifts from the nobles she took as clients, but I figured she siphoned that into her people smuggling. If she had enough left over to buy this manor, along with all the businesses I'd seen in her financials, and employ these servants, how much was she actually making as an escort?

And more importantly, how much was she hiding from Rigel? Escorts paid a tax to the guild on their earnings, and it wasn't light. It was somewhat amusing that he'd become suspicious because of how little she spent instead of how much she seemed to hold back.

I wasn't sure I wanted to know, but... "Are you cheating Rigel that much? Is that why you're keeping this a secret?"

She grimaced. "I was cheating a little bit. At first. We all do. But the investments I was making to get people out of the city started bringing in more than I expected. It let me purchase little stores and inns outside of Sangarie so I could relocate even more people and help them start fresh. I ended up needing someone I trusted to manage it all, so I found a pair of very bright women to seek out and obtain opportunities when they presented themselves.

"Eventually we decided I needed a true presence in the city, so the persona of Lady Josyna was created. Her past was fabricated and emissaries acted on her behalf to obtain this manor, then it was relatively simple to become the paid companion of the sickly noblewoman."

I shook my head. I had no idea she was doing all this. "How long?"

She blushed. "Things have been building for the last seven years or so. After the ordeal with Beth and Loring is when I started hiring others to help me. I knew I couldn't do it on my own anymore."

"You couldn't have mentioned any of this to me?"

She set her teacup on the low table and shifted to face me. "At first I didn't want to risk bringing anyone else in, even you. I mean, the Six know half the time you're being watched by the Yellows just so Rigel can keep his eye on you."

I raised an eyebrow and shrugged in agreement. I was good at giving them the slip when I wanted to, but now that I was a Hand of the Master every beggar in the city took note of my passage just so they could locate me in a pinch. I wouldn't say they were actively following me, but Neffrey could string a whisper and two farts into a solid picture of my comings and goings if he wanted to. Or so he claimed.

"Not to mention Rigel has you marked to take over for him someday."

I glared at her. "That isn't going to happen."

She sighed. "I know you don't want to, but he's preparing you for it whether you like it or not. I couldn't risk him turning his eye on your relationships. He's a meddler, and I don't want him meddling in my affairs just to manipulate you."

I settled back into the couch, not looking at her. Did she realize how suspicious Rigel had grown of her? Did I tell her the real reason I was investigating here? "Why tell me now?"

"Mainly because Senyr and Neffrey have been snooping into Lady Josyna." She looked to the study. "And because I located Loring."

A shudder went up my back and I felt like the shadows behind the furniture were watching me, even though I knew that was ridiculous. "You did?"

She nodded. "He's encamped east of the city. I got a message with his location this morning."

I twisted to sit sideways on the couch, focusing entirely on her. "How many people are with him? Did they see an elf there? Did they find out what he's up to?"

She shook her head and set her cup on the low table. "There were less than a dozen people in the camp. I don't know if there are more nearby, but as far as they could tell he's only brought a small retinue. They never mentioned an elf. Although…"

I waited, watching the lines tighten on her face as she pondered. It took all my patience not to grip her hands and urge her to tell me whatever she knew.

She sighed and bit her lip. "He's involved in something. I'm not sure what it is, but a cloaked figure is always at his side, so maybe that's the elf you're talking about. My reports say Loring is losing his grip on reality, screaming and ranting about shadows and destiny. He must have something or someone powerful on his side, otherwise why would he think he could take over a city with just a handful of men?"

My brow furrowed. "I don't think he needs any men. I just haven't figured out how he plans to do it."

"We should go to Rigel. Maybe we can find a way to stop him before he gets to the city."

"Sure." My mind whipped back to the situation at hand, and my reason for being in this manor. "We could do that."

She narrowed her eyes. "What aren't you telling me?"

Was it even worth telling her at this point? Everything was on the table, but if she knew about Rigel doubting her would it change anything? For that matter I wasn't even certain this was enough evidence to satisfy his suspicions.

"What is it?"

I glanced down at her fingers twined in mine. "You said Senyr and Neffrey were snooping."

"Yes… There's a Yellow downstairs, and the break-in had to have been on Senyr's orders. I'm sure they've grown suspicious of Lady Josyna's—"

"It's not Josyna I was looking into. Well, not entirely."

A little crease appeared on her brow and she frowned. "Me."

"Rigel noticed some inconsistencies. Your close relationship with a mysterious noblewoman. Your refusal to talk about her. They thought

Josyna was making a play at the baroness and you were helping her do it."

She scoffed and looked away. "Did you think so too?"

"No. I asked to be the one to come, to clear you. I just couldn't find anything." I squeezed her fingers. "You're too good at covering your tracks."

"You can't live with a thief this long and not pick up some tricks."

"I was worried Josyna was using you, though. Making some kind of play that would get you hurt. Involving you in something dangerous."

"I won't deny I have ambitions, Gray. I want to make a difference in this city and be able to walk the hill on my own merits instead of on the arm of someone paying me to be there. If I use their money to do that, all the better. But I would never betray the guild."

"I know."

"Well Rigel apparently doesn't."

I bowed my head.

After a few moments she sighed and moved her teacup to the tray. "If we're going to talk to Rigel, we should finish eating and get dressed."

She rose and I looked up at her. Her smile was back, determined and dazzling. Some of the knots that had been tightening through my chest over the last week loosened and I found myself smiling back.

***

By the time we strolled down the main stairs and out the front door of the manor it was an hour or two past noon. I walked next to Deidre, holding her hand with our fingers twined together. It felt good to be beside her and I focused on that as we walked down the street past quiet manors. Her fancy cloak was draped over my other arm, since it was sunny and warm. We took our time, and it was calming just shuffling along and smiling when she occasionally bumped into me with a flirty glance. The memory of the previous night warmed me almost as much as the sun.

When we neared the crossroad that would take us to the gate at Market Street I glanced in that direction and froze, gripping her hand tighter and bringing her to a stop beside me. The gate was blocked by Silvers, at least a dozen of them, holding their spears at the ready.

"Let's try another gate." I pulled her around, turning and starting quickly back the way we'd come.

She glanced over her shoulder at the guards. "What did you do?"

"I don't know. Nothing I can remember." Of course I'd lost a good chunk of the previous afternoon due to Loring's elf friend and his mind magic. I had a feeling that might have something to do with it.

The Silvers were shouting and following. I passed Deidre's cloak over. "Keep going and find someplace to lay low."

She clutched the garment to her chest. "What are you going to do?"

"Try to slip past them. Just don't get involved."

She scowled, but I pulled her to a stop and took her face in both hands, kissing her then touching my forehead to hers. "I need to know you're safe, okay?"

She huffed and glanced behind me, but nodded. "Go."

I slipped past her and ran. The sound of clanking armor grew as the guards increased speed to match, and they shouted at me to stop. I didn't dare risk looking back to make sure Deidre was okay, but she wasn't yelling either so I was hoping she'd just stepped aside and they'd ignored her.

There were probably Silvers at every gate. My guess was they'd reported my attempted entry to the Warden last night and she'd deployed them to round me up. The estates were difficult to get out of in a hurry. The secret ways through the wall took time to use, and weren't supposed to be revealed to the guards. The gates would be blocked.

But if I could get into the back passage and double back they may have left only a few men behind them at the Market Street gate. It would still be too risky to rush them, but they wouldn't expect me to run past it and up the stairs to the top of the wall. A few hundred feet beyond the gate I could jump to the roof of one of those rickety buildings along the crooked street that circled the wall, and once I climbed down I could disappear into the city.

It was the best option I could come up with.

I swung into the little alley that led between manors to the back passage and the guards shouted even louder behind me at my unexpected move. I burst into the back passage and circled wide back to the gate. Clanking reached my ears from the street beyond the row of manors where some of the Silvers had pivoted to return to the gate while others kept up the pursuit. I'd have to beat them to it.

I counted three guards still at the gate. Two of them spaced themselves in front of the opening, while the third was smart enough to begin unlocking the massive doors from their open position so he could swing them shut. I tried to make it look like I was preparing to rush them, then swerved past and clattered onto the bottom of the stairs.

I threw a hand out to keep from toppling forward with my momentum, climbing as fast as I could. A spear flew past my hip and thwacked into the steps in front of me then clattered down, and I barely managed not to trip over it. The guards were all shouting and I could hear at least one coming up the stairs behind me.

I shot onto the six foot wide battlements on top of the wall and kept running, choking back the panic when I saw a guard sprinting toward me from the direction I was going. He staggered to a stop and held his spear out sideways to block me from going past him. I put a burst of effort into speeding up, and just before I would have collided with him I twisted and dropped to the stone walkway, sliding feet-first past him right under his spear.

I lurched back to my feet as he staggered around, then I was running again. Just ahead on the left there was a rooftop about ten feet below the top of the wall, but this guard was right behind me. No time to slow and lower myself down.

I swerved toward that side, jumped to the low barrier of stone that acted as a railing, took three more steps along the narrow rim, then leaped for the edge of the roof.

It was a long way down at this speed, and as my feet touched the rough planks I folded into a roll to take some of the impact. I bounced as my shoulder touched down, did two more complete rolls trying to keep my arms and legs tucked in, then grabbed for the far edge of the roof as I rolled off it.

The momentum pulled the edge out of my grip, but it had slowed me. I dropped about six feet to another section of roof, landed awkwardly on my heels, and toppled onto my back. The breath was knocked out of my chest and dust billowed around me, but I was still alive, and as far as I could tell I wasn't broken.

I crawled to the edge of the lower roof and looked down. Another fifteen or so feet to the ground. No ladder or handholds. The buildings along the wall weren't permitted to have them for obvious reasons.

There were guards shouting above me and guards going through the gate nearby. Not much time to get down and disappear. I swung myself over the edge until I hung from my hands, then dropped.

I bent my knees when I landed, but still the force of it sent pain up through my shins and I dropped to my ass, catching myself with both hands on the dirty cobbles. I had to get up. I had to move.

I staggered to my feet and turned away from the gate. One of the Silvers was quicker than the rest and clattered up behind me, but there wasn't much I could do about it other than leap forward. His arm shot out and he grabbed the back of my vest, dragging me down with him.

I was gasping for breath at this point, but swung my elbow at his nose, wincing at the snap of cartilage when it connected.

He howled and let go.

I pushed myself to my feet, staggering to the side before reorienting myself in the direction I needed to go. Armored hands grabbed my arms before I could move, then yanked me backwards and drove me to the ground. They knelt on my arms to either side, pinning me down.

My chest heaved and I struggled to catch my breath, tugging uselessly against their hold. The guard that had tackled me pushed himself to his feet, spun and growled at me, then stalked over. Blood flowed from both nostrils and he looked like he wanted to bash my head into the cobbles, but one of the two holding me yelled at him to stand down.

I closed my eyes and coughed as I sucked dust kicked up from the street into my lungs. It probably hadn't been the best plan I could have come up with. Maybe I should have fled deeper into the estates and hid with Deidre.

The guards shifted their hold and dragged me to my feet. I was pretty sure nothing was broken, but I'd have bruises all over, especially the shoulder I'd landed on when I hit the first roof.

They shoved me chest-first into the side of a nearby building and wrenched my arms back, closing metal cuffs over my wrists. Pain flared through my shoulder and I winced. "Easy."

"Should have thought of that before you ran." He gripped my collar and yanked me around, then shoved me toward the gate.

I stumbled and fell to my knees, but managed to lurch to my feet again before they could get hold of me. I walked on my own, a little unsteady, toward the Silvers that milled around just outside the gate. One stood apart from them, waiting, and the guards prodded me in that direction.

He was familiar, but it had been a crazy week. I think I'd seen him ordering people around during our little forays into the city with the Warden. An officer of some sort. He stared down at me with as much disdain as anyone I'd ever pissed off.

"By order of the Warden, you are under arrest."

I glared back. "What for?"

He grinned. "For ignoring her summons."

Shit. That was probably one of the things I didn't remember about the previous afternoon. I doubted the Warden would believe my explanation, and I wasn't sure Rigel could buy me out of this one. She was too eager to get her hands on me right now and he'd warned me to play nice. It certainly looked like I was doing the opposite of that.

To be honest, I probably shouldn't have run in the first place. It had been instinct, and I hadn't even questioned the decision until now. If I'd gone quietly I may have been able to avoid all the pain now coursing through my bruised body.

The officer began giving orders, forming up the Silvers around me as if they expected me to try to escape. My legs were a little wobbly and I ached all over, so I doubted I could outrun a dozen guards right now anyway. I'd just have to go along with them and hope I could talk my way out of this.

After all, I had a city to destroy.

32 – Arrested

They didn't take me to the Warden's office like I expected, but led me directly to one of the side doors and into the jail part of the building. A wide aisle went down the center and both sides were lined with ten-foot-square cells. They had stone walls except for the wall facing the aisle, which was close-fitting bars with barred doors. The ceiling and floor were also stone, and the floor was sloped with a groove in the center of each cell which extended into the aisle where a trench ran down the middle for the full length. The smell wasn't as bad as the jail in the Lower Yard had been, but it was still unpleasant with the mingled scents of piss, vomit, and blood.

They shoved me ahead of them, sending me down the aisle. Most of the cells were empty, but the people that were there watched with either suspicion or the dead stares of those who'd given up already. It was small consolation that I didn't recognize anyone.

The Silver directly behind me shoved again and I stumbled, then glared over my shoulder at him.

He raised an eyebrow, daring me to complain.

I bit my cheek and looked forward. At the end of the aisle was a heavy wooden door set into the stone wall. It had iron bands on it and the surface was stained with something dark that looked as if it had splattered.

One of the guards used a key to open it, then pushed it wide and stepped away.

They prodded me forward.

The room inside was large. It ran the entire width of the aisle and cells, and was that deep as well. Maybe thirty-five or forty feet square. A few long tables were against the walls, and a few smaller ones scattered around the room near heavy chairs or platforms with straps mounted on them to restrain prisoners. Torture implements hung from the walls and ceiling, or were scattered across tables.

I swallowed the lump that had risen in my throat and hoped the guards couldn't tell my heart was racing. They shoved and prodded me to a ring in the floor with a chain attached to it, then one of them spun me to face the door and another attached the chain to the metal cuffs I wore. I heard a lock click and the added weight dragged at my arms.

Two of the Silvers came forward to search me. The first thing they took was my belt with the knives and picks, along with my pouches. Then my boot knives. They found a few coins from various hidden pockets, the key to my apartment, and the crumpled note Deidre had left for me. They were very thorough and patted down every inch of my clothing, even checking my palms in case I'd hidden anything. Which I hadn't. I kept my mouth shut throughout the entire thing, even though some of the hands weren't very gentle.

One by one the Silvers filed out, the officer waiting until all the rest had left. He looked at me then and smirked. "We'll let the Warden know you've arrived. Make yourself comfortable." He laughed and slipped out the door after his men, then it was slammed shut.

A shiver ran up my back.

The room was well lit by lamps, but I wished it hadn't been. All the various methods of torture were on full display and I wasn't sure if this was a scare tactic or if the Warden was just waiting until the time opened up in her schedule to get around to me. The stuff seemed used, which wasn't a good sign.

I twisted my hands and moved my fingers over the end of the chain. It was a simple enough hinged lock. Even without being able to see it I could probably have picked it if I had any of my tools.

I sighed and bowed my head. The threat of the room pressed down on me, working to drive me into a panic. I couldn't let that happen. I needed to keep my head and try to figure out some way out of this.

After standing for what seemed like hours but was probably more like twenty minutes, my legs started to shake. The adrenaline was all gone and my muscles were demanding rest. I knelt on the floor and sat back on my heels, wincing at the ache in my knees, but it was better than falling over.

Time crawled by. The longer I knelt there, the more certain I was that she was trying to let this room get into my head. I deliberately kept my eyes closed and tried to think about nothing. When thoughts did intrude, I turned my attention to simple things... Deidre laughing, Ruena walking the streets beside me, cards with Sans.

When the door finally opened it startled me out of an exhausted doze. I looked up at the Warden, followed by a handful of Silvers. She was sneering and took a moment just to stand inside the room and stare at me.

I narrowed my eyes and broke the silence. "I heard you wanted to see me."

"I told you what would happen if you disrespected me again."

"I must have forgotten. It's been a long week."

She moved forward, coming to stand just within arm's reach. I looked up at her from my knees, my heart pounding in my chest. I couldn't help but tremble and it pissed me off.

I'd been afraid of this moment my entire life, but five years ago I'd walked into the labyrinth and faced true nightmares. I could sure as Six face the Warden without begging for mercy. I relaxed the best I could, leaning back on my heels.

She stared down her crooked nose at me. "The city is full of whispers. People are closing their shops and packing up their valuables, but nobody will tell the authorities what's going on."

I smiled.

She scowled. "They're running from something, and I think you know what it is. I think you're involved with it."

"What do you want me to tell you, Warden?"

"The truth. I think this chase for a thief is a ruse. I think the guild is planning to overthrow the baroness and this is a distraction. We know the people closing their shops have had dealings with the guild. They're being warned ahead of time, aren't they? Getting out of the way to avoid the coming violence of your coup."

I snorted. "Rigel wouldn't upset the balance like that. You're grasping at straws."

"Am I? You've been in and out of the estates a lot lately."

"I've had business there."

"With an eccentric nobleman who's obsessed with your past indiscretions. Are you trying to convince him to get you closer to your target? Trying to recruit him to pass information from the inside?"

"I doubt Lord Barty could be discrete enough for spy work."

She held up a crumpled piece of paper. "And that new noblewoman. Lady Josyna. She's been gathering quite the army of servants from all the houses. Shows up here suddenly one day, buys a house, nobody knows her or ever sees her. Is the Lady Josyna part of Rigel's inner circle?"

My cheek twitched. If she figured out Deidre was Lady Josyna, she'd send the Silvers after her as well. I shook my head. "Rigel sent me to investigate her. She's not part of the guild at all."

"Is he trying to recruit her? Using Lady Midnight to turn her head?"

"No. Fucks sake, I already told you it's Loring that's after Sangarie."

"You want me to believe some exiled nobleman is going to return when we've had no sign of him other than the words you spew into people's ears? I'm inclined to think you staged this entire investigation to keep us busy. Your so-called assassination attempts, the confused farmer at the gate, that foreign woman that so conveniently fills the baroness's head with paranoia. Your lies are obvious."

I glared up at her. "Just because you don't understand what's happening doesn't mean it's a lie!"

She took a swing at me.

I reacted out of reflex, bending backwards so her fist whooshed in front of my face instead, close enough I could feel the air of its passage.

It threw the Warden off balance and she staggered, then turned furious eyes on me.

Shit. I swallowed the lump down again and wished I'd been a little slower.

Her hand shot out and gripped my shirt, twisting and lifting under my chin, pulling me up on my knees. "Tell me what the king of thieves is planning."

I tensed. "Nothing."

The blow hit the ridge over my eye and stung like a bitch. I stared at the floor to one side for a couple of seconds, blinking at the pain spreading across my skull. I was going to have another very bad headache after this.

"Why are all the people closing their shops?"

"Because Loring is coming, and you won't take it seriously."

She hit me across the jaw and my teeth cut open the inside of my cheek. I tried to bring my arms forward, forgetting they were chained behind my back.

She bent closer so her face was right in front of mine, still smelling of onion. "How do you plan to get into the baroness's treasury?"

Blood was pooling in my mouth and I swallowed what I could. I wanted to clench my jaw, but it fucking hurt so I settled for chuckling as I glared up at her. "If I wanted inside that treasury I wouldn't need a convoluted plan. I'd just do it."

Her fist hit my sternum and drove the wind out of me. She dropped her hold on my shirt and I doubled up and fell to my side on the dirty floor, my arms wrenched behind me. My entire chest was on fire and I couldn't get my lungs to work. Eventually I dragged in a thin, ragged breath, tried to cough, sucked in a little more air.

A kick to my gut drove it all out again. I'd have groaned if I had the breath for it. I pressed the side of my face into the floor and concentrated on opening my chest to bring in air. It caught and I coughed and wasn't sure if the blood was from inside my chest or my cheek. But I was able to breathe even if it was painful.

The Warden dropped to one knee beside me and rolled me onto my back. With my arms still chained behind me it left my hips propped awkwardly in the air and the strain on my chest sent pain shooting all the way around to my spine. I squirmed, trying to find some relief from the pressure.

"Tell me what you know, thief."

"I already told you. Loring is back." I gagged on the blood running into the back of my throat and did my best to swallow it. "He's east of the city right now, waiting for everyone to be distracted by the Night of Shadows. If you don't believe me, send someone out to look."

She growled, staring at me with narrowed eyes. "I will. And when I find nothing, I will order them to build the gallows." She leaned closer and put her weight on my chest until I couldn't breathe and was afraid my ribs would snap and cave in. "The morning after the Night of Shadows you'll hang, so everyone will know you're a liar and a traitor."

I merely narrowed my eyes and ground my teeth.

She pushed herself up and wiped off her hands as she walked away.

I rolled to my side as I started breathing again, trying not to move my ribs too much. The door opened and closed, then the Silvers were there to unchain me, lift me up, and drag me out to the cells.

I was given my own, and they even removed the cuffs. Once I'd recovered from being pushed inside I noticed it was at least clean. Or as clean as a stone floor in a cell could be. Someone must wash them out between prisoners.

I wrapped my arms around my chest and curled up on my side in a back corner. Once again I was sitting in a cell waiting for the Night of Shadows. I'd have been happy that at least this time they didn't plan on forcing me out of it to steal anything, but staying in here while the city was blown to ash wasn't any better.

If Nissa really believed I had to be there for the destruction of Sangarie, she'd better start thinking of a way to get me out of here.

33 – Waiting

There were windows in many of the cells. They weren't big, they were too high to reach, and they had bars mortared into them, but they let in the light. I watched the shadows crawl across the floor until a guard brought in a bowl of gruel and a thick slice of bread.

At first I wasn't going to eat it, but I'd barely eaten the fancy lunch at Deidre's secret manor, and I couldn't remember whether I'd eaten at all the day before because of that elf's fucking compulsion spell, so I was starving. While it wasn't good by any means, it also wasn't spoiled.

Then I huddled in the corner again and waited for it to get dark.

Would Deidre have gone to Rigel? Would he come? Would Ruena try to do something on her own and get in trouble? Would Nissa have a plan? I kept thinking about any number of things that could happen, but when something finally did it wasn't what I expected.

An urgent hiss came from the window and I looked to see a shadowy hood peering inside by the light of the few lamps that shone in the aisle. I frowned and pushed myself to my feet, carefully stretching my chest before crossing to stand under the window.

The voice hissed down, barely loud enough for me to pick it up. "Gray?"

It was Elias. My shoulders slumped and I leaned against the wall below the window and gazed out at the aisle while I whispered back. "Did Rue send you?"

"Deidre, actually."

A piece of paper fluttered to the floor in front of me and I held my chest as I crouched to pick it up. With one hand, I flipped it open and turned it to the dim light to read. It was difficult to see, but I caught enough to piece the message together.

I'm okay. I'll be waiting in the underground, so you better get through this.

I sighed in relief and tipped my head back against the wall. "Thanks."

"Should I try to get you out?"

"How?"

There was a long pause. "I'm not really sure."

I smiled despite the pain in my jaw. "Have you talked to Nissa?"

"Yes. She's going to the baroness to convince her to evacuate the city."

"I don't think that's going to work. The Warden has her own theory on what's happening."

There was a soft sound of frustration from the window. "What do you want me to do?"

What *did* I want? I'd spent the last few hours daydreaming about a rescue, but that was risky and not likely to work. Nissa was going to do whatever she thought best, no matter what message I tried to pass on. If Senyr was willing to come for me, Deidre would have already gone to him. I sighed and looked around the little cell.

"There's no point in waiting. Go to Rigel and tell him we need to spread the word *now*. Get Senyr to talk to Lord Bartholomew and have him warn the hill. Deidre can talk to Lady Josyna and send her army of servants out to warn people as well. Get all the Yellows and Blues screaming it from the streets."

"Screaming what?"

"That a deranged nobleman has found a powerful magical weapon and come to destroy the city, and they have until the Night of Shadows before the streets will burn. They can go underground or leave, but if they stay they die."

"Do you think they'll believe it?"

I sighed and shifted my back against the rough stone of the wall, holding my ribs. They'd believe the lie if I could just prove it to them. But how could I prove it? I almost wished Loring would attack early, driving the people from the city, setting fire to the streets.

That was it. The attack had to start early. I spun to look up at the window again, gasping and taking a moment to let the pain in my ribs pass. "Tell Rigel to dig out that fire powder we stole a few years back.

He needs to get people to set it up tonight and light it off at noon tomorrow. Make it look like the attacks have started."

"You want to start the city on fire?"

"Yes."

"You think he'll actually do that?"

Did I? It was a desperate and reckless move—something Rigel would have sighed disapprovingly about if he were here—but I didn't know a better way to prove to the citizens that the danger was real. Not early enough to make a difference at any rate.

It was a gamble. We'd never tested that powder, and fires in a city like this could quickly get out of control. People could get hurt. It could cause another distraction and create even more chaos. It could give the baroness fuel to turn the people against the guild if she found out.

Would he trust me? I set my forehead against the cold stone of the wall. "Tell him…" I grimaced, the need to get all these people moving to safety fighting against my aversion to Rigel's goals for me. "Tell him it's my call."

Elias was quiet a moment, then shifted at the bars. "Is that everything?"

"Make sure Ruena doesn't do anything stupid like trying to rescue me."

"I'll try."

I snorted softly and shook my head. After a few minutes I realized he'd left, so I went back to my corner to rest. I hoped it was enough.

***

Morning was slow in coming. I slept fitfully when I did manage to doze off, but the pain in my chest and head kept bringing me back to consciousness. As light from the windows crawled across the floor I grew too restless to bother trying to sleep.

Today was the last day. At sundown the Night of Shadows would be upon the city and this year it wasn't some echo through time, but the destruction that would cause it. People should be moving by now, spreading the word.

The guild would have locked up their private rooms and the halls and caverns would be filling with people who may not have realized the extent of the city beneath their feet. I couldn't imagine what it'd be like packed in a crowded underground corridor for the entire night, barely room to move, the stink of fear around you as death and shadow monsters roamed the streets above, but it was better than being topside in it.

I grunted and shifted on the hard stone floor. Part of me wished I'd thought to check the underground when I was in the labyrinth five years ago. Would I have seen the terrified faces of citizens staring back at me? How many had fled? How many wouldn't have listened and had probably been blown to ash in the magical explosion?

Then my thoughts turned to the vision given to me by that damned stone. I was meant to be in the baroness's manor tonight, carrying the stupid fucking rock and climbing to the battlements to look out over the city as the sun set. I was sure it'd take more than Nissa's arguments to get me out of this jail cell.

I mulled over these thoughts—interspersed with worries about the people I cared about—for hours. At times I could hear shouting in the distance because of the open windows, like the city was beginning to riot. Mostly I heard rats, or the rattling cough of another prisoner. I watched the light move across the floor like a sundial. Around midday there was a series of rumbles and the mortar flaked from the wall as the building shook gently with each one. Silvers shouted outside and the Warden's bells sounded from somewhere nearby. I hoped it was enough.

When the door leading out of the prison finally opened, I was pretty sure it was late afternoon. From my place at the back of the cell I couldn't see the door, but I could pick out the sound of a handful of armored guards entering by the sharp clank of their boots. Then a familiar, entitled voice rose above the noise that I recognized as Lord Barty's.

"Quickly now! The baroness will not be kept waiting! Whatever crimes Mister Gray may have committed, you will have to pursue them another day, for the city itself is under attack and we must look to the—" He stepped in front of my cell and paused, moving forward to grip the bars.

His eyes lit up, and he nearly quivered with excitement. "Here he is! Release him, I say!" He gestured grandly, then noticed his hand was dirty from grabbing the bars and wiped it on the tunic of the guard next to him, who glared back.

One of them grumbled as he stepped forward to unlock my door.

What in the ever fickle whims of the Six was he doing here? I sat against the back wall and waited.

As soon as the door was open, Barty strode past the guard and up to me, reaching down for my shoulder with an eager expression.

I narrowed my eyes. "What's going on?"

"Come now, Mister Gray. The baroness requires your service."

"I don't serve the baroness. What are you talking about?"

He bent lower, then thought better of it and tried to crouch, but his coat tails dragged on the floor so he stood up again and dusted them off with a scowl. "Well, Master Senyr came to speak with me, and told me a very disturbing tale about that fellow Loring that was involved with Lord Firmin's death. Apparently Loring is planning on destroying the city. Did you know about this?"

I raised an eyebrow.

He waved his hands. "What am I saying. Of course you knew about it. At any rate, the guild is leading an evacuation of the city, and the populace is in a panic. I went out to see for myself, and then we went to visit the baroness to see what could be done. Much to my surprise an elf was in the audience hall! She was holding a large scythe-like weapon and looked very menacing, and she was appealing to the baroness for your release."

"I bet the Warden loved that."

"No actually, she didn't."

I rolled my eyes and rubbed a hand through my hair, but continued listening to his manic retelling.

"The Warden argued that you and the guild were to blame. Then Master Senyr came up from behind me and began to speak. He is really very eloquent, isn't he? Essentially he pointed out that the city was in an uproar, and to turn against the guild right now and throw away the treaty would prove to the citizens that the baroness didn't care whether they lived or died. They would flock to the guild for protection, and the baroness would lose all control over the masses. He told her there was no time left, and she could either play her part in things, or stay out of the way."

I grabbed the wall and dragged myself up. Senyr had done that? He'd stood in the baroness's own hall and called her out? By the Six... I wished I could have seen that.

Barty steadied me and continued. "The baroness asked what he wanted, and Master Senyr told her to have you brought to the manor immediately, and to order everyone to evacuate to the surrounding countryside or to the underground. She didn't seem very happy about it, but she did it." He put his hand over his chest where the ruffles peeked out of his coat. "I offered to fetch you myself."

I stared back at him, amazed that everything had fallen into place. "Thank you, Lord Bartholomew, for all your help."

The nobleman beamed. "Don't mention it! Happy to be part of your current adventure, yes?" He snapped the lapels of his coat. "Now, it's time to be the heroes of this story. We're off to see the baroness!"

I followed behind him as he breezed past the scowling guards. His pace was quicker than I'd have liked, but I gritted my teeth and pushed past the pain in my chest to keep up.

It didn't surprise me that the streets of Varinston district were nearly empty. If the city was rioting, the Copper and Silverguard would have been called out to maintain order and most of this district was taken up by barracks and other government buildings. I could smell smoke, and a look at the horizon showed a few thin pillars rising in the sky from various parts of the city. There was even a hint of shouting on the breeze.

We went directly north to the gate that led into the estates. The gate was closed and I frowned as we waited for them to open it for us. They never closed the gates unless they believed the hill was being threatened. The Warden must be very worried about the reaction of the citizens…

Or Loring had already entered the city.

I stepped up beside Barty. "Has anyone seen Loring yet?"

The nobleman glanced to the east. "Silverguard were sent outside the city to find him."

The gate opened and the Silvers waved us through. I held an arm over my chest as I kept pace. "Where is Nissa?"

"Last I saw, she was standing in the baroness's audience hall, looking like an avenging goddess." He shook his head. "I would have liked to speak with her, but first I'm to deliver you to the hall and then I must see to my own house. I do apologize for the lengthy walk, but all my carriages are occupied with the evacuation."

"You're evacuating?"

"Of course. My household staff will be leaving the city by the north gate, but I have accepted Master Senyr's invitation to descend into the underground. I'm looking forward to a lovely tour."

I snorted, but covered it up with a very real and somewhat painful cough. I doubted Senyr would be giving tours while the halls were crowded with huddled shopkeepers and craftsmen, but if that's what it took to get Barty to safety, so be it.

I scowled then, keeping my gaze locked on the street in front of us as we wound through the estates. Why did I care if he made it out or not? Or any of the rich assholes on the hill for that matter? I glanced to either side, seeing evidence of a few manors being boarded up, and others with guards standing in the lawns. "How many nobles are evacuating?"

Barty looked around as well. "A few, but not many. Most are sending their families out of the city for safety from the riots, but the nobles themselves prefer to guard their wealth and power. They're ordering their servants to fortify and defend their property, hiring outside guards."

I shook my head and kept walking. The memory of the devastation in the estates was hard to hold back. Whatever had destroyed Sangarie had ripped through this area the hardest, flattening everything, washing the buildings up against the inner wall like a tide washes debris onto a beach.

As we went, Barty asked questions about what I knew of the coming attack, but I mumbled noncommittal answers and tried not to think about it. I glanced at the location of the sun often, worried about how little time we had left until this would all be gone.

Finally we approached the gate that led to the gardens surrounding the baroness's manor. Irons guarded the entrance, but gave us only a cautionary glance before resuming their stoic postures. Barty stepped out ahead and turned to face me.

"This is where we part, Mister Gray. I have a great deal yet to do before nightfall, but I wish you the best of luck." He held out his hand.

I looked at it, all the ingrained distrust of nobility burbling to the surface. But as much as Barty's obsession irritated me, he was doing his best to be helpful. I clasped his hand and he pumped my arm enthusiastically, causing me to hiss through my teeth and clench my arm over my ribs. Then he brushed past me and was quickly winding his way back through the estates.

I looked up at the manor beyond the gate and took a slow breath, mindful of my bruised chest. This was it. This was the end.

34 – Room to Hang Myself

I wasn't sure where to go. The Silvers turned to leave as soon as I stepped through the gates, and the Irons wouldn't even look in my direction after their initial scrutiny. I walked up the main path, following the same route through the gardens I'd taken when Rigel had brought us to see the baroness.

Two Irons at the main doors into the manor itself watched my approach, and when I got close enough to wonder what I should say they reached in unison to open both doors. Their eyes were accusing and their mouths drawn into a grim line.

It felt like a trap.

I made an effort to slow my breathing, forced a polite smile, then stepped inside.

The last time I'd been in this hall I was overtaken by how similar it felt to the ruined version, but I'd been wrong. That day had held only an echo of it. Today, servants were scurrying about and guards were rushing through, both Irons and Silvers. Here and there I saw a dropped item hastily picked up, or just kicked aside. I stood in the middle of the entrance hall, fighting the shivers crawling up my back as I picked up on the undercurrent of panic.

Off to my left the sound of breaking pottery brought everything to a halt. My gaze was pulled in that direction and a feeling of dread settled into the pit of my stomach as I set eyes on a broken vase next to a pillar it had been displayed on. It was a sight I remembered from the labyrinth.

It was happening. It was all happening. The panic rose in my throat.

"Gray!"

Senyr's voice dragged me back to the present and I drew a shuddering breath and gestured at a passing Silver, muttering softly. "You should get someone to clean that up."

He scowled at me and moved on.

Senyr reached my side and took hold of my arms, turning me to face him. "Glad you're still with us, boy."

I grimaced and glanced past him at the rest of the group. Deidre was there, Ruena with Elias hovering protectively behind her, and Nissa stood a few feet away. I met the elf's eyes. "Where else would I be? The future calls."

She dipped her head minutely, her face expressionless.

Deidre came up and wrapped her arms around me and I groaned at the pressure on my chest. "Careful. I'm still recovering from my conversation with the Warden."

She raised a hand to the side of my face, turning my head so she could get better light on the cut over my eye. The dried blood on my temple and cheek probably made it look worse than it was.

There were tears brimming in her eyes. "Are you badly hurt?"

"No. I think it's mostly bruising."

She clutched my arm and turned back to Nissa. "Do you have anything to help him?"

The elf frowned, but reached into the satchel at her side.

Deidre pulled my attention back. "We can't stay long, but we wanted to see you before–" A tear trailed down her cheek and her chin trembled.

I grimaced and folded her gently into a hug. "Before I save the city?"

She pressed her face into my shoulder and gave a snorting sob, squeezing my arm. "Being the hero again?"

"I'm no hero. I'm a greedy, self-important, manipulative son-of-a-bitch. My game's just a little bit off today."

She squeezed me tighter. "You're an idiot."

"That too."

Nissa cleared her throat. "We should speak with the baroness. Time is growing short."

Deidre gave me a light kiss and smiled past the tears. "We'll be waiting in the underground for you to come home."

I nodded and let her slip away, my fingers sliding across hers as our hands separated. I don't think either of us wanted to say what we were afraid of.

Deidre bowed her head and motioned at Ruena. "Come on, you and Elias can come home with me."

Ruena pulled herself up and shook her head. "I'm staying. I'm supposed to be here too, remember?" She caught my gaze and I nodded back.

Elias looked like he wanted to argue and glanced between Ruena and me, but in the end he moved to Deidre and took her arm. "I'll keep you company."

As they made their way out I gave Senyr a final look as well and he nodded briskly with his face drawn into a grim mask, then turned to follow them.

Nissa slipped the tin of ointment into my hand. "Apply it later. First we should talk to the baroness and get into position."

"Right." I slipped the tin into a pocket and followed her through the entrance hall, deeper into the manor. Ruena fell into step beside me and I set my hand briefly on her shoulder, then focused on the doors to the audience hall.

The Irons opened them for us, but didn't bother with introductions. I paused to take in the scene.

Very few courtiers were present, and those that were looked curious or amused by the spectacle. They gazed around like parents tolerating the misbehavior of children. The chaos itself was due to the intermittent line of servants and guards that approached the throne and were admitted one at a time by the ring of Irons surrounding their leader. Whispers traveled up and down this line, and occasionally someone would break from it and go darting off as if they'd gotten sick of waiting.

The baroness looked haggard and frail, her jewels and burgundy gown coming off more as an attempt at looking regal than actually adorning her. The imposing figure I remembered from my last visit was now struggling to maintain the image of authority.

Off to one side, but close enough to step in should the need arise, stood the Warden. As I met her glare she drew her lips back in a silent snarl, baring her teeth. Her hand gripped the hilt of her sword, but she didn't go so far as to pull it out in the baroness's presence.

I tore my gaze away and looked again at the baroness.

Lady Karyn had noticed us and she waved the current pair of Silvers away. Her face was as grim as always, but the Silvers that hurried past us on their way out of the hall looked spooked. I locked gazes with one briefly and took note of the panic in his eyes. What would they be so afraid of? The real fight hadn't even started yet.

Faces peered in our direction and an aisle opened up leading straight to the throne. Nissa's voice came beside me, so quiet only Ruena and I could have heard it. "This will be your discussion. We are only here to support you."

I grimaced, but began walking through the ranks of waiting servants and guards, Nissa and Ruena at my sides. I didn't know what I was supposed to say. Somehow I needed to be on the roof of the manor soon, but did I tell the baroness what was going to happen? Did I lie and try to move around in the chaos that was coming? The vision hadn't shown me any of this.

When I reached the edge of the dais I stopped and bowed low at the waist. It hurt a lot, and I pressed a hand to my chest as I came back up with a grimace. "Lady Karyn."

She pursed her lips and glared back. "It's impossible to get rid of you, isn't it?"

"I hope you don't expect me to apologize for that."

She scowled even harder. "Come closer, thief, so I don't have to utter unladylike words too loudly."

I absolutely did not want to get closer, especially since I caught the Warden moving forward as well, although I wasn't sure whether it was to hear better or protect her boss. For a moment I felt as if my feet had turned to stone and the air was getting thicker and harder to breathe. The baroness tilted her head, raising her eyebrow in an expression of impatience.

I measured my breath as I stepped onto the dais and concentrated on walking forward. Each step felt like I was heading toward a gallows.

The baroness's dangerous tone stopped me like a wall. "That's far enough."

I had to keep breathing. Stay calm. Think about how I could get myself onto her roof so I could unleash a torrent of destructive magic. My cheek twitched.

She lowered her voice so the assembled masses wouldn't hear. "Your master has me at a disadvantage. I underestimated his cunning and deceit."

"I'm as impressed as you are." I was more than happy to give Rigel the credit for this and avoid her wrath.

She wrinkled her nose at me and clenched her hand on the padded arm of her throne.

I hastily added, "My Lady."

Ruena sighed from the edge of the dais behind me. Little shit. Maybe she should come up here and do the talking if she had such strong opinions.

"Tell me, thief, what do you know of the exiled nobleman?"

I shot a glance at the Warden, who was watching with barely contained fury, then returned my eyes to the slightly less frightening baroness. "As I mentioned before, we heard of Loring's return and his ambitions. We believe he's after not only your riches, but your city. In the past few days we located him east of the city, along with a few close allies."

I resisted the urge to look behind me at Nissa for confirmation. "I've been indisposed for the past day, so I don't know much more than that. My friends might know more."

"Why is he so interested in *you*?"

"I think that should be obvious. You share the same interest, after all."

Her eyes narrowed. "Indeed. Tell me, thief, why is your false king calling for the evacuation of the city? Surely a disgraced nobleman with a small band of hired soldiers couldn't threaten the entire city."

I was tempted to be a smartass and tell her they were evacuating so I didn't kill them when I leveled the place, but that would get us nowhere. "He carries a powerful magical artifact. It has the potential to destroy the entire city. We have reason to believe he'll use it."

"Is that so?" She stared at me, chewing on the inside of her cheek. "My Silverguard report he has breached the east gate and is moving into the city, accompanied by half a dozen monstrous beasts that seem to be made of shadow or smoke but with claws like knives. They made short work of the gate guards."

A knot of anxiety rose in my chest. Behind me Nissa cursed under her breath and I heard the creak of her armor, but she didn't move. If Loring was already coming we didn't have much time. I glanced at the ceiling where a few stained glass windows let in some light, trying to tell how close to sunset it was. I thought we'd have a couple of hours yet.

"Why shouldn't I give you over to him? Maybe if I chained you to the wall like a sacrificial goat he'd take his revenge and leave."

I took an involuntary step back, then stubbornly held my ground. I couldn't run from her. I needed to be here. "He wants more than just me."

"Are you sure? According to my reports, he's been trying to kill you, and only you. Could you be making everything else up, using this city's resources to defend yourself from a well-deserved repercussion?"

I ground my teeth. There was a long silence in the hall as the baroness waited for my response and the assembled masses strained to hear what was being exchanged. As I met her glare and tried to think of an argument she'd accept, I realized I was more irritated than afraid.

Loring was bearing down on us with a handful of pet shadowbeasts, the original Night of Shadows was less than a couple of hours away, and I hadn't figured out how to avoid destroying the city I called home. This entire conversation was pointless. I growled in the back of my throat and took back the step I'd given her, speaking in a low tone that wouldn't carry.

"Look, I don't give Six flying fucks what you believe. If you're so sure I'm lying, then sit there in your throne and watch the show. If the dust clears in the morning and this was all some elaborate game, I'll put the noose around my neck myself and step off your wall. Until then let me and my friends try to protect *our* city."

Her face had paled, then gone very red. She tapped her fingernail on the arm of the chair and narrowed her eyes. "Very well." She beckoned an Ironguard forward. "Go with them. Make sure they don't run off."

The Iron bowed crisply and backed away, motioning at a few others to form up behind our group. I took the opportunity to look over my shoulder at Nissa and Ruena, and they both looked surprised.

I turned to face the baroness again.

She leaned back in her chair and it made her seem even more frail. "Go on then. Play out your ruse. It'll be all the more sweet when your excuses run out and your master can't protect you. Then I shall make an example of you, to the king of fools and all others who would dare oppose me."

I spun on my heel and walked painfully off the dais with Nissa and Ruena falling into step behind me, followed by half a dozen Irons. As we exited the audience hall I thought about nothing. Absolutely nothing.

I didn't want to think about anything. It felt like someone was silently screaming inside my head, and my body was tense with anticipation and worry. I knew it was probably panic, but there wasn't much to be done about it.

Nissa took my arm and drew me aside. "Interesting approach. Not how I would have addressed it."

"Would you rather still be in there when Loring showed up?"

She ignored the comment, pulling me toward a sitting room to the side of the audience hall doors. "Take some time to use that ointment."

The room was large and full of clustered groups of chairs and couches surrounding low tables. It was currently empty, other than us and our escort of Irons. I walked to the nearest couch and sank into it, leaning my head back.

Nissa removed a pouch from her satchel and set it on the table in front of me. I immediately felt the tingle of the stone and wondered why I hadn't noticed it before now. Maybe I was too anxious. She stared down at me.

"You know what you have to do."

I looked at the pouch, my skin crawling. "What if I can't?"

"You can. You have seen it."

I sank deeper into the plush cushions, wishing I could go to sleep. This was much more comfortable than the stone floor of the prison and sleeping seemed infinitely better than destroying Sangarie. The very thought sent a rush of fatigue through me.

Nissa set a hand on Ruena's shoulder and turned her to the door. "We will wait on the battlements."

I continued to stare at the pouch as they left, chewing back all the doubts and objections, since voicing them wouldn't do me any good. Three of the Irons had stayed behind, and three went with them.

After a few minutes I sighed and pulled the tin of ointment out. Barely paying attention to what I was doing, I lifted my shirt to smear it on my chest, then rubbed some on the ridge over my eye and along my jaw. It took most of the ache away.

I slipped it back into my pocket and rose from the couch, staring down at the wrapped stone. May as well get it over with.

Just picking up the pouch made the hair lift on my arms and I gritted my teeth as I loosened the knots and dumped the stone into my other palm.

It sent a jolt of energy through my hand to my elbow and I nearly dropped it, but clenched my fingers and waited until I got used to the pulsing. The stone was giving off a faint glow, just enough to make it obvious it wasn't something I'd picked up out in the garden. Hopefully nobody tried to stop me and question it.

Speaking of noticing it, I turned to look at the three Irons that had remained in the room with me. They had been staring, but quickly averted their gazes and returned to the typical pose of watchful attention. One of them was sweating and cast a last worried glance at my hand before firming up his grimace.

I was contemplating a snide remark when the stone in my hand suddenly throbbed and my vision darkened along with it. Wispy voices bled into my ears, fading in and out as I bent and clutched my forehead.

–from the depths of the earth–

–abyssal shadow–

–summon to my side–

–sate thy hunger–

I gasped and shook the voice off, staggering and blinking to bring the room back into focus. One of the Irons was holding me upright by the arm and I tugged out of his grip and peered down at the stone I was still clutching.

It looked the same as it had when I first dumped it out of the pouch, glowing faintly, obviously magical, but nothing more. It had certainly never done *that* since I plucked it out of the labyrinth. Was this something akin to the vision it had given me back then?

Noises erupted from outside the door and I exchanged worried glances with the Irons before hurrying forward and bursting into the entrance hall. They followed right behind me.

35 – Red Sunset

The manor was chaos. The doors to the audience hall had been flung wide and people were pouring out, panic on their faces. Silvers were trying to calm everyone down and direct people deeper into the building.

I was pushed back against the wall by the movement of the crowd and waited until I could snag a passing Silver. "What's happened?"

"Some kind of enormous beast has appeared at the eastern gate district. They said it's like a giant sea monster made of shadow."

The blood drained from my face. Shadowkraken? Already? I glanced up at the windows high above the hall, and while the light coming in was definitely tinted orange, it was still light out. It wasn't sunset yet, why were the shadowkraken here?

The Silver broke away and I stared out at the panicking servants and courtiers for a moment, then clenched my jaw and straightened my shoulders. It didn't matter. I needed to get to Nissa and Ruena.

I knew from the maps the guild kept that the twin corridors leading away from the entrance hall would eventually take me to corner towers with stairs that went all the way to the battlements. There were other routes, but these were the widest and quickest. I took off to the right, not really caring if the Irons followed me or fled with the others. They wouldn't be able to do anything anyway.

I pushed through the crowd, yelling at people to flee and get to the underground, but I doubted any of them would listen. Even if they tried, the nearest opening to the underground was outside the inner wall, and that was a long run to make for cover. I tried not to think about all these people still being here when the stone exploded.

Occasionally I had to shove people out of my way, or push through a cluster blocking the corridor. I was glad I'd taken the time to fix my wounds. I picked up snatches of panicked conversation in the din about shadow monsters and evil magic, and heard some of the Silvers trying to shepherd the servants into the lower levels of the manor.

Would that work? Would they survive the blast there? For their sake I really hoped so, but in my gut I felt the churning guilt as they pushed and shoved around me to get to what they thought was safety. I tried not to look at faces, to plunge through them like they were just obstacles.

When I finally had the tower door in sight, the stone in my hand throbbed again and my surroundings went fuzzy as the voice whispered in my head. I hunkered against the wall, hoping I didn't get run down while words hissed through my brain.

–kill–

–devour–

–hunt–

Then it was gone and I gasped and shook my head to clear it. That voice was familiar. I took a moment to catch my breath and slow my racing heart as I tried to remember where I'd heard it before. It had a strange lilting accent, like Nissa's when she was casting spells, and I realized it had to be the elf Loring had brought with him. Broken memories of the conversation in the alley surfaced and I was sure I was hearing that elf's voice.

Six be damned. He was summoning the shadow creatures and somehow I was connected to it with the stone I held.

I had to get to Nissa. She'd know more, wouldn't she? I glanced down the hall at the tower door and grimaced as I pushed away from the wall and back into the tide of people. The stone was uncomfortably warm in my hand, magic pulsing up my arm.

When I reached the tower and started up the stairs, the crowd thinned. I realized I had lost two of the Irons, but the third followed me with a pale-faced determination. His dedication to his orders was impressively stupid.

I paused once at the third level to catch my breath, then barreled up the remaining stairs to the battlements and burst through the door.

My vision in the past hadn't prepared me for the details of the situation. What had once been a military feature of a castle was now essentially a rooftop patio complete with potted plants, benches, and tea tables. The parapet remained, the crenulations modified to have decorated iron railings between them painted a bright white. Leaning against this railing on the east side, where the wall turned back to the building, were Nissa and Ruena, along with a gaggle of Silvers and Irons.

Beyond them I could see the city. The bulk of the battlements looked north, and gave me a clear picture of the situation in Sangarie. To the west, in the direction of the river, the sun was getting ready to set, painting the sky in bright orange and deep red, glazing the rooftops with warm light.

To the east was fire and death. Multiple buildings were ablaze, filling the sky with thick pillars of smoke. Between these pillars were darker blotches as the shadowkraken heaved and crawled their way toward the center of the city.

Nissa turned to look at me, the reflection of the sunset making her armor look like it was touched with flame. The wind blew her short white hair wildly around her head, and though her face had no expression to give away what she was thinking, her eyes were wide and sympathetic.

Ruena twisted to look at me from Nissa's side, Her hands were tight on the railing in front of her and her jaw was clenched hard. Her eyes looked even paler than usual, but when her gaze met mine they steadied. She nodded once and I could see the trust she was putting in me.

I joined them at the parapet, standing between them and looking out at the oncoming monsters as the old familiar fear crawled over me. "I thought we'd have until sunset."

Nissa sighed. "The portals appear at sunset. That doesn't mean the battle starts then."

I bit off a snide comment, then cringed as the far off east gate of the inner wall burst inward in a cloud of debris. The guards around us uttered curses and many of them went back to the stairs and hurried inside, presumably to reinforce the troops below, or possibly to run away. It didn't really matter, since they wouldn't survive in either case.

I could barely make out the bounding shadowbeasts entering the estates, quickly disappearing behind manors, but the shadowkraken was clearly visible. It didn't bother with the gate, simply heaved its body to the top of the wall. I was grateful for the distance that separated us as I caught my first clear glimpse of the creature in its entirety, lit by the setting sun. Masses of tentacles spread out and groped ahead of it, dragging its bulk along. The body was soft and bulbous, big as a two story building, dragged behind it like it wasn't used to being in this environment. Some kind of black slime was left in its wake, which was quickly evaporating into hazy pockets of shadow that hung in the air like smoke.

A group of Silvers that looked like tiny metal ants charged up to it on the wide street and the stone in my hand throbbed again, the voice whispering through my head, uttering a string of broken words I didn't understand. It could have been a spell, or just something he was shouting in elfish. I held tight to the stone so I wouldn't drop it over the edge of the parapet and clutched my head in my other hand.

"Gray!" Ruena clutched my arm and kept me from falling off as I leaned over the low rail. "What's wrong?"

I shrugged off the echoing whisper as my vision returned. "I'm not sure, but I think the stone is showing me what's going on. I've been hearing a voice off and on ever since I picked it up and I think it's that elf with Loring."

Nissa glanced in the direction of the attackers, then frowned at me. "Ailred? How are you hear–" Her eyes widened. "The stones. He must have the other, and it connects you. They are the same stone, after all."

I glared back at her. "Whatever it is, I'm not fond of it. He summoned the shadowkraken. I heard some creepy chant, and he's ordered them to hunt and kill."

Her brow was creased and she turned her gaze to the stone in my hand. "He is tapping into the power of Dakara. Only the god of darkness can command the shadowkraken."

"He's using the power of a god? How are we supposed to fight that?"

"It does not matter. We know what has to happen here."

The sound of shouting in the garden below drew my attention and I watched the shadowkraken breach the garden wall off to one side, flattening trees and bushes beneath its huge black body. The tentacles look like a nest of massive snakes beneath it, waiting to snap out and grab anything that came near.

It was so close. My heart was racing and I swallowed against the lump in my throat, gripping the pulsing stone with shaking fingers. I should have insisted that Ruena go with Deidre. Fuck the future. What did it matter to the world if one kid lived or died?

"So this is where you ran off to."

My eyes widened and I glanced over my shoulder to see the Warden stalking across the battlements from one of the tower doors. She snapped commands at the terrified Silvers and Irons, sending most of them into the tower to go below, the rest over to surround us.

Nissa let out an exasperated growl and tugged on my arm. "Do it now!"

I looked at the oncoming shadowkraken, then at the advancing Warden. The stone pulsed in my hand and I held it out between myself and the Warden as if it could somehow stave her off. Ruena flinched from the brightness of the magic and ducked behind my arm.

My chest tightened. I pushed her further behind me, but it wouldn't be enough to shield her from the destruction caused by the stone. She clung to the back of my vest like she'd done five years ago when I'd dragged her through a ruined city filled with deadly shadows. I grimaced and reached back to grip her hand over the side of my vest, my other hand shaking as I held out the stone.

The Warden drew closer, her eyes dark and her lip curled back in a snarl. I ground my teeth, sucking in a breath and trying to push all thoughts out of my mind, brandishing the stone like a knife in front of me. If I did it now, it would take her out. It would take us all out.

Memories flashed in my head of Ruena growing up, hours spent on the rooftops in the dark telling stories and laughing, teaching her to pick locks and throw knives, quiet dinners at home with her and Deidre.

I couldn't do it. The stone would kill her too.

A shove from behind sent me stumbling forward, and I caught my balance as Nissa and Ruena shouted in protest. The guards forced them to their knees, holding them in place.

The Warden drew her sword, growled, and took a swing at me.

I bent backward and staggered to the side, barely avoiding the tip of the weapon. "What the *fuck* are you doing?"

"My job. Protecting this city."

She thrust again and I darted to one side, then ducked under another wild swing. "If you kill me now, the city is lost."

"Liar. You're drawing those things here with that stone you're carrying."

287

It certainly looked like that. Even this far back from the battlements I could see the shadowkraken making its way through the manor's gardens, intent upon us. But I'd be damned if I was going to let her skewer me now.

I darted into her range, sliding to one side as she thrust at my chest so the blade slipped past, then hooked my arm under hers and twisted sharply to bend it backward at the elbow. She screeched as she lost her grip on the sword and it clattered at our feet.

But that's where my advantage ended. She grabbed my arm before I could scurry away and jerked me back into range, where my face met her fist with such force that it knocked me off my feet.

As I landed sprawled on my back, the stone slipped out of my grasp and bounced across the patio stones with a startlingly loud *tink tink tink*, then rolled toward the open iron railing that looked out onto the garden below.

I swore and scrambled after it on my hands and knees. If I lost it... If Loring and Ailred got their hands on it...

It wobbled into a joint in the patio stones and rolled to a stop, inches from falling out of reach, pulsing gently. I flung myself forward, but the Warden caught my leg and yanked me back, dragging me away before I could grab it.

Nissa and Ruena were shouting in the background, but I focused on the furious face of the Warden above me. A face I'd feared for most of my life, now twisted in rage and intent upon killing me. She'd recovered her sword and screamed as she swung it down like a hammer, without any finesse or skill.

I hunched to one side, the blade sparking off the stones where I'd been, then I kicked out with my boot heel and connected with the side of her calf, staggering her but not doing nearly as much damage as I'd hoped.

I scrambled away and lurched to my feet, spinning back to face her as she took a wild swing at my head with the sword. I ducked and grabbed a delicate metal side table from between a cluster of chairs, bringing it around to meet the next swing of the sword.

The blade bounced off the rim, vibrating my hands and arms up to the elbow.

"Hold *still*!" She swung again and I knocked it aside. Then she thrust at my chest and I hurriedly brought the table up but the blade went through the fancy metal scrollwork on the legs and sliced into my upper arm. I hissed and yanked the table sideways, ripping the blade from her hand, then flung them together as hard as I could across the battlements.

As I caught my balance again she slammed a fist into my side, followed quickly by a punch across the face that spun me around to crumple face-first to the stones.

Everything was spinning in my vision. I lifted myself up, but tipped onto my side, then tried to get up again, only to fall back down. It was like the whole manor was turning sideways.

Ruena's furious scream made my heart skip and I looked up to see her charge the Warden's unprotected back. Somehow she'd squirmed free of the Iron that had been holding her. He was hunched over on the ground near the others, doubled up in pain.

With both hands, Ruena slammed one of her throwing knives into the crease under the Warden's arm, screaming as it went in. The Warden recoiled, then shot out a hand to pick the girl up by the throat, lifting her entirely off her feet.

The sight of Ruena in the woman's grasp sent my mind into a panic. "*Hey*! Let her go!" I pushed myself to my feet and staggered, catching hold of a nearby chair to keep myself upright. "It's me you want!"

Ruena kicked and squirmed, clinging to the arm that held her and trying to pull it loose. The Warden shifted her gaze to me, then flung the girl across the patio into a stone bench.

Rue's scream of surprise was cut off abruptly as she crashed into it and dropped to the floor, motionless.

No. My heart dropped and I started to run to her, but the Warden swung her arm in front of my throat and flipped me onto my back again. My head cracked against the patio stones and for a few seconds I couldn't see or move.

When my vision cleared the Warden was standing over me, one foot on either side of my thighs. Her armor creaked as she dropped to one knee and reached for my throat.

I pushed her hand away and tried to drag myself free, but she caught hold of my vest and jerked me back. One of her calloused hands slapped onto the stones beside my head and she let go of my vest to grab my throat again. I shoved at her and my fingers caught on the dagger sheathed at her waist.

She leaned over me, spittle flying from her mouth as she grinned past clenched teeth. Her eyes were bloodshot and bulging with anticipation.

I yanked the knife out of the sheath and plunged it into her side, angling it up and twisting. Her fingers tightened on my throat, cutting off my air entirely. I gripped her arm with my other hand, trying to pull it away.

Her hand clenched and I scraped my feet against the stones and arched my back, trying to shove her off, but she was too strong. Her eyes had a fierce hatred still blazing from them and she coughed blood that splattered my cheek as she gasped, "Die... *thief.*"

I pulled the knife free and stabbed her again. And again.

The hand continued to tighten and for a terrible moment I was worried she'd break my neck before she died. I stabbed her once more, shoving the knife in as far as it would go.

The light slowly went out of her eyes and her full weight dropped onto me as her fingers finally loosened. I coughed and gasped for breath, my bloody fingers slipping from the handle of the knife lodged in her ribs.

For a few moments all I did was breathe, pushing with shaking hands at her limp shoulders so my chest could move to draw in air.

The sound of trees snapping in the garden and stones tumbling from the wall reminded me it was far from over. I heaved at the body, my arms threatening to give out, and managed to drag myself free and crawl toward Ruena.

What guards remained were heading for the tower door, but I ignored them. I rolled Rue onto her back and the soft groan she let out made me want to cry in relief. After a few light taps on her cheek, her eyes fluttered open and took a moment to focus on my face.

"Gray?"

I smiled. "I bought you those knives for throwing, not for stabbing." My voice cracked and I fell into a sitting position and coughed some more, rubbing at the pain in my throat as she sat up beside me.

From below the wall a rage-filled voice drifted up on the wind. *"Thief!"*

I looked sharply at the battlements where Nissa stood, holding the glowing stone and looking down into the garden. She turned to gaze back at me.

Ruena used my shoulder and the nearby bench to get to her feet, then tugged on me until I pushed myself up as well. Things still weren't quite stationary around me. As we went to join Nissa, the voice drifted up again, even more angry and desperate. "I know you're there, thief!"

The sun was finally setting, giving everything that unreal gray tone that played tricks with the eyes, and spreading orange and red across the burning city. When I stopped in front of Nissa she held the stone out to me.

I stared at it a moment, knowing I wouldn't be able to do what she wanted.

She shook it, glaring at me.

The blood on my fingers smeared onto the faintly glowing surface as I picked it up, and I gripped it carefully so it wouldn't slip out. With a steadying breath I looked over the battlements to the ground where two figures stood, seemingly unconcerned to be surrounded by the waving tentacles of the waiting shadowkraken.

The elf had his hood flung back and stared up at me with a wide grin, holding a stone that matched mine in his hand. Beside him stood Loring, his eyes rimmed in red and his cheeks gaunt. He laughed in a manic, high-pitched tone. "There you are. Time to *die*."

Nissa set a hand on my shoulder, muttering under her breath. "*Do it!*"

I merely stared below. Not at Loring and his insanely hungry expression, but at the elf beside him. Specifically at the glowing stone in his hand. It pulsed in time with mine, slow and steady, building its power.

My eyes widened. "It's not mine."

Nissa scowled beside me. "What are you talking about? Time is up. Do it!"

"No." I reached back for Ruena, pulling her between Nissa and myself. "This stone doesn't create the labyrinth. That one does."

"But you saw it."

"I saw myself raise the stone and everything exploded. The *vision* exploded." I glanced at the bloody stone in my hand, the magic tingling

291

all through my arm, then finally met Nissa's frantic stare. "I can't do it."
I let out a strained chuckle. "I never could have done it."

Her brows creased and she just stared back at me.

Ruena leaned close and I put an arm around her shoulders, hoping I
was right. "That's the stone that belongs in this time, and the stone that
needs to be in the treasury for us to bring back. And someone has to put
it there."

"What are you saying?"

Loring's voice rose from the ground level below. "*Listen to me when
I'm threatening you!*"

I stared hard at her. "We have to be here to put it there."

Nissa glanced below, then back to me, her eyes uncertain.

The sound of a scuffle broke out below and I looked over the edge to
see Loring wrench the stone from Ailred and thrust it aloft, screaming
out. "Destroy it all!"

The stone in my hand went quiet, like a breath being held.

This was it. I didn't know how to do magic, but I suspected Loring
didn't either, and if his rage could destroy Sangarie, then my
determination could save our lives.

I raised the stone to the sky and concentrated on it as hard as I could,
clinging to my thoughts of Ruena and how I couldn't let her die. How I
refused to let Loring win.

Please, let us live.

***

When you plunge underwater the silence pushes in as the river
envelopes you, and all you can hear is the beating of your own heart.
The magic closed around us like that, trying to crush us. To drown us.

Then it was reflected back and flung outward in every direction. The
force of it tore the air away as well and I staggered against Nissa on my
left. She flung her arms around Ruena and I, ducking her head against
the sudden rush of returning air buffeting us.

I opened my eyes, squinting against the gale to watch the shockwave
as it reached the very edge of the city and a little ways onto the plain
beyond before dissipating. The sound of collapsing timbers and stone
rose from the destroyed districts, and the estates were hazy with dust
blowing back from the inner wall. The fires had all been snuffed out.

The wind died.

I took a long breath and lowered the stone as Ruena and Nissa let go of me.

The stone in my hand was glowing in the dying light of the sun and as I focused on it pain flared through my bloody fingers, into my hand, and up my forearm. I gasped and tried to drop it, but my fingers wouldn't move. I staggered back and sat heavily on the stone floor of the battlements, trying to pry my fingers open with no luck.

A stiffness crept over my wrist and the glow of the stone bled into my skin almost to the elbow. It burned like ice and the ache of the cold went all the way to my shoulder. Flakes like frost appeared on my hand, spreading across skin and stone, and I groaned in pain past clenched teeth.

Nissa took my arm and tried to pry the stone loose as well, but only ended up huffing in frustration. It was frozen in my hand and I couldn't move anything below the elbow. I couldn't feel anything below the elbow at this point either, and the cold ache that stretched to my shoulder made me gasp and shiver.

I glanced around the battlements for Ruena and saw her huddled on the ground against the railing, her hands pressed over her eyes. I couldn't imagine what that explosion had looked like with her sight. Other than that—to my intense relief—she seemed unhurt.

I clutched my frozen arm to my ribs and climbed to my feet, staggering to the wall to look out over the city. The sun was finally setting, and with the revealed darkness the shadowkraken blended into the shadows and groped its way around the side of the manor, away from us.

Then the gateways began flaring up. They ripped open closest to the manor first, spreading in all directions like the city was a piece of stretched fabric. A blue glow gave me the outline of the districts and streets, and sent the familiar shudder across my skin.

Nissa touched my shoulder. "We have to get the other stone into the cavern."

I glanced down at my hand, thinking about the rope maze that had connected the pillars beneath the manor. "That might prove difficult." I leaned over the battlements to look, catching sight of a faintly pulsing light at the bottom of the wall, nestled in a pile of ash. Loring's stone.

Ruena still huddled by the wall, sniffling.

I took a deep breath. "Let's go. You said there was a back way into the cavern?"

Nissa nodded. "Outside the city."

"That's even better. You can put the stone on the pedestal in the cavern, then go back out and hide."

The first scream from the labyrinth tore through the darkness then, high and frantic at the edge of my hearing. We weren't safe here and I didn't have so much as a pick or a razor on my person. They'd taken everything from me at the Warden's jail, and there had been no opportunity to rearm myself.

Nissa helped Ruena to her feet and led her toward the tower stairs. I clutched at my frozen arm just above the elbow, gritting my teeth at the ache that throbbed into my shoulder, and followed after them. Then the scrape of a bench across the stone alerted me to the fact that we weren't alone.

I froze and scanned the patio, catching the faint glimmer of a darker shadow inside the shadows.

36 – Night of Shadows

The shadowbeast inched closer, sniffing soundlessly. Hesitating?

How had it gotten up here so quickly? Was the manor full of them? Fear tightened my throat and I groped to the side for Ruena and pulled her behind me without taking my eyes off the beast.

Nissa brought her scythe to bear and stepped in front of us. With a few words in elfish it glowed green and the blade tripled in length. The beast reared up in response and leaped forward.

One shadowbeast didn't stand a chance. She spun her scythe and ripped it open, gut to forehead, turning it to ash before it even hit the ground.

I sighed in relief and motioned them into the tower ahead of me, shutting the door and throwing a bolt on the inside to lock it. For a moment I leaned against the heavy wood door, taking a couple of steadying breaths.

They were already halfway down to the next level and I clutched at my arm as I shuffled down after them. The cold was making it go numb and ache at the same time. I was trying hard not to think about whether this was permanent. Surely Nissa could figure something out once we had the other stone in place and could take a moment to rest.

I caught up to them by the time they reached the ground floor because Nissa had paused to look down the wide corridor. I looked as well, taking the opportunity to try to rub feeling back into my upper arm. My hand came away bloody and I was confused for a moment before I remembered the Warden's sword had cut me there.

I didn't even feel it now.

Then I noticed the dust-covered floor beneath our feet, scuffed by our passage. I frowned, thinking back to the first time I'd been in the labyrinth.

295

It had bothered me that the treasury was so easy to find. The baroness had built it and kept it a secret for a couple of years, yet we'd gone straight to it when we entered the manor. Of course we'd followed Culley and that shit-for-brains knight, but how had *they* found it?

How many tracks had there been? Four people with Culley's group, but I was sure there'd been more than that. Culley had been there before with another crew. How many bodies had we found?

Nissa started for the entrance hall and I called out. "Wait!"

She stopped and looked around for the danger before glancing back at me with a raised eyebrow. "We have to hurry."

"Not that way. We didn't see any tracks leading down this corridor, did we?"

She frowned and looked at the corridor again. "I do not remember."

"I do." I took a moment to orient myself, thinking back on the maps I'd studied. "You need to get to the north garden." I crouched to sketch in the dust on the floor and groaned as the stone sent a pulse of cold up my arm. Shrugging it off, I motioned her closer. I drew lines as I spoke.

"Take the second left ahead of us. Take that corridor all the way to the rear wing and turn right into the back corridor. From there just try to find a large dining hall. Go through the dining hall and into one of the sitting rooms beyond, and you should find a door that leads out to the garden."

Nissa raised her eyes from the dust sketch to meet mine. "You sound as if you are not coming with us."

"I'm not."

Ruena gripped my collar. "I'm not leaving you."

"Yes, you are." I lurched to my feet, falling against the wall to steady myself as the pain in my arm spiked. I pushed her hands away. "I have to make sure Culley finds the treasury. There were at least five or six people with him the first time he came here when they worked through all the traps ahead of us. Then three of them plus Rue the second time. Yet the tracks all led pretty much straight to where they needed to be."

Nissa scowled. "Perhaps they knew where it was located already."

"And if they didn't? We barely made it out in time five years ago. Do you want to risk them not finding it ahead of us? Culley not surviving the first time through? Having to navigate those traps on our own? Maybe it was easier because they got a hint."

She shook her head. "You play a dangerous game, trying to outguess the future."

"If I'm wrong, I'll just hide." Another jolt of pain went through my arm and I grimaced through it. "Besides, I'm not sure I could make it through the city. You have to move fast. You can slip by the shadowbeasts with Rue's sight. We did before."

Ruena was biting her lip and I wasn't sure if the tears were from seeing the magic earlier or if they were fresh. As I met her gaze, she shook her head. "I'm not leaving you."

"You need to get Nissa out of the city so she can get the stone where it needs to be. I'm counting on you. Come back for me afterward if you want. Deal?"

She looked at Nissa and sniffled, then nodded and dropped her gaze.

"Go." I wrapped my good arm around her shoulders and gave her a brief hug. "Be careful."

I leaned against the wall and watched until they disappeared around the corner, bracing myself to move again. My arm was all but immobile, and I still didn't have any weapons or tools, but I had my memory of the layout of the place and I could get to that library from the other side and make a few tracks to the front door. It'd give them something to follow, as long as they weren't all idiots.

I knew Culley was an idiot, but I hoped some of the others Beth had recruited were more perceptive.

***

I found my way to the library with the disturbing light of my glowing hand and stood looking inside the room that hid the secret stair. I hadn't crossed the threshold yet, because I'd intended to leave some footprints for them to follow, and if I went inside they might just follow my prints back out this direction instead of finding the lever. I hadn't yet figured out how to get through the thick dust to the actual secret stair.

The door I stood in front of was at the back of the room, opposite the one they'd be coming in. The lever was on the wall to my left about a quarter of the way down from the back wall. The opposite door was closed.

As I looked around for a solution I was struck by how tranquil everything seemed. This room had been chaotic when I arrived last time, with Ruena screaming in the knight's arms, Culley desperately searching for the lever he knew was there, scuffed footprints and books strewn across the floor, and Waren being killed by a shadowbeast. Right now it was quiet and the dust and ash coated everything like a fresh fall of gray snow. The light from the stone gave it a bluish glow.

Hold on. The books.

I tried to think back on the details, but I'd been a little preoccupied by Ruena at the time. I could understand there being books where Waren was being rammed into the shelves by a slathering beast, but there had been others all over the floor.

An idea was beginning to form on how I could avoid leaving prints back to this door. If I was careful to avoid walking in a pattern, I could cover my tracks by throwing books out over them. I just needed to make sure it didn't look like a row of stepping stones leading across the room. Whoever came in here needed to think I left through the secret staircase.

Some of the jumps to space things out were difficult to take with my arm numb and aching, and my head throbbing from the fight with the Warden, but I did my best to hop across the room like a deranged mystic.

I relaxed a little in front of the lever, leaning on the shelf and squeezing my eyes shut until the throbbing dropped to a more tolerable level. There would naturally be a cluster of prints here anyway as I "searched" for the lever. Now to leave the proper trail, which would look like two people going into the library and nobody leaving.

I'd done this only a few times before, but I knew the key was to shift my weight and adjust my pacing while walking backwards. Usually a backward walk put most of the weight on the toes, while a normal stride was either heel heavy or evenly spread. A decent tracker could spot the difference on bare earth, but it was hard to tell on solid floors.

I wound my way backward out of the library, to the entrance hall, and all the way to the front doors, which were already hanging open like I'd found them five years ago.

Well, five years ago for me. A few hours from now for the manor itself.

I stumbled through the debris there until I was sure my footprints were lost in it, then started walking forward to the library. Short strides, like I was being cautious, and alongside the prints I'd already left. When I was once again standing in front of the lever I looked back through the room, nodding in satisfaction at the tracks. Even an idiot would be able to tell someone went this way.

Now for the books.

I pulled a few out of the nearest shelf and tossed them at the scattered half-prints I'd made coming in from the back. They slid through the prints and the dust, leaving little furrows behind them and obliterating my tracks. When I was sure I'd gotten all of them I scattered more, throwing them over my shoulder to both sides as if I'd been impatiently searching the shelves. I made sure I had enough of a spread to walk across them on the way to the back door when I left.

As a final touch I ran my hands all over the nearby wall, and especially on the lever. Just for good measure I pulled on it, shuddering at the noise when the hidden panel slid to the side to reveal the dark stairs spiraling down. I walked to the first step and stood looking down. No dust in there.

I shifted to the side and backed away, pushed the lever to close the door, and noted with satisfaction that there was a trail along the floor where it had opened. Good enough. I stepped onto a book and hopped my way out of the room through the back, closing the door behind me.

***

The ache in my arm was creeping across my shoulder and making me want nothing more than to lean against the wall and shudder. Instead I started making my way toward the back door I'd pointed out for Nissa and Ruena. Maybe I could still catch up to them.

I was halfway there when a shifting in the shadows ahead made me pause. I peered into the darkened hallway, trying not to let the fear take over. A long, scraping noise echoed back to me, like claws on tile.

I turned and ran, hearing the scrambling of the beast behind me. There was no roar, no growl. Shadows are silent. I raced down the wide corridor, desperately trying to think of how to escape the beast. I had no weapons, no way to fight back, I could only run. If I tried to hide in a room it would only break down the door eventually.

I saw the base of the tower ahead, the door open as we'd left it. At least it wasn't a dead end.

The beast was having trouble on the smooth tile and in the confines of the manor, but it was gaining. By the time I reached the tower door I had just enough time to grab it and pull it shut behind me as the beast smashed into the other side. Mortar crumbled from the walls and fell as dust around me.

I fell back onto the first couple of stairs, leaning against the wall to catch my breath. The shadowbeast banged against the door again and it shook in the frame, but was made to repel attackers and reinforced with iron. Thank the Six for paranoid nobles with too much money on their hands.

After one more attempt to break through by the shadowbeast everything fell silent. I wasn't about to go back out and risk it being there waiting for me, so I pulled myself up and headed for the battlements once again. By the time I unbolted the door at the top of the tower and stumbled onto the stones of the patio, I was huffing in pain. I crossed to the railing on the right and looked down, seeing no stone and two trails leading there and away again. They'd found it, and were on their way out.

I sighed and leaned heavily on the stone tooth of the battlements, wincing as the cold spread across the top of my shoulder toward my neck. My elbow wasn't locked up yet, but it was stiff and I couldn't feel it. I turned my back to the city and dropped to my ass with a grunt, leaning against the stone rail while my numb arm rested beside me.

I wasn't sure how long I sat there, breathing through the pain, squashing down panic whenever the aching cold advanced a little farther. Was this how I died? Overtaken by the magic of the stone?

Movements in the shadows caught my attention now and then, but they weren't as frightening as the thought of this creeping paralysis. It was now advancing into my upper chest and neck, making it hard to breathe and leaving me shivering with cold. So much for leaving the ruined city with Nissa and Rue.

For a long time the only thing that broke the quiet was the occasional thready scream, floating through the haze of darkness, or the crash of rubble as something large moved out in the garden. Once I heard the death cry of someone much closer, cut off abruptly. It sounded like it came from the other side of the manor where the main doors were.

Was it the source of the blood smear we'd found in the path on our way through? That meant Culley's first group was almost inside the manor.

Later on I heard the pleading cries of a little girl echoing faintly off the stones and had to squeeze my eyes shut at the thought of Ruena being dragged inside by the knight. I'd be there soon to rescue her. There was nothing I could do about it now, even if I'd wanted to. The cold was up in my jaw and spreading across my chest and into my gut, I couldn't lift my arm anymore and it was a struggle just to pull in shallow breaths.

I was going to die here.

On the other side of the narrow patio that made up the battlements two hulking beasts crept over the side near the wall of the manor. I could only see them now that they were moving, and my heart thudded painfully against my frozen ribs. I tried to use my good arm to push myself up, but my legs didn't want to move either.

The shadowbeasts crawled closer, then stopped to stare at me, nearly disappearing in the haze. Only the faintest shimmer as they flexed their muscular shoulders told me they were still there.

The stone throbbed, sending a wave of pain through me that made me groan.

I glanced down at it, noticing a blackness that fluttered inside like a flame in a lamp. My brow creased and I peered closer. As I stared at that flickering shadow the edges of my vision closed in and I felt myself falling.

37 – Six in One

I stood in an empty space filled with darkness. There was no light source, but when I looked down I could see myself just fine.

And there was no stone in my hand.

I lifted my arms, staring at both perfectly normal hands, and breathed in relief. My headache was gone, and even the blood on my hands had disappeared.

A voice rumbled from the empty space around me, smooth and vibrant as the night itself. *"I've been waiting a long time for you."*

I spun in place, looking for the source of the voice, but there was nothing but darkness. "Who are you?"

It came again, like a whisper next to my ear, raising goosebumps and evoking a yearning that startled me. There was just a hint of amusement in the tone. *"Don't you know?"*

I did. With a strange certainty more akin to instinct. "Dakara."

A chuckle shook the very air around me and I circled again, trying to catch sight of anything it might be coming from.

"That is one name given to me, but I have many."

"What do you want?"

"You, of course."

I scowled and stared so hard into the darkness my eyes watered. "Well that's too bad, isn't it?"

"You would refuse me?"

"I'm not interested in serving anyone."

"You wouldn't be a servant. You'd be my vessel."

The voice whispered across the back of my neck, making me spin around again to see that nothing was there. I rubbed a shaking hand across my neck. "That sounds like a lot of work, and I'd rather not."

"Would you rather die?"

A freezing ache pulsed in my chest and dropped me to my knees, and for a moment my arm was numb again, my ribs wouldn't let in air, and what breath I still had caught in my throat. Then the ache was gone. I could breathe. I could move.

I dropped forward onto my hands, shaking. This wasn't real. Somewhere I was still being slowly paralyzed by that fucking stone.

The voice of Dakara shivered up my spine. *"I'm the thief's friend. You thrive in the shadows, why not join them? Bring me back into the world."*

I snorted. "You think it's just that easy? You thrust yourself into my head, threaten my life, and I become your loyal stooge?"

"You have no other choice."

I stood, still shaking a little, and pretended to dust myself off to regain some semblance of composure. "I'm done with people forcing me into things. Fuck you, and fuck your magic rock."

"I could give you everything you've ever wanted. You'd be the greatest thief who ever lived, able to command the shadows. The shadows would protect you, empower you, give you access to riches beyond even your wildest dreams."

The space began to get deeper to one side of the emptiness, growing darker and more solid. I faced it and backed away, glad to have a direction to focus on at least. It drew together, pulling shadow from all sides like fog until it was a mass of moving darkness. Then a tentacle at least six feet thick rolled out of the seething mass and slapped to the floor with the force of a falling tree.

"Holy *fuck*." I staggered back, nearly falling on my ass.

Another tentacle rolled out, and another, shaking the ground like an earthquake each time. Eventually a bulbous body with a humanoid torso wreathed in flickering black flame rose from the center of everything. Faintly glowing purple eyes peered down at me from an otherwise featureless face. Massive arms stretched forward and it leaned down to brace itself on the floor as it loomed over me.

I thought my heart would beat itself right out of my chest. My mouth was dry and I trembled in place, waiting for the thing to kill me.

The smooth voice slid into my brain. *"All you have to do is accept me."*

T. Olsen

I grasped at the first thing that popped into my head. "What about that elf? Things didn't turn out so well for him, did they?"

A spark of irritation bled through in the answering whisper. "*The elf was weak.*"

"Weak, huh?" I glanced to either side and backed away, but there was nowhere to hide. How could I do anything to a god? How could I even hope to survive? The only thing that could fight a god was... another god.

If the stone worked just by wanting something enough, maybe... Fuck, what was the name? Lux—Luxali. I filled my head with the name, putting all my fear and need into it. *Luxali! I need Luxali! Come and fight the shadow!*

I broadcasted the desire the best I could as I backed away from Dakara. "I don't think you were looking for me. I think you just desperately proposition anyone stupid enough to use the stone."

The answering chuckle started slowly, then morphed into something more manic as the god bent closer, crouching over the top of me and casting the area around me into near complete darkness.

I flung my arms over my head and dropped to my knees, grinding my teeth so hard I thought I'd break them. I fully expected the final blow to come right then. Maybe one of the flopping tentacles, or the massive hand flickering with black flame, or just the full weight of the presence above me smothering out my life. *Luxali, please.*

I huddled and breathed, feeling a pulse of cold wash through me. How long did I really have out there? If we talked long enough would I just snuff out as I died from the stone's leaking magic? Would Nissa and Ruena find me there on the battlements, dead and frozen?

The god spoke again, its breath ruffling my hair and pressing my clothes to my back. "*You want to live, don't you? You want to go back to your friends. To your lovers.*"

I didn't answer. *Luxali. The shadow is escaping.*

The god crouched above me, close enough the shadow leeching off its skin enveloped my body. "*Little thief. All I need is a spark. All I need is something to follow back to the world.*"

I forced out my reply through clenched teeth. "Then why not force me?"

There was silence from the writhing mass around me. I counted my breaths, trying to regain control of myself. As shitty as it was to know I was dying on top of the baroness's manor, that meant I was in no danger here, right?

Dakara hadn't hurt me. Even the pain before had only been the reality of my situation bleeding through into this place. Maybe they couldn't actually do anything.

Or maybe I was doing something incredibly stupid, which was just as likely.

I gathered myself and stood, looking up at the monster and clenching my hands at my sides to keep them from shaking so much. "I said... why not force me?"

A second voice, sweeter and ringing in my ears, spoke aloud. "Because they can't."

Light spilled out beneath my feet like a rush of water and the monstrous form of Dakara raised itself up, glaring at something behind me. A yellow glow touched it, making little wisps of shadow rise into the air like smoke.

I turned and squinted as a creature just as monstrous pushed back the dark and replaced it with a bright nothingness on its side. I couldn't tell what its main body looked like because of the powerful light, but dozens of golden wings lifted it up and made a fluttering noise that slithered around me. I expected a warmth to come from it, like from sunlight, but there was no heat at all.

It spoke again. "If they forced their way out, we would all follow."

Dakara faced the god of light, wisps of their shadowy form stretching out and making the other god's light dim enough that I caught sight of a barrel-shaped body with a long, whip-like tail and at least a dozen multi-jointed legs like a monstrous scorpion covered in fluttering wings.

What the fuck had I done... I didn't want to get caught in the middle of this. I backed quickly away from both massive figures, praying... well, praying wasn't probably the best thing to do at the moment.

The god of light surged forward and I stumbled as I tried to dodge away, falling to the strange solid surface below me with a pained grunt. One of the spindly legs moved over me and a vaguely human-looking foot on the end of it crashed down within inches. The foot was as big as I was, and each of seven toes ended in razor-sharp claws.

My head hurt from how bright everything got as the god crouched over me. The ground shook as multiple monstrous feet and massive tentacles slammed down. The two opposing deities shifted and entwined, shadows swallowing the light, and light burning back the shadows. Golden wings flapped and beat against the black flames of Dakara while tentacles wrapped the barrel-shaped body of Luxali.

They staggered to the side and I tried to dart out from underneath them, but a tentacle shot in front of me and wrapped quickly around my chest, trapping my arms at my sides and yanking me into the air. I grunted in surprise before the panic rose up and I tried to wrench my arms free.

I wasn't sure if Dakara was even paying attention to me. They seemed to be very focused on each other, but the tentacle around my chest tightened with each move the god made. In my mind, I heard the slithering whisper of the god.

"*Where are you going? We aren't finished yet.*"

I squirmed, trying to work my arms loose. At this rate they were going to kill me on accident as they flailed around.

I didn't belong here. All I wanted to was to be home in Sangarie. Home with the people of the city, even if I had to die with them. At least I wouldn't die in some empty place, crushed by rampaging gods.

The light god thrust its tail forward, directly under the tentacle holding me up, and I saw the gleaming tip of a barb on the end of it just before it pierced the writhing mass of tentacles that made up Dakara's lower half.

The god of darkness convulsed and howled in rage. The tentacle holding me spasmed, tightening briefly and cracking my ribs before it lost strength and I slipped out of its grasp.

I flailed madly and hit the solid surface feet first, pitching forward and landing on my shoulder, I wanted to curl up and scream, but one of the disturbing giant feet was coming my way and I heaved myself up and staggered as far as I could from the entwined gods. Weirdly, while I was sure my ribs had cracked at the time, they didn't feel damaged now, and though I'd been certain I'd broken something in my shoulder, it moved freely.

I wasn't sure if this place was in my own mind or inside the stone or something else entirely, but it definitely wasn't the real world. There wasn't even anything to hide behind. I turned my back on the gods and sprinted away, feeling strangely nauseous without any kind of visual reference for my movement. When I eventually had to pause and catch my breath I looked over my shoulder to find them still there, as if I hadn't even moved.

"Fuck." My shoulders dropped and I tried desperately to think of anything else I could do, but without catching their attention there was literally nothing here. I wanted to go home. I closed my eyes and wished for it as hard as I could, desperately hoping it was the way out. *Home.*

I shook my head as a buzzing grew in my ears, looking around for the source. It got louder, almost painful in its intensity, then I found myself plunged into a vision once again.

It was the same as when I'd first picked up the stone five years ago. I saw flashes of myself running through the manor, bursting onto the battlements to meet Nissa and Rue, then holding the stone up as a magical explosion blew outward.

It was gone as quickly as it had come on and I staggered, trying to ground myself in the vast expanse of emptiness Dakara had brought me to. Why was I having that vision again? Unless it was that late, and the other me had just picked up the stone... maybe I was sharing the vision since I was being consumed by the stone in real life.

As I took another step back my thigh met a hard surface and I nearly jumped out of my skin. I reached back and grabbed—the edge of a worn table? I glanced at it, then raised my eyes to find the familiar sight of the bar at the Devil's Throat. A few scattered tables stood between the bar and me, and behind it was Sans, wiping out a mug.

Conflicting emotions raced through me, quicker than the thoughts at least, which seem to have gotten stuck somehow. I wanted more than anything for this to be real, for the crazy nightmare to be over. Had the stone granted my wish? Could I really just walk back into the Throat right now?

As I watched, freshly swept floorboards expanded from beneath the bar, spreading under the tables, all the way to a couple of inches in front of my boots, where they stopped. A low, greasy ceiling with heavy cross braces grew overhead, groaning and creaking as it also stopped just short of where I stood. The warm glow of lamps lit the interior.

Sans set the mug he'd been wiping behind the bar and picked up another. "Good to see you, boy." He didn't seem at all concerned with the god-battle raging behind me in the expanse of nothingness.

I frowned. "You aren't real."

He snorted. "I'm real, just not usually dressed like this."

I glanced over my shoulder at the towering mass of light and shadow, twining together and flinching apart, caught in some conflict bigger than me. Then I looked back at the bar. "Are you one of them?"

"I am." He gestured at a barstool. "Come. Sit."

Why not? I stepped onto the floorboards and felt the comforting thump of my boot against wood. The noise that had been echoing through my head from the two gods lessened somewhat and I sighed in relief as I walked to the bar and stood looking at the figure that looked like my friend. "Why appear like this? Are you trying to make a deal with me too?"

He smiled and shook his head. "I appeared like this because this is your hearth. Your home." He glanced around the little corner of the Devil's Throat he'd recreated. "It's a good one."

"You're the god of fire. Hone."

"That's right. Since the first beings rose from the earth, my power has given them comfort and protection. Like they always say... Hone is where the heart is."

"Nobody says that."

His face fell a little, his eyes troubled. "They don't? Well, they used to."

I narrowed my eyes. "So what do *you* want from me? Are you looking to ride me out of this rock too?"

He chuckled. "No. I don't want anything from you, boy."

"You don't? You're happy being trapped in here or wherever you are?"

"Oh I wouldn't say happy. But it's restful."

I looked past the missing wall of the fake Throat and watched the two gods pitting themselves against each other. "Restful, huh?"

Hone-Sans shrugged. "Mostly."

I leaned on the bar out of habit. "Then what do you want? Why show up like this?"

"Because you called for me, in a way. And to remind you the First Stone is capable of both destruction and creation. Much like fire."

I rested my elbow on the bar and rubbed my forehead. "Is this why mystics are so fucking cryptic?" I gestured out the gaping hole in one side of the room. "Two gods are banging chests out there and you're pulling me aside to mutter great truths. If you want to be helpful, maybe help me get—"

The freezing ache pounded into my chest again and I squeezed my eyes shut and collapsed against the front of the bar. Hone-Sans gripped my upper arm, holding me up with more strength than the real Sans had ever shown in reality. I couldn't breathe. I couldn't move. The cold burned.

Hone-Sans leaned close. "You don't have much time left before the First Stone consumes you too, but you can change that."

I couldn't speak. I forced my eyes open and stared at him through the pain.

He leaned closer. "*We* tried to take the power for ourselves, but you can guide it instead. It only wants an outlet. There's a balance that must be maintained. *Create something*." Then he shoved me backward.

38 – Create Something

I fell back, readying myself to hit the fake floor, but that didn't happen. Instead I found myself lying on the battlements of the manor, staring into the frightened face of Ruena looking down at me. I could barely breathe, and I couldn't move. Beyond her the sky was painted in the reds and pinks of sunrise. The Night of Shadows was over.

"Nissa! He's awake!"

The elf knelt beside me, her face troubled. "I tried to stop whatever this is, but it seems to be beyond my magic."

I tried to speak, to tell her what I'd seen, but my words were breathless and weak. I was so cold. So cold I wasn't even shivering anymore. This fucking rock was going to kill me.

I thought about the god of fire, and the image he'd worn of Sans. How warm his hand had been on my arm before he pushed me out of wherever I'd been. I closed my eyes again, ignoring Rue's sharp intake of breath.

Please. Please just a little while longer. Create something? What the fuck was I supposed to create? If I had my way, I'd recreate Sangarie. Put it all back together. Just the way it was.

A warmth flowed up from the stone. The first thing I'd felt in that hand since Loring's attack. It coursed up my arm and into my chest, not quite thawing me, but giving my chest room to breathe, letting me think.

I'd bring back the Throat, with the smell of ale and grease, the worn and thickly varnished bar, the swept stone floor, the heavy tables with ale stains and knife gouges in the tops, the crumbling hearth that needed patched every spring, the rickety stairs leading up to the few tiny bedrooms... the chimney with a smooth spot worn in it from all the times I'd leaned on the warm bricks and stared out across Old Town and dreamed.

I'd bring back the Old Market with its patchwork stalls, the docks that smelled like slime and booze, the Crispy Catch that had the best fried fish in the city, Red Roan's smithy where I brought anything I needed fixed because he looked the other way, Mama Kithie's apothecary where I got the tea Deidre loved.

The brothels. May's with the tasteful red and gold and the tiny fireplace off to the side where she sat and visited with people. Tanji's and Nolan's where I felt like family. Even Odele's. The bars. The Black Bottle, the Three Barrels, the Running Hart, the Wolf and Bear... so much song and laughter. The maze of rooftops, the twisting alleys, the broken cobbles, the loud markets. The smells of lamp oil, garbage, and the river.

And the hill. The manicured lawns and extravagant back gardens, the fancy parties and rattling carriages, the façade of importance.

I'd remake it all, just as it was. Dirty and broken and fiercely alive.

Create something?

Ruena's voice, calling my name, brought me out of my thoughts again. I looked up at her tear-streaked face. That thread of warmth trailed from the stone to my chest, holding the cold at bay. How much power did the stone have?

I lifted my other hand. "Help me up."

Nissa pushed at my back and Ruena pulled on my arm, and together they sat me up and helped me stand—wobbling—at the battlements. We looked out over the ruined city. The early morning sun revealed moving shadows on the streets, and the monstrous forms of the shadowkraken squeezing between buildings that crumbled under their weight, trying to hide from the daylight, the sound of falling stone barely heard on the breeze.

Were the people of Sangarie somewhere under that? Had they remained safe in the underground? Was Deidre out there, holed up in our apartment with Elias... waiting?

I looked at the stone in my hand and clenched my teeth. Create something. I hope I was fucking doing this right.

I raised the stone above me, squeezed my eyes shut, and thought very hard about Sangarie. "Bring back my city."

The warmth that had been trailing through my body flared, burned through my arm and into my chest. I groaned with the new pain, but

311

continued to hold up the stone. Nissa and Ruena supported me to either side, much as they had when I tried to shield us from Loring's attack.

Images of Sangarie flashed through my mind, too fast to focus on. A dizzying barrage of buildings, streets, people… Memories I didn't recall. Things I couldn't have seen. I didn't fight it. The magic ripped through me, banishing the numbness from my limbs and lighting every nerve on fire. And behind it all, wearing Sans' face but seeming much *much* older, was Hone.

I think I screamed? I'm not sure how long the stone held me, but when the last of the magic flowed out through me it took whatever strength I had left and I crumpled. I was vaguely aware of my arms dropping and the stone slipping from my bloody fingers to bounce and roll across the battlements, then Nissa and Rue slowed my backward fall to the stones. Everything closed in.

39 – Prince of Fools

"Gray. *Gray!*"

The voice was familiar. I dragged myself back to consciousness with a groan and blinked in the morning sunlight to see Ruena's face above me once again, her pale eyes red and puffy, her face streaked from dried tears. I flashed her a tired smile. "This is becoming a bad habit."

She made a little squeaking noise and her chin trembled. It looked like she wanted to fall onto my chest and sob—and I prepared myself for the brunt of that—but instead she drew herself up and glared down her runny nose at me.

"What's becoming a bad habit is you almost getting yourself killed because you're an idiot. I can't believe you'd just throw around such powerful magic like that. Don't you know—"

I snorted and took stock of my physical state while she continued to berate me. There was surprisingly little damage, but a great deal of bone-numbing weariness. My arm itched a little from the fucked up paralysis the stone had caused, but otherwise seemed back to normal. Even the sword cut was gone. Had that been the stone or Nissa's work?

I pushed myself onto my elbow and Ruena helped me sit while calling me a stupid, selfish, reckless, infuriating asshole.

I sighed. "I'm sorry."

She clenched her jaw and nodded. "At least nothing I ever do will be nearly as stupid as this."

"I wouldn't be so sure." I glanced along the battlements and saw Nissa with her hands resting gently on the stone rail, staring over the city. She looked shocked and a little overcome by the view.

I wondered how different the ruins looked in daylight for her to be gazing out at them like that. Then the thought of all the people in the underground surfaced and I scrambled to my feet, brushing away Ruena's hands. Had they survived?

My first glance across the city took my breath away. I had to look around and make sure we were still stranded on top of the baroness's manor, and that everything hadn't been a nightmare. Ruena stepped up beside me and slipped her hand into mine, squeezing briefly as she matched my gaze.

Everything was back. The garden below us was bursting with green. The estates spread out around the manor wall, their sloped roofs glistening in the morning sun, each a little different than its neighbor. The wall surrounding them was completely intact, gates and all. Beyond that… the city of Sangarie stretched in a chaotic jumble of buildings and streets, the main thoroughfares piercing through to the far off city walls to the north, east, and south, and to the river in the west.

A lump formed in my throat and I gripped the stone rail hard, making sure it was real. "What happened?"

Nissa spoke with a softened tone of respect. "You somehow rebuilt it with the power of the First Stone. How? I do not know."

I didn't either. I'd thought about it… dared to hope for it… and something else had done the rest. But what about the people? I looked over my shoulder at the stone surface of the patio. There was no sign of the Warden's body and the manor seemed unnaturally quiet.

A pang of guilt blossomed in my chest. Had it been because I didn't think of them? I'd thought of the crowds in the marketplaces, and the patrons in the bars… I looked over the city again, peering toward the New Market square, and thought I could see figures moving there.

"Let's go see who survived."

***

The manor was eerily empty, fueling my panic, as were the streets on the hill, but as we neared the inner wall separating the estates from the main city I saw people at the gates. Coppers and Silvers, to be exact. They were blocking people from coming in, trying to close up the gates and hold back a small mob with thoughts of looting the deserted homes of the rich. I didn't blame them.

They looked at us with a mixture of surprise and suspicion as we pushed our way out, probably wondering where we'd come from or why we weren't clamoring for entrance, but they let us through. As I passed

314

beneath the arch I took a closer look at it. The gate opening seemed taller. Wider. And the gate itself was definitely thicker. The guards were struggling to close it with confused faces, cursing at each other. I looked over my shoulder after we shoved through the crowd and swore the wall itself was a few feet taller than it had been.

A glance to the side revealed the crooked alley to be a chaotic mess. Had it been so ramshackle before? Some of those buildings actually leaned into the alley, almost touching in the middle. I couldn't see far down it because of the crooked walls.

Ruena dragged me on, down Market Street, heading for Old Town. Most of the people we saw were dirty and confused, a few wore haunted looks or sported cuts and bruises. And there weren't nearly enough of them. I grew more and more certain that whatever magic I'd worked hadn't brought back anyone that died in the blast.

Here and there I had to look twice at a building or street, because everything was just a little bit off. Some of the shops were a little fancier. Some of the alleys a little deeper and darker. At one point I paused and looked up to see a rickety bridge spanning between two buildings where I'd always wish there was an easier crossing on the Thieves Way. It was like the entire city was just a little bit... more. Of everything.

Ruena pushed me forward, muttering about wanting to see Elias and Deidre.

We made it halfway through the city before a Yellow found us and insisted we follow him. He wouldn't say what was so important, only that they'd been ordered to search me out and bring me to the guildmaster. So we trekked to an entrance close to the guildmaster's quarters and went below.

In the underground things were more as I remembered them, other than the debris scattered in the corridors. So many people in such an enclosed space left a mess. But they were all topside now, and the tunnels were quiet as we reached the guarded door and were ushered inside.

Rigel's quarters were in shambles. The big front room that had been full of seating and carefully placed displays had been cleared. All the couches and little tables were pushed to the sides, the collected artifacts scattered across the floor, most of them visibly broken. Ruena gasped at my side and stared wide-eyed around the room. She wasn't squinting from the glow of magic, and I realized I couldn't feel the usual buzz either.

The room was full of high ranking criminals who all turned to look at me as we stepped further in. Slowly, a path cleared to the middle of the room where Senyr, Neffrey, and Deidre stood over a prone figure.

A nervous pit formed in my stomach.

Every master criminal in the guild had to be in this room, all watching me. Someone prodded me in the back and I shuffled forward, searching out Deidre's gaze. She looked grim and worried, the front of her dress over her knees dirty from having knelt on the floor. I wanted nothing more than to run to her and fold her up in my arms, make sure she was really okay and we'd both made it through all this, but a dreadful expectation hung in the room that made me stuff all that away.

When I broke her gaze and looked down I wasn't surprised that it was Rigel I saw on the floor. He was lying on his back with one hand on his chest and the other held by Toleny, one of the three Attendants of the Master. The other two Attendants cried softly in each other's arms. As I neared, Toleny looked up with red eyes and gently nudged him.

"Rigel, my dear. Your thief has arrived."

I stepped around him and into his field of vision. He looked haggard, and much older. His face was gaunt and pale, his eyes dulled. His expression held neither the jaunty smile of his good humor or the severe, tight-lipped frown of his bad moods, it was just... tired.

"I'm glad you made it, Gray." The voice was weak, but the room had settled into an eerie silence and I had no trouble hearing him.

The sight of him there, on the floor like a used up mystic, felt wrong. I wanted to leave. Instead I curled my fingers into my palm until my nails were almost piercing skin. "What happened to you?"

A ghost of the smile returned. "It was more difficult than I anticipated, protecting the entirety of the underground. That blast was impressive." He coughed and Toleny leaned down to support his head.

Neffrey stepped up beside me, leaning close to whisper. "Lord Rigel used his gift to shield the tunnels."

"His gift?" I narrowed my eyes and stared at the guildmaster, who was speaking softly with the woman beside him. Nissa's story about him

316

being raised with the elves came back, and I tried not to let on that I knew what he was talking about.

The spymaster's tone was angry, as if he was insulted not to have known something. "He's an elfblood. He can shield things with magic."

It was tempting to insinuate that I'd known about his heritage already, since it was so rare I'd have information like that before Neffrey did, but something about the weariness in Rigel made me keep the comments to myself. "What's wrong with him?"

"He said he couldn't do it with the power he had, so he used all the contraband shit he's acquired over the years to boost his ability. It burned through him."

Rigel spoke up from the floor again. "Gray. My spies tell me the city has been restored. How did that happen?"

I tried to search out Nissa and Ruena, but the people surrounding us were hovering close, hanging on the guildmaster's words, and I couldn't see them in the press of bodies. "Well, I—" I looked at Senyr, then Deidre, both of them watching me from the other side of Rigel. "Loring's stone destroyed the city. Mine brought it back."

Thoughts of Dakara threatened to bubble up and I stubbornly shoved them down deeper. They were trapped in the stone, and I was out here. I was safe. I sought out Deidre again, grounding myself in her return gaze.

Rigel sighed. "I won't waste much time with grand speeches. I don't think there's a lot of time left, and if the city is to continue then arrangements need to be made."

The small noises that had been coming from the gathered criminals stopped entirely as they all listened, waiting on every word coming from their leader. I had a terrible feeling in my gut, like being cornered on a hit.

Rigel tried to rise and Toleny pressed him to the floor, scolding under her breath and warning him not to move. He brushed her weakly away, but remained on his back. His next words came a little louder, and took more effort.

"I rebuilt this guild to benefit those cast out of society. To give them safety and community. Some of us remember the old days all too well, and I fear in times of challenge we would slip back into clawing at each other instead of working together."

A coughing fit took him and Toleny supported him through it as everyone in the room waited, whispering and shifting uncomfortably. I glanced at Deidre, but she was watching him with a troubled expression on her face.

Rigel spoke again, somewhat weaker. "I chose my successor long ago. Someone born here on the streets, raised by the guild, but with the vision needed to carry the city to a brighter future. Someone I believe the undercity will follow."

He turned his wavering gaze on me. "The guild must carry on, and it will do so with you as its leader."

Anxiety flushed through me, making my hands sweat and my legs shake. I didn't want to run this guild. I didn't want to be responsible for all these people... again. Just the thought of it made my throat start to tighten.

"It's time for you to take your place."

No. I didn't care what he thought was best for the guild. I didn't care what he'd planned. This wasn't me. Anger rose up and drowned out the anxiety, and I ground my teeth and shook my head. How dare he just make that decision for me? "No. I refuse." I turned and tried to walk away.

Neffrey stepped in front of me. "What are you doing?"

My hands were shaking and the blood was pounding in my head. "Get out of my way, Neff."

He gripped my arm and stepped in front of me again as I tried to sidestep him. "You were raised for this, boy!"

Rigel's voice drifted up, stopping us both. "Let him go."

Neffrey grunted and shot me a dirty look, but backed away. I glanced behind me at the guildmaster, his tired gaze meeting mine.

Rigel's mouth quirked with a wry smile. "You enjoy ruining my plans."

I glared back. "Then stop making my life part of your plans."

"As much as you dislike the idea, I know you're ready. Please..." He gasped faintly and pain crossed his features before they once more smoothed out. "Reconsider. You were meant for this."

I thought of all the times he'd pushed me. All the times he'd lectured me, protected me, or laid opportunities at my feet. He'd given me more freedom than anyone in my station deserved. He'd sent me to Senyr. He'd given me Old Town.

I ducked my head, the anger warring with guilt. My face flushed, but my voice rang steady in the silence of the packed room. "I have *never* wanted this."

There was a long pause, then the guildmaster sighed. "Very well." He pulled a ring from his finger and held it up, casting me one last regretful look as Senyr stepped into view. Rigel raised his voice, though it was still thready and weak, addressing the gathered criminals. "I pass on my legacy to Senyr, and ask that you give him the same loyalty you gave me."

Senyr looked at me as Rigel continued talking, nodding once in a signal I recognized as telling me to go.

I nodded in return and slipped behind two Greens. Everyone was paying attention to what Rigel was saying, not concerned with me sliding past. A few glanced my way, shook their heads, and turned back to the new speech being given in halting, pain-filled words.

When I reached the edge of the crowd I was joined by Nissa and Ruena. Rue's face was shocked as she stared at me, but Nissa's was more curious and she kept an eye on the cluster of people.

Ruena leaned close. "Did you just give up the chance to be the boss?"

I frowned and ignored her question. I wasn't able to pick out what Rigel was saying, surrounded as he was by criminals hanging on every word, and I couldn't see him either. I couldn't even see Senyr and Deidre past the throng. My chest tightened at the thought of her, but the danger had passed. She'd survived, and she looked fine. Big things were happening and I could wait to talk to her now that I knew she was safe.

Ruena nudged me. "What now?"

I didn't want to stick around and have to explain myself to any of these people once the excitement had died down, and I certainly didn't want to have to explain myself to Rigel. Surely he wasn't dying, right? He wasn't bleeding or anything. He'd get some mystics in here and dodder away into retirement and let Senyr run things. That had to be what was going on. They didn't need me for that. "Let's get out of here."

Ruena and Nissa led the way. Before I could join them at the door, someone tugged on my sleeve and I glanced back to see Deidre.

She ran her eyes over my body and smiled as she bit her lip. "You made it."

I peered over her shoulder at the crowd, feeling a desperate urge to be anywhere else. "Not here." I slid my hand into hers and tugged her along after Rue and Nissa.

In the tunnel outside the guildmaster's quarters Elias joined us, embracing Ruena briefly before looking at Deidre with his eyebrow raised in a question.

She clung to my hand with both of hers and said, "To the hill. Market Street gate."

I frowned and tried to meet her gaze, but Elias started off and she pulled me along after her. We worked our way through the underground most of the way, coming topside a few blocks from the wall, then pushed past the rioting people we found in the streets.

It was worse than when I'd been through not half an hour ago. It looked as if the Coppers had been drastically depleted in number, which made sense considering the baroness hadn't believed our story and had ordered them to fight. I was surprised even this many had fled, and even more surprised they'd gone straight back to being pains in the ass once morning came. Strangely, there were people in common clothes helping the Coppers try to maintain order. Odd for so many people to be acting rationally in a situation like this, unless—

I pulled away from Diedre's hand and stopped one of them. "What's going on here?"

Recognition dawned in the man's eyes and he straightened a little. "We're trying to do as the masters instructed, but people don't like to listen to us without uniforms or something. Just trying to keep all these people from looting and killing each other." Then he grinned slyly. "Coppers are a little confused about it. It's kind of funny."

They'd rallied the guildmembers to keep the populace in check? Who'd managed that on such short notice? Unless it was part of Rigel's plan for protecting everyone in the underground. Had he foreseen the riots come morning if everyone survived? I hadn't been around the last couple of days to know what rumors were spreading, so it was possible.

Diedre tugged me into motion again and we eventually reached the inner wall, now heavily guarded against rioters. The gate was shut and Silvers stood before it. When I looked down the crooked alley to either side there were Silvers stationed there as well. It seemed they'd left the streets to the Coppers and decided to protect this wall with the more experienced troops. I doubted there were many nobles inside the estates, so they were just guarding the empty houses of the nobility.

Diedre left me standing with the others and walked up to the guard that stepped out to face us. "We need to be let through. We have business inside with Lady Josyna." She pulled a piece of paper from the folds of her dress and held it out impatiently.

The guard ripped it out of her hand and looked it over, frowning, then waved at the gate and a pair of Silvers rushed to crack it open. I was shocked that her claim had worked so well, but managed to keep my jaw shut as she returned to me.

She led us all through, then in the direction of the manor she kept as Lady Josyna. The streets on the hill were empty except for patrolling Silvers, and there was no movement in the manors.

I leaned closer to her. "What are we doing?"

She replied back in a subdued tone, as mindful as I was of the eerie feeling given off by the rows of empty houses and armored guards. "I thought the best place to be alone would be my manor. Plus I have to begin sorting out a few things."

"What things?"

She gave me a wicked smile. "You'll see."

40 – Lady Midnight

Josyna's manor was startlingly occupied, if only because every house around it looked so empty. I shuddered to think of how many people had lost their lives on the hill, bidden to remain and guard the manors of the elite while the families of the nobles themselves fled the city. Deidre, of course, had sent her servants to the underground with orders to return as soon as it was safe.

Plainly clothed guards stood in her garden with crossbows, casually watching us near the front gate, but Deidre merely nodded at them and led us through. One even jumped to open the front door of the manor for her. A quick glance at Ruena's shocked face reminded me that I was probably the only one not on her payroll who knew the Lady Josyna's true identity, but that was her secret to tell in her own time.

She led us into the manor and paused at the bottom of the grand staircase, suddenly looking worried and frantic. I instinctively set a hand on the small of her back and moved in to comfort her, then caught myself.

She wasn't biting her lip, and she always bit her lip when she was really worried. Her hands fluttered uselessly in distress until she gathered her skirt and took three quick steps on the stairs, peering up and calling out for someone named Kebron.

She was faking it. I schooled my expression into one of concern, but held back. I wasn't entirely sure what was going on yet, but she was here as Lady Midnight, not the lady of the house. Things to take care of, huh?

One of the upper floor servants I recognized from the night of my break-in came trotting down the steps. Kebron, I presumed. Deidre clutched his arm and spoke softly with him, then passed him by and hurried up the stairs.

I started up after her, but Kebron put a hand out.

"You'll have to wait down here. There's a sitting room just there." He pointed to the left through a pair of open doors into a room dotted with plush chairs and couches.

I frowned and started to take another step to be on the same level as the servant-guard, but Elias spoke from behind me.

"We'll wait."

I shot a dirty look at him over my shoulder, but his face remained firmly neutral. He didn't back down. Had Deidre told him what was going on while they waited out the night in our apartment? If she had some kind of plan she was hatching it was very likely he was in on it.

I let my posture relax and dropped down off the staircase. "Of course. We'll wait."

Kebron narrowed his eyes at me, but retreated up the stairs.

I watched him go, then glared at the Red as I led the way into the sitting room. I could ask him, but if Deidre didn't want anyone else knowing he'd just refuse to tell me and I'd get angry. I had to trust she had everything in hand and would bring me up to speed when she could.

We waited at least an hour, and I paced the entire time. Toward the end of that hour I realized how very tired I was after waiting out the Night of Shadows and recreating the entire city with a magic rock, but before I could decide if it'd be improper to take a nap on one of the couches, Deidre walked in.

Her eyes were red and her cheeks were puffy like she'd been crying. I crossed to her and she flung herself into my arms and leaned close to whisper into my ear in a voice that was not at *all* distraught.

"How does it feel to hold a noblewoman in your arms?"

I stiffened and scowled, but she pulled away before I could find an answer.

She took my hand and led me out of the room, into a foyer growing increasingly crowded with servants. Kebron cleared the way for us to the stairs and she let go of my hand and asked me to wait as she climbed up enough stairs to be looking out over the people alongside Kebron.

He spoke in a voice that probably carried through the entire house. "The Lady Josyna has passed on, taken by the destruction of the city along with the home she created for all of us. On the eve of the Night of Shadows she made her first and final appearance to us here on these very steps to name her successor."

323

I frowned at Deidre, but she wasn't looking at me. She was artfully wiping a tear from her cheek and steadying herself on Kebron's arm.

He continued, "Today, with the unexpected miracle that restored our home to us, we also welcome its new Lady." He shifted to hold Deidre's hand and took a knee on the stair. "Welcome your mistress, Lady Deidre Maywither, adopted daughter of the late Lady Josyna Maywither."

Cheers filled the foyer and Deidre's face flushed a deep red. I was watching closely, or I might not have caught the quick squeeze she gave Kebron's hand, or the steadying breath she took before smiling through her fake tears. She stepped down to the floor level once more and people swarmed her, swearing their loyal service to her as they had to their beloved Lady Josyna, and Deidre took it all with grace.

Once the foyer began to clear and the servants went back to their duties, Diedre stepped in front of me with an apologetic smile, still glowing with the excitement of her sudden rise in station.

I raised an eyebrow. "Lady Josyna made an appearance, did she?"

The blush on her cheeks grew a little brighter and she stepped close to not be overheard. "An acquaintance from outside the city. She was very sick and was more than willing to spend her final days being cared for and pretending to be nobility. I promised I'd give her grandchildren a place here. Sadly, she passed on during the evacuation. I had her body sent quietly back to her family."

I pitched my voice to match. "A move worthy of Rigel. Perhaps he should have made you the guildmaster."

She grinned a little wider. "I have larger aspirations."

Before I could question her the main door opened and a servant peered inside. "Lady Midnight, a carriage has arrived for you from the Henrick estate."

She beamed back at him. "I'll be there in a moment."

I felt completely out of the loop and it was irritating. I glared at the door as the servant closed it, then muttered at Diedre. "Lord Barty?"

She rose on her toes to kiss my cheek. "I didn't expect the city to still be here. I thought I was going to have to relocate everything and start all over, which is why I gave myself the title before the Night of Shadows. But now... Plans have shifted drastically, and I have to make my move."

"What move?"

She gripped both my hands, squeezing them excitedly. "If I'm successful, you'll find out soon. But in the meantime you look like shit. Why don't all of you go upstairs and find someplace to rest. I believe you know your way around." Her eyebrow raised in amusement and she spun away.

I reached out to catch her but she was too quick, or I was too tired. "Deid! Be careful!"

She looked back once at the door, blew me a kiss, and was gone.

I wanted to sink down on the stairs and not move for at least a day. As I took stock of myself again I realized how wobbly my legs were and how heavy my eyelids had become.

Kebron's voice echoed down the stairs. "I'll show you to your rooms, sir."

Ruena stepped up beside me and wrinkled her nose. "Sir? He doesn't know who you are, does he?"

"Shut up."

"You need me to help you up the steps, old man?"

I merely started climbing and called up to the man waiting for us. "Make sure the mouthy one gets a room all to herself. We must protect her purity."

Ruena made an indignant noise behind me and I chuckled as I trudged up the stairs. As much as I was worried about what Deidre was hatching, I knew I was in no position to do anything to help her. I'd just have to be patient and wait for her to come back.

And sleep. By the Six, I needed a *week* of sleep.

I frowned at the phrase that had reflexively entered my thoughts, but I was too tired to do much else. Each of my companions was deposited in a room of their own, despite Ruena's grumbled protests that she wanted to share with Elias, and Kebron brought me further down the hall to the room Deidre used when she was here. I stood uncertainly as he opened the door and stepped aside.

How much did this man know about who I was? About who Diedre was? I really needed to sit down with that woman and get all this secret life stuff sorted out.

"Sir?"

I scowled. "Don't do that."

"Do you want a different room?"

325

I didn't move. "Is she being protected?"

"She has Sybil and Ogden with her, and Lord Bartholomew sent an escort as well."

There were so many questions, but they all flitted in and out of my thoughts. None of them were quite as pressing as that one had been, so I let them go. I sighed and stepped into the room, glancing back as the door closed softly behind me.

At least I could get a little sleep before having to deal with anything else.

***

I was standing on a rooftop, looking out over the sprawling city, but this was no fortified manor on the hill. It was the roof of the Throat with the worn chimney behind me. The inside of the low parapet that ringed the building was scarred by little chips from rocks I'd thrown at it over the years. It seemed odd that it was the center of the city now, but I couldn't put my finger on why, and it didn't seem to be all that important.

As I watched, the sky darkened until the streets were lit only by lamps and beams of light coming from windows. A familiar and comforting sight. Then a deeper darkness surrounded the city and began to creep inward, flowing along the streets and swallowing buildings. Lights winked out as it advanced and the first fingers of panic gripped my chest as the feeling of being trapped and surrounded intensified. I set my back to the chimney.

The front edge of the shadows looked like a bank of thunderclouds moving across the ground, billowing forward and filling in the last clear space around the Throat, climbing up the exterior walls, pouring over the parapet onto the graveled rooftop.

There was no place to go. It was coming at me from every side and the roiling edges crept closer just ahead of the looming wall of darkness. It wash over my boots first, completely obscuring the solid surface so that it looked like I stood in a bubble surrounded by inky clouds, just me and the chimney at my back. Then it rose to my knees, and to my hips, and over my waist.

The panic fully settled in and I groped for the edge of the chimney that had just been swallowed up, hoping to find an anchor of some sort, but where I should have felt stone my hand passed through with no resistance. I flailed wildly about, searching for the chimney as the darkness reached my neck, then I sucked in a deep breath as it surged over my head.

I couldn't see anything.

For a few moments I tried not to breathe, but eventually I blew out my remaining air in a rush and inhaled with a sense of dread.

It was cold, but it was air. I took another breath, and another, reaching out for anything solid and finding nothing. I didn't dare move from the place I stood in case I stepped off the side of the roof.

A voice came out of the darkness, bypassing my ears entirely and going straight to my mind, causing my entire body to vibrate. *"Gray."*

I knew that voice.

It was the god of darkness. Dakara.

"Gray."

I shook my head, closing my eyes to keep the pressing darkness at bay. I couldn't feel anything around me except the hard surface below my feet, and I wondered if the rest of the world had disappeared.

Then a thick, cold, leathery appendage moved against my chest.

I reacted instantly and violently, throwing myself back, and in the darkness I came up against a writhing mass of tentacles. They wound over my arms and around my thighs and waist before I could jerk away. I strained, tugging one arm free only to have it grappled again. They wrapped around my chest, sliding against my skin and clothing, tightening to hold me in place.

I was breathing fast, trembling all over. I had the terrifying thought that they could constrict and crush me in an instant, spraying the darkness with blood and shards of bone.

"Did you think you could escape me?"

The tentacles tightened and I heard my joints crack and felt the stretch in my shoulders and hips. One of the tentacles wound across the front of my throat, forcing my head back and making it even harder to catch my breath.

"I am everywhere. I am watching you from the shadows."

They pulled a little tighter and I made a strangled noise of pain as one of my shoulders dislocated, then the other. I sucked in the next few breaths past my teeth, groaning and realizing I was beginning to lose feeling in my arms and legs.

"You are mine, thief."

I summoned what sense I had left, forcing as much air into my chest as I could, and answered. "Fuck. You."

The tentacles convulsed and there was a terrible tugging, and a ripping pain as my limbs were torn from my body.

***

I woke in a cold sweat, gasping for air as I sat up and tried to get my bearings in a mound of fluffy pillows and thick blankets, in a room much different than my underground apartment. As the panic gave way to reason I remembered where I was and dropped my head into shaking hands.

I'd lived with nightmares my whole life, but the words of the god of darkness had chilled me and clung to my mind like burs. The pain had felt so real, and I wondered if it had only been a nightmare, or if some part of that place had stayed with me after my use of the stone.

I flopped back onto the pillows, sighing and throwing an arm over my face. I could just go back to sleep, pretend it was three days ago and Diedre was here beside me.

I'd just started to doze again when a knock startled me awake.

"Mister Gray, your presence is requested by Lady Diedre."

I groaned and wondered if this was the beginning of a very irritating turn of events. What was life going to be like now that Deidre was real nobility?

41 – The Baroness

The carriage rattled through the garden surrounding the baroness's manor, rocking to a stop just to the right of the main doors. All the bouncing and vibrations from the cobblestones had been enough to make me nauseous and jar my spine, so I was glad to be able to get out of the damned thing. I hoped I'd never have to use one again and couldn't imagine why someone rich enough to afford one would want to use it either.

I straightened the respectable shirt and vest I'd been given, glad at least that it was a cut I was used to, even if it was a little more embellished than I liked. Deidre had obviously chosen it specifically so I would have to be petty not to accept. Someone had even been so good as to find my lost possessions in the Warden's jail, though Deidre's servants couldn't tell me who had retrieved them or how. So I had my back sheaths, my picks, and all my hidden knives. Just having them made me feel a little more normal again.

I stared up at the double doors with the Silvers posted to either side, wondering how many Irons had survived the Night of Shadows. Most of them had been in the manor, and to my knowledge anyone who perished in the blast was still gone.

One of Deidre's servant-guards, whose name I hadn't caught, stepped up beside me. He looked a little out of place, tugging on the collar of his tunic in a gesture I was familiar with. He was a good ten years older than I was, his hair and thick moustache streaked with gray and his face weathered. He spoke without looking at me.

"Lady Deidre said you should join her in the audience hall when you arrived."

"Care to tell me what's going on? Maybe prepare me for what I'll face in there?"

His cheek twitched, but he remained staring dutifully forward. "She wanted it to be a surprise."

I raised an eyebrow and sighed loudly. "Of course she does. Because I haven't been through enough surprises in the last couple of days." I moved to take the first step and realized I was shaking.

Nothing good ever came from entering this building. As I climbed the short set of stairs and passed through the doors opened by the Silvers I reflexively started to invoke the Six, then thought better of it and just hoped everything would work out on its own.

I honestly couldn't remember what the manor had looked like on the way out after recreating everything. Between the weakness and stress of facing Dakara I hadn't been paying attention until we were well into the estates below. What I saw now was a strangely bare foyer. Many of the expensive tapestries and décor were missing, possibly from having been removed before it was destroyed, and things I remembered as torn and broken had been restored with whatever I'd done. Servants were busy cleaning or scurrying through rooms, and Silvers stood everywhere watching them all.

I didn't know what to expect as the Silvers at the doors to the audience hall swung them open. I was pretty sure the baroness had been turned to ash with the rest of the nobility that remained in the manor, so someone must have claimed her title and moved to set themselves up to rule Sangarie.

I stepped through into the massive room to find clusters of wide-eyed courtiers whispering in groups and craning their necks toward the raised dais. It wasn't much different than the scene from Rigel's stateroom, and I knew there was definitely a change of power happening here.

I strode through them, the dutiful guard beside me, until the last of the courtiers parted to reveal a surprising group standing at the front. Deidre was there in a beautiful gown of midnight blue, her hair done up and a sapphire necklace at her throat that sparkled in the light of the lamps. Her face was flushed and nervous, but when she caught sight of me she smiled.

Next to her was Lord Barty, holding a large book in his arms and breaking off whatever he'd been saying to also watch my approach with a pleased grin. Three other nobles I didn't recognize completed the group.

Deidre lifted her skirt and met me at the base of the two steps leading up to the waiting chairs where the baroness had held court. She gave me a quick hug, then began talking in a hushed tone as she poked her fingers through my hair to arrange it.

"I'm so glad you made it before we started. I was worried you'd refuse and miss everything. Is your outfit okay? I tried to find something just a little nicer than what you normally wear, but the clothiers aren't really up and running yet so it was difficult."

I brushed her twitching fingers away. "What's going on?"

She took a deep breath and beamed back at me. "I'm taking an opportunity."

I frowned, glancing at the nobles behind her with a growing anxiety. She couldn't mean... "What opportunity? Slow down and tell me what you're doing."

She grabbed both my hands, pulling them up between us and holding them tight. "When Lord Bartholomew and I realized the city had been restored we knew there were a number of empty chairs here. The baroness had no heirs, and no family. Someone would be stepping in and claiming her seat. We thought, why not us?"

My gaze darted to Lord Barty, who was talking with the other three nobles nearby. "Go on."

"I had word sent out to the nobles friendly to me or to Lady Josyna, and told them to meet me at her—my—manor. I asked for their support, in return for status in the new court."

"By the Six... Deid what have you done?"

"With the support of the lords and ladies who returned at my call, and most of the other houses in disarray because of the deaths of their heads of house, I've taken control of the city myself. I've claimed the title of baroness, and in a few moments Lord Bartholomew will announce it to the gathered court."

The blood had to have run all the way out of my face. She set a hand on my cheek and gazed up at me with furrowed brows. "There will never be a chance like this again." Her breath shuddered and she bit her lip. "I can do something good here."

I raised my hands to cup her face, swallowing back the nerves and doing my best to smile. "I know you can. If this is what you want, then do it. I'm here for you, even if you wear a crown."

Tears welled in her eyes and she snorted softly. "A baroness doesn't wear a crown."

"I'll steal you one, if you want."

She leaned into me, resting her forehead briefly on my shoulder. "Just trust me. Senyr will be here soon, and I know what I'm doing."

I raised an eyebrow. "Dare I ask?"

Lord Bartholomew's voice thundered through the hall, surprising me with a ring of authority I didn't think the noble capable of.

"We have gathered here today to name a new ruler of Sangarie, as outlined in the laws of the Free State of Elisar." He held up the thick book for all to see.

Deidre squeezed my hand, then let go and moved to stand with the other three nobles on the dais. I glanced around, catching sight of my gray-haired escort, and stepped back to stand near him and out of direct sight of the assembled court.

Bartholomew continued. "I hereby put forth Lady Deidre Maywither as candidate for the position."

One of the nobles behind him spoke up. "I second the candidacy."

Bartholomew nodded and peered around the room. "Does anyone else put forth a candidate?"

The room buzzed, and people shoved one another and whispered furiously, arguing amongst themselves, but nobody spoke out.

Bartholomew spoke over the din. "In that case—"

A voice shouted from the crowd. "This is too fast! There needs to be deliberation!"

A supporting noble stepped up beside Lord Barty. "There's no time for lengthy deliberation. Sangarie has been weakened by the loss of nearly half its population, including a great many of its guard. Power must be restored now, before we fall prey to outside forces."

Another voice from the crowd: "Isn't that the escort? Lady Midnight? How can she run the city when she's part of the guild of thieves?"

Deidre stepped forward at that, casting me a quick glance as she did so with a warning look that was very familiar. She was telling me not to get involved.

She stepped in front of Barty, her dark blue dress swirling at her feet dramatically. "I *was* an escort. But I have brought the king of thieves here today so that I may formally renounce my place with the criminal guild."

Scattered laughter greeted that and I could sense the crowd turning on them. Their point had been valid, and the nobility would never nominate a prostitute as their leader. She'd lost them. I glanced up at her with concern, but her face was clear as she stared them down.

"Master Senyr, would you please step forward."

Senyr walked out of the crowd, dressed in his finery and flanked by Neffrey and Rohgart in their usual attire. The beggar was in rags, the assassin in creaking leather and a tattered cloak. The nobles gasped and hurriedly gave them a wide berth, although they looked on in fascination. Senyr walked to the dais and gazed up at Deidre. His first words were soft, just loud enough for me to pick up off to the side.

"Are you sure about this?"

Deidre nodded briskly.

Senyr sighed and closed his eyes briefly before addressing the room, his voice carrying through the hall as easily as Barty's had. "She has denounced the guild. She is no longer under my protection, and may no longer practice in this city." He motioned Rohgart forward.

The hulking assassin moved to the steps of the dais and set down an iron box at the end of a thin rod so that it clanked on the marbled floor. Deidre stepped in front of him and they exchanged a few whispers I couldn't make out, then she turned her back and knelt on the edge of the dais.

I glanced at Senyr, but he was staring at them with a carefully neutral expression. I didn't know if he'd seen me or not, but he looked uncomfortable.

The ripping noise of cloth brought my attention back to the dais and I caught my breath as Rohgart stepped back, having torn open the back of Deidre's gown to expose the blue hand tattoo on her shoulder. Her arms were across her chest, holding the fabric closed for modesty's sake, and she was trembling.

Rohgart gripped the rod's handle and twisted, releasing a catch in the iron box so the top opened up. Light came from glowing red coals within, and on the end of the rod was a brand already heated to a bright orange.

My heart dropped and my mouth went dry. "No!" I started forward, but the gray-haired escort grabbed me around the chest and held me back, hissing into my ear.

"Don't ruin this!"

I hissed right back, struggling in his grip. "I can't let them hurt her."

"Trust her."

Fuck. I stopped fighting, but the escort kept hold of me. I wanted to run to her and protect her, even if I faced the Butcher, but I knew he was right. She'd asked me not to interfere. She'd known this would happen and she was using it.

She was right. The nobility loved spectacle. This would shock the fuck out of them and they'd have to accept her severed ties with the guild, but how could I watch it happen?

Rohgart was quick. The brand touched the smooth skin of her shoulder and sizzled, smoke curling from the edges. Deidre shook, her face screwed up for a moment, and I thought she'd endure it without crying out, but a high-pitched screech echoed through the stunned silence of the hall.

I surged forward again without thinking, but the escort had been ready and held me back.

Rohgart pulled the brand away and I had a brief glimpse of the angry red X across her tattoo before a servant scurried forward with a wet cloth and covered it. Deidre slumped into their arms briefly, then gathered herself and stood on shaking legs to face the room.

She was breathing heavily, her dress still held together in the front with one arm, but she glared defiantly out over the assembled nobles. Her voice rang through the room. "I leave behind my old life, and accept my place here."

There were a few moments where the only sound was the soft click of Rohgart's boots as he stepped back and the whisper of cloth as the crowd shifted, then someone in the back started to clap and it was picked up by others until the entire room was clapping and shouting approval.

The escort holding me spoke in my ear over the din. "Is it safe to let go of you now?"

I scowled. "Yes." I shook him off and straightened my shirt, watching as Lord Barty led Deidre back to the center of the dais.

He then turned and addressed the court. "I ask those assembled today to approve Lady Deidre Maywither as the legal and rightful Baroness of Sangarie. All those who approve, call out."

The room roared in response. I sucked in a deep breath and gazed out at them. How was this even happening?

Barty's voice quieted the crowd. "All those in opposition?"

A few voices rose in anger, but were quickly cut off.

Barty pierced each one with a hard stare, as if to say he was making note of them. Then he held his hand out and Deidre took it. He raised it in the air and called out, "May I present the new Lady of Sangarie, Baroness Deidre Maywither!"

Deidre smiled brightly and pulled her hand free to wave at the court as she clutched her ripped gown to her chest with the other. Senyr, Neffrey, and Rohgart quietly slipped into the crowd and disappeared from sight.

I just stood there, dumbfounded.

42 – Goodbye

I stood on the same battlements where everything had happened the night before, watching the sun as it lowered on the horizon until it looked like it was balanced on the city skyline. It wasn't where I wanted to be, but it was the only place I'd found that wasn't full of scurrying servants or guards. Only a single young man was here, sweeping ash from the stones into a sack as if it was merely the remnants of a dust storm. I wondered if it was what remained of the Warden.

I glanced down again at the wrinkled piece of paper in my hand, the short message on it scrawled in Senyr's handwriting.

Rigel passed early this morning. He said to tell you he understands, and to continue protecting what you care about.

I took a step forward and looked down into the garden where Loring had raised the stone and unleashed his dying rage. My mind was surprisingly numb about the entire thing. Somewhere in the city there was music playing loud enough the melody drifted all the way here, and it made me feel strangely cut off from everything.

One of the heavy doors leading into the manor opened and I glanced over to see Deidre, trailed by Kebron and a besotted-looking Silverguard that couldn't have been old enough to shave.

I sniffled and crushed the paper in my hand, then shoved it into a pocket. I'd deal with it later.

Deidre spotted me and sighed in relief, then picked up her skirt and rushed toward me. She'd changed her gown and now wore a sheer dress of dark blue with a train of silver filagree. The sleeves were long and flared at the end, and the bust was embroidered in silver as well. Kebron held back the over-eager guard with him, giving us a little space.

I raised my arms and wrapped them around her waist as she hugged me close, mindful of the bandage peeking through the edge of the dress at her shoulder. The scent of some kind of sweet perfume clung to her and made my nose itch, alongside the smell of whatever ointment they'd used to dress her burn. It wasn't how she normally smelled, and I was surprised how irritated I felt about that.

After a few moments she spoke. "You're upset."

I watched the servant diligently brushing ash out of the cracks between the stones and the guards doing their best not to look like they were listening. "What happens now?"

She chuckled. "Well, now the rumors will fly about how the baroness has had her heart stolen by a master thief."

I grunted softly and stepped back to lean my ass against the stone rail of the battlements, crossing my arms over my chest. I couldn't meet her gaze.

She leaned against the rail beside me, close but not touching, her hands fidgeting in her lap. "I'm sorry I didn't tell you what was going on, but it all happened so fast. We had to take action before someone else tried to."

I knew she was right, and I wasn't even sure why I was upset, just that I felt like I was losing something. I'd been so concerned with the destruction of the city for the last week, but now that it was whole again it seemed worse than if it *had* been leveled to ruins. It all seemed so different, like it was completely foreign to me.

Lady Karyn was gone, along with all her Ironguard. Most of the pompous nobles were gone. Their families remained to pick up the pieces, but for the next few years the court would have a great many children and cousins trying to figure out how to be rich assholes with more responsibility than before.

Fuck. The Warden was gone. The sense of relief only made me feel more disconnected from everything. It all seemed like a dream I'd wake up from any minute.

Deidre's voice was low and uncertain. "Please talk to me?"

I dropped a hand to hers, squeezing her fingers to stop her fidgeting. "I'm happy for you, and proud of what you've managed to do. The city will be a better place with you at the top of the hill."

She twined her fingers in mine. "But?"

I snorted. "I don't know where I belong in it anymore. What am I supposed to do, sneak into the baroness's manor whenever I want to see you? Live here with you and sneak out to do guild work?"

She leaned against my shoulder. "You'd make a terrible nobleman. I'd never ask you to do that."

"What happens to us? I imagined spending the rest of our lives together."

"Oh dearest, we can still do that." She set a hand on my cheek and guided my gaze to hers. "It just might look a little different than you pictured it."

I pulled her hand down and looked away. "I don't even know what I'm supposed to be doing now. I haven't talked to Senyr since before the Night of Shadows and I might not even have a place in the guild anymore after refusing Rigel. After all that happened I—"

Visions of the encounter with Dakara flitted into my mind and I swallowed back the instinctive panic, reminding myself it was done. They were locked in the stone and I'd fixed everything.

Almost everything.

Deidre stepped in front of me and wrapped her arms around my shoulders, pulling my head to her shoulder. For a moment I stiffened and thought about slipping away, but a whiff of her familiar moonflower scent clung to her skin beneath the other sweet smells and I pulled her closer and squeezed my eyes shut to fight the sting of tears.

Her fingers slid through my hair, stroking the back of my head in a calming motion, and her voice was soft. "We'll figure it out. This was never going to be easy for us, but if we want it then we'll make it work. Besides, someone has to take care of you."

I snorted and quickly wiped at my eyes as I pulled back, then dragged up a smile. "Just make sure whoever you pick to be the new Warden doesn't have anything against me."

She laughed. "That's asking a lot."

The door to the tower stairs opened and we both looked to see Nissa appear, followed by a Silverguard who slipped off to the side to stand at attention. It was going to be difficult getting used to having the Silvers around all the time and not worrying about them trying to arrest me for something. I straightened and tugged my vest back into place, pushing the roiling emotions aside for now.

Deidre raised herself to tiptoes and kissed my cheek. "We'll talk again when you're ready. I have to go pick out some Irons and meet the new nobility."

"Lucky you."

She smoothed a hand down the front of my new vest, then patted my chest, lingering. "Make sure you talk to Senyr. It might help."

"That's not a conversation I'm eager to have."

"It's a needed one."

I grunted and she gave my chest one last pat before joining her guards and striding back into her manor. I watched her go, ignoring the elf that had stopped nearby and was staring at me with her familiar scowl.

Nissa let the silence go on for another minute before holding up a fat pouch. "I will be taking this with me."

I waited for the tingle of magic to wash over me, but there was nothing. A nervousness tugged at my gut at the thought that maybe my gift was gone, then I remembered I hadn't been able to feel the stone from this far away when I'd first picked it up out of the labyrinth either. Only recently had it been so powerful it made my teeth ache.

I sighed. "I hope that's your magic rock."

"It is the First Stone. Specifically it is the Enhali Voga Surai. Calling it a magic rock is disrespectful."

"It's a rock. How can I disrespect a rock? Especially one that's tried to kill me more than once."

She frowned, but moved on. "The power seems to have been greatly diminished, but I suspect the elders will still want to protect it from being abused again."

No doubt because the power of six gods was mixed up in it. I shuddered to think of what would happen if Dakara tried to bargain with someone else to gain his freedom. The elves would know not to let him out, wouldn't they? I hadn't said anything about my conversation with Dakara inside the stone. I'd been a little afraid to say it out loud.

She continued. "If your guild has cast you out, you are welcome to accompany me. The elders would be eager to speak with you about your experiences."

I raised an eyebrow. "First of all, I haven't been cast out." At least not that I knew of. Maybe I did need to talk to Senyr sooner rather than later. "Second, being poked at by your leaders isn't my idea of a great retirement. I'm afraid I'll have to decline."

Her emerald gaze lingered, and for a moment I thought she was going to question me. She'd pushed for details a few times about how I'd remade the city, but I kept telling her the same thing: I didn't know how I'd done it. I'd simply wanted it to happen and it had.

She slipped the pouch into her satchel and out of sight. "Whatever your future holds, may you find it with a steady heart and a clear mind."

"Thanks. I wish the same for you."

She turned on her heel and began walking for the tower door.

The guards had all disappeared with Deidre, and the servant that had been sweeping ashes was in the far corner, so we were essentially alone out here. A chill breeze blew up from the garden, bringing with it the smell of greenery and flowers, and just a bit of ash.

If I had told her about the vision the stone had given me five years ago, would it have made a difference?

She kept walking, the tattered hem of her traveling cloak billowing around her legs, her short white hair fluttering in the breeze.

"Wait."

She paused and glanced back at me over her shoulder.

Shit. I sat against the cold stone of the battlements once more, staring down at the flagstones. "There's something I should tell you."

She returned without comment and stood in front of me, waiting.

"Right." I ran my hand through my hair and took a steadying breath, then plunged into the retelling of my encounter with Dakara and the other two gods. I tried to focus on the words and not the emotion they threatened to evoke within me, so I think everything came out a little breathless and confusing, but Nissa remained intently listening through it all.

When I trailed off and was merely staring at the stones beneath my feet, trying not to think about anything, she finally spoke up.

"Thank you for telling me this. I can see it was difficult for you."

I grunted. "You have no idea. I have brand new nightmares now. I didn't think anything could be worse than the Night of Shadows until I met the one who'd created it."

"If you need help, find me."

I took a deeper breath, trying to shake the lingering thoughts and chuckling. "Find you? How am I supposed to do that? Don't your people actively hide from humans?"

She grimaced, her tiny fangs dimpling her lips, then pulled a ring off her finger and set it in my offered palm. "This will help you, if you truly desire to find me."

I raised an eyebrow and looked it over. It seemed like a simple little thing a child would make out of supple twigs, all wound tightly together into a band, but it tingled against my skin with some kind of magic. "How in the—"

It shifted against my palm, the strands sliding against each other and one visible end curling and releasing again, like it was stretching. "*Sh—*" My hand twitched and it was all I could do not to fling it away like a bug that had landed on me and tried to bite.

Nissa closed my fingers around it and I paled as I felt it moving inside my grip. I swallowed thickly. "I hate you."

She chuckled. "I know. It will not hurt you, but it will show you the way, should you need it." She patted my hand and turned away. "Fare well, Gray."

I grumbled a goodbye in return, stuffing the strange ring into a pocket of my new vest. With any luck I would never have to use it, and it could sit in the back of my closet along with the black knife I'd taken from the labyrinth.

Once Nissa had left I briefly glanced at the city behind me, telling myself it was all worth it as I mentally prepared for a difficult conversation with the new guildmaster about my future. Hopefully a future that contained a lot less shadow and nightmare, and maybe a little more time spent on the hill.

I snorted at the irony and turned to go back inside. There had to be a drink somewhere in this fucking manor. *Then* I would talk to the new king of thieves.

341

Black Hand of Sangarie